Praise for Nadeem Aslam's

Maps for Lost Lovers

"Brave. . . . Affecting. . . . Beautifully written . . . with passages of gorgeous sensuality."
—*The Washington Post*

"Exquisite. . . . A work of almost suffocating beauty. . . . Like an epic written on a grain of rice, this is a novel about macro issues . . . written in almost microscopic detail. . . . The tale he has to tell rises above it all—the iridescent language making it possible to tell a story at whose heart there is so much darkness, so much longing."
—*San Jose Mercury News*

"Provocative. . . . Bold. . . . Remarkable. . . . Rich and beautifully wrought. . . . Saturated with the mythic figures, the colors, and the scents of the subcontinent."
—*The Boston Globe*

"Rich in detail, languid in cadence and iridescent with remarkable images. . . . This is that rare sort of book that gives a voice to those whose voices are seldom heard."
—*The Observer* (London)

"Poetic, sensuous, precisely descriptive and lavishly allusive prose. . . . The prevailingly tragic atmosphere is shot through with luminous gleams of beauty, hope and light, making *Maps for Lost Lovers* not only an important and memorable achievement, but a book that is deeply satisfying to read."
—*The Washington Times*

"An extraordinary work, echoing Rohinton Mistry and Salman Rushdie, but entirely, and unmistakably, the product of a wholly original mind."
—*The Herald* (London)

Nadeem Aslam

Maps for Lost Lovers

Nadeem Aslam is the author of a previous award-winning novel, *Season of the Rainbirds* (1993). He was born in Pakistan and now lives in England.

INTERNATIONAL

Also by Nadeem Aslam

SEASON OF THE RAINBIRDS

Maps
for
Lost Lovers

Maps
for
Lost Lovers

Nadeem Aslam

Vintage International
Vintage Books
A Division of Random House, Inc.
New York

FIRST VINTAGE INTERNATIONAL EDITION, MAY 2006

The Library of Congress has cataloged the Knopf edition as follows:
Aslam, Nadeem.
Maps for lost lovers / Nadeem Aslam.—1st ed.
p. cm.
1. Muslim women—Fiction. 2. Married women—Fiction.
3. Pakistanis—England—Fiction. 4. Murder victims' families—Fiction.
5. England—Fiction. I. Title.
PR9540.9.A83M37 2005
823'.914—dc22 2004059428

Vintage ISBN-10: 1-4000-7697-8
Vintage ISBN-13: 978-1-4000-7697-0

Book design by Pamela Parker

www.vintagebooks.com

Printed in the United States of America
10 9 8 7 6 5 4 3 2

for My Father,
who advised me at the outset, all those years ago,
to always write about love
and for
Faiz Ahmed Faiz
1911–1984
and
Abdur Rahman Chughtai
1897–1975
two masters who taught me, each in his own way,
about what else is worth loving

Acknowledgements

During the long eleven years that I spent working on this novel I was grateful for the assistance I received from the Arts Council of Great Britain, the Authors' Foundation, and the Royal Literary Fund.

While writing *Maps for Lost Lovers,* a book into which elements from numerous myths and legends of the world have been woven, I had, quite fittingly, guardian angels and guiding spirits of my own: Nicholas Pearson, Richard Beswick, Esther Whitby, Alexandra Pringle—thank you.

I am grateful to Arif Rahman Chughtai—of the Chughtai Museum Trust in Lahore—for allowing me to use in this book the deer-and-cypress illustration from the dust-jacket of his father's 1934 picture album *Naqsh-e-Chughtai* (Aivan-e-Ishaat Press, Lahore). The poem on page 277 is by Abid Tamimi. The verses on page 148 are by John Berger. The italicized passages on pages 77 and 78 are adapted from *The Proudest Day* by Anthony Read and David Fisher (Cape). The chapter named "You'll Forget Love, Like Other Disasters" takes its title from an etching by Anwar Saeed, that named "How Many Hands Do I Need to Declare My Love to You?" from a painting by Bhupen Khakar.

For help and advice with the manuscript and for their kindness and generosity, I must also thank Sara Fisher, Kathy Anderson, Anjali Singh, Leyla Aker, Vrinda Condillac, Riaz Ahmed, Haneef Ramay, Salman Rashid, Martijn David, Ulrike Kloepfer and everyone at the Faber and Faber extended family: Walter Donohue, Stephen Page, Noel Murphy, Rachel Alexander, Charles Boyle, Helen Francis, Angus Cargill, Kate Burton, Will Atkinson. Thank you to Tim Pears for the decade-long friendship and care.

A special thanks to Jon Riley in London and Sonny Mehta in New York for believing in my book.

My deepest and most profoundly felt debt is to Victoria Hobbs: Dear Victoria, my own words fail me so I must reach for Ghalib—

Aisa kahan se laoon ke tujh sa kahen jise

A human being is never what he is but the self he seeks.
Octavio Paz

Contents

WINTER

The Night of the Great Peacock Moths

Metaphor

Shamas stands in the open door and watches the earth, the magnet that it is, pulling snowflakes out of the sky towards itself. With their deliberate, almost-impaired pace, they fall like feathers sinking in water. The snow-storm has rinsed the air of the incense that drifts into the houses from the nearby lake with the xylophone jetty, but it is there even when absent, drawing attention to its own disappearance.

This is the first snow of the season and the neighbourhood's children will be on the slopes all day today, burning candles to heat the runners of toboggans to make them slip with increased fluency, daring each other to lick the frozen spikes of the railings around the church and those around the mosque, smuggling cheese-graters out of the kitchens to refine the symmetry of the snowmen they will build, oblivious to the cold because everything is a sublime adventure at that age; an oyster tolerates the pearl embedded in its flesh, and so the pebbles on the lake shore don't seem to pain the soles of the children's bare feet.

An icicle breaks off from above and drops like a radiant dagger towards Shamas, shattering on the stone step he is standing on, turning into white powder the way a crystal of sugar loses its transparency when crushed. With a movement of his foot, Shamas sends this temporary debris into the snow-covered front garden where in May and June there will be rose-buds the size and solidity of strawberries, into the corner where one of his children had buried a dead finch many years ago, not allowing anyone to set foot on that spot afterwards lest the delicate bones crack under the weight, the tiny skull as fragile as the eggshell within which it had formed the previous spring.

The house is on a street that runs along the base of a hill. This street is linked by a side-street to a shelf-like road higher up the hill and, in late summer, when the abundant dropped fruit of the wild cherry trees gets trodden on, the footpaths up there are stained with red and dark-blue smears.

In the mornings the adolescents from down here can be seen keeping an eye on the elevated road for the bus that takes them to school, eating breakfast on the doorstep if the parents and the weather permit it, racing up the side-street when they glimpse the vanilla-and-green vehicle coming between the cherry trees—up there between the gaps in the trunks where a small figure is walking through the snow now. Fishing for carp one night, Shamas's younger son had catapulted into the lake a mass of flowers from those trees, hoping they would prove an alternative to the expensive hyacinths which drew the fish to the surface within moments, but the cherry blossom was a failure, as were the dandelions that lit up the dark water the following night with a hundred vivid suns; perfume was the key and only the clusters of lilac were a success but their season was soon gone.

According to the children, the lake—as dazzling as a mirror and shaped like the letter X—was created in the early days of the earth when a towering giant fell out of the sky; and he is still there, still alive, the regular ebb and flow of the tides being the gentle rhythm of his heart still beating, the crashing waves of October his convulsive attempts to free himself. Just inside the water's margin the stones are covered in tufts of wet moss, bringing to mind the broken pulp of a squeezed lemon, and to stand up to the waist in the calm summer water is to become two-headed like the jacks and queens on playing cards, right side up either way. On the shore the winds rush from every direction during the winter months to twist themselves around the body like a sari, and he remembers one of his children saying that his biology teacher dispatched a pair of boys with cellophane bags to the lake whenever she needed a frog for dissection. Very occasionally in the past, the lake has frozen over and then the children have walked on it, "pretending to be Jesus."

Even though it is not yet daybreak, the dawn-like translucence of the fallen snow enables him to see clearly the person walking on the road up there, and he decides that it is someone on his way to the mosque for the day's first prayer.

Or it could be Queen Elizabeth II. Shamas smiles, in spite of himself. Once, marvelling at the prosperity of England, a visitor from Pakistan had remarked that it was almost as though the Queen disguised herself every night and went out into the streets of her country to find out personally what her subjects most needed and desired in life, so she could arrange for their wishes to come true the next day; it was what the caliph Harun al-Rashid was said to have done according to the tales of the *Thousand and One Nights,* with the result that his perfumed Baghdad became the most easeful and prosperous place imaginable.

Perspective tricks the eyes and makes the snowflakes falling in the far distance appear as though they are falling slower than those nearby, and he stands in the open door with an arm stretched out to receive the small light pieces on his hand. A habit as old as his arrival in this country; he has always greeted the season's first snow in this manner, the flakes losing their whiteness on the palm of his hand to become clear wafers of ice before melting to water—crystals of snow transformed into a monsoon raindrop. Among the innumerable other losses, to come to England was to lose a season, because, in the part of Pakistan that he is from, there are five seasons in a year, not four, the schoolchildren learning their names and sequence through classroom chants: *Mausam-e-Sarma, Bahar, Mausam-e-Garma, Barsat, Khizan.* Winter, Spring, Summer, Monsoon, Autumn.

The snow falls and, yes, the hand stretched into the flakes' path is a hand asking back a season now lost.

The person on the hill is indeed a woman and, whoever she is, she has left the high shelf of the road and is coming down the side-street towards him, one arm carrying an umbrella, the other steadying her descent by holding on to the field maples growing at regular intervals along the edges of the inclining street. With that umbrella she is a riddle personified: the solution being *a foetus attached to a placenta by the umbilical cord.* She would soon be near and would no doubt consider him lacking good judgement: a man of almost sixty-five years standing here with his hand thrust into the path of the snow—and so he withdraws into the house.

The front door opens directly into the kitchen. One blue, one strawberry pink, one the yellow of certain Leningrad exteriors: these were the colours of the three rooms in the olive-green house in Sohni Dharti—the small place in Pakistan where he was born and had lived permanently until his mid-twenties—and a few years ago, by mixing ground-up chalk and rabbit-skin glue with the appropriate pigments, he had painted the rooms in this house with those three colours, surprising himself by reproducing the three shades precisely. It's almost as though when he stood facing a corner as a child during a game of hide-and-seek, it was for the sole purpose of committing its colour to memory, to be able to conjure it up in the years of exile and banishment.

During the school holidays he would approach the bookcase in the pink room and stand before it, his hand alighting on this or that volume with the arbitrariness of a moth, half deciding on something before sliding it back in place and moving on, as though experimenting with the keys of a piano, all briefly opened books eager to engage his eye, each flickeringly glimpsed paragraph enticing him hurriedly with its secret, and having made his choice he would drift through the house in search of the coolest spot to read through the long summer afternoons that had a touch of eternity to them, altering the arrangement of his limbs as much for comfort as for the fear that his undisturbed shadow would leave a stain on the wall.

There is someone at the door. Three informal taps are given on the glass panel instead of the doorbell being pressed, the bell that has a little amber light burning in it, the moths dancing around it all through the summer nights. As though he has sucked too hard through a paper straw and flattened it shut, he inhales but cannot find his breath, his chest solidifying into heavy stone, in terror. Who could it be? However enriched with light this hour is—this pause between night and day—it is still too early for a call not to be out of the ordinary. But he is aware that he would have reacted similarly had it been the middle of the day, imprisoned as he has been in a shadowy area between sleep and waking for almost five months—ever since his younger brother, Jugnu, and his girlfriend, Chanda, vanished from their house next door.

Almost five months of not knowing when time would stir again and in which direction it would move, tip him into darkness or deliver him into light.

He doesn't know what to do about the knock.

There it is again, the knock, the sound of finger-bone on glass, louder this time, but he is in a paralysed trance, his skull full of moths. Garden Tiger. Cinnabar. Early Thorn. Nail Mark. He loves the names of moths that Jugnu taught him. Ghost Moth.

The sound of the doorbell runs through him like an electric current, jolting him out of his funk.

"I am sorry to trouble you this early, Shamas . . . Good morning. But my father has had to spend the entire night on the floor because I can't lift him back into his bed." It is Kiran—a ray of light. "Could you please come with me for a few minutes, please." She indicates the direction of her house with a turn of her head—up the sloping side-street with its twenty maples, and then along the high road with the cherry trees where he had seen her earlier without recognizing her.

He opens the door wider for her to step inside, handfuls of snow on a gust of wind rushing in inquisitively either side of her and then past him into the house, sticking softly to the linoleum in whose pattern of ivory-and-green roses a peeled almond is hard to find once it has slipped out of the fingers, or out of which, as though one of the green roses has shed a petal, a mint or coriander leaf curling at the edges strangely appears when the floor is swept at the end of the day, having lain undetected against the pattern since lunch.

"You should have telephoned, Kiran."

She doesn't enter the house—uneasy no doubt about encountering Shamas's wife, Kaukab. Kiran is a Sikh and had three decades ago wanted to marry Kaukab's brother, a Muslim. The two were in love. He was a migrant worker here in England, and when during a visit to Pakistan he told his family of his intentions of marrying Kiran, they were appalled and refused to allow him to return to England. Kiran boarded a plane in London and arrived at Karachi airport to be with him, but her telegram had been intercepted by the young man's older brother who was waiting at the airport to tell her to take the next flight back to England, any reunion—or union—between his brother and her an impossibility. A marriage was hastily arranged for him within the next few days.

Shamas asks her to step in now. "Come in out of the rain, I mean, snow, while I put on my Wellingtons. Kaukab is still in bed." This is a narrow house where all the doors disappear into the walls, except for the two that give on to the outside world at the front and back, and he slides open the space under the stairs to look for the shoes, stored somewhere here amid all the clutter at the end of last winter. There are fishing rods leaning like stick-insects in the corner. Soft cages for her feet, there is a pair of jellied sandals that had belonged to his daughter, lying one in front of the other as though he has surprised them in the act of taking a step, the straps spiralling like apple peel.

"I apologize again for having troubled you so early. I was hoping one of your sons would be visiting, and I would bring him with me."

"All three children are far away, the boys and the girl," he says as he rummages. There is a lobster buoy from Maine, USA, that is used as a doorstopper at the back of the house on hot mornings, to let in the sun and the trickling song of the stream which runs beside the narrow lane there; the stream that is more stones than water as the summer advances but a great catcher of pollen nevertheless, the stones white as chalk in the sun, black underwater. During autumn the speed of the water is so great that you fear your foot would be instantly sliced off at the ankle if you stepped into it.

Outside, as he walks behind Kiran in that below-zero monsoon, there are gentle skirmishes between the falling snowflakes now that the wind has risen a little.

Two sets of Kiran's footprints lie before him as he follows her to her house. Each perfect cylinder punched into the deep snow has at its base a thin sheet of packed ice through which the dry leaves of the field maples can be seen as though sealed behind glass. They are as intricate as the gold jewellery from the Subcontinent—treasures buried under the snow till a rainy day.

Planted between two field maples on the slope, the telephone pole has had several of its wires broken during the night, and, encased in thick cylinders of ice, they lie snapped like candles in the snow. The chilled air is as keen as a needle on the skin and the incline is forcing him to take a hummingbird's 300 breaths per minute. A frozen buried clump of grass breaks under his weight and the cracking sound is the sound that Kaukab produces when she halves and quarters cinnamon sticks in the kitchen.

"I lay next to him on the floor all night, distracting him with talk," Kiran says over her shoulder. "But when he began to grow despondent I set out for you. He said, 'I want to leave this life. My bags are packed, but the world won't let me go: it fears the report I'll present to Him on my arrival.'"

Shamas wants to say something in response but a snowflake enters his mouth and he almost chokes.

Kiran is now ahead of him by a few determined yards. His own progress is decisive but full of inaccurate moves.

Kiran never saw her lover again—until perhaps last year when, now a widower, he visited England; Kaukab was apprehensive that the one-time lovers shouldn't encounter each other, and, as far as Shamas knows, she succeeded in keeping them apart, but—he is quite sure—Kiran must have caught glimpses of him.

The street rises. On one side is the hundred-year-old Parish Church of St. Eustace, nestling in a wedge cut into the hill, circled by lindens and yews. Missing for as long as he can remember, the tail of the weathervane had turned up two months ago when the lake was dragged unsuccessfully for the bodies of Jugnu and Chanda. And on the other side of the street is the mosque. The crescent faces the cross squarely across the narrow side-street.

Pakistan is a poor country, a harsh and disastrously unjust land, its history a book full of sad stories, and life is a trial if not a punishment for most of the people born there: millions of its sons and daughters have managed to find footholds all around the globe in their search for livelihood and a semblance of dignity. Roaming the planet looking for solace, they've settled in small towns that make them feel smaller still, and in cities that have tall buildings and even taller loneliness. And so the cleric at this mosque could receive a telephone call from, say, Norway, from a person who was from the same village as him in Pakistan, asking him whether it was permitted for him to take an occasional small glass of whisky or vodka to keep his blood warm, given that Norway was an extremely cold country; the cleric told him to desist from his sinful practice, thundering down the line and telling him that Allah was perfectly aware of the climate of Norway when He forbade humans from drinking alcohol; why, the cleric had asked, couldn't he simply carry a basket of burning maple leaves under his overcoat the way the good Muslims of freezing Kashmir do to keep themselves warm?

A telephone call could also come in the middle of the night from Australia, a despondent father asking the cleric to fly immediately to Sydney all-expenses-paid and exorcise the djinns that had taken possession of his teenaged daughter soon after an end was put to her love for a white schoolmate and she was married to a cousin brought hurriedly over from Pakistan.

Having reached the summit of the street, Kiran is looking down the slope waiting for him to catch up. He arrives and they stand side by side, motionless for a short moment, looking down at his house.

The town lies at the base of a valley like a few spoonfuls of sugar in a bowl. At the very top are the remains of an Iron Age fort to which a tower was added to mark Queen Victoria's Golden Jubilee.

"All night I have tried to lift him to put him back into bed," Kiran says, "but I wasn't able to." Her hair has silvered with age but her skin is still the colour of rusting apple slices. The beads hanging from her earlobes are tiny and clear, as though she has managed to crack open a glass paperweight like a walnut and somehow managed to pick out whole the air bubbles suspended within it. "All night I tried."

"You should have come for me immediately." Encrusted with snow, the hawthorns behind his house seem to be in flower this morning.

"Your elder boy is married now? To the white girl with the green Volkswagen Beetle?"

"They referred to it as 'the Aphid.' They *were* married, but are now divorced." They've set off again, along the road through the cherry trees towards Kiran's house. "I can't really remember the last time I saw the grandchild."

Seven years old, the little boy is "half Pakistani and half . . . er . . . er . . . er . . . human"—or so a child on his English mother's side is reported to have described him in baffled groping innocence.

As he walks, his foot shatters an iced-over puddle (he's neither a child nor Jesus); the thin sheet breaks, releasing the loud sound that was lying trapped underneath, the water coming out to mix with the snow in a sapphire slush.

Kiran's house is one-half of a stone box set at the edge of the road, interrupting the cherry trees. It is his understanding that the woman next door is a prostitute. Kiran was a girl of thirteen back in the 1950s when Shamas had arrived from Pakistan. Her father had lost all other members of his family during the massacres that accompanied the partition of India in 1947, and so he had brought her with him when he migrated to England from India. She was a mysterious withdrawn creature: to look at her eyes was to wonder immediately what myth it was that contained a being of identical spell-binding powers, the blood stopping dead for a beat or two.

A child in a house full of lonely migrant workers, she was the focus of everyone's tenderness. It was a time in England when the white attitude towards the dark-skinned foreigners was just beginning to go from *I don't want to see them or work next to them* to *I don't mind working next to them if I'm forced to, as long as I don't have to speak to them,* an attitude that would change again within the next ten years to *I don't mind speaking to them when I have to in the workplace, as long as I don't have to talk to them outside the working hours,* and then in another ten years to *I don't mind them socializing in the same place as me if they must, as long as I don't have to live next to them.* By then it was the 1970s and because the immigrant families had to live *somewhere* and were moving in next door to the whites, there were calls for a ban on immigration and the repatriation of the immigrants who were already here.

There were violent physical attacks. At night the scented geraniums were dragged to the centres of the downstairs rooms in the hope that the breeze dense with rosehips and ripening limes would get to the sleepers upstairs ahead of the white intruders who had generated it by brushing past the foliage in the dark after breaking in. Something died in the children during those years—and then, one night, Jugnu had come, his passport swollen with the New England wildflowers he had picked at the last minute before boarding the plane, the pages damp with sap and dew—he soon filled the days and nights of his niece and two nephews with unexpected wonder.

They have arrived at Kiran's house and he goes in after her.

A vase of roses has dropped a few crimson notes onto the piano keys.

The heat in the room leaps at the sensitive parts of Shamas's face: the brow, the eyes, and the upper cheeks—the area onto the reverse of which dreams are projected during sleep. Kiran's father, lying where he had fallen next to the bed, acknowledges their entrance by a faint movement of the body, a movement allowed him by the elasticity of the skin; otherwise, he is pinned to the floor by his great bulk and by the weight of his illness that is greater still. Being a Sikh, he has never cut his hair and the locks are collected in a bun at the top of the head. "Shamas? I am sorry to disappoint you but I am still alive. I know you cannot wait for my death to get your hands on my jazz records." The wood these walls are made of has soaked up more music than the birdsong it had absorbed as trees in the forest.

Shamas approaches and drops by his side. "I pray for it every day but you are stubborn." Blood vessels creep close to the surface on the man's cheeks as on the bodies of shrimps. Together in the harness of their arms, he and Kiran lift the old man as heavy as a stone Buddha onto the bed.

"Thank you, *sohnia.*" His eyes droop close as Shamas arranges the quilt around him. *Sohnia:* the Beautiful One. "I want to leave and go up there. The temptation on my part is strong to arrive and watch with these eyes all the greats playing music together."

"God's very own backing band!" Shamas smiles. Through his socks he can feel a zone of greater warmth on the carpet where the body had lain next to the bed all night.

"God's very own backing band. Yes." Loose strands of his dishevelled beard are softly bristling away from his skin, some short, some long, the colour of mist on a spring morning, floating above his face as though he is below water. The room expands and contracts with the unfocused dazzle thrown off the white crumbs falling past the window. Tenderly, the old man places a hand on Shamas's sleeve and whispers, "Thank you for coming, my friend." And then, mischievous once again, he shouts: "Watch him on his way out, Kiran. Don't let him steal. I'll count the records this afternoon just to be sure." He shuts his eyes, the lips keeping the shape of the last word.

Shamas closes the door quietly behind him as he leaves the room.

"They are three weeks old." Kiran, who had been in the kitchen, comes out into the hallway where he stands looking at the roses on the piano. "Duke Ellington taught me to put an aspirin in the water to make them last." She presses a key without sounding it, exposing the dull yellow wood of the adjoining key beneath the gleaming lacquer. "He mentions it somewhere in the 'self-interview.' "

"Sidney Bechet uses the word 'musicianer' in his book. It's lovely. I don't think I have come across it anywhere else, but 'a practitioner of music' *should* be called a 'musicianer.' "

"Come through. I am making tea." The kettle is whistling back there like a toy train. Around her wrist there is a gold bracelet composed as though of a series of semicolons—

;;

He declines her offer. She doesn't know this but her lover eventually named his baby daughter after her—Kiran, it being a name acceptable to both Sikhs and Muslims. A ray of light.

She plucks open the front door for him. "I'll tell him you failed to steal anything."

It was this father and daughter who had introduced Shamas and the other migrant workers to jazz in the house they shared all those years ago. She would stop suddenly on hearing the pulse of sound coming out of the Woods music store. "Unless I am mistaken that's Ben Webster."

At home she would take out the new record that would look painfully vulnerable out in the air, and examine it carefully for imperfections, blowing on it quietly as though it were on fire, and then place it onto the turntable with the caution of a mother setting a baby in a cradle, while, an open book of faces, the others would be sitting in a semicircle around the gramophone, waiting for it to begin—Louis Armstrong "calling his children home" with his trumpet, or the genius of Count Basie so unmistakable that the stylus would seem to be travelling around the very whorls of his fingerprint.

The record would begin and soon the listeners would be engrossed by those musicians who seemed to know how to blend together all that life contains, the real truth, the undeniable last word, the innermost core of all that is unbearably painful within a heart and all that is joyful, all that is loved and all that is worthy of love but remains unloved, lied to and lied about, the unimaginable depths of the soul where no other can withstand the longing and which few have the conviction to plumb, the sorrows and the indisputable rage—so engrossed would the listeners become that, by the end of the piece, the space between them would have contracted, heads leaning together as though they were sharing a mirror. All great artists know that part of their task is to light up the distance between two human beings.

"Thank you," Kiran says, standing in the door. "I approached the mosque earlier—knowing there would be people there, hoping I would bring one of them back with me but they were busy with their own troubles."

"Troubles?"

"Someone left a"—Kiran hesitates—"a pig's head outside the door during the night. A lot of noise and shouts outside the building as people discovered it."

A quill of vapour emerges from Shamas's mouth. He has just been to the mosque to assess the situation, the building that was an ordinary home until a decade ago when it was bought to be converted into a mosque. The widow who had lived here had slowly lost her reason after her husband's death. She was alone: her husband had brought two of his nephews into England in the 1960s, declaring to the immigration authorities that they were his sons, and when she miscarried complicatedly five times in the 1970s, the doctors did not see why they should not suggest a hysterectomy since the couple already had two children. The husband had consented and persuaded her to consent: knowing very little English and nothing about how the law operated in this country, he feared their refusal to have the operation would somehow result in the doctors' alerting the immigration authorities and landing all four of them in prison.

The nephews did end up in jail once they grew up. They were briefly brought to the funeral of their uncle in handcuffs: one was serving a sentence for breaking-and-entering, the other for possession-with-intent-to-supply. She flew at them with her nails at the ready and then went into convulsions and the women had to prise open her clenched teeth with a spoon to get at her tongue.

Losing weight rapidly over the coming months—there were reports that there were spiders' webs on the hobs of her cooker—she went about in rags, her veil as wrinkled as a poppy, having locked all her other clothes and jewellery in a trunk and thrown the key into the lake. Within the year she became convinced that someone had been tampering with the sun: "I can't find it anywhere, and if ever I do it's in the wrong place." That was when her brothers came and took her back to Pakistan, putting the house up for sale.

Shamas pauses outside the mosque, having gone in there looking for the cleric. He had to offer help, talk to the cleric—even though he didn't want to initially. After the previous cleric died last year, the father of Jugnu's girlfriend Chanda had taken up the reins at the mosque. Chanda's family had disapproved of her "living in sin" with Jugnu, and so Shamas would rather not face the missing girl's father.

But then he remembered being told by Kaukab last week that the missing girl's father is no longer headman at the mosque: he had stepped down recently, unable to do anything about the talk in the mosque about his "immoral," "deviant," and "despicable" daughter, who was nothing less than a wanton whore in most people's eyes—as she was in Allah's—for setting up home with a man she wasn't married to.

And so Shamas had gone in and found the worshippers weeping. They were in tears at the realization that Allah does not consider them worthy enough to have placed them in a position where they could have prevented this insult to His home.

The director of the Community Relations Council, Shamas is the person the neighbourhood turns to when unable to negotiate the white world on its own, visiting his office in the town centre or bringing the problem to his front door that opens directly into the blue-walled kitchen with the yellow chairs.

Had the CRC existed back then, the fears that led to the woman agreeing to the hysterectomy would have been allayed.

Breathing quills of vapour he stands outside the building where plastic bags containing the animal's head and the blood-soaked crystals of snow are lying against the stump of the apple tree that had been cut down because, according to the cleric, it was the seat of the 360 djinn whose evil influence was responsible for the widow's lonely bewilderment.

He must go and see if anything has happened at the Hindu temple—responsibility to his neighbourhood driving him on.

Snow creaks underfoot as he goes back towards Kiran's house once again. Torn pages in a wastepaper basket, the new snowflakes have partly filled the oblong cylinders his feet had made in the snow earlier. It is January in England, and it is January in Pakistan too. When they arrived in England, some of the migrants had become confused by the concept of time zones, and had wondered if the months too were the same at any given time in various continents. Yes, it's January in Pakistan too. January—the month of Janus, the two-headed god, one looking towards the future while the other looks back.

His father worked in Lahore and came home to Sohni Dharti, on the banks of the river Chenab—Pakistan's moon river—only on Saturday nights, walking his sons to school on Monday morning before catching the train to Lahore where he was the editor's assistant at *The First Children on the Moon,* an Urdu-language monthly for children that had a Bengali sister-publication in Calcutta and a Hindi-language one in Delhi. Shamas has two brothers—one elder, one younger, Jugnu—but Jugnu was fifteen years younger than Shamas, so Shamas had only one sibling during his school days. "Solve this riddle," their father would say to the boys as they walked: "*Twelve or so princesses deep in conversation in their palace, huddled in a circle.* What's the answer?" He still remembers his delight at being presented with such puzzles. The eye that in the adult sees the rough material for metaphors and similes all around it, comparing one thing with another, that eye was already half open in the child. "An orange!"

Shamas wants to get to the Hindu temple as quickly as he can but the snow makes for hard walking, the air itself an obstacle to be overcome, and he fears he's catching a chill, having heard himself coughing in the night. A mass of dislodged snow slides rapidly down the tiles of the St. Eustace roof, burying with a subdued thump the beehives that are standing apart from the rest, perhaps waiting to be mended. During June and July, the bees work the many thousand flowers of the lindens that are dotted around the churchyard, and under whose fissured bark Hummingbird Hawk moths may be hibernating now—immigrants from Southern Europe that arrive in vibrating clusters each summer to breed here; their wing-beats are said to produce a sharp-toned noise audible only to children, whose ears can still register the higher pitches.

He goes past Kiran's house and the house that belongs to the woman who may be a prostitute, continuing along the road with the wild cherry trees, towards the river where the Hindu temple is situated. Someone had once asked him if the prostitute was Indian or Pakistani. She is white: had she been Indian or Pakistani, she would have been assaulted and driven out of the area within days of moving in for bringing shame on her people. And so had Chanda brought shame on her family by living with Jugnu: Chanda and Jugnu—the two missing bodies that were not found in the lake when it was dragged, the lake where the many hearts carved on the poles of the xylophone jetty enclose initials in Urdu and Hindi and Bengali as well as English, and where the colour of the waves is that particular blue grey green found on the edge of a sheet of glass, that bright strip of colour sandwiched between the top and the bottom surface.

In another few hours the surface of the snow would harden to a fragile layer of ice that would give out a knife-on-toast scrape when stepped on, but for now it is still powdery.

He comes to the end of the road through the wild cherry trees and begins to walk along the wider road it gives on to. On its way into the town centre, this road—planted with mighty horse chestnuts on either side, its surface patched like a teenager's denim jeans with lighter and darker triangles and squares of tarmac—leaps over the river. The temple, dedicated to Ram and Sita, is on the riverbank where in early summer the reeds and flag irises stick out of the water in tight bunches as though being held in fists just below the surface.

Just at the place where the road briefly becomes a bridge, the double-helix of a metal staircase drops down from the footpath to give access to the riverbank thirty feet below. A lepidopterist by profession, Jugnu, keeping himself alert with a flask of the coffee into which he had dropped a curl of orange peel and two green cardamoms, had spent many nights here, standing on the riverbank up to his waist in yellow daisies, calling the moths out of the darkness with his upraised hand, the fingers closing around each creature like the collapsible petals of a flower. They were unable to resist the pull of his raised hand and more and more would arrive out of the black air to spin around it like planets bound to a sun through gravity. Sometimes the three children accompanied him on these nocturnal gathering trips; and during the day the children were often sent out to collect specimens from around the town and across the surrounding countryside, guided by exactly sketched maps, the precisely worded instructions removing every possibility of error.

. . . The greenish-grey twigs of the Guelder Rose tree are angular and smooth, and the leaves are covered with a silver down. I had pointed one out to you during the drive to see the beached minke whale last year, so you will remember the flower heads . . .

. . . Do not be tempted to help the butterfly out of the chrysalis, should you find one that is about to emerge. It would come out grey if you do. The effort to split open the chrysalis forces the blood into the wings, imparting colour and pattern . . .

Once a week, the information about the county's butterflies and moths was typed up and one of the boys bicycled with the pages to the offices of the local evening newspaper—*The Afternoon*—where it ran as a column with India-ink illustrations by the elder boy. The typewriter—the keys arranged in rows one above another always reminding Shamas of faces in a school photograph—was bought by Shamas when he arrived in England all those years ago, with the thought that one day soon he would write poetry again, but it had remained unused on the whole until Jugnu came from the United States and began producing his pieces for *The Afternoon*.

The river is black as tar against the surrounding snow, a rip in the white scarf tossed down by the sky. Miles downriver, beyond the outskirts of the town, the river passes the ivy-clad ruin of the abbey where the Sikhs ceremonially cast the ashes of their dead into the water; when the practice began a decade or so ago, the inhabitants of the nearby all-white suburb had been outraged, but the bishop had settled the matter by saying he was delighted the site was being put to a spiritual use, rather than the open-air dog lavatory he was sorry to say those who were now complaining had turned it into.

Filled and concealed by snow, a depression in the earth has swallowed his left leg up to the knee, and in pulling himself upright he disinters segments of rowan leaves and red berries, the limb bringing them up to the surface as it emerges from the ground, and there are some blue fish scales, each resembling a boiled sweet sucked down to a sharp sliver between tongue and roof of mouth.

Shamas can see the large pea-green hut that is the Hindu temple, a simple structure set beside the river like something in a join-the-dot book belonging to a very young child, the pine trees reaching towards the sky behind it. Wooden steps lead to the water's edge from the door.

Nothing untoward appeared to have occurred here.

Icicles are dripping brightly at the edge of the roof, drilling holes in the snow the size of half-penny coins. The pipes must have frozen during the night because Poorab-ji is collecting water from the river to wash his hands, leaning from the lowest step and selecting a wave before holding the lip of the shiny brass *garvi* vessel in its path to let it swirl home. It's more a wooden path to the river's edge than a series of steps: wide square treads with very short strips of verticals in between. From there Poorab-ji lifts one earth-covered hand at him in greeting. "I have just buried a goldfinch, Shamas-ji. It broke its neck on that windowpane. See if you can spot where." Delicate in visage, he is soft-lipped and has a long neck, and like a large number of middle-aged men from the Subcontinent he dyes his hair a startling pure black.

The canopy of each rowan tree growing along the river is perfectly spherical, like a firework exploding in the sky.

"Here." Poorab-ji has approached and pinpoints the tiny notch the bird's beak had tapped out on the glass. From his pocket he takes a clumsy rhinestone and fits it into place on the pane, holding his palm under it in case it falls out. "I found it in its beak."

As an explanation for this unusual visit Shamas relates all that has transpired at the mosque, but Poorab-ji tells him that there has been no incident here since the vandalism back in October which Shamas already knows about. The feuds of the world. The feuds of the world.

And now, suddenly, in a gesture of intimacy Shamas is not prepared for, Poorab-ji gently places his arm around his shoulder:

"This morning I saw a mass of snow that had slid off a roof and was lying in a heap on the ground, and from the distance I thought it was Chanda and Jugnu's bodies. You cannot know how sorry I am, but at least now we know the truth about what happened to them."

"The truth?" The steel trap around his heart springs shut.

"You don't know yet, Shamas-ji?" Poorab-ji's face over the next few instants is a mirror reflecting his own confusion and dread. "Am I to be the first one to tell you? The police obviously haven't informed you."

Shamas looks down and his feet appear far away. "The telephone lines are down." He has a specific desire to stretch out on the white snow.

Poorab-ji is talking fast: it appears that the police have arrested both of Chanda's brothers, charging them with the double-murder of their sister and Jugnu.

The almost five months since the lovers disappeared have been months of a contained mourning for Shamas—but now the grief can come out. He is not a believer, so he knows that the universe is without saviours: the surface of the earth is a great shroud whose dead will not be resurrected.

The quails injured in the secret fights organized by some Pakistani and Indian immigrants of the neighbourhood are regularly brought to Poorab-ji, who, threatening to expose the illegal activity each time he receives the damaged birds, nurses them back to health, the turmeric powder on their wounds making them appear as though they have thrashed through clumps of Madonna and Easter lilies, the mango-coloured dust-fine pollen of the flowers coming off on the feathers.

"I have two cock birds in there, and when it began to snow at two o'clock last night I left the house to come here to see that they were warm enough . . . I passed the family's home . . . There were policemen all around . . ."

Official confirmation of disaster has made Shamas nauseous.

The mind rejects the idea and the body joins in so that the stomach goes into convulsions as though it too has been administered a poisonous substance that must be vomited out. His flesh is armoured in plates of searing heat and the hands burn through the snow like branding irons. There is nothing much in the stomach to be expelled since he has had no breakfast, but the body insists on going through the spasms of gagging, each gruesome surge a prolonged slowed-down hiccup. *We'll drink from your veins.* When Chanda had moved in with Jugnu next door—leaving behind the home she shared with her family above the grocery shop they owned—the brothers had threatened revenge to preserve their honour. *We'll make you lick our injuries.* They had broken in and put out a cigarette in their bed.

But after the disappearance they had denied any knowledge.

Shamas now finds himself on all fours, looking for something, shifting fistfuls of snow so that the area around the wooden hut is grooved and churned a pale lilac-blue, as though by the jabs of an aimless rake. The wind stirs a yellow feather stuck in the whiteness, a wisp of filaments—as bright as something to be found in a bazaar—that had belonged to the bird which had died with a diamond in its beak. Each melting icicle drills a hole in the snow the size of a half-penny piece, a coin now discontinued and missed so badly by Shamas in this moment of madness that it now represents all that has gone away never to return, his mind convincing itself that to be able to locate just one of those copper discs small enough to fit in a doll's purse would solve every difficulty in life. The skin peels away from his fingers in strips of accordioned rice-paper as his hands dig the ground in their urgent search for a worthless bit of metal that has suddenly become the price of sanity.

"I should never have let him out of my sight," he hears himself say; these were the words of Kiran when she returned dazed from Pakistan all those years ago, having been turned away from Karachi airport. "I should never have let him out of my sight," he repeats.

Poorab-ji convinces him to be still and he closes his eyes in order to conquer his turmoil and, drained, leans his head against the temple wall, unaccountably thinking about the night that Great Peacock moths had hatched in the blue-walled kitchen, letting himself imagine the likely sequence of events after they had emerged from the cocoons. Their search for a way out of themselves finally over, the nineteen males had hatched in the blue kitchen during the night and, still damp from the chrysalis, fluttered into the adjoining drawing room where the vase Shamas had brought from Pakistan in the 1950s—as a reminder of home—was on the glass table arranged with sprays of yolk-coloured mimosa, the fine layer of dust he had picked the vase out of all those years ago continuing to cry out across the years with an agonised O for it to be put back exactly where it had been set by his mother's hand.

As large as a bat, with wings made of deep-paprika velvet and a necktie of white fur, a moth looped the thready globes of the mimosa, but food wasn't what it sought as it had no mouth and was born to die; it alighted on a guava that had leaves and stalk attached to the crown as though it had been picked in a hurry, and then flew out of the strawberry-pink drawing room with its eighteen companions, arriving in the kitchen again.

The absolute darkness was light enough for them and with passionate impatience they floated up the stairwell to the Leningrad-yellow room where Shamas slept beside Kaukab.

Their tufted antennae questioning the air, they lingered indecisively above Kaukab—she who remembers even today the morning a butterfly had tried to lay eggs in her plait, drawn by the scent of the oil she applies to her hair—and she opened her eyes in the darkness for an instant or two, more asleep than awake, and sharply expelled air from her nostrils three times, because the Prophet had said, "If any of you wakes up at night, let him blow his nose three times. For Satan spends the night in a man's nostrils."

She sank back into sleephood almost immediately and the moths moved out to the elder boy's room, having first made sure at the open window that the summons was not coming from out there.

The thirty-eight eyes painted on the thirty-eight red wings blinked in the darkness as the insects then fluttered into the room shared by the two younger children, and here they tried to pass through a circular opening only to discover that others were trying to emerge from it just as frantically—it was a mirror.

A slippery spew of Indian movie magazines was at the foot of the girl's bed.

Through the open hatch in the ceiling of this room, the Great Peacock moths entered the attic that was embraced on the outside by the back garden's purple beech, and in a blur of near-misses they went into the space above the adjoining house, bought newly by Jugnu, the two hatches open for his stored possessions to be zigzagged across from here to there and then handed down. A number of his belongings were still scattered about the house: these included the hatbox containing the nineteen chrysalises. It was left in the blue kitchen till tomorrow because everyone had decided to leave things as they were when night fell and they realized that they had been working without a rest for ten hours, helping Jugnu move.

Like kites whose strings have been cut, the moths swooped down out of the attic into the room wallpapered with twisted leaves and tiny indigo berries.

Here, the Great Peacocks ignored the sleeping Jugnu even though his hands weren't covered by the blanket, the hands that had the ability to glow in the dark. No moth could resist being drawn to his hands, but that night the interior was noisy with another call that only they could hear—that of a female moth. It had hatched the day before and hung in the cage Jugnu had constructed by knitting copper wire around a bottle and then smashing the glass.

The female was motionless except when it swished its wings gently to disperse the odour that had gradually flooded the two houses with the faint electricity of a yearning inexpressible any other way, undetected by the humans but pulling the nineteen males towards its source slowly at first and then hand over hand a yard at a time as they learned to distinguish truth from lie and arrived to drape the entire cage in reverberating velvet.

A Breakfast
of Butterfly Eggs

Walking home from work at the end of the day, with *The Afternoon* under one arm, Shamas hears the echoes of his own footsteps on the snow as though he is being followed.

For almost a week now the country has been draped in daisy chains on the television weather maps. During the nights, the condensation on the windowpanes has frozen into sparkling patterns of bird feathers, insect wings and leaf skeletons, as though each home contains within it a magical forest, tangled with fables and myths, the glittering foliage growing pressed against the glass. Each street has become a row of books on a shelf.

Shamas no longer feels the pain in the fingers that he wounded the other morning, scrabbling for half-penny coins in the snow on the riverbank. He no longer feels the wasp-sting soreness. The skin is mending itself fast. Under the hard scabs on his fingers, the new skin has the fine buffed sheen of mother-of-pearl. Pale pink. Jugnu—the lepidopterist—said that because there are no pink butterflies in nature, the ones that were released into the air during the Rolling Stones concert in Hyde Park in July 1969 were in fact white ones dipped in pink dye.

Shamas doesn't know what led the police detectives to name their investigation into the disappearance of Jugnu and Chanda "Operation Ivory."

The officers who came to the house that morning to inform him officially of the arrests said that the two men were being held separately—to highlight inconsistencies in their tales—and he has visited the police station twice since then, talking first to the Detective Chief Inspector and then to the Detective Superintendent, both of whom are in charge of the case. The Detective Superintendent said that the lack of bodies is a stumbling block but it will not prevent the team from battling on to secure a conviction. He has been told that the trial will be in December. There are numerous legal precedents in which the murderers who thought they had covered their tracks had been brought to justice. As long ago as 1884 there were cases in which the courts were prepared to bring in convictions without a corpse: that year, two seamen who had eaten cabin boys while drifting for hundreds of miles at sea in an open boat, were found guilty of murder. A more recent case concerned a wealthy woman kidnapped for ransom, and although she was never found, the police had charged two brothers with her murder. The court heard that she had probably been fed to pigs.

Suddenly he understands why the investigation was called "Operation Ivory": the police knew that there was every possibility of there being bones to gather up.

Language can provide some refuge from terror, as when the words "lethal injection" are employed to refer to "poisoning"; to "send someone to the electric chair" means to "burn them alive"; and to hang is to "strangle."

The rumours concerning the missing couple—he must try to think of them as dead now—are many (they had turned into a pair of peacocks!), but these are the facts. Last summer, Chanda and Jugnu went to Pakistan for four weeks. It was the last week of July and they were expected back in August. Chanda—the daughter of a nearby grocery-shop owner—had moved into Jugnu's house back in May, against her family's wishes. They did return from Pakistan—the passports and luggage were found in the house, the documents showing that they had come back a week earlier than expected—and were murdered sometime over the next few hours or days. Neither Shamas nor Kaukab saw them arrive, nor were they aware of their presence in England—right next door.

Inside Chanda and Jugnu's house, there are numerous glass-topped cases containing moths and butterflies of every colour, from the dull and inconspicuous to the glossily enriched, the visual equivalent of a nightingale's vibrant note, the long pin impaling each body reminiscent of the shaft that passes vertically through the wooden horse of a carousel.

Button-shaped or bottle-like, truncated cones or spheres full of spines like sea urchins, or domed as though intended for the roof of the smallest mosque imaginable: sometimes the eggs of butterflies are laid on tree bark, in neat groups like vases in a potter's courtyard, and sometimes they are positioned on the surface of a leaf, as far apart as the tastebuds are on a human tongue, or they may run around a twig like a spiral staircase. They come in as many colours as contact lenses, as disposable cigarette-lighters, and possess a similar translucence. They may be left exposed, glued to the selected base, while the females of some species cover theirs with a blanket of hairs which they free from their abdominal surface.

And if Kaukab was puzzled one brightly hot summer morning as she came across her three children intently licking off tiny beads from their hands and arms, she was appalled on being told that they were butterfly eggs, her eyes narrowing critically, her endurance reaching its limit when Jugnu told her, in all seriousness, that there was no cause for anxiety because he had made sure that the eggs were safe. "Some butterfly eggs do contain poisonous chemicals as protection against predators, especially those species which lay their eggs in clusters and produce brightly coloured eggs . . ." Such information was second nature to him and he often forgot that he could not assume a similar learning in others. ". . . And nor is there any need to worry that the children may jeopardize a species by eating its eggs: these came from the butterflies that scatter them during flight, the Skippers and the Browns. They had no chance of hatching any way, so don't worry—"

He stopped there, having noticed the look on his sister-in-law's face.

One of the children said: "They landed on us while we were out by the lake."

After that morning Kaukab tried on a few occasions to prevent the children from going out to the hills with Jugnu to collect butterflies and moths, but her wish proved a net of weak threads.

Paper turns yellow over the years because it's burning very slowly due to contact with the air. Stacked chronologically, the photographs of Jugnu in the various boxes in the house the police had termed "the house of death" would form a spectrum of pale browns.

The earliest photograph, showing the gentle nineteen-year-old boy their mother always said was Allah's way of compensating her for the daughter she had always wished for, dates from 1966, the year he arrived in Moscow to study at the Patrice Lumumba People's Friendship University. Learning Russian and obtaining a bachelor's degree would take him five years; and afterwards he would return to Pakistan briefly, shortly before their father died. There followed a few months in a damp cold house in England with Shamas and Kaukab, and then he moved to the United States.

"Who is this green woman in a sari?" Kaukab had held up the Statue of Liberty postcard he had sent from New York, a short note informing them of his safe arrival and asking about the seven-year-old nephew's tuberculosis, with love to the baby niece—the girl who would try to contain her laughter in a decade's time, when he had returned to England, as she asked him to explain the large moustache a photograph showed he had grown during his six years in the United States.

On the day she spotted a bottle of whisky in one of them, Kaukab had had all the photographs sent up to the attic, away from the impressionable eyes of the three children in the house, and they would remain there until Jugnu moved out to live next door.

On the road with the chestnut trees he hears footsteps behind him on the snow, but there's no one there. There have been moments over the past few days when he has felt that it is he who has died and been buried—and he hears his own footsteps as though someone has come to find him and dig him out.

Two months after Chanda and Jugnu disappeared, the police had contemplated extending their investigation to the United States but the passports of the two lovers were here in England, in the house next door to Shamas's.

From Tucson to the orange groves of California and then on through Oregon towards Washington, the journey Jugnu made during his first three springs in the United States with migratory beekeepers took him two whole months, stopping along the way to let the bees pollinate the crops. As he drove, the truck hummed with the three-million bees in the back and he reeked of banana oil long into each year. He painted radium dials in a clock factory one winter and it was there that a spillage had left his hands with the ability to glow in the dark, making them irresistible to moths.

He had briefly married an American woman whose trade it was to marry illegal immigrants and divorce them after they had been granted legal status. He never knew how lonely he was during those six years until the news of his mother's death reached him in Boston where he was working on a doctorate. The following year he flew to England.

It was 1978, and the cry in Britain was that immigrants should be sent back to the countries they had come from: *Just look in the telephone directory: there are thousands of them here now.* He was thirty-one; and the children whose spirits he began to revive immediately upon arrival were thirteen, eight and four. "The droppings of a moose look and smell the same as deer droppings," he told them, "and if you try you'll find that they taste the same too."

Perhaps the most recent photograph in the bundle which was consigned to the attic is the one that shows the three children sitting cross-legged beside a beached minke whale, its pink corduroy belly resting on the wet packed sand, the reflection of the setting sun stretching like a golden path from the sea's edge to the horizon, the sky above them a combustion of emerald feathers that were, perhaps, the tattered outer-edges of the thunderstorm that happened to be raging here in this inland valley town that afternoon. As evening passed and night descended, Shamas and Kaukab had looked out of the rain-lashed windows of their house with rising panic:

Lightning strikes without caring whose nest it burns: Shamas and Kaukab were terrified that the four of them would not make it home in time before the pubs shut and the streets were full of drunk white people.

On the road through the cherry trees, Shamas enters a sphere of street-light like a day and emerges from it as though into night, again and again. He turns into the sloping side-street between the church and the mosque. Verses from the Bible translated into Urdu, especially those extolling the virtues of Christ as saviour, are regularly pinned to the noticeboard in the churchyard and they are torn down in the middle of the night just as regularly.

From the incline between the church and the mosque, Shamas sees the faint shimmer of heat haze clinging to the roofs of all but one of the houses in his street—Jugnu's. *The Darwin*—Jugnu's Sheridan Multi-Cruiser speedboat—is still there in his front garden, covered by a faded tarpaulin.

As in Lahore, a road in this town is named after Goethe. There is a Park Street here as in Calcutta, a Malabar Hill as in Bombay, and a Naag Tolla Hill as in Dhaka. Because it was difficult to pronounce the English names, the men who arrived in this town in the 1950s had re-christened everything they saw before them. They had come from across the Subcontinent, lived together ten to a room, and the name that one of them happened to give to a street or landmark was taken up by the others, regardless of where they themselves were from. But over the decades, as more and more people came, the various nationalities of the Subcontinent have changed the names according to the specific country they themselves are from—Indian, Pakistani, Bangladeshi, Sri Lankan. Only one name has been accepted by every group, remaining unchanged. It's the name of the town itself. Dasht-e-Tanhaii.

The Wilderness of Solitude.

The Desert of Loneliness.

In Darkness

Kaukab looks out of the window and watches a little boy climb the sloping side-street lined with the twenty maples. The six-year-old is on his way to the mosque and his grandmother has just telephoned Kaukab from three streets away: "Keep an eye on him, sister-ji. He won't let me walk him to the mosque anymore. He is becoming independent and wants to go alone. I am telephoning everyone I know along his path because you have to be careful—every day you hear about depraved white men doing unspeakable things to little children." And the woman rang off with a sigh: "We should never have come to this deplorable country, sister-ji, this nest of devilry from where God has been exiled. No, not exiled—denied and slain. It's even worse."

Kaukab remains at the window after the boy has disappeared from sight, and then she blots her eyes with her veil. It has been seven years and a month since she and Shamas heard from their youngest child, her beloved son Ujala. She lifts a small framed photograph from the shelf and looks at him, his hair falling on his shoulders, the body beginning to stretch in adolescence, his mouth grinning, and she recalls that the Prophet, peace be upon him, had said that Allah had revealed Himself to him in the beautiful guise of a long-haired fourteen-year-old boy. She presses the picture to her breast. He was always recalcitrant—everything she did seemed to disgust him—and he left home as soon as he could. The daughter Mah-Jabin calls every month or so and visits once or twice a year. Charag, the eldest child, the painter, came during summer last year, and hasn't telephoned or visited since. He is divorced from the white girl—which means that Kaukab hasn't seen the grandson for two years and seven months.

Her children were all she had, but she herself was only a part of their lives, a very small part, it has become increasingly clear to her over the past few years.

Alone in the house, she looks out in a daze. Snow has begun again.

Kaukab knows her dissatisfaction with England is a slight to Allah because He is the creator and ruler of the entire earth—as the stone carving on Islamabad airport reminds and reassures the heartbroken people who are having to leave Pakistan—but she cannot contain her homesickness and constantly asks for courage to face this lonely ordeal that He has chosen for her in His wisdom.

She often reminds herself that Allah had given Adam his name after the Arabic word *adim*, which means "the surface of the earth"; he—and therefore the whole of mankind, his descendants—was created from earth taken from different parts of the world. His head was made from the soil of the East, his breast from the soil of the Mecca, his feet from the West.

She lowers herself into a chair, the veil pressed to her eyes, remembering how the fridge door feels lighter these days because it is not as weighted with bottles of milk on the inside as it once was, when the children were here and Jugnu was still taking his meals with the family, as he would continue to do even after he went to live next door. How grateful she was at the beginning for Jugnu's being here in England! When he was in America, he used to send coin-like postcards and, like a jukebox, she would sing a lengthy song in return, page upon page detailing the family's life, asking him to come back, telling him that circumstances had improved a little since his first short visit to England. He did return and Kaukab found it hard to contain her pride when the neighbourhood women wanted to know who that flesh-and-blood Taj Mahal was they saw sitting in her garden yesterday. She recruited them in her search for a bride for him but he said he needed to find his feet in England first. She was grateful to him for being here in Dasht-e-Tanhaii because the move to England had deprived her of the glowing warmth that people who are born of each other give out, the heat and light of an extended family. She prepared for him all the food he had been missing during his years away.

Bamboo tubes pickled to tartness in linseed oil, slimy edoes that glued the fingers together as you ate them, *naan* bread shaped like ballet slippers, poppy seeds that were coarser than sand grains but still managed to shift like a dune when the jar was tilted, dry pomegranate seeds to be patted onto potato cakes like stones in a brooch, edible petals of courgette flowers packed inside the buds like amber scarves in green rucksacks, chilli seeds that were volts of electricity, the peppers whose stalks were hooked like umbrella handles, butter to be diced into cubes reluctant to separate, peas attached to the inside of an undone pod in a row like puppies drinking from their mother's belly: she moved through the aisles of Chanda Food & Convenience Store and chose his favourite foods. Coriander was abundant in the neighbour's garden and it was just a matter of leaning over the fence with a pair of sewing scissors. If the ingredients were heavy as hailstone in the carrier bags, the final dishes were light as snowflakes, so delicate and fleeting was the balance of spices and the interplay of flavours. She feared her successes were accidental but with the help of Allah she repeated the error-free performances, and the diners proclaimed her to be the eighth, ninth, *and* tenth wonder of the world.

He was her husband's brother, her children's uncle, her own brother-in-law. Daily and deeply, she loved these words and what they meant. It was as though, when the doors of Pakistan closed on her, her hands had forgotten the art of knocking; she had made friends with some women in the area but she barely knew what lay beyond the neighbourhood and didn't know how to deal with strangers: full of apprehension concerning the white race and uncomfortable with people of another Subcontinental religion or grouping.

She had had no schooling beyond the age of eleven, but when she arrived in England all those years ago, bright with optimism, she had told Shamas she planned to enrol in an English-learning course as soon as their material circumstances improved, and, in anticipation, she filled a whole notebook with the things she overheard, words whose meaning she didn't know, proverbs jumbled up, sayings mistakenly glued to other sayings:

The grass is always green with envy on the other side.
Love is in the air but is blind as a bat.

Blood is thicker than water through thick and thin.
It will be a cold day in Hell when Hell freezes over.
A friend indeed is a friend, indeed.
Heaven is other people.

This last she had heard and remembered correctly, *Hell is other people*, but she had later begun to doubt herself: surely no one—no people, no civilization—would think other people were Hell. What else was there but other people?

She never did take that language course. But when they bought a television in the 1970s—it was a Phillips because her father had owned a radio made by that company back in Pakistan so she found it a reassurance and also knew it could be trusted—she began to watch children's programmes with her children, but each one of the three moved on eventually, leaving her and her rudimentary grasp of English behind.

Now she stands up and moves towards the telephone. Dialling carefully, she waits for the call to connect but then hangs up after the first ring, her courage failing. A minute later she dials again and, bravely, keeps herself from walking away. She lets it ring. The answering machine at the other end has a message in Ujala's voice. He has refused to speak to her personally for years now, but she rings his number every few days to hear his voice, always afraid lest the boy himself pick up the phone and proceed to say something unpleasant to her, something abusive, telling her she is heartless, is partly or wholly responsible for the deaths of Jugnu and Chanda, having been outraged when they set up home together.

Overcome by fear, she hangs up for the second time.

Yes, she had objected to Chanda moving in with Jugnu, but she is not heartless and hadn't disapproved of their love. When she heard the rumour about the pair, she remembers being secretly relieved that Jugnu had chosen a Muslim this time, all his previous women having been white. Jugnu was in his late forties, and Kaukab knew he must marry this girl and settle down. But then they began to live together in sin and Jugnu refused to listen to her no matter how reasonably or passionately she tried to make him see the error of his ways.

She was already anxious to see Jugnu settle down and raise a family long before Chanda appeared. Shamas—unwilling to think about such things unprompted—agreed with her whenever she insisted on raising the subject. They would then talk to Jugnu together. The last time the two of them broached the subject with him, seven years or so ago, he startled them both by replying: "Good. I have been meaning for you to meet her." He was referring to the white woman Kaukab had seen with him in the town centre on two occasions during the last month.

It was high summer, and on the day of the dinner Kaukab worked in the kitchen all morning. She went to sit out in the sun for a few minutes as the afternoon wore on, all the summer foliage giving a sea-tinge to the light in Dasht-e-Tanhaii as though a green scarf had been draped over the sun. That was when Charag came home on an unexpected visit: Charag—the son whom she had sent away to university in London to get an education—had come to inform her that he had a *girlfriend* who was not only *white* but also *pregnant*. The news stunned and repulsed Kaukab, and she held Jugnu responsible for her misfortune. Once, on seeing a diagram of a moth's innards in one of Jugnu's magazines, Kaukab had wondered how there could be room in so small a creature to house so many mechanisms, and that summer seven years ago, her own despair was immense although she was tiny: she accused Jugnu of leading her children astray. After Jugnu, her mind, flooded with bitterness and sorrow, had turned on Shamas because Shamas himself had confused the children with his Godless ideas, undermining her authority and devaluing her behaviour as though it was just neurotic and foolish—Jugnu only finished the job Shamas started years ago.

And then she held her own father responsible for having chosen an irreligious husband for her, the father whose impeccable judgement—she had said at other times—could be counted on to remain unclouded during all circumstances, uncowed even by the most monumental of world events so that he had sent a nine-page telegram to Ayatollah Khomeini following the Iranian Revolution to ask him to reconsider his zeal, quoting from the Koran and the sayings of the Prophet, peace be upon him, against his excesses.

She accused her father of not checking what kind of people he was handing over his daughter to: surely, the clues were everywhere if he had cared to look. Just after the engagement, Shamas's mother had wondered whether Kaukab would like to rub bird shit into her face, claiming it would enhance her complexion, and she sent her a cage of Japanese nightingales which Kaukab kept just for their song!

Charag, after giving her the devastating news, stayed for less than an hour, leaving her alone with her grief and tears.

She wept as she prepared the food in honour of Jugnu's white woman—a feast celebrating the fact that they were sinners! The two guests would come after eight, around the same time as Shamas, who had a Communist Party meeting that night; and since Ujala was staying with a friend, Kaukab was alone in the house, alone in the house just as she was alone in the world, alone to let out a noisy sob whenever she felt the need, and as though in harmony with her own state the sky darkened around six and it began to rain noisily. It was just after seven that she happened to see herself in the mirror: the whites of her eyes were veined with blood, her face was red, her eyelids were swollen, and her hair was in disarray (she had beaten her head with her hands several times in a fit of grief ten minutes ago).

She did not have the energy to clean herself up—let Shamas come home and see what he and his family and his children had done to her—but she washed her face nevertheless and oiled and combed her hair because the white woman was coming.

She sprayed perfume into her armpits, and rubbed moisturiser into her flaky grey elbows. She had never met a white person at such an intimate level as she would tonight, and for several days now she had been wondering which of her *shalwar-kameez*s she should wear, settling on the blue one that had a print of white apple blossoms. She clicked open the lid of the face-powder container for the first time in ten years and the smell the cracked pieces of powder gave off took her back to her younger days. Delicately, she patted the fawn-coloured powder over the eyelids, to hide the dark circles and the wrinkles, to bring out the eyes that had sunk into her skull over the years. Allah, the pores on either side of her nose were deep enough to lose coins in. She plucked hairs out of her eyebrows. (Must remember to take out exactly the same number from the other brow.) She wondered which earrings she should wear as she painted her mouth with the pale reddish-brown lipstick. Too much? She wiped it off and started again, and wondered whether she should try eyeliner and just the smallest hint of mascara, wishing her daughter was still living at home to provide guidance on such matters. She struggled hard not to cry at that but failed; in the end, however, she had to restrain herself because she had also to practise her English in the mirror. And it too was hopeless: what was a person to do when even *things* in England spoke a different language than the one they did back in Pakistan? In England the heart said "boom boom" instead of *dhak dhak;* a gun said "bang!" instead of *thah!;* things fell with a "thud," not a *dharam;* small bells said "jingle" instead of *chaan-chaan;* the trains said "choo choo" instead of *chuk chuk* . . . The eyebrows were still a little unruly, she decided towards the end, and rummaged in the cupboard where Ujala kept his things: she managed to locate the jar of hair gel and smoothed a little of it on each brow to tame the hairs. Shouldn't she take some of the powder off her face: the layers looked so thick she could've scratched a message on her forehead with a nail. After she was ready, at last, there was just enough time to attend to the few last details of the meal: she went into the back garden with her sewing scissors to clip leaves of coriander to sprinkle over the *mung dahl.* And that was when a ten-year-old girl from the neighbourhood saw her from the other side of the lane, crossed over, looked at her contemplatively for a few seconds, and then said quietly in the flat tones of one making an innocent observation:

"But surely, auntie-ji, you look like a eunuch."

Shooing the child away, who must have seen eunuchs dancing at a wedding during a visit to Pakistan or India, Kaukab rushed indoors burning with shame and humiliation, wondering whether she hadn't in fact got carried away with the cosmetics, and she pleaded with Allah for help because now there was no time for her to correct her appearance: the doorbell rang to announce the arrival of Jugnu and the white woman, she who no doubt had a perfectly made-up face framed by perfectly arranged hair. She stood frozen in the middle of the room and heard the key slide into the lock of the front door: Shamas must be with Jugnu and his guest.

"My Allah, come to my help! Save the honour of your servant, O *Parvardigar,*" she mouthed to herself because the door was about to open any second and disgrace her. But had she forgotten that the Almighty had nothing but compassion for His creatures? The moment the front door opened, the electricity in the entire street happened to fail and—praise be to Allah—the house plunged into darkness. Kaukab managed to move and clambered upstairs to wash her face while Shamas brought in Jugnu and the white woman.

Most of the meal was taken by candlelight, the wet prints the white woman's high-heeled shoes had made on the linoleum of the kitchen floor shining like exclamation marks in the yellow light. The kitchen table was carried into the pink room next door and there was a vase of flowers at its centre. The spoons had been polished and the meal was among the best Kaukab had cooked. The white woman wore a lilac blouse of shimmering silk that Kaukab couldn't resist the urge to finger just for the pleasure of it—it looked like a fabric known in Pakistan as *Aab-e-Ravan*, the Flowing Water—but despite all that the evening was not a success: what happened during the get-together would eventually lead to the end of Jugnu and the white woman's relationship.

Trying to keep Charag's revelations of the afternoon out of her mind, and trying not to dwell on the fact that the white woman's legs were bare below her knee-length skirt (made, incidentally, of a checked fabric that reminded Kaukab of *Bulbul Chasm*, the Eye of the Songbird), Kaukab busied herself with the food and was reluctant to sit at the table with the other three, saying she must bake the chappatis freshly, that the *aloo bhurta* had to be *turka*'d moments before it was served, that the sweet *zarda* rice had to be got going so that they would be ready just in time for the end of the dinner. The candle flames corrugated each time she arrived in the room with another tray, another bowl, another tureen. The white woman praised Kaukab's skill as a cook whenever she took a mouthful of something new on the table, the candlelight throwing dark shadows under her breasts, emphasizing them obscenely. Kaukab's stomach twisted into a knot when Jugnu shamelessly planted a small kiss on the woman's cheek in passing, and she gritted her teeth at Shamas's expansive behaviour towards the white woman and towards her own self: "Come sit with us, Kaukab, and talk. Let's prove to our guest that Pakistanis are the most talkative people on earth. My goodness, we use *seven* syllables just to say hello: *Assalamaulaikum*."

Kaukab was glad Ujala was out of the house: she wouldn't have wanted him to think there was anything normal about a Pakistani man bringing home a white woman to meet his family.

And that was when she panicked. Ujala! She had already lost one son to a white girl; wouldn't Jugnu marrying this white woman make it possible for Ujala to marry white one day too? Outside the rain intensified, and she shook with fear as she heard the sounds of conversation from the table, the clinking of glasses, the cutlery on the plates: it sounded like a normal family gathering, yes, but she herself—and everything she stood for—was excluded from it. They were talking in English and too fast for her to keep up. She tried to follow the conversation and her fear began to turn to anger. "I was born into a Muslim household, but I object to the idea that that automatically makes me a Muslim," Jugnu said. "The fact of the matter is that had I lived at the time of Muhammad, and he came to me with his heavenly message, I would have walked away . . ." Stunned, Kaukab knew that it was the white woman's presence that was really responsible for this utterance of Jugnu (she who herself didn't add anything disrespectful, just listened intently): he felt emboldened to say such a thing in her company—he may have *thought* these things before, but the white person enabled him to say them out loud. And sure enough, soon Shamas too was dancing in that direction:

While Kaukab was in the kitchen—adding to the refilled salad bowl the radishes she'd carved into intricate twenty-petalled roses with the tip of a knife—Shamas laughed above the conversation in the pink room and, raising his voice, addressed her in Punjabi: "Kaukab, you should really come and talk to our guest: she's just said something which I have often heard you say, 'But, surely, the rational explanations of how the universe began are just as shaky. Every day the scientists tell us that their long-held theory about this or that matter has proved to be inaccurate.' " Yes, Kaukab had indeed made this observation when defending religion, and now she tried to follow Shamas's words as he switched to English and said to the white woman, "I am still inclined to believe the scientists, because, unlike the prophets, they readily admit that they are *working towards* an answer, they don't have the *final* and absolute answer." Kaukab had still not recovered from this when Jugnu added (to Shamas, in Punjabi, proof yet again that the white woman's presence was just a catalyst for the two brothers to air their blasphemies):

"And anyway, the same procedures and the same intellectual and analytical rigour that went on to produce the car we've driven in this evening, the telephone we talk on, the planes we fly in, the electricity we use, are the ones that are being used to probe the universe. I trust what science says about the universe because I can *see* the result of scientific methods all around me. I cannot be expected to believe what an illiterate merchant-turned-opportunistic-preacher—for he was no systematic theologian—in the seventh-century Arabian desert had to say about the origin of life."

It took Kaukab several minutes to understand what she had just heard, and then she had to steady herself against a wall because she realized that Muhammad, peace be upon him, peace be upon him, was being referred to here.

Praising things like electricity: the very thing that's failed this evening, she had fumed inwardly, *making you all sit in the darkness!*

Soon her children would be further encouraged towards Godlessness.

What would she tell her father-ji? She remembered how horrified her entire family had been when her brother had wanted to marry a Sikh woman back in the 1950s, despite the fact that the Sikhs were a people of the Subcontinent, a people whose habits, language, skin colour and culture were somewhat familiar. Who was this white woman? How clean was she, for instance: did she know that a person must bathe after sexual intercourse, or remain polluted, contaminating everything one came into contact with? She had an image of Jugnu and the woman stopping by at the house next door to fornicate before coming around to dinner here: and she felt nausea. And all this had been going on with her own son too, Charag. Kaukab had touched the white woman and would have to bathe and change her clothes to be able to say her next prayers. She refilled the bowl of *raita* and took it to the table in the pink room, and she had just placed it next to the vase of roses when the electricity returned. The abrupt brilliance so surprised Shamas that he let drop the bottle of wine he had been holding: the liquid splashed onto the carpet and Kaukab stepped back to avoid being touched by the repulsive stuff.

So they had been drinking wine in the darkness. Kaukab had a sudden illumination: she was hoping to get some sympathy later that evening from Jugnu and Shamas, concerning Charag's news, but now suddenly she saw how mad that hope was—they wouldn't see it as debauchery. She was the only one who thought there was anything wrong with the pregnancy, and for that they would silently accuse her of being inhuman, moribund, lifeless. It wouldn't surprise her if they weren't all secretly longing for her to die so they could start to "enjoy" their lives.

The bottle rolled across the floor and came to a stop. There was silence and then Jugnu stood up and said, "Salt is what you need for a red wine stain—isn't it?"

"I wouldn't know, never having allowed that abominable thing into my house," Kaukab had said, trying to control her rage and disgust. "What else have you learnt from her and her people," she wanted to ask him, "what else do you plan to pass on to my children?"

Jugnu remained where he was but Shamas got up to retrieve the bottle, despite Kaukab glaring at him. The white woman leaned over and tried to place a hand on Kaukab's arm, but she shrank away: "Don't touch me, please. May Allah forgive me, but I don't know where you've been." She remained standing where she was, now about to break down and cry, now ready to sweep everything from the table onto the floor and begin shouting, but had then turned around to go back into the kitchen: "I'll get the *dahl*. I completely forgot to serve it." She lifted the lid off the *dahl* and tested a grain of it between her fingers to see that it had cooked to perfection; it had, and so she picked up the ladle and looked for something to serve the *dahl* in.

Shamas came and stood behind her. "I thought they would enjoy wine with dinner."

Aha! Kaukab nodded. *"Enjoy"—just another word for the works of Satan the Stoned-One!*

"I didn't mean to upset you."

"You yourself seem to be enjoying yourself a good deal too this evening," Kaukab said, doling out the *dahl,* her back towards Shamas. "Conversing away, using big words to show off to the white woman."

"Showing off? How old do you think I am?" He had sighed, and on hearing Kaukab's sobs had approached her. "What do you want me to say to you?"

"Nothing. I want you to listen to me."

"I will. Why won't you let me help you with the food? Go and sit down." And when she pushed him away he added: "Please don't throw a tantrum."

"Who is the one treating the other as a child now? I am not throwing a tantrum: I am *angry*. Take me seriously."

"What are you doing? For God's sake!"

Kaukab had arranged four shoes on a tray and was pouring *dahl* into them as though they were plates.

Shamas was unable to stop her as she slipped from his repulsive wine-contaminated grasp and carried the tray into the pink room and placed it on the table before Jugnu and his white woman with a loud bang—*dharam!*

Kaukab rings Ujala's number and stays on the line until the answering machine has played the two sentences spoken by him, and then she quickly replaces the receiver. Just then the doorbell rings.

"Jugnu?" Kaukab whispers to herself and then rushes across the room on legs trembling with excitement to let him in. *Ujala? Charag and his little son? Mah-Jabin?*, but it's a neighbourhood woman, the matchmaker, come to ask Kaukab if she has a veil that would go with the mustard-coloured *shalwar-kameez* she's brought with her.

"I'll need to borrow it just for one day, Kaukab. Moths chewed out holes the size of digestive biscuits from my own mustard-coloured veil and I haven't been able to find the replacement of the exact shade," she explains.

"I think I *do* have a veil of that colour upstairs. Its edges are crocheted, though—that won't be a problem, will it? A row of little five-petalled flowers. Quite discreet."

Standing at the bottom of the stairs, the matchmaker talks while Kaukab goes up to her bedroom, taking the mustard *kameez* with her. Of course the woman wants to talk about the arrest of Chanda's shopkeeper brothers.

From the stairs, Kaukab says, "They are saying, sister-ji, that the police got the breakthrough completely by chance. They had spent hundreds of hours investigating the case but the main clue came not in England, but in the Pakistani village where Chanda's parents are from. A white Detective Sergeant from here in Dasht-e-Tanhaii had flown to that village to make enquiries into a suspected fraud case—a case totally unrelated to the lovers' *alleged* murder, I say 'alleged' because *I* don't believe Jugnu and Chanda are dead—and there he happened to hear a chance remark: apparently Chanda's brothers had confessed everything to their relatives in the village. The Detective Sergeant flew to England and informed his colleagues who then went to Pakistan to collect witnesses. Sister-ji, the white police are interested in us Pakistanis only when there is a chance to prove that we are savages who slaughter our sons and daughters, brothers and sisters."

The matchmaker narrows her eyes: "Imagine, they flew all the way to Pakistan just to be able to brand us Pakistanis murderers, at £465 a ticket, £510 if they minded the overnight stop at Qatar and went direct."

Kaukab brings her the veil. "I know Chanda's brothers are innocent because those who commit crimes of honour give themselves up proudly, their duty done. They never deny or skulk. I am certain they will walk free after the trial in December."

The matchmaker nods vehemently. "And as for Chanda: What a shameless girl she was, sister-ji, so brazen. She not only had poor Jugnu killed by moving in with him, she also ruined the lives of her own poor brothers who had to kill them—if that was what happened, of course. Let's hope they are found not-guilty in December. But what I fail to understand is how Shamas-brother-ji could have allowed the two of them to live together in sin? And how did you, Kaukab, manage to tolerate it, you who are a cleric's daughter—born and brought up in a mosque all your life?"

The matchmaker holds her mustard *kameez* against the veil that Kaukab has brought. "This is a perfect match, Kaukab." She holds the soft veil against the back of her hand. "It's not georgette. Is it chiffon?"

Kaukab nods. "Japanese. From the shop way over there on Ustad Allah Bux Street. I don't go there often—white people's houses start soon after that street, and even the Pakistanis there are not from our part of Pakistan."

"I have just been to that street. Do you remember years ago I tried to arrange a marriage between your Jugnu and a girl from that street, a girl named Suraya? No? Well anyway, nothing came of that, of course, and so I found a man for her in Pakistan. But now unfortunately she has been divorced. The husband got drunk and divorced her, and although he now regrets doing it, she cannot remarry him without first marrying and getting a divorce from someone else. That's Allah's law and who are we to question it? Poor Suraya is back in England, and I am looking for a man who will marry her for a short period."

If her children were still living at home, or if Shamas was back from work, Kaukab would have asked the matchmaker to lower her voice to a whisper, not wishing her children to hear anything bad about Pakistan or the Pakistanis, not wishing to provide Shamas with the opportunity to make a disrespectful comment about Islam, or hint through his expression that he harboured contrary views on Allah's inherent greatness; but she is alone in the house, so she lets the woman talk.

"I'll bring the veil back the day after tomorrow," the matchmaker says as she leaves around five o'clock and Kaukab gets ready to cook dinner. "Shamas-brother-ji would be home soon from work—from this year onwards he'll be able to put his feet up now that he's sixty-five and retiring from work." She laughs. "No retirement age for us housewives though, Kaukab. Anyway, I must leave you alone now because if you are anything like me, you too can't bear another woman watching you while you cook."

Mung dahl. As she washes the *dahl* she recalls the disastrous evening with Jugnu and the white woman, the *dahl* in the shoes, and she begs forgiveness from Almighty Allah yet again for having wasted the food that He in His limitless bounty and compassion had seen fit to provide her with, a creature as worthless as her. But the fact of the matter is that she doesn't really remember doling out the portions into the shoes and carrying them to the table; she remembers coming to her senses only once all the actions had been performed and she was standing in the room with Jugnu and the white woman staring at her, aghast.

Kaukab can remember the evening as though she is reading it in the Book of Fates, the book into which, once a year, the angels write down the destiny of every human being for the next twelve months: who'll live, who'll die, who'll lose happiness, who'll find love—Allah dictates it to them, having come down especially for one night from the seventh heaven to the first, the one closest to earth.

Allah gave her everything, so how can Kaukab not be thankful to Him every minute of the day when He had given her everything she had, how could she have not tried to make sure that her children grew up to be

Allah's servants, and how could she have approved of Jugnu marrying the white woman, or later, approve of him living in sin with Chanda? For the people in the West, an offence that did no harm to another human or to the wider society was no offence at all, but to her—to all Muslims—there was always another party involved—Allah; *He* was getting hurt by Chanda and Jugnu's actions.

She sets the *mung dahl* on the cooker and adds turmeric, salt, and red chilli powder, shaking her head at how that whole affair with Jugnu's white woman turned out. After the dinner that night, Jugnu didn't come around to Shamas and Kaukab for about two weeks, though they both heard through the walls the sounds of arguments between him and the white woman, and Kaukab once saw the white woman emerge from the house in tears. Several weeks of silence followed, and she knew Jugnu had broken relations with the woman, but he still refused to come see Kaukab; she gathered all the information from Shamas. Ujala had recently moved out of the house (forever—she would realize as the years passed), after yet another argument with Kaukab, so Kaukab only had Shamas as her source of information about Jugnu. And it was Shamas who told her one day that Jugnu and the white woman were back together again, and it was Shamas again—his face drained of blood, his voice full of panic—who told her a few days later that Jugnu was in hospital with glucose drips attached to his arms and painkillers being injected into his bloodstream every few hours.

"That diseased woman, this diseased, vice-ridden and lecherous race!" Kaukab hissed as she sat by Jugnu's bedside at the infirmary. Apparently the woman had decided to go on a short holiday after breaking up with Jugnu and had one night drunkenly slept with someone who had given her a disease, a prostitute's vileness which she had unknowingly passed on to Jugnu when she returned to England and got back together with him. The disease was found in Jugnu's manhood but also in his throat, and Kaukab tried to control her nausea when she realized how it must've got there. Such accursed practices, such godlessness! That disease was surely Allah's wrath and punishment for such behaviour.

Jugnu had to stay in hospital for eight days and Kaukab nursed him back to health when he came home, bedding down on the floor next to him at night in case he needed something. She could do nothing about Jugnu's insistence that the news of his ailment be kept from Ujala: the boy hadn't visited the house even once since he moved out, and a small part of Kaukab—may Allah forgive her!—had been secretly pleased that Jugnu was so severely ill; surely that would bring the boy home to his beloved uncle immediately. But she had to respect Jugnu's wishes in the end, and told him that the first thing he had to do after his recovery was to locate and bring back Ujala.

And she told him squarely that she didn't believe him when he said that the white woman had picked up the disease in Tunisia. "She's lying," she said firmly. "Tunisia is a Muslim country. She must've gone on holiday somewhere else, a country populated by the whites or non-Muslims. She's trying to malign our faith."

She attempted to keep any neighbourhood women from entering the house during Jugnu's convalescence, lest a careless word by someone in the house led to the disclosure of the true nature of Jugnu's affliction.

The neighbourhood women. Kaukab stands at the kitchen window now and looks out, and she can hear them all around the neighbourhood, this neighbourhood that is noisy: it manages to make a crunching sound when it eats a banana and its birds bicker like inter-racial couples. Speaking up is a necessity because the neighbourhood is deaf after thirty years of factory work, and it stirs its tea for minutes on end as though there are pebbles at the bottom of the cup instead of grains of sugar. But the neighbourhood is also quiet: it hoards its secrets, unwilling to let on the pain in its breast. Shame, guilt, honour and fear are like padlocks hanging from mouths. No one makes a sound in case it draws attention. No one speaks. No one breathes. The place is bumpy with buried secrets and problems swept under the carpets.

Kaukab hears the women. One is cursing the inventor of the wheel and ruing the day she came to England, this loathsome country that has stolen her daughter from her, the disobedient girl who doesn't want to go to Pakistan for a visit because males and females are segregated there, "Everything's divided into His and Hers as if anyone needed a reminder of what a great big toilet that country really is, Mother; no wonder you get the shits the moment you land."

The women are dreamers. No, their sons certainly can't grow up to become footballers for Manchester United. If they are *that* interested in the team, they can become the team's doctor.

Kaukab, a picture of loneliness, waiting for Shamas to come home, remembers how the Tannoy announcement at the bus station always makes her think she's in Pakistan and a Friday sermon is being conveyed over a mosque loudspeaker, and the other women tell her that it's happened to them too. One woman tries to hold back her tears because she's beginning to realize that she would never be able to go back to live in her own country (she has started monthly payments for funeral arrangements at her mosque near her house), a country that's poor because the whites stole all its wealth, beginning with the Koh-i-Noor diamond. And though the heart of every woman in the neighbourhood sinks whenever there is an unscheduled "newsflash" on TV, making them think the government is about to announce that all the Asian immigrants are to be thrown out of Britain, just like they had been expelled out of Uganda two decades ago, and though the women's hearts sink for a moment, they plan to put up a fight and say they'll go back with pleasure as soon as the Queen gives back our Koh-i-Noor.

And, yes, as she waits for Shamas to come home, Kaukab can also hear the women talk about herself and Shamas, about how Shamas has insisted on remaining in this neighbourhood even though he can afford to move out to a better area. The whites were already moving out of here by the end of the 1970s, and within the decade the Hindus became the first immigrant group to move out to the rich suburbs, followed slowly over the next few years by a handful of Pakistanis. Doctors, lawyers, accountants, engineers—all have moved out of the neighbourhood and gone to the suburbs by now, leaving behind the Pakistanis, the Bangladeshis, and a few Indians, all of whom work in restaurants, drive taxis and buses, or are unemployed.

Only the good Shamas-brother-ji has remained—thinks a woman preparing the dinner—despite the fact that he works in an office and can no doubt move away ten times if he chooses but he is not the kind of man who believes you see through your window what you deserve because *nobody* deserves this rundown neighbourhood of one suicide attempt a year, twenty-nine people registered insane, and so many break-ins a month that the woman unplugs the video-recorder that had cost two-years' savings and brings it up to bed every night, and when she isn't lying awake waiting for the sound of a window breaking downstairs, she is lying awake wondering where her two boys are because more and more of the burglaries are being done by the sons of the immigrants themselves, almost all of whom are unemployed.

Next door, this woman's neighbour wonders why her children refer to Bangladesh as "abroad" because Bangladesh isn't abroad, *England* is abroad; Bangladesh is *home*.

Kaukab hears them gossip about Jugnu, he whom they had all loved from the beginning, encouraging their children to seek his company because he was educated and they wanted some of his intelligence to rub off on them, Jugnu who had lived in Russia and in the United States and had gone on butterfly collecting trips to western China, India, Peru and Iran. He told the neighbourhood children that in Oklahoma he had seen the white funnel of a tornado turn red as this apple as it pulverized a nursery full of geraniums. And the children had wanted to know why he didn't stick around to see if the tornado passed over a dye factory because they certainly would have.

The women were pleased that the children were spending so much time with a civilized person and they stopped him in the street to tell him how happy they were that he was among them, and to chastise him gently for telling the children that there are no references to butterflies in the Bible because it might make the children curious about that book and become Christians.

That was, of course, before he was seen with white women, long long before he began living openly in sin with that shopkeeper's daughter, Chanda.

They asked him to secure the shoelace that had come undone or he would trip. And only later—at home—would they smite their foreheads in regret for having made that comment about the children converting to Christianity because the confusion of faiths was exactly what had torn to pieces the life of his and Shamas-brother-ji's father. Their father was born a Hindu and had lost his memory as a ten-year-old boy and drifted into a Muslim life, remembering his true identity only in adulthood, by which time it was too late.

Yes, the women would nod, among the many things the white people stole from the Subcontinent was that ten-year-old boy's memory, back in 1919.

Kaukab, having just finished her prayers, hears Shamas's key turn in the front door, and the sound takes her back to the day Jugnu had brought the white woman home for dinner, and she remarks to herself that it had been a sign from Allah for the electricity to have failed the moment the white woman had stepped in, the house plunging into darkness.

Women with Tails

Shamas doesn't remember his dreams, but on some mornings, like today, he awakens with a gentle deliberateness to his gestures and from that he knows that his father has managed to infiltrate his dreams, just as a lover long gone and not allowed to surface in the waking thoughts comes to place a flower in the mind during sleep, not settling for being forgotten.

Alone in the blue kitchen, Sunday morning, he reflects on the nature of his father's drift into Islam, part dream, part nightmare, back in 1919 when he was a Hindu child of ten years and on his way with his sister to witness the wonder of women who had tails.

In the India of the Raj, the clothes the white women wore were an announcement that they weren't going native. Although it may not have been convenient and certainly was not comfortable, some British women kept firmly to their corsets well into the twentieth century, even after they had passed out of fashion back in Britain. And in the nineteenth century they had insisted on the rigidly swaying crinolines and ruched bustles even during the muddy and humid monsoon, and during the tandoor-hot heat of the months preceding it, making the natives wonder about the nature of the secret concealed under the yards of fabric, a belief spreading across the Subcontinent that white women had tails.

It was to see them that two Hindu children walked along the lanes of their Punjabi hometown of Gujranwala one spring afternoon in 1919. The brother was the true child but the sister who was older than him by three years had enough of childhood's exploratory initiative still in her to have agreed to the expedition.

What kind of a tail does a white woman have? they wondered in excitement. Not dissimilar to a peacock's, capable of being jerked up to form a giant fan of five-hundred feathers? Or a small twitchy one, resembling a deer's, needled with white hair? The boy—his name was Deepak but he would have no memory of it or of anything else by the end of the day—wondered if perhaps it was long and packed with powerful muscle for the mem-sahib to lean back on, kangaroo-like, as she lifted her feet into the air to remove her shoes. The girl—Aarti—desperately wanted it to glow in the dark like a firefly—the frilled and ruffled skirts irresistibly bringing to mind a lampshade—and there were two quarrels and three reconciliations between the pair as they made their way to the *dak* bungalow—the rest-house where the white people lodged when they travelled through Gujranwala. It was surrounded on three sides by the groves of blood-oranges for which the region was famous, and the sahibs were said to climb over the boundary wall in the middle of night for an orange to squeeze into their drinks. So intensely perfumed was the air that in winter a single curl of fog plucked from outside the window and stirred into the glass was enough to impart the flavour of six of the fruit's segments.

It was a Tuesday in April. The jackals and wolves in the nearby jungles had howled throughout Sunday night, roused by the smell of warm human blood that the winds brought to Gujranwala from forty miles away, and by dawn on Monday the news had spread to the human population also: hundreds of men, women, and children had been gunned down at the Jallianwallah Garden in Amritsar.

Enraged by the news, the inhabitants of Gujranwala had stoned a train and set fire to railway bridges, and several buildings along the Grand Trunk Road which passed through the town—the telegraph office, the district court, the post office, and an Indian Christian Church—were reduced to ashes. The white superintendent of police was attacked and escaped with his life only when he ordered his men to open fire on the rioters.

Today, Tuesday, there was no smoke in the air but it was still unsafe to be outdoors. Lacking clear facts and news, the women who had relatives in Amritsar had kept up their wails of assumption all night last night. Hindus, Muslims and Sikhs had forgotten their differences and rioted together and the British knew from experience that such amnesia meant only trouble for them.

The path forked ahead and when Aarti told him that they would be taking the left branch, Deepak placed his hand on his chest—the easiest method of distinguishing between left and right was to remember that the heart was located on the left.

As they walked past a blue house with three *peepal* trees in the courtyard he attempted to insert his fingers into his sister's grip because he had ventured only so far from home previously and would be in un-explored territory beyond this point. Soon Aarti too was in alien terrain and linked hands with Deepak to receive and offer courage in a two-way transfusion.

Now and then as they moved forward they consulted the guidebooks of stories and hearsay (without realizing that they were getting closer and closer to the pages of history).

They arrived, but in the place where the *dak* bungalow was said to be situated, up a path lined with stones painted a bright green, they found nothing but the perfunctory sketch, charcoal on sky: only the framework of the building had survived yesterday's conflagration; the walls and roof had fallen to the ground in a black heap. The outline reminded them of the drawing of the house their father had made on the floor with a piece of coal, the house he said he was building for them, the house that was wrested by their father's family from their mother as soon as she was widowed, leaving her homeless with no alternative but the brutal charity of her sister's husband.

Deepak and Aarti circled the remains of the *dak* bungalow, Deepak attempting hard to contain his disappointment. The women with tails had been so real during the journey that he had expected footprints around himself as he walked but now the apparitions had vanished.

Aarti saw that he was close to tears, and since she could not propose raiding the orange grove—men could be heard digging water-ditches just over the wall—she tried to distract him by constructing the *dak* bungalow from the clues scattered around the site. Up there had been a balcony splashed by a hibiscus vine, and down here there was a tiled veranda with a frangipani tree at its edge, the leaves the shape of a ram's ears. Bride-red, indigo, emerald—the place glittered with fragments of stained glass. Violence unleashing violence, the fire had liberated the hundred deadly edges each pane had contained harmlessly within it when whole. In the heat breathed out by the burnt debris, the clarified butter smeared on

Deepak's skin gave off a pungent smell. He had lubricated himself before setting off on the adventure to maximize his chances of escape in case of discovery: before entering a house or a train, thieves and robbers greased themselves similarly to become as difficult to hold as fish, as melon seeds.

Smallpox had pockmarked Deepak's skin during infancy and as he stood in the kitchen applying the clarified butter to himself, Aarti had joked that there wouldn't be any left for her. She had only just begun to grease her arm when they were discovered by their uncle. The beating woke the two women from their nap but their appeals for moderation were ignored. Instead he imprisoned the two sisters in the back room by trapping their long plaits in a trunk lid, locking it, and pocketing the key, a smile of vengeful delight on his face on seeing both these women in torment as they sat tethered on the floor, one of them dark, the other pale— the first he was married to, the other he had *wanted* to marry but had been deemed unworthy of because only a wealthy man was good enough for such a pale-rinded beauty, but now that the rich man had died *he* was burdened with having to clothe, feed and shelter her and her children— that bitch daughter whom he intended to hand over to the first toothless man to ask for her hand in marriage, the poorer the better, no matter that she was as pale as her mother who dreamed of educating her bastard son when it was clear to everyone that the only education that street-loving loafer was ever likely to acquire was the skills of a pickpocket.

He dragged the children across the courtyard and shut them out of the house while the voices of the two women continued to plead for clemency from back there because it was dangerous for the children to be out on the streets today.

Their fear was not misplaced. There were disturbances across the province as the news of the Amritsar killing spread farther and farther. All the urban centres in the Gujranwala district were on fire—Ramnagar, Sangla, Wazirabad, Akalgarh, Hafizabad, Sheikhupura, Chuharkana, and the rebellion had also spread north along the railway line into Gujarat and west into Lyallpur.

Requests for help from Gujranwala had left the governor of Punjab, Sir Michael O'Dwyer, in a predicament: he could not send large numbers of troops without severely depleting the garrisons in Amritsar and Lahore where the army was already overstretched. He turned to the Royal Air

Force who made available three First World War BE2c biplanes, each armed with a Lewis machinegun and carrying ten twenty-pound bombs.

They were under the command of Captain D. H. M. Carberry who had flown the reconnaissance mission over Amritsar for General Dyer on Sunday, pinpointing Jallianwallah Garden as the location where a public meeting of natives was taking place. This afternoon, Tuesday, his instructions were that he was not to bomb Gujranwala "unless necessary," but that any crowds in the open were to be bombed, and that any gatherings near the local villages were to be dispersed if they were heading towards town.

Aarti and Deepak—and the men working in the orange grove on the other side of the wall—heard the drone of the biplane engine and the tension singing in the strut-wires before they saw the machine itself, gliding steadily at an altitude of three-hundred feet, the wind of oxygen in its propeller igniting a few hidden embers in the sooty rubble around the children.

It was a *vie jaaj,* a ship-of-the-air, Deepak understood immediately.

He had heard about these flying vessels from his Muslim and Sikh friends whose fathers had gone to fight the War in France for the King.

It grew in size as it approached them and began to diminish once it had gone over them. The four flat projections—two on either side of the body—were the ship-of-the-air's horizontal sails, the crisscross of wires the sails' rigging. He wished it would drop anchor so he could examine it carefully but it had gone as quickly as it had come.

A species prone to turbulence at the merest provocation, the crows were filling the air with their noisy uproar.

Drops of sweat slid down Aarti's arm and moved across the one stolen stripe of clarified butter, above the wrist, in the same curvilinear lines they described on the untreated areas but faster this time, like a cobra leaving coarse ground to swim across a river.

The shadow of the returning biplane poured itself down the *dak* bungalow's boundary wall and advanced like a sheet of unstoppable black water undulating along the ground's gentle rise and fall.

It had lost height and made Aarti feel she had grown taller in its absence.

Perhaps, she thought, the metal bird was about to flex two gracefully-aligned legs like a stork and alight on the *dhrake* tree which was now suddenly on fire.

A red lily grew out of her arm.

The sharp images blurred like a carousel gaining speed and suddenly she was so tired she had to sit down against the wall she found herself against and close her eyes.

Uprooted, lifted high onto the contours of expanding air, Deepak saw the ground rushing under him and smelled oranges being cut open before he forgot everything, the last sensation being the flesh-eating heat of his hair on fire against his scalp.

The bomb, like a foot stamped into a rain puddle, had emptied his mind of all its contents.

Shamas looks out at the snow lying on the street outside, hearing Kaukab at work in the kitchen.

In most minds, Sir Michael O'Dwyer, the governor of Punjab at the time, carried the ultimate responsibility for the Jallianwallah Garden Massacre of 1919. He was shot dead in London in March 1940 by Udam Singh, who had been wounded in the Massacre as a child; he was hanged in Pentonville for the murder.

But one of the stories that began with the RAF's bombing of Gujranwala two days after the Jallianwallah Massacre would take considerably more than twenty-one years to find an ending of sorts, an ending equally brutal.

The child Deepak, having drifted through the provinces for a year, fetched up at the shrine to a Muslim saint where in the courtyards in the evenings the drum-skins would be beaten with such devotion that friction often rose to dangerous levels and set the hands on fire. He was given the name Chakor, because he seemed fascinated by the moon, and *chakor* was the moonbird, the bird that was said to subsist on moonbeams, flying ever higher on moonlit nights until exhausted, dropping onto roofs and courtyards of houses at dawn, close to death. A *chakor* is to the moon what the moth is to the flame.

"You are appropriately named," his future wife would say, when he met her at the shrine in 1922. "My name is Mahtaab. The moon."

Shamas moves to the pink room and opens the album containing the photographs of his father and mother. They were great lovers, even in old age, Chakor smiling good-humouredly and saying to Shamas and his elder brother, "Come on, bring your wives here and make them stand next to my woman: let's see if she isn't the most beautiful of the three despite being the eldest."

Mahtaab's eyes shine blindingly in the grainy pictures—a light reaching the present from the distant years, the way light from long-dead stars continues to arrive on earth.

He puts the picture album away, sliding it next to one of the butterfly books that Jugnu had given to his nephews and niece, the children quoting things from them to each other during the day.

Having gently stroked the spine of the butterfly book for a few seconds, he returns to his seat and takes up the newspaper. He has thought about his parents all morning, due to some dream he must have had last night, and in about an hour it'll be time for him to go to the Urdu bookshop situated at the edge of the lake, near the xylophone jetty; he spends most of his free weekend hours there.

Kaukab comes in from the kitchen carrying a tray and takes the chair opposite. Flat, round, the size of pebbles on a doll's beach, a small cupful of black *masar* seeds lies in an uncertain mound in the centre of the tray: enough for two. They are to be cleaned and then soaked for a few hours prior to cooking. These days—less out of loyalty to her own family than the fact that the grief of Chanda's mother shames and unsettles her— Kaukab has taken to visiting the grocery shop twenty-minutes away on Laila Khalid Road. She feels shame because her brother-in-law Jugnu is partly, no, not partly, *entirely,* responsible for the woman's distress.

Chanda, the girl whose eyes changed with the seasons, was sent to Pakistan at sixteen to marry a first cousin to whom she had been promised when a baby, but the marriage had lasted only a year and her mother had been devastated by the news of the divorce. But another cousin in Pakistan took pity and agreed to marry her even though she was no longer a virgin. But he too divorced her a few months later and the girl came back to live in England, helping the family at the grocery shop all day. Then they found an illegal immigrant for her to marry: he wanted a British nationality and wasn't concerned that she had been married twice already. But he disappeared as soon as he got legal status in England. Chanda remained married to him because there had been no divorce.

And then one day last year she went to deliver the star anise that Jugnu—the man with the luminous hands—had asked for over the telephone, an ingredient for his butterflies' food. She was twenty-five, he forty-eight. It was March and the sparrows were about to begin shedding the extra five-hundred feathers they had grown at the start of winter to keep warm, to return to their summer plumage of three-thousand feathers each. The apples had not yet put out their shell-white flowers. The blossom would be out in May—when she would move in with Jugnu—and both Chanda and Jugnu would be dead by the time those very flowers became fruit in the autumn, the apples that would continue to lie in a circle of bright red dots under each tree until the snows of this year's January.

Jugnu had said he would marry Chanda but since she had not been divorced by her previous husband, Islam forbade another marriage for several years—the number differing from sect to sect, four, five, six. All the clerics she and Jugnu consulted stated firmly that the missing husband had to be found, or they had to wait for that prolonged period for the marriage to annul itself. If the husband did not return after those years, she could consider herself divorced, and marry whomever she wished.

All these consultations were, of course, to gain favour with Chanda's family and with Kaukab. If only she could obtain a *Muslim* divorce and marry Jugnu *Islamically*—they could cohabit then, regardless of the fact that she was still legally married to someone under British law.

Gently, Kaukab shakes the metal tray containing the heap of *masar* seeds until she has lined the surface evenly in a layer the thickness of one grain. Clearing an arc on this doll's beach with the back of her fingers, she begins to look for insect damage, pieces of real stone, and millimetre fragments of chaff. She surveys the room, eyes going on brief sorties along the various surfaces and returning to the tray where something unusual is being kept in sight. She gives up at last and stretches out her hand: "One second, please."

Shamas lowers the newspaper and looks over its top edge that is serrated like a carnation petal, and at the flicker of her fingers he takes off his
spectacles and passes them on to her.

During the weekends they like to settle in this room whenever they
can, leaving it and returning to it, each going about his or her own habits
at the periphery of the other's consciousness. The disorder of the day's living is tidied away at night and the pink room—filled with books in five
languages—is made immaculate once again as though all the slack strings
of a musical instrument have been pulled tight.

"Look what I found," she removes the spectacles, her inspection complete. "A *ravann* seed. Here." In the palm of her hand is a shiny blue bead,
the outer skin flaking away to reveal the ivory within. "The packet said
Product of Italy. That probably means they grow *ravann* in Italy. Is Italy
somewhere quite close to Pakistan?"

As she passes it to him, he holds her hand without looking at the grain.
He smiles at her, trying to catch her eye, and strokes her wrist with the
other hand, sending the fingers up under the sleeve.

She is shocked by the overture, and knows she mustn't look at him
from this point onwards—but he holds her hand suggestively and tries to
bring it closer to him, while she tries to pull it back decisively. There was a
time when in the mornings she sometimes stood over him and twisted her
wet hair into a yard-long rope, letting beads of water fall onto his face,
waking him with her body scented with the dawn bath, eyes glittering
with mischievousness. His "beautiful wife," he called her, "the heroine of
the story of his life."

But now? No, no. It's too late in life to be rutting like animals. Kaukab
had heard that to go to Shamas's house in Sohni Dharti was to often find
his parents in bed together, lying next to each other contentedly or talking, joking, the door open, in full view of the children playing out in the
courtyard. Well, *she* was born and bred in a mosque, and that wasn't the
norm in her household.

Shamas releases her with a soft groan, barely audible, and then they sit
in silence, too ashamed, embarrassed, and distressed, the both of them.

The blue grain is discarded into the glass that contains the other debris
from the *masar*. "Your father-ji, may he forever rest in peace, used to love
ravann, with a corn-flour chappati thick as cardboard." She is trying to

convince herself that his holding her hand just now wasn't a request for intimacy: she's relieved that she had managed to avoid the look in his eyes. The open rattle of seeds in her lap is given a final little shake and deciding glance before the tray is placed on the carpet. She adds a little tea to the dregs in Shamas's cup, swirls and empties it out into the glass of *masar* debris, and refills the now-clean cup. No it wasn't a sexual touch. There is a burst of sandalwood from the tray where the warm teapot has been resting. "Have the police found out who left that . . . that . . . *thing* outside the mosque last month?" She stirs milk into the cup and subdues the whirlpool with a little counter-circle of the spoon.

He answers only after a while. "It's not difficult to guess who it was but there is no proof." An English girl had converted to Islam in December and had been given shelter in the mosque because her family was hostile towards her decision to change her faith.

Kaukab sips her tea in silence. Unable to understand the lovers' mysterious vanishing, she has wept over Jugnu's absence (perhaps the reaction with which his love for the girl was met has made him take her somewhere and start a new life?) and she prays for their safety after each of the day's five prayers (perhaps something dreadful *has* happened to them?) but she refuses to believe that Chanda's brothers had anything to do with it.

While Chanda and Jugnu were away in Pakistan last year, Kaukab had asked Charag to visit Dasht-e-Tanhaii. He and the white girl were no longer together and Kaukab had had several meetings with the match-maker with the thought of finding a girl of Pakistani origin for him. Thirty-two, he was still young—a mere boy—and it wasn't unheard of for Muslim men to marry white girls and then divorce them quickly upon learning how difficult and shameless they were, and then having an arranged marriage to a decorous and compliant Muslim girl, preferably a first cousin brought over from back home. Her Allah told her to be optimistic: let the rope of breath snap, but never the thread of hope. Charag had no suitable first cousins in Pakistan, but Kaukab had made a list of four girls from amongst the three dozen the matchmaker had told her about. She planned and dreamed for weeks and she had the photographs of the four beautiful girls in her hand as she telephoned Charag to ask him to come home the following weekend because she missed him. ("It's not a lie," she told herself, "I do miss him!") And it must be said that a part of

Kaukab was somewhat relieved when Jugnu and Chanda had decided to go to Pakistan for the summer: she didn't want any interference from the uncle when she suggested a second marriage to Charag.

"A vasectomy! You've had a vasectomy!"

It was against Allah and everything the Prophet, peace be upon him, had said. He had mutilated himself. Unmanned.

"My Allah! When did you have it done?"

"A while back. I don't want another child. Ever. I can't even look after the one I already have. I resent him sometimes when I want to paint but must look after him instead."

"That's what a wife is for! Looking after the children is the *woman's* job while the man gets on with his work." A man, a man—she lamented in her heart—something you no longer are! If that white girl had done what a woman is supposed to do her son would still be a man.

"I slapped him once when he moved some of the drawings I had laid out on the floor. No, I didn't slap him—I *hit* him, hard."

"So? Parents are supposed to hit children."

"I remember."

"What do you mean by that remark? Parents are *supposed* to hit children, disciplining them. The Prophet, peace be upon him, said that when you send a camel out to graze, make sure one of its legs is doubled up and tied securely with a rope, so it can't wander too far. Too much freedom isn't good for anyone or anything."

A marriage to a Pakistani girl was now an impossibility—who would want a neutered husband for their daughter?—and Kaukab was to be denied the ally the Pakistani daughter-in-law would have proved to be.

"How could you have made such a big decision without first consulting me and your father?"

"What?"

"If you don't want any more children, then why couldn't you have been just careful, instead of doing something as drastic as that?" She couldn't believe she was having to conduct this conversation with her son.

"You can never be sure. That first time was an accident."

"Really? It wasn't planned? I *have* sometimes wondered whether that white girl hadn't trapped you by deliberately getting pregnant."

"I am sorry, but I can't listen to any more of this."

Charag went back, leaving her alone with the four photographs and her thoughts. She kept having the same dream every night: she was hanging from a noose and also standing beside the scaffold. "I can't help wondering it's all my fault," said the corpse. "Stop wondering," said the executioner-self. But during the waking hours, as usual, she could find no one other than the old culprits for this new disaster that had befallen her. Shamas. Jugnu. England. The white race. The vasectomy was a Christian conspiracy to stop the number of Muslims from increasing. Her parents were responsible for marrying her to an infidel. Her in-laws were Godless. Afflicted with loneliness and maddening fury, she finally accused Shamas of not being a Muslim at all, the son of a Hindu, whose filthy infidel's corpse was spat out repeatedly by the earth no matter how deep they buried it the next day—a phenomenon which she had up until then ascribed to the angel of death regretting his action in having removed that most-virtuous and -loving man from the world, a man whom she loved as much as her own father.

Chanda and Jugnu were staying in Shamas's parents' olive-green house—and were pretending to be just friends during their stay there; and it was to that olive-green house that Kaukab made a telephone call after Charag's departure: she could talk to the people in the house and tell them they had two sinners under their roof.

She hasn't revealed this fact to anyone, not even Shamas.

Her telephone call was probably why the pair had returned to England earlier than expected: they had been asked to leave. They came back to England and . . . disappeared.

Kaukab's anger and distress were beginning to subside somewhat as the time drew closer for the couple's expected return. But the day of the expected arrival passed. And then another, and another . . . When the police eventually forced their way into the house, the passports revealed that the couple had come back to England thirteen days earlier. A peacock and a peahen burst out of a room and escaped to the freedom of the street—this would eventually lead to the talk that Chanda and Jugnu had been transformed into a pair of peacocks. The corpse of another peacock was found in one of the downstairs rooms, the injuries revealing that it had been pecked to death by the other two. A dozen-strong flock of peacocks had appeared in the neighbourhood a fortnight or so previously:

they had escaped from the menagerie of a stately home on the other side of the lake, and they would be rounded up eventually—the foliage falling from the trees in the coming months of autumn meaning that they would have no groves or clusters of bushes to hide in. For the time being, however, no one could tell where they were from. They roamed the streets, scratched the paintwork of the cars and attacked the cats and sparrows. How three members of the flock had managed to enter Jugnu's house and how long they had been in there could not be determined. There were sweeps on the dust on the floors, made by the males' tail-feathers. On a white plate on the dinner table there was a puddle of urine the pale-green colour of gripe water. The hen had laid an egg in one of the open suitcases that lay on the bed upstairs.

Jugnu had put up a framed photograph of a peacock on one wall and for a moment it was as though the live peacock had left its reflection in a mirror in the house.

She finishes her tea and says, "I am soaking some rice for you to eat with the *masar* this evening. I'll have to make chappatis for myself because there is a little dough left over from Friday and it'll spoil if not used today."

"Won't it keep until tomorrow? The weather is cold enough," Shamas says quietly; it could almost be a thought being passed into her head from his.

"Perhaps you should have chappatis also. You had rice last night too and it's bad for the bones two days in a row, especially in this cold country." She pauses, waiting for him to dreamily say that now that he has reached the year of his retirement they would soon move back to the hot climate of Sohni Dharti, as they had planned decades ago. They have discussed the matter several times over the past few months and each time she has told him he would have to leave without her—she would remain in hated England because her children are here.

"If only Jugnu was here, there would be no leftovers—" She stops, having got carried away with her thoughts, and looks at Shamas, but he doesn't react. Quietly she turns to the work at hand, and sighs:

Dear Allah, if only things had gone another way. Only the other day the matchmaker was talking about one of the young women she had suggested for Jugnu all those years ago, someone called Suraya, who has now been divorced by her drunk husband and is now looking for someone to marry temporarily. Kaukab shakes her head: she doesn't remember who that woman was, but if only Jugnu had married her the poor woman wouldn't be in this predicament, and he himself wouldn't now be missing. Instead, he took up with white women. Kaukab knew that the few nights a week that he spent away from home were spent in the arms of one of his white girlfriends. Kaukab lived in fear of such contemptible and unforgivable behaviour rubbing off on her three children, but there was nothing she could do. He was discreet and she liked him for that—he was secretly colluding with her, preventing her children from seeing immoral conduct.

Years passed and then one day a little boy stopped her in the street and asked her whether it was true that Jugnu's "place of urine" was also glow-in-the-dark like his hands. She puts the boy's obscenity and impertinence down to the corrupting influence of Western society, but within hours she learned what some of the neighbourhood's adults had known for about a week and its children for about a fortnight. A group of boys had peeped into the upstairs bedroom of Jugnu's house—where the cage containing the female Great Peacock moth had swayed one night with the passionate wing beats of the male velvet clinging to the wires, the bedroom papered with twisted leaves and indigo berries. Those children had dimly seen the two secret lovers in bed, the light from his hands illuminating her skin.

And, just as the king of Samarkand had come upon his wife locked in the embrace of a kitchen boy and set into motion the *Thousand and One Nights,* what the five young boys espied through the window that afternoon—when they climbed up to the boughs of the purple beech to bring down a kite—became the starting point of another set of tales.

The children told them to each other, adding and subtracting this or that detail, and it eventually reached the adults' realm. Kaukab was on her way into town when the boy had stopped her to ask about the light-giving properties of Jugnu's manhood; coming back from the town centre the bus was crowded so she had to sit next to the white woman who had burnt her Muslim husband's Koran, but when a few stops later a seat next to a Gujarati woman became vacant, she had moved. The Gujratan gave her the news that Chanda and Jugnu were lovers.

She waited for Jugnu to come home from work that night. "I may only be a woman and not as educated as you, but I won't stand by and let you damage further that already-damaged girl. Have you considered the consequences for her when her family finds out about this? You men can do anything you want but it's different for us women. Who will marry her again when people find out that she has been engaging in intercourse with men she's not married to?"

Chanda moved in with Jugnu a few days after that.

Over the coming weeks Kaukab began to time her trips outdoors in order to avoid the girl, because that was what Chanda was, a girl. Instead of the drawstring that adults use, she used elastic in the waistband of her *shalwar;* Kaukab could see her clothes hanging out on the washing line between two of the five apple trees. She sensed the girl's own reluctance to let her gaze meet hers.

And it was by that washing line that Kaukab, having crossed over into the adjoining garden, had eventually told the girl to move out of Jugnu's house.

Chanda tried to pull her arm back but Kaukab tightened her hold: "If truly offered, repentance is honoured even on one's deathbed and wipes out a lifetime's worth of sins to deliver the sinner into Paradise along with those who led virtuous lives. Only on the day that the sun would rise out of the west, the Judgement Day, would the gates of forgiveness be barred shut."

The girl freed her arm with a jerk, her green eyes igniting. "There is no alternative. He says he'll marry me but I am not divorced and my husband cannot be located." She flicked the dripping *muhaish*-work *kameez* back on the line—like flipping a giant page—and went back into the house, but not before stopping at the doorstep to say to Kaukab: "We love each other deeply and honestly."

Kaukab had looked her directly in the eyes: "I care about what it is, yes, but also about what it looks like."

"And I care only about what it is."

It was Kaukab's first and last conversation with Jugnu's lover. His own visits to the house were already dwindling. It was a sin to offer food to a fornicator, and Kaukab—the daughter of a cleric, born and raised in the shadow of a minaret—stopped soaking that third glassful of rice and peeled two aubergines instead of three. And then on a July afternoon heady with the pine-soup heat of the lake, Jugnu and Chanda left for Pakistan for four weeks, and Kaukab busied herself with trying to arrange a marriage for Charag.

After the hopelessness and despair that resulted from the disclosure about the vasectomy had settled a little (she had startled herself by abusing her father-in-law, that loving and beloved man, he who was so good that when he visited a saint's shrine the holy man's hand was said to have emerged from the grave to shake hands with him) and, stunned and repentant at her thoughts, feeling Allah's spit land on her soul because she was so evil-minded, feeling so small in her own eyes that she would have had to fight to subdue a beetle, she had told herself that she must try to accept the world's realities; it was almost time for the couple's expected return to England. By complete chance she ran into Chanda's third husband in the street and told him he had to release her by divorcing her: "Immediately contact her parents to tell them that that is what you plan to do. Allah will never forgive you if you don't. If not out of the fear of Allah, then do it out of gratitude towards the girl who made you a British citizen."

Chanda and Jugnu could now get married!

She propped open the back door with the lobster buoy from Maine to keep an eye on the activity in Jugnu's back garden: the front door of his house was always locked because *The Darwin* filled up his front garden. The boat's actual price was £3,000 but he had bought it, a battered wreck, for £650 in 1985, and then spent the following few years renovating it with the help of the three children. It lived at the front like a huge clothes iron and so the back door was how everyone always entered the house.

As the days passed without the couple appearing, she telephoned Pakistan and was told that they had left a week earlier than planned. She asked a boy in the street to climb the purple beech in the back garden to look into the upstairs bedroom. She then dragged a ladder and put it to the upstairs windows at the front. Were they in England or still in Pakistan? Perhaps they had left the house in Sohni Dharti and gone butterfly collecting around Pakistan? The boy she had sent up the ladder shouted down that he could see open suitcases through one of the windows.

And then Kaukab suddenly knew what had happened: the couple had returned from Pakistan and gone straight to Chanda's family's shop to ask for their forgiveness. The decadent and corrupt West had made them forget piety and restraint, but the countless examples in Pakistan had brought home to them the importance and beauty of a life decorously lived according to His rules and injunctions, Pakistan being a country of the pious and the devout, a place where boundaries are respected. She rushed to the shop, absolutely sure that Chanda and Jugnu had gone there in repentance and—Oh, the miracles of Allah!—Chanda's parents had in turn told them that the girl's third husband had been on the telephone recently to say he was ready to divorce her. But when she got to the shop Chanda's brother told her bluntly:

"Stop bothering us with all that, auntie-ji. As far as we are concerned, that little whore died the day she moved in with him."

She returned, shocked by the vehemence. All the way there she had been thinking that the family would have forgiven the couple, that the parents would have remembered that everyone loved someone before marriage, love being a phenomenon as old and sacred as Adam and Eve. Women joked amongst themselves: "Why do you think a bride cries on her wedding day? It's for the love that this marriage is putting an end to for all eternity. Men may think a woman has no past—'you were born and then I married you'—but men are fools."

The size of a matchbox, the old piece of cooked fish in the fridge is stiff with the cold and ought to be thrown away but Kaukab wraps it in a slice of bread and eats it, bending forward at the second bite because she has neglected to check for bones. It's like a metal hook in her throat. She coughs and splutters, gasping for air, and manages to swallow, her throat raw. She takes a glass of water and sits down to steady her nerves, the danger passed, her mind returning to what she was thinking about earlier.

Love.

Islam said that in order not to be unworthy of being, only one thing was required: love. And, said the True Faith, it did not even begin with humans and animals: even the trees were in love. The very stones sang of love. Allah Himself was a being in love with His own creations.

In their youth Chanda's parents themselves must have loved someone other than the person they were married to now, for Kaukab certainly had, she who was the daughter of a cleric . . .

But it seems that the danger from the fishbone has not passed: she leans forward and watches in horror as a small wrinkled kerchief of blood issues from her mouth and spreads on the table before her.

Before she has had time to realize what is happening, Shamas has called for a taxi to take her to the hospital, another small pool of blood on the stairs as she goes up to the bathroom, feeling faint.

Suspicious at first, she lets Shamas hold her hand in the taxi as she presses the bloody tissue-paper to her lips with the other.

She is examined and X-rayed and it turns out to be only a minor injury. "Nothing to worry about," says the white doctor. "Date of birth?" he asks her, flipping through the forms before him.

Shamas looks at her to be reminded of it, and she whispers it. It hurts her to speak.

"On your birthday you should have had trouble with swallowing cake not fish," the man laughs good-naturedly.

"It's your birthday?" Shamas asks quietly.

"You didn't know?" The doctor looks at him, amused.

"I didn't remember myself," she interjects. She scrutinizes Shamas's face. Surely, he is more embarrassed about what the white man is thinking of *him* than upset that he'd forgotten the date, that *she* would be hurt by it. But then she drives the wicked thought away.

Back home through the snow-covered roads and streets, she wants him out of the house so she can ring Ujala's voice, but he is reluctant to leave her and go to the bookshop as had been his plan. She pretends she is in less pain than she really is. There is also the fear in her that he might become amorous again, this time in repentance for having forgotten the day, as though she cares in the least about frivolities like birthdays.

The trip to the hospital had taken more than an hour but it had passed blankly for her: there's nothing for her out there in Dasht-e-Tanhaii, to notice or be interested in. Everything is here in this house. Every beloved absence is present here.

An oasis—albeit a haunted one—in the middle of the Desert of Loneliness.

Out there, there was nothing but humiliation: she's hot with shame at what the white doctor would now think of Pakistanis, of Muslims—they are like animals, not even remembering or celebrating birthdays. Dumb cattle.

She convinces Shamas to go at last and watches from the window as he walks away between the twenty maples, her husband—who, all those years ago, very nearly wasn't her husband. Kaukab hadn't seen a man up close without there being the gauze of her *burqa* between him and her since the age of twelve—she had been made to wear it because it was well known that certain men marked out beautiful girl-children and then waited for years for them to grow up. Her vigilant mother lifted the stamp of every letter that came into the house to make sure no clandestine message was being passed. And then on a certain monsoon Thursday when she was in her twenties, and sitting in the back room working on the articles that would one day soon become part of her dowry, for her parents had begun the preliminary negotiations for her marriage, she heard a short tap on the window. She put aside the fabric she was cutting up into a *kameez* and went to open it, expecting it to be the little boy she had seen through the same window wandering through the street earlier and sent to the shop at the corner with a swatch of fabric the size of a teabag to buy a spool of thread "matching exactly that colour, or I'll send you back to exchange it. And show me your pocket so I can make sure there's no hole in it, otherwise you'll lose my money and come back with a long face."

Only after he left had she regretted not having told him to get an adult—preferably a woman—to match the thread with the cloth.

She opened the window and recoiled, barely managing to hide behind the casement leaf because there was a grown man standing on the other side.

She was shaking. She heard his voice but it was many seconds before she made out his words: "The newspaper. Can I have our newspaper back?" It must be the son of the family from whom her father borrowed the newspaper each morning, she understood, and felt terror at the thought that someone might have seen her opening the window to him: a woman's life was ruined as easily as that. People might not believe that she was innocent.

And then suddenly she felt anger at him: how dare he knock on a window during the daytime when there was every possibility that he might catch the daughters of the house unawares.

"The newspaper was sent back at eleven o'clock, brother-ji."

She was about to close the window when the voice said: "The literary supplement is missing. Could you check that you don't still have it in there somewhere. I'd be grateful."

She closed the window and bolted it shut noisily with a "Wait there, brother-ji," more and more furious at him for neglecting to refer to her as "sister-ji," which would have decriminalized the glimpse he had caught of her face, and in a panic because she hadn't checked the date on the paper she had found on the table earlier and had spent the past hour practising the pattern of her *kameez* on it: there it lay on the floor now, today's literary supplement, cut up into geometric shapes.

She collected the boats and heron's beaks from under the bed—off-cuts the ceiling fan had scattered—and stood motionlessly, holding all the pieces in her fist, wrinkling the paper further, hoping the stranger would tire and leave. But he tapped again, and she opened the casement just enough for her hand to pass through and handed him his beloved literary supplement, the pages that did not mention the name of Allah or Muhammad, prayer and peace be upon him, even once because she had checked before spreading them on the floor.

"Here it is, brother-ji. I am sorry it is a bit creased but the iron isn't working today," she said, as though all he would notice would be the creases and not the chopping up. And she shuddered that a daughter of the mosque was handing over her vital statistics to a complete stranger. There were no limits to the depravity of the world and all this man had to do was to spread the whole thing out on a bed and with a bit of sense put together a cut-out of her upper body like a jigsaw.

He received the pieces and left without another word.

The following Thursday, oppressed by a sense of remorse about last week, she ran the hot iron over the newspaper just before it was due to be sent back, to smooth over the few creases her father had made whilst reading. Somehow she managed not to make a sound when the words *I see the iron is working today* appeared suddenly along the margin of the literary section. It was a schoolchild's trick: the sentence had been inscribed with a clean bamboo pen using onion water as ink—upon drying it was invisible to the eye, but the iron scorched it a deep manila, revealing it.

Later that year, she locked herself into the bathroom and wept when her parents informed her that her engagement had been finalized. The instant the first onion-water message had materialized she had ripped it off the newspaper, relieved that no one else had seen it, but she regretted her action during the week because the missing strip was a signal to the sender that his words had been received. Having successfully shunned the literary section for the two Thursdays that followed the first message, she had plugged in the iron on the third and was troubled as to why she felt inconsolable because no message appeared on the paper. And there would be none over the next two months, but, today, now that she was engaged to be married to another man, there was a cruelly mocking, *I heard the good news. Congratulations.*

Her mother interpreted her tears as the ordinary reaction of a girl who had just been told that she would soon leave her parents' house forever, and she was proud at having raised such a modest girl when she ran away upon being told her fiancé's name. When the relatives of the fiancé came for a formal viewing of the girl, she offered the women her needlework to admire, the chain stitch, the satin stitch, lazy daisy, herringbone, the French stitch and the German stitch, the cross-stitch pillowcases and long smock-work caterpillars, embroidered Koranic samplers, bedspreads with borders encrusted with glass beads tiny as grains of sugar, and she poured tea for the men, speaking only once and so softly that it was difficult to make her out above the cutlery.

She cried in secret for the man she wanted. Throughout the months of her engagement the iron revealed the literary pages to contain a love poem every Thursday which she memorized before the paper went back. She turned the lines of the poems into curlicued and tendrilled vines and then embroidered them onto her wedding-day clothes. She hoped someone in the house would notice the revealed poems on the newspaper, or ask her to explain why the arabesques on the hems and cuffs and veil-border of her dress looked like actual words—she would tell the truth, the alarm would be raised, precipitating a crisis that would bring her engagement to an end.

On the day the wedding clothes were ready, sparkling so much they made people think sequins were collected free of charge from beaches and that beads were cheaper than lentils, she became resigned to her fate.

And the day before the wedding, sitting under the cage of the Japanese nightingales that her future mother-in-law had brought for her on the occasion of the formal viewing—the droppings of the birds contained lime and were to be rubbed onto her skin to enhance her complexion, the birds as though feathered tubes of beauty-cream, automatically dispensing measured amounts three times a day—she clicked open the small locket containing the photograph of her fiancé that her mother had passed wordlessly into her hands months ago, and, as she would tell her own daughter Mah-Jabin many years later, red with laughter, it was like opening the casements of the window all over again and getting caught unawares because her fiancé and the handsome stranger were the same person, my Allah, it was *him* all along!

She is about to telephone Ujala's voice, but the doorbell rings: she opens the door, her heart thumping, swallowing hard against the searing pain in her throat, and finds a white man on the doorstep. He holds a bouquet of Madonna lilies, their whiteness undiminished even against the falling snow, the sight of them bringing a smile to her face. Glory be to Allah who has created beauty for the eyes of His servants.

The "thank you" she murmurs to the flower-deliveryman is her third exchange with a white person this year; there were five last year; none the year before, if she remembers correctly; three the year before that; . . . She places the Madonna lilies on the draining board. Three pithy stems, each with a sparrow-foot-like division at the top bearing the hollow coffin-shaped buds and the already-open heavy blooms, white as the flesh of a newly-split coconut. She reads the card—a birthday greeting. It seems her daughter was the only one in the family to have remembered it. Tears well up in her eyes—someone loves her.

The gold in her earlobes and nostril is chilled from the blast of snowy air that the opening of the door had exposed it to.

Each containing a miniature image of the lilies, the small pieces of mirror stitched along the front of her *kameez* feel as though they are discs of ice.

Passingly, she wishes some neighbourhood woman would drop by so she could show off the flowers to her with pride: "My daughter sent me these for my birthday. I am always telling her not to waste money on me, but she loves me—as you can see."

Holding the glass vase under the tap she fills it with water. The bubbles seethe and lift themselves into a jostling heap and then subside.

Carefully using one of the flowered stems she stirs an aspirin tablet into the water and she counts the flowers because an arrangement must always have an odd number of blooms. Her Koran is full of lilies dried flat as cut-outs, the colour of tea-stains. She thins some of the leaves where they would crowd together at the vase's rim; peeled off with the leaves, the thin strips of green skin contract slowly and neatly come to rest in perfect spirals like the tin coils inside a wound-up toy taken apart by children. Why hadn't the boys also remembered her birthday? She wipes her tears: her life is over and yet there is still so much of it left to live. She briefly rinses each lily stem before it takes its diagonal place inside the vase and the rope of water frays whenever it scrapes against the edge of a leaf, the fluttering splashes reminiscent of a bird in a pool of rain.

Their scent is strongest at night, and since there is a hedge plant back in Sohni Dharti whose buds, like the Madonna lilies, not only open in the evening's whispers but also release a perfume as hazy as them, Kaukab's affection for the lilies has increased over the years.

Compared with England, Pakistan is a poor and humble country but she aches for it, because to be thirsty is to crave a glass of simple water and no amount of rich buttermilk will do.

She carries the nodding Madonnas to the table and places them next to a bowl full of apples whose skins are covered in yellow and red brush-strokes like the plumage of tropical parrots.

She stands in the blue kitchen, gently swaying: Shamas will be at the bookshop all afternoon and she wonders what she herself would do over the next few hours. Let me talk to myself, she whispers, an old fool talking to an old fool.

With her children absent from her life, she feels as bewildered as a child whose dolls have been stolen. She is sure she hadn't felt this bereft even when Shamas had moved out of the house to live on his own for nearly three years, all those years ago, when the children were younger.

She lifts the vase and takes it into the pink room where there are books in five languages on the shelves, the books she had one lonely afternoon opened at random one after the other, madly, to see if she could find in any of them an explanation of her predicament. The framed verses of the Koran hanging on the walls provide her with solace. She places the lilies on the coffee table, and goes to the window to look at the falling snow, the mirrors on her breast reflecting the snowflakes as though they are little windows and it's snowing inside her body.

She dials Ujala's number and listens to his voice.

He was here in the neighbourhood soon after the couple vanished, she knows. The rumours about Chanda's family being involved in the disappearance had begun almost immediately, and one day Kaukab received a phone call from the girl's panicked mother: "Your son is digging up our back garden, sister-ji, saying we buried his uncle there!" The woman had been startled by him and his pickaxe when she went out to the back of the shop to discard an apple crate. Kaukab rushed to the shop but he had gone by then; there was nothing but a small hole in the ground and the pickaxe which she had dragged home, closing her fingers around the warmth in the wooden handle where he had held it only moments before. The steel point of the pickaxe tinkled on the pavement like ice-cubes in a glass of water and scored a dotted line on the stone slabs, knocking off sparks.

The following week he attacked the shop's display window with a cricket bat.

He was never an easy son; but Jugnu had been his companion since his earliest childhood. She remembered them together, Jugnu telling him about an Irish law of 1680 which decreed that a white butterfly was not to be killed because it was the soul of a child, and how in Romania adolescent girls made a drink with the wings of butterflies to attract suitable partners. And as he grew up and entered his teens, she found butterfly dust in his underpants and vest one day: Jugnu was puzzled when she told him about it but then smiled and said: "Along the Ivory coast, pubescent boys hunt butterflies to gather the colours from their wings, which they rub into their armpits and genitals in the belief that pubic hair will grow, that it would bring on manhood and bestow virility. I told him about it last week. Now I know where one of my Apollos and my Two-tailed Pasha have gone." She was shocked, as much by what the boy had done as by the fact that Jugnu seemed to find the whole thing amusing.

Kaukab had dreamed of her sons graduating from university, first the elder, Charag, and then a few years later the younger, Ujala, and she planned to send the graduation-ceremony photographs to the local newspaper, standing proudly next to her gowned boy in her Benaresi *shalwar-kameez,* the names printed in the caption below. She had already bought the two 12 x 12 gold frames in which she would display the photographs at home.

She did get her name in *The Afternoon,* but for entirely different reasons. The police had obviously wanted to know why it had taken almost thirteen days for the family to go around and see where Chanda and Jugnu were. They had wanted to interview all three children in case they had any information about the missing uncle. And Ujala had told the officers and *The Afternoon* that it was all the fault of his cunt of a mother who had decided not to speak to Jugnu because he was offending her religion and that his fucking spineless father must've just gone along with what she said because she was a poor immigrant woman in a hostile white environment who deserved everyone's compassion, what with her sons and daughter away, leading their own lives, and to cap it all she was also going through the menopause.

He must've heard this last from his sister because, yes, he is in touch with his siblings—the only ones he can't bear are his parents, or, rather, Kaukab. She shudders now, remembering how angry he used to become before he left home, seven years ago. He ruled the house as an entire forest vibrates to the movements of a tiger. Although living in fear of him, Kaukab often pretended not to notice his rage in an effort to deceive him into thinking he was not having any effect on her. One day as she came to ask him whether he wanted her to make anything for breakfast, the covers had slid off him a little where he lay in bed and exposed a section of his bare thighs. He was in bed naked, one arm tucked behind the head to reveal the long armpit hair. She demanded he get up and put on his pyjamas: she could not bear the thought of him being alone with his nakedness! He glanced at her in contempt but did not stir as she raised her voice the way she used to when he was a child throwing a tantrum in Woolworth's over a costly toy, rolling around on the floor, indifferent to the threat that he would be handed over to a white person if he didn't behave, a threat that had reduced his siblings into submission when they were his age. It was the weekend and Shamas was home so she shouted for him to come upstairs, keeping her eyes fixed on Ujala the while. His own eyes were on the ceiling, unmoving. Shamas came up and stood behind her and she explained the situation to him.

"Get up, right now," said Shamas, "and do what your mother says."

Immediately after what happened next, Kaukab's first thought was of death, that whenever Allah decided to take her, He should take her while Shamas was still alive, because were he to go ahead of her she would be totally alone in the world. But it was equally unbearable to think of him stumbling around the no-man's-land of old age without her hand to steady him, a widower whose children were past caring, his corpse awaiting discovery at the bottom of the stairs for hours, days, perhaps even weeks.

What happened next was this: Ujala brought out his hand from under the covers and jerked his fingers at them where they stood in the door so that the swipe of semen flew across the room in an arc to spatter their faces, smelling of bleach, runny like the whites of a quarter-boiled egg.

The Most-Famous Tamarind Tree
in the Indian Subcontinent

Shamas picks up the package that had arrived yesterday from India, containing foliage from the most-famous tamarind tree in the Indian Subcontinent, the tree that spreads over the tomb of the legendary singer Tansen, who had brought on the rains just by singing about them, and whose golden voice had led the Emperor Akbar to proclaim him one of the nine gems of his court. Even today, Tansen's renown is such that singers travel to his tomb in the city of Gwalior to pluck foliage from the branches of the tamarind tree to make into throat concoctions, in the hope that their voices will become as pure as that of their illustrious predecessor, he who had caused the palace lamps to light up by singing the *Deepak Raag*, four centuries ago.

This one bent into the arc of cursive script, this one leaping back on itself to form a bangle—the long feathery leaves have come from India, and although their final destination is Pakistan, they have been sent to England. The hostility between the two neighbours makes it necessary for a letter to Pakistan from India, or one to India from Pakistan, to be posted to a third country—to a friend or a relative in Britain, Canada, the United States, Australia or the countries of the Persian Gulf—from where it is forwarded to the intended recipient in a new envelope, the entire procedure reminiscent of a rubber ball being made to bounce off a wall by the left hand to be caught on the return journey by the right one. Direct correspondence is often destroyed out of pettiness disguised as patriotic duty, or violated by the authorities who are quick to see a regular communicator with the other side as a traitor. Countless thousands of families wait for the news of their loved ones from the other side of the border—a wall that also effectively cuts the whole of Asia in half—but what they feel is less important than nationalistic ideals.

A friend of Kaukab's a few doors down is originally from Gwalior: the foliage has been sent by her and will be passed on to Kaukab's father—so he can maintain the suppleness of his vocal cords with which he calls the faithful to prayer.

If Shamas's aunt Aarti had been located over there in India he would have arranged the supply of foliage through her. The thirteen-year-old girl who had become separated from her brother during the bombing of Gujranwala in April 1919 would be ninety-one this year—if she's alive. At the time of Partition she must have left the Gujranwala—which was part of Pakistan now—and moved to India. Shamas's parents would try to find her and the rest of the family shortly after his father's true identity and early past came to light, but there was little access to India. Nor was there any way of knowing whether they had survived the Partition massacres during the move to India.

She is lost forever. It is conceivable that, as a grown man, he would not have felt the loss of an aunt with as much intensity as he sometimes does Aarti's—but she's linked with the tragedy of his father, and his mind keeps returning to her for that reason. And also, it could have something to do with his advancing years: has he, perhaps, come to see life as little more than darkness and separation?

Shamas uncovers the window and looks out at the dawn. His back teeth still warm from the tea of five minutes earlier, he steps out of the house as he does early morning each Saturday and Sunday, to go into the town centre and intercept the bunch of newspapers that the newsagent otherwise drops into his closed office. He brings the office keys in case the papers have already gone out, but that rarely happens because he leaves as early as possible, sometimes setting off before dawn, these leisurely strolls in the empty roads and streets being a pleasure much looked forward to during the week. He carries the newspapers back to the office on Monday, and the stories and articles—concerning race relations—that he has circled during the weekend are clipped and filed by the secretary.

The sky is beginning to pale, but a mournful darkness still clings to the world down here.

Locking into each other like the facets of a jewel, the tilting surfaces of the neighbourhood have channelled away the water that the snows released upon melting.

When the snows began to melt, receding to lie on the sides of the roads, the white mounds looked as though they were dead bodies covered in white sheets.

Where are they? They are nowhere and yet he feels as though he is handcuffed to their corpses. It has been many months since their disappearance but Kaukab cannot be swayed: "They will return, safe and sound. What are months and years in Allah's plans? For all we know your own father's sister will contact you one day, after half a century."

The truth about his true identity had returned to Chakor slowly over the years, the truth that he hid from his family for as long as possible. He had known that truth in its entirety long before he introduced into *The First Children on the Moon* a regular section called "Encyclopaedia Pakistanica," inviting the readers to write the histories of their towns, villages and neighbourhoods, and a boy from Gujranwala had sent in the details of the 1919 bombing. He had looked up the accounts of that April Tuesday in history books too.

The three First World War BE2c biplanes, under the command of Captain D. H. M. Carberry, arrived over Gujranwala at 3:10 p.m. that Tuesday. He dropped his first three bombs on a party of 150 people in the nearby village of Dhulla, who looked as though they were heading for the town. One bomb fell through the roof of a house and failed to explode. Two fell near the crowd, killing a woman and a boy, and slightly wounding two men. The rest of the crowd fled back to the village, encouraged by 50 rounds from the Lewis machinegun.

A few minutes later, Carberry dropped two bombs—one of them a dud—and fired 25 rounds at a crowd of about fifty near the village of Garjhak, without causing any casualties.

Returning to Gujranwala, he attacked a crowd of about 200 in a field near a high school on the outskirts of the town, dropping a bomb which landed in a courtyard, and followed up with 30 rounds of machinegun fire: a sweet-seller was wounded by a bullet, a student was hit by a bomb splinter, and a small boy was stunned.

In the town itself he dropped a further four bombs—two of which failed to explode—and fired between 100 and 150 rounds at crowds in the streets.

When asked later why he had machinegunned the crowds even after they had been dispersed, Carberry replied, "I was trying to do this in their own interests. If I killed a few people, they would not gather and come to Gujranwala to do damage."

His idea was "to produce a sort of moral effect upon them."

He claimed he could "see perfectly well" from the altitude of 200 feet and that he did not see anybody at all who was innocent . . .

Deepak confessed everything to Mahtaab eventually, the truth that Chakor had kept from his family. The first very-brief and confusing flash of recall had occurred as early as 1922, just three years after the bombing, when he saw a white woman and inexplicably found himself staring at her feet. But in the years to come—the years during which he married Mahtaab and had children—the details of his past life would return more fully, making themselves visible in the gentle and gradual manner of objects taking shape with the slow arrival of dawn. When the British began selling the contents of their homes in preparation for their official departure from the Subcontinent in 1947, Mahtaab had returned home one day with a crinoline to make into a quilt (along with six suede hats to take to the shoemaker to have slippers made out of them), but he had not needed that prompt to remember that his name was Deepak, that he was a Hindu, or that he and his sister had been on their way to see whether it was really true that white women hid tails under their crinolines.

Mahtaab gave no indication that she minded his not having shared it all with her much earlier. He said he hadn't known what to do so he had ended up doing nothing.

Not for a single moment, Mahtaab wrote in answer to the letter in which Kaukab had asked whether she felt betrayed by her husband. *Imagine how much he must've suffered with that secret gnawing at his innards.*

Shamas is standing on the bridge, looking down into the water. And a woman's voice calls to him, softly, from behind:

"Brother-ji."

He is startled, and, turning in a near swoon, sees Chanda's mother standing there, hesitating about approaching him.

"I wanted to tell you something, brother-ji."

Shamas doesn't know how to react, his head a perfect vacuum.

"It is something important. I thought of going to the Urdu bookshop by the lake yesterday afternoon, but I couldn't make time. Instead, because I know you always go to collect the newspapers from the town centre very very early, I left the house this morning to talk to you . . . I was walking behind you but couldn't catch up. Then you stopped here to look at the river . . . Brother-ji, a woman from near our house returned from a visit to Lahore yesterday. She says she thinks she saw Jugnu in the crowd at the Data Darbar mausoleum last Thursday."

He looks at her without making eye contact. In her earlobe there is an emerald that would fill the cupped paws of a mouse—a berry of solid green light. He clears his throat, confused by what he is being told, but then the power of reason and the ability to conceive coherent thought fly back into his skull. "Both their passports were found in the house," he says quietly. "Have you forgotten that, sister-ji? No one saw them upon their return from Pakistan but they *did* return."

"She thinks she saw him, brother-ji." Roses suddenly bloom on her cheeks.

He feels himself soaked in profoundest grief: when she speaks it is as though all the sorrow in the world has been given voice. The words float out of a deep loneliness he recognizes. "The passports are here in England, sister-ji." He must state the facts but feels himself cruel for doing so, vindictive, as though he is swinging at her hopes with a club.

The sun lights up the course of tears on the fraught melancholy mask of her face. "Everyone in that country wants to come to the West, brother-ji, so the two of them probably sold the passports to another couple and decided to live in Pakistan themselves . . . Everyone made their life difficult here . . . No one at the airports checks to see if the passport photographs match exactly . . ." She is searching his face to see if some little thing can be salvaged from the wreck of her ideas.

He shakes his head. "That other couple entered Britain, came to this town, let themselves into Jugnu and Chanda's home, and deposited the passports and luggage before disappearing. Forgive me, sister-ji, but is that what you are suggesting?" She resembles her daughter; it is as though the father had made no genetic contribution towards the absent perished girl.

"Yes ... No ... Yes ... I know it sounds foolish but ..."

"Forgive me, but that is as absurd as that talk about them turning into a pair of peacocks. Don't you agree?"

Standing immovably, she tries again. "Brother-ji, people are lost and found in so many ways ... Your own father-ji was separated from his family members in a strange manner ..."

Coloured motes fill the sunlit distance between him and her.

Shamas wonders what expression he's wearing on his face—is he frowning, does he look angry, distressed?

She is silent for a few moments and then, defeated, says, "Yes, it *is* foolish. I am terribly sorry to have troubled you, brother-ji." On her head is a veil transparent as water and her upper body is wrapped in a yellow shawl printed with white penny-sized stars; her arms are crossed under the shawl. He is not sure if he has ever conversed with her before but he knows she has the long slender fingers of a piano player, has seen her using them to manipulate with sensitivity and graceful importance the cash register at the shop.

"Would you like me to walk back with you?" He is not sure whether he should have made this offer: what would people think if they saw her walking beside a man not her husband at this early hour? If someone has seen them talking there is already a possibility of gossip. The breeze is coming from her direction and he realizes now that the sorrow he had sensed within him earlier was partly due to the woman's smell— the mother *smells* like the daughter. All he has to do to be reminded of Chanda is to draw a breath. Once, during the brief few months that the couple lived together—in radiant ignorance of the fate that awaited them—Jugnu had tacked one of Chanda's veils to the window to keep out insects, and Shamas had walked into a space saturated with a scent he had understood to be the scent of Chanda's body and hair.

She shakes her head to decline his offer to see her home. "No, thank you, brother-ji. I'm not going far." And before walking away, she says, "But you yourself should be careful: I don't like the thought of you going out of the house at an hour when there is no one around. As I was waiting for you earlier I felt like the only one out in a town under curfew. You must try to break this habit. Anything could happen: you should remember that this isn't our country."

There is silence all around and the whole town lies wrapped in dreaming. He must continue with his own journey. He straightens as though shifting a yoke. The exchange of words could not have taken more than two minutes but it had felt longer: shocking or stressful events and incidents are said to concentrate consciousness to a single point and that slows down the time. Dying, over within seconds, supposedly takes forever.

He's been left shaken by the encounter, and as always in times of stress he thinks of his younger days in Lahore and Sohni Dharti, when he was writing poetry, beginning to develop political awareness. An unmarried young man's sexual life, in those days and in a segregated country like Pakistan, began late, and so they were also the years of his sexual initiation, exploration, and gratification—in the "Diamond Market" district of prostitutes in Lahore. (During the past few years here in England, at the other end of his life, he has occasionally thought again about paying for sexual contentment, to alleviate his physical loneliness, but he hasn't gone beyond looking at telephone numbers and addresses in the classified pages of *The Afternoon.*) He was twenty-six and awaiting the publication of his first book of poems. The rumour in the publishing world in Lahore was that of any two rivals competing for the love and attentions of the same woman, the one who owned a copy of his book would have the upper hand. But then, in 1958, he had had to leave Pakistan for England, fleeing the military coup. The new government began hunting for Communists and he came to England a month after police raided the offices of his publisher and noted down all the names they found there before torching the place. He stayed in England until he was thirty-one, working in the mills and factories around Dasht-e-Tanhaii.

After five years in England, he returned to Sohni Dharti in 1963 and married Kaukab, doing all he could to catch a glimpse of her after the negotiations had begun, and succeeding finally when he knocked on her window one monsoon afternoon to ask for the literary pages of the newspaper. When he learned that he was to be a father, he decided to go back to England, having failed to gain meaningful employment since his return to Pakistan. He was back in England at the beginning of 1965, and Kaukab joined him at the end of that year, wearing a long chocolate-brown coat he had sent her from here, and carrying the baby Charag in her arms.

Shamas was working in a factory and that was when the word of his father's past reached him. It was 1970. Shamas did not return for a visit until the following year when news came that Chakor was dying of pancreatic cancer.

And as death drew near he became delirious, asking Mahtaab to promise she would cremate him on logs of the flame-of-the-forest tree, like a Hindu, instead of burying him in the ground like a Muslim.

Difficulties had arisen soon after the identity became known but the letters to Shamas had hidden the news of this harassment. He would learn later that a shopkeeper whose hand had accidentally brushed against Chakor's had immediately washed it, saying, "I wouldn't touch a Hindu even with a meat hook." Women began to send back the rose essence Mahtaab sold—in bottles the size and shape of a bicycle's light-generator—claiming it was contaminated with onion. Things were made difficult for him at *The First Children on the Moon* until he had no alternative but to resign; the "Encyclopaedia Pakistanica" series was seen by some to be nothing more than his excuse for publishing detailed maps of Pakistani towns and cities which the Indians could use during war—a war with India being always a possibility, the most recent only five years ago, when, to distract the attention of the public who had become disaffected following that election back in 1964, the government had sent the army into Kashmir, and India had retaliated by crossing the border into Lahore.

An Indian Hindu scholar claimed that Anarkali, Pomegranate Blossom—the servant girl with whom the Muslim prince Saleem had fallen in love, and whom Saleem's father the Emperor Akbar had had buried alive as a result in 1599—was not a girl at all, but, in fact, a boy, a fact the Muslim historians of the Mughul era had suppressed till now: the claim was published in Pakistani newspapers and Chakor was manhandled in the street that week and told that the Hindu gods were "pretty boys," what with their rouged cheeks and lipsticked mouths.

The cancer of the pancreas was in the last stage when it was diagnosed, and as death drew near, Chakor's raving became constant, wanting cremation instead of burial. Fearful that Mahtaab might act upon the words of a dying man out of his mind with pain, Kaukab had sent Shamas to Pakistan:

"I want you to go there and see that what needs to be done is done." She pointed to the one-year-old daughter, Mah-Jabin: "No one will marry her if your mother-ji does what he is asking. She herself never had any daughters so she doesn't realize how important it is to remain on the good side of society. But you *do* have a daughter now, and must place her before everybody else. A scandal like that would do irreparable damage to her chances."

It was November 1971, and the West Pakistani army had been in East Pakistan since March, spreading death and destruction: the general election last December had been won by an East Pakistani leader and the West Pakistani powers had refused to allow him to form the government, sending in the soldiers to suppress the unrest that followed. These soldiers had been told that the East Pakistanis were an inferior race—short, dark, weak, and still infected with Hinduism—and junior and senior officers alike had spoken of seeking in the course of the military campaign to improve the genes of the East Pakistanis: women and girls were raped in their hundreds of thousands. On the day in December that Chakor vomited dark-brown half-digested blood, grainy like sand—the aorta had ruptured and spilled its contents into the stomach so that now his body was consuming itself—the Indian army moved into East Pakistan, and Pakistan surrendered after a two-week long war: East Pakistan was now Bangladesh—India had not only defeated Pakistan, it had helped cut it in two.

At night Shamas would sit beside Chakor, the basket of bloody rags set by his chair leg. Sometimes the twenty-four-year-old Jugnu would be there with them, back from the Soviet Union.

The *harsinghar* tree in the courtyard, which dropped its funereal white flowers at dawn, had more flowers than usual under it during those mornings, as though the branches had been disturbed during the night. Shamas was no believer, but imagination insists that all aspects of life be at its disposal, the language of thought richer for its appropriation of concepts such as the afterlife. And so as he looked at the carpet of blossoms he couldn't help entertaining the thought that during the night Izraeel, the Muslim angel of death, had wrestled in the branches above with the Hindu god of death for our father's soul. Shamas looked up and imagined the branches twisting around the two supernatural beings, the flowers detaching from twigs and forming a thick layer on the ground.

The excessively heavy drop of blossoms was caused in fact by Mahtaab, who had lately taken to chewing the *harsinghar* foliage: the betel leaves, which were her lifelong addiction, and without which it was impossible for her digestive system to function, grew mainly in East Pakistan, and when their price went up at the beginning of the civil war she had reduced her intake to just a two-inch section at dawn; but now that East Pakistan was another country, the supply of betel had stopped altogether, and while a few people had given up the habit as a patriotic gesture, all over Sohni Dharti men and women were experimenting with any leaf they came across in case it resembled the betel in bitterness and flavour.

"I am sure the government is happy at last," Mahtaab had said, "now that it has turned us all into donkeys."

Both Shamas and Jugnu had smiled but their elder brother had taken exception to the comment. He had become increasingly religious in his forties and the news that his father was a Hindu had devastated him. He had accused the man of betraying them all by concealing the secret from them, prolonging the sin he was committing by living with a Muslim woman.

As a young man he occasionally attended the mosque run by Kaukab's father, his attendance increasing when he fell in love with Kaukab's young aunt who lived with the cleric's family beside the mosque. He hoped to catch a glimpse of her each time he went to pray: she was often at a high window overlooking the prayer hall—waiting to catch sight of him, surely? And through his piety he hoped to be seen in favourable light by Kaukab's father, hoping that one day he would think him an appropriate match for his sister. When he heard that the young woman was soon to be married off to the man to whom she had been betrothed at birth, he was heart-broken and stopped going to that mosque, attending instead another one, one operated along a more strict interpretation of Islam. It was here that he would meet the people who would eventually lead him towards the austere and volatile form of the faith that was alien to his parents and brothers.

After his father's origins became known, he pushed aside the recommendations and gentle reassurances of Kaukab's father, and wrote and talked to some friends and scholars he himself trusted, and the news they gave him nearly pushed him over the edge—the children of the union between Mahtaab and Chakor were all illegitimate. He smashed the furniture on the veranda and hurled the water pitcher against the wall when he heard that Chakor wanted to be cremated. He shouted that Chakor should not have produced children if he was not sure about his religious standing, that on Judgement Day he would be hauled in front of his children in chains to ask for mercy from them.

He was against their efforts to locate Aarti. He said the cancer of the pancreas was Allah's punishment and stood over the dying man while he coughed up blood and asked him to beg forgiveness from his wife and children and from Allah, "Only then would Allah stop the pain." The war with the Hindus over East Pakistan was the final blow, and the defeat, when it came, traumatized him (and most of the rest of the country). He became silent, jaws working in rage as he went about the house, eyes aflame, spitting into the plate and walking away if the food was not to his liking, beating his son almost unconscious for flying a kite which he considered unIslamic, or for blowing on his whistle or dribbling a ball in the courtyard—asking a child to apologize for being a child.

Shamas fell asleep beside Chakor's bed one night and woke at the sound caused by the opium addict next door throwing stones at the moon. He was alone in the room and it would be several decades before he would know fully what had happened while he slept. While he was asleep Jugnu too had nodded off, waking up only at a sudden blast of chilled air. The door to the courtyard was open—the pale light indicated that dawn was near—and the *harsinghar* was shedding its petals. Jugnu looked at his father's bed and found it empty. Shamas was asleep on the mat on the floor. Going out into the courtyard, Jugnu saw that the front door was open and there was a bloody rag in the street, just outside the threshold. He went and picked it up—the blood was wet. Soon he found himself walking towards the ruin of the Hindu temple, following the trail of blood drops. The building had fallen into disrepair since 1947, when the Hindus of Sohni Dharti had left for India.

He went from room to ruined room, shouting his father's name. He thought he heard sounds but they were the birds waking up. The smell of the smoke had intensified and he ran towards it but it was too late: his father had doused himself in kerosene and set himself on fire. Knowing himself to be near death, out of his mind with the excruciating pain, he had decided to cremate himself.

The charred face, the lack of gleaming moisture on the teeth, the marriage ring melting and fusing with the finger the way meat sticks to the grill during roasting: Jugnu would try over the years not to think about these things, try not to put them in their sequential place in the story of the next two hours in the temple.

And he—like Shamas—would try not to think of the fact that someone in the night went into the cemetery and dug up the corpse no matter how deep they buried it; it happened three times.

Jugnu beat the flames out with the *loi* he had wrapped around himself before leaving the house and then he covered the burnt man with it, he who was producing growl-like low sounds at the back of his throat, and was in too fragile a state to be lifted. A crow swooped down from a low branch above Jugnu and picked up a glistening red piece of meat from the dusty floor. Just after the bird took off—disappearing through a gash in the wall—Jugnu recognized what it was: Chakor had cut out his tongue before setting fire to himself lest the pain cause him to call out for help.

He is returning home through the empty town centre, having been to the newsagent and collected the bundle of newspaper.

He climbs down to the riverbank, to listen to the river. The leaves of the rowan trees resemble the tamarinds'. Even if found, Aarti would not have been able to attend her brother's funeral—it would have been too soon after the war with the Hindus for her to be granted a visa.

Drowned grass-blades whip like tails of sperm in the shallow edges and it is on reaching a secluded curve where the bubbles are like a tumbling spillage of glass beads that he looks up to find the two lovers staring fixedly at him, and the unexpectedness of it is as though a syringe of adrenaline has been emptied into his body.

It is obvious that they saw him before he saw them: they've flown apart and are already somewhat composed but their faces retain traces of the look they must've borne only moments earlier—*show me where and I'll taste you there.* The boy's back arched, he has almost refastened the buttons of his fly, and the girl is shrugging her shoulder back into the *kameez* that had been undone at the back—or had it magically come undone at his touch?—and peeled to expose a breast.

They must have taken great care to select a secluded enough place for this rendezvous, and no doubt the condom he would have unrolled onto himself sometime soon had they remained undisturbed is patterned with battle-fatigue camouflage.

"Hello, Shamas-uncle-ji," the boy—twenty-odd, a Hindu—says with a smile. "It is Shamas-uncle-ji, yes?"

Shamas knows him vaguely from the neighbourhood. Knowing no English on the first day of nursery school, having spoken nothing but his parents' Hindi up until then, he had demanded to know whether his mother was being called a liar by the teacher who insisted that this fruit was an "apple" and not a *saib* as he had been taught to call it till then.

A smiler, he stands there now, the shirt straining at the wide shoulders. The force of puberty had struck from within the plates of his face with differing intensity in different places: the nose has become disproportionately longer; the cheekbones are flat, remaining where they were in childhood; the chin and jaw are more angular.

"Let me get my lid": he nods backwards where his baseball cap lies on a boulder. It is a pretext: he wishes in reality to check on his lover—she, the nipples the size of vaccination scars embossed on the fabric of the shirt, had vanished when the boy came towards Shamas, tenderly giving her the time to correct her appearance somewhere discreetly out of sight, even though the jut and swell of his own erection was still there and he had had to thrust his fists into the trouser pockets to make it less obvious.

She is now married to a Muslim, but this love is much older than the marriage.

Shamas is suddenly tired from the jolt the encounter has given him. On the luminous edge of his fevered senses, he waits, feeling slightly stoned, dreamily stilled. The sky is almost all light now, the water sparkling. There is the beginning of cataract in his eyes, but the faint milkiness has to be endured for now because nothing can be done about it until it has grown more opaque, setting like glue, shutting out vision, the doctor informing him that surgery would be performed in about a decade, surprising him by how long he expected him to live.

He brings her to Shamas now. Poised and graceful, marked by distinction at every pore, as she comes she pats her hair and consults her shadow on a boulder as she would a mirror.

"You know Shamas-uncle-ji, of course? He and his brother are the coolest adults I know. He lives near St. Eustace's Church. When we were children we used to call the vicar Bo Peep: the whites have moved out, so he's lost his flock."

She is a girl from the edge of the neighbourhood, and her face concentrates with the effort to place Shamas—the intruder on stolen rapture. She has freshly applied scent to herself and it drifts to Shamas in surges as though gardenia flowers are opening in rapid succession somewhere nearby.

"A heart was found here yesterday, uncle-ji," the girl tells him—she has obviously decided to believe her lover and trust Shamas, understanding that he is not the kind of adult who would report this sighting to others and make trouble for the pair. "About half a mile in that direction, beyond the pine trees. There were detectives everywhere. We came just out of curiosity . . ."

"A human heart," says the boy. "Some children went home talking of something they called a 'beat box.' The parents called the police."

Shamas looks at them without understanding what he is being told. A heart? The lovers stand facing him, still as if painted in a picture, though the fronds of the bracken they had walked through are still moving from that disturbance as though ghosts are passing through. His words, when he speaks, come out ragged from the throat that has remained unused for a while: "Whose heart was it?" Chanda's? Jugnu's? He hears himself give out a small cry. A wren on a tree that overhangs the boulders has been watching Shamas and now flies away with a shrill whistle. He turns and begins to walk away.

The soft distortion of tiredness polluting his blood, Shamas moves under the high nave formed by the pine trees, the trees occasionally shaking drops of yesterday's rain onto him, the clusters of needles dripping like saturated paintbrushes, producing a mud thick as mayonnaise. No, it can't be Jugnu's heart or Chanda's, he tells himself as he hurries, his breathing settling somewhat.

He is embarrassed by the manner of his departure from the two lovers, and looks back to see if he can locate them. In love with a Hindu, she was married off against her will to a cousin brought over from Pakistan, but the couple divorced because she remained distant from him—the cousin moved out as soon as he got his British nationality, no longer having to put up with her. Though she was still young, no one was willing to marry a girl who was not a virgin—"Why not marry a blue-eyed English blonde if virginity is not an issue?"—and the parents could only find an older man for her, who, it has now turned out, has three other wives: one is under the British and also the Islamic law, the other three are under Islamic law only. He wants a son but they keep producing girls, so he has married again and again. The fertility clinics run by Pakistani doctors often place advertisements in the Urdu newspapers, saying, *We tell you the sex of the foetus while you wait*; this is innocent-seeming, yes, but Shamas knows what message is being conveyed—*so that if it's female you may have it aborted quickly.* He wonders if the husband of this particular girl has used these services.

Shamas gives a final glance in search of the lovers but they are nowhere to be seen. When her mother discovered that she had refused to consummate the marriage with her cousin after sharing a bed for almost a week, she took the bridegroom aside and told him in a whisper,

"Rape her tonight."

He goes past Kiran's house. The sight of the young girl's flesh—the soft brown body, bright in the sunlight, glimpsed in sections—is hard to shake off. There have been times over the past few years when he has found himself visiting Kiran and her invalid father, but each time he has known— the guilt lying heavy as lead on his thoughts—that he had set out in that direction with the initial intention of encountering and, perhaps, beginning a conversation with, the prostitute who lives next door.

spring

The Madonnas

Mah-Jabin's train, bringing her to Dasht-e-Tanhaii, passes through tunnel after tunnel like a needle picking up beads to thread a rosary. Their number increases as the valley draws near and the ground corrugates to resemble a tempest on land, heaving, convulsing, the troughs deeper with each turn of the rails, the peaks higher in each new view.

And as the air caught between the stiffened waves pours into the compartment—filling it to the brim with England's warm April—a moth the size and shape of the cursor arrow on a computer screen also enters, to loop and spiral against the window.

She'll be twenty-seven this year and lives and works in London, divorced from the first cousin she had gone to Pakistan to marry at sixteen, living with him in the pale-green house in Sohni Dharti. Her decision to divorce him had devastated—and enraged—her mother. The two-year marriage is strange to her as though someone is telling her a story.

Kaukab submerges the apples one at a time in the basin of water, rubbing each with her hands to polish away a breach in the slight greasiness on the peel, and then works her way around the fruit until she meets the whistling clean beginning.

The orb of the bunched-up tissue paper in which Mah-Jabin has brought Madonna lilies is continuing to rustle as it expands and opens complicatedly inside the bin out of which dead tulips lean like necks of drunk swans, limp. The Madonnas have replaced them in the glass vase; the shrivelling and the separation of petals that had come to the tulips in drying out has made each cup resemble a live honeysuckle blossom, in size and shape.

"Did you get the flowers I sent you on your birthday, Mother?"

The apples have already begun to yield their fragrance to the warmth in the room, soft and lazy—smoky autumn days. "Yes. They lasted two whole weeks."

She brings a knife to Mah-Jabin, seeing that she is holding an apple. "Is that how white girls are wearing their hair these days?" Outside, the sun suddenly slips out of a gash in the clouds and lights up the room like magnesium detonated.

Mah-Jabin squints and returns the apple to its hexagonal space among the others, accepts the knife, and gestures with it at the peppers—red as birth—lying on the draining board. "I just felt like a change." The cutting off is quite recent, and she still finds yard-long strands clinging to the clothes she hasn't worn for a while.

"It was nearly eighteen-years' worth of growth." Kaukab's lips assume a smile, fixed, as a smiling statue would continue to smile regardless of the violence which might be done to the rest of its face or body. "Eighteen years."

All the more reason, Mah-Jabin thinks but doesn't say. Calmly, the blade cuts through the pepper with a hollow sound, creating red hoops that would acquire a wax-like transparency on cooking.

Kaukab nods to postpone the subject, for now. "I saw the peppers by chance yesterday. From Spain, I think. At this time of the year they are the size of tulips so I had to get these big ones when I saw them. A little expensive, but,"—and here she examines the girl's face for signs of forgetting—"you know your father likes them."

With the back of her fingers she touches the silk Mah-Jabin has brought her—the green of the dome on Muhammad's (peace be upon him) mausoleum in sacred Medina—for her to sew a *kameez* for herself, and which she has rejected because she would not be able to say her prayers in it: it is patterned with butterflies and Islam forbids pictures of living things.

"It is a pity about this," she says. "Perhaps I could make you a *kameez* of this, but you probably don't wear Pakistani clothes these days." The words are spoken with the back turned; the listener is being tested, to see if she can guess what expression of the face accompanies the words, as a lover would suddenly close both eyes and demand to know what colour they are: the right answer would be a proof of love.

Mah-Jabin was allowed to wear "Western" clothes to school but only if they mirrored *shalwar-kameez* in cut and style: the shirts had to be long-tailed and had to remain untucked whenever she wore trousers. Aswirl with pleats like the *ghagra*s of Pakistani desert women, and because it was floor-length, a skirt had been allowed her once, though skirts on the whole were forbidden because they were an easy-access garment. When someone they met at a wedding ceremony was considered "skimpily dressed" by Kaukab, Mah-Jabin had said, "She was wearing a sari! Six and a half yards of fabric." "The number of yards in itself is immaterial when it comes to modesty," had been Kaukab's response. And so she intercepted the secret codes and signals before they could be transmitted and under-stood. She saw it all as cats' eyes see in the dark. Despite the fact that Mah-Jabin said she had lost the receipt, she was made to return to the shops a blue sweater that had a broad paler stripe running from armpit to armpit, calling attention to the chest.

Mah-Jabin—chalk-green suede trainers at one end and an uncovered head at the other, black trousers gently fluted at the ankles, and a daz-zling purple-collared shirt made out of a marigold sari fabric—brings the plateful of pepper rings flecked with ivory seeds to Kaukab. "I once cooked myself a meal of what my friends at university were about to throw away—the stalks of the peppers, the seeded heart. They were aston-ished, but you've taught me well." She is afraid of sounding casual about her new familiarities, anxious not to hurt Kaukab by presenting herself to her in any capacity other than a daughter, *her* daughter. There is so much outside the house that may not be brought into the house, and the mother is quick to construe any voicing of opinion or expression of independent thought by the girl as a direct challenge to her authority.

After almost twenty years of doing without, Kaukab had found a friend when Mah-Jabin reached puberty. "My Allah," she would say, biting the corner of her veil to stopper her laughter, "I didn't tell even my mother or mother-in-law half the things you've coaxed out of me, you wretch. How can you ask me what was the first thing your father said to me on our wedding night? Have some shame." They could discuss and dissect anything with ease once Kaukab's feeble protests against her impropriety had died down.

Mah-Jabin would ask questions about Grandfather Chakor: she wondered why it was not considered strange by the other Muslims at the shrine that the little boy in their midst was uncircumcised, as he must have been because he was born a Hindu. Kaukab explained that during those early days of the century, when disease and infection were rampant, it wasn't uncommon to find a Muslim boy of that age with his foreskin intact because he was deemed too weak from the smallpox he had caught last year and the typhoid of the year before, and then the cholera the following year would cause yet another postponement: "They circumcised him at that shrine he found himself in, and that was that. In Sohni Dharti there was a *twelve*-year-old in *my* time whose mother had eight other children and therefore had never had the time: afterwards he walked around with a hole in the front of his shorts like an elephant in a balaclava, and what am I doing talking to you—and that too of such matters!—when I should be doing something about the bottom of the washing basket where the less-urgent bits and pieces have been lying undisturbed for weeks like an invitation to centipedes and silverfish."

Once, during a disagreement, Mah-Jabin had shouted, "And don't come running to me the next time those sons of yours upset you or Father says something you consider contrary to Islam": these three had been within earshot and Kaukab's eyes had boiled over with tears at the shock and humiliation of the betrayal.

The kettle shrieks like a squeaky toy caught underfoot, and Kaukab takes two cups from the six hanging at regular intervals from the hooks at the edge of the shelf, like ripe pears on a branch, or an arrangement of bells. "I usually cook in the evening when your father gets home—he doesn't like reheated food—but today we'll cook now. I remember when I was a girl my mother used to say that when it comes to food a woman should neither end something nor begin it: meaning, she must never take the last of something in case someone else needs it, and she must never take the first helping or cook something especially for herself because it indicates an indecent lack of restraint. But these ideas are considered old-fashioned now. People are different these days." She brings Mah-Jabin the cup the colour of a lotus bloom.

"Mother, I think we should cook at six o'clock, but since I left without breakfast this morning, and it was such a long journey, I *would* like to eat something for lunch—a sandwich perhaps." She takes the tea and catches again the scent her mother is wearing and which she had caught earlier, on arrival, in a pocket of air above the garden gate: by it she had known that her mother was outside only moments earlier, either leaving the house or returning.

"I'm sure your father wouldn't mind: let's have the peppers and chappatis now." Kaukab opens the door to the back garden, propping it in place with the lobster-buoy from Maine, and suddenly heat-veined air is being breathed into the kitchen.

Hugging the narrow lane that is full of moist shadow and that lies between garden and slope, the blue-and-pink trickle of the stream will dry to brilliant-white stones by midsummer. It flows from right to left like Urdu.

"You make the chappatis, Mother, and I'll do the peppers. How shall I cook them?" She can already sense the pleasure of the flame-cored spices on her tastebuds like atoms dancing in a reactor, but her mother's reply sears her heart:

"Whichever way you cook them at university."

Kaukab stands facing the back garden, the green grass that only a month ago was the orangey-gold of the foil that orange-flavoured chocolate bars come wrapped in, listening to the stream's mother-tongue that is constant in the house like the babble of blood in a human ear. When she arrived in England all those years ago she had thought the reason this country lacked blossom-headed parakeets, lorikeets, mynahs and bee-eaters was that its inhabitants did not plant the correct trees and vines in their gardens, did not know that acacias were needed to coax weaverbirds out of the skies, that grapevines were required for golden orioles, that rose-ringed parakeets had a penchant for mangoes and *jamun*. She knew that paradise flycatchers were heartbroken when coral trees were cut down and that the tiny sunbird would quarrel with a butterfly to feed on the lustrous hibiscus bloom that dwarfs them both.

And so she had written back home to ask for seeds, and seedlings and cuttings, none of which had flourished here, leaving the hoopoes and the blue-jays and the red-vented bulbuls circling above the clouds of England for want of somewhere to perch, and later she had wondered whether this country's soil itself hadn't been responsible for the failures and contemplated requesting sacks of Pakistani soil which was hospitable to everything as the century-old public parks and gardens of Lahore—planned and opened during colonial times—were said to testify, containing as they did every plant from every country the British had ever ruled. This land is warmer now however, and she knows someone not far away on Benazir Bhutto Road who had raised a banana tree successfully, though it never survived the denuding it suffered when—soon after a television programme on Madrasi cooking was aired—some schoolgirls followed the recipes and decided to eat their *dosa*s off banana leaves for added South Indian authenticity.

Mah-Jabin rises, stretches her body until she feels the spine pulled taut as an iron chain, goes to rinse her cup and hangs it from its empty hook. She notices that there is a dead moth like a pinch of powdered gold in one of the other cups (undiscovered by her mother because there has been no occasion to use all six for a while?), and now recalls seeing, earlier, on the curtain close to where the vase is set, the stale discoloured pollen from the Madonna lilies she had sent Kaukab for her birthday.

Once upon a time this would have been unthinkable.

The girl reaching puberty had been a turning point in the appearance of the house: many improvements were made to the interiors which until then had been seen only as temporary accommodation in a country never thought of as home—the period in England was the equivalent of earthly suffering, the return one day to Pakistan entry into Paradise.

The growing daughter's irritation at her economized surroundings had made the mother agree to the transformation of the home, and she followed the girl into shops she would not have entered on her own, watched her ask the white assistants if this thing came in that colour and whether that other thing was available in a smaller size but with snap-fasteners instead of these tasselled ties like the one in this picture that I clipped from a magazine. She watched dumbfounded as the girl spoke English sentences at the rate she herself spoke English words, as she said let's get rid of the tablecloth because I want to be able to "enjoy" the grain of the wood.

Mah-Jabin remembers Kaukab's disappointment at the two "over-dependent" neighbourhood girls, one of whom had told her mother in great distress that her husband wanted to "do it from the back," and the other who told her mother that her husband wanted to "discharge in my mouth," and she remembers also her saying that the first fifteen to twenty years of marriage belong to the man but the rest to the woman because she can turn her children against their father by telling them of all his injustices and cruelties while they are growing up, patience being the key to happiness: and so Mah-Jabin has never revealed the truth about her marriage to Kaukab, to the extent that there are times she herself believes that her husband—the cousin she had gone to Pakistan to marry at sixteen and lived with for two years in the pale-green house in Sohni Dharti—was in desperate love with her, that he asks the trees of the forest where she has gone. In these fantasies he does not grab her by the throat—in a grip as strong as a tree root—to call her a "wanton shameless English whore" for secretly touching herself towards climax after he himself had finished, rolled over and begun to fall asleep, having wiped himself on the nearest fistful of fabric in the darkness dark as the grave.

She knows the truth that her daughter had suffered would cause Kaukab more pain than the lie that she had selfishly and scandalously abandoned someone loving. How Kaukab would react to the truth would be a proof of her love, that she is being spared it is proof of Mah-Jabin's.

"You should rest," Kaukab says. "Leave everything to me." And within ten minutes the work-top is littered with broken onion skins—crisp fractured bowls of conch-pink tissue—and resembles a song thrush's "work-shop," as Jugnu had referred to a flint ledge in a chalk meadow where a thrush had been smashing open snails. Pinching her eyes against the fuming sulphur, Kaukab cuts the onion into crescents and drops them into hot oil where they disappear under a rugby scrum of bubbles, lets them sputter until they begin to lose firmness and the tips turn a pale red and yellowish-brown—the shapes and colours of the decorative tendrils on Venetian glass ornaments. Kaukab points to the butterfly-patterned silk: "Mah-Jabin, put that into the next room, in case a drop from all this sputtering oil falls on it. I've just remembered that some days ago I saw a girl wearing a *kameez* made out of this very fabric. It was the girl from Faiz Street who had wanted to marry a Hindu boy but was made to see sense and married to a first cousin. Of course that didn't work out because she didn't get on with him—she was very young then and still influenced by the ideas she must've picked up from school and her teachers and friends, from life in general in this country, but she agreed to be married off a second time and is perfectly happy now."

"I saw her earlier, just near Omar Khayyám Road," Mah-Jabin says, withholding the fact that she was with her Hindu lover. And she wonders at the ease with which she has slipped into thinking of the roads and streets of this town by the names the immigrants of her parents' generation had given them, the names she grew up hearing.

Kaukab is at the cooker with her back towards her, and the turned-away body in that corner of the kitchen produces a surge of homely familiarity in the girl: her mother standing over a pot, expressing her fears about what she is cooking, or attempting to tighten the loose screw on a panhandle with the tip of a butter knife during the washing up at the sink next to the cooker.

"How do you know her? Some days ago I couldn't ease apart a plastic bowl that had got stuck into another one during the washing up, and— since I don't have my own children around me—I looked out and walking by was the Hindu boy she had wanted to marry, so I called him in to help me. As I said, the girl is perfectly happy with the new husband her parents found for her." She falls silent and then adds: "Ending up with an obedient daughter is a lottery, I suppose."

Mah-Jabin does not wish to enter this perilous game that recognizes no rules, where a mere comment may be a lure to entice the other into a confrontation. "Would you like some help, Mother?"

Kaukab shakes her head but all the same brings the wooden stirring-spoon to Mah-Jabin: "You'd better taste this and see if the salt and spices need adjusting. My own tastebuds are mangled from the fasting I have just finished doing."

"Fasting! Was it Ramadan recently?" Mah-Jabin is aghast. "I had a feeling that I had missed the Eid festival. Why didn't you phone?"

"No, the Ramadan is in the autumn. I just fasted for two days to ask Allah to bring me peace." She shakes the spoon to draw the girl's attention to the matter in hand. "And you *have* missed *two* Eids. We didn't celebrate anything last year because Jugnu was missing; but the one the year before, you did miss that. Why should I phone you: you shouldn't have to be reminded."

"Mother, I'm so sorry I wasn't here." The problem, of course, is that the Muslim festivals are based on the lunar calendar and it's hard to keep track of them from year to year. Mah-Jabin wipes a trace of the sauce onto her tongue. "Perfect. But I phone every month: you could have said something." The response when it comes is devastating:

"It happened to be Eid the day you phoned that year."

Kaukab has returned to the cooker. "It's my own fault for having brought my children here: no one would need reminding in Pakistan when Eid is, or Ramadan, the way no one can remain unaware of Christmas here. The only way you'd know it was Ramadan here was that the catalogue shop in town does a brisk business in alarm clocks so that Muslims can wake up before dawn to begin the fast." The wall before Kaukab's eyes dissolves in her tears and the wooden spoon stops its circular motion. Mah-Jabin's languishing feet are tangled in the thick forest of the chair-legs under the table but she frees herself in time to rush across the room with the lightness of a tugged balloon, or a paper-boat borne on a sudden downward current, to stop her mother from sinking to the floor, her young arms strong enough to hold the woman upright.

"This house is so empty," Kaukab sobs in tight breaking heaves as Mah-Jabin had earlier, at the moment of arrival, letting the white lilies tumble to the floor with a rustle and herself falling into her mother's arms without a word needed as explanation that she was weeping for Jugnu and Chanda, this being her first visit since the news of the two brothers' arrest in January. So have mother and daughter always laid claim on each other, consoling to be consoled in return.

Kaukab continues to weep. "I am sure none of you will come to pray on my grave when I am dead. Sometimes I become so frightened that nobody would ask Him to have mercy on my soul."

The porous white steam above the pan begins to turn into black smoke. Kaukab swallows her trembles neatly and rapidly back into her body, loosens Mah-Jabin's grip from her stomach and pushes her away to give herself space. "You are going to have to check for salt again," she attempts a smile that comes out grotesque in the chaffed face, "because my tears have fallen in."

Mah-Jabin smiles weakly and, looking for a diversion, says after a silence, "Mother, the hair on the back of your neck is completely grey. Why don't you dye it properly?" It is like a patch on the fur of a cat.

"Is it obvious?" Kaukab says after a while, twisting her neck as though a glimpse of the back of the head is achievable. "The white people on the street must think we 'fucking Pakis' are ridiculous, don't know how to do anything right. Your father has stopped colouring his hair, you see. Before, we used to do each other's on the same day but now I do mine myself, not wishing to trouble him or get stains on his hands . . . I hope this food isn't spoiled . . . So do you think the hair looks strange? Really? But it doesn't make much difference at my age: a red harness is not very becoming on an old mare."

"I'll put the dye on it properly for you after lunch." Mah-Jabin plays with her own hair: there haven't been enough days since for her to have discovered all the possibilities of the new cut. "I'd like to put henna on mine to get rid of its complete darkness, though it's so black that I wonder if it would take the colour. And, by the way, I bet Father doesn't think you are an old mare."

"Hush, you wretched girl!" Kaukab blushes. "Sometimes I wonder if you are mine." She leaves the cooker and rummages in a cupboard: "I *think* . . . Yes, I *have* a packet of henna here." The little sachet lands on the table before Mah-Jabin. "No, wait, there are two. Here, take this one as well. We'll do each other's heads this afternoon. And squeeze half a lemon into the henna: that will bleach the hair a little and then the henna will show."

Mah-Jabin mixes the henna in a bowl. Like four cut-off spectral hands the transparent cellophane gloves that came with the two henna sachets have floated to the floor to lie invisibly on the linoleum arabesques.

"Only one chappati for me, Mother. Your chappatis are heavier than mine: I can usually eat two of mine." Mah-Jabin had begun to be tutored into making chappatis at about twelve years old, the boys complaining and laughing in brotherly amusement at her efforts, feigning sickness as she removed one misshapen disc after another from the baking-iron, once or twice reducing her to tears, the elder calling her Salvador Dalí, but

Kaukab was firm that a girl's family must endure the earlier efforts so that the husband and in-laws can enjoy the skilled creations in the future.

Having broken three handfuls of dough from the mass in a enamel basin, Kaukab now presses one back. "Your father always says how lovely and light your chappatis are, the way they puff up on the iron. And he's been saying it a lot recently because I'm still not used to this new baking-iron—the handle came off the last one—and my chappatis have been mediocre at best as a result. I remember when I came to England I had a baking-iron in the luggage: your father had written especially, since they were not available here then. Men used to make chappatis on an upside-down frying pan—"

"Yes I know, you've told us. But I think there is a thing called a 'griddle' in Britain that resembles Pakistani baking-irons, and of course the Mexican tortillas are cooked on—"

"If we'd had you to guide us during those early years we would have done things differently, and I apologize if I repeat something I've already told you but I don't lead a life as varied as yours." It wouldn't tip the scales on a pin, the amount by which a comment has to fall short from the ideal in the listener's head for it to be regarded an affront, an offence—a crime. "If I tell you something every day it's because I relive it every day. Every day—wishing I could rewrite the past—I relive the day I came to this country where I have known nothing but pain." Immediately after taking it off the iron, Kaukab polishes the chappati with a pat of butter that melts and is propelled forward on the hot surface like a snail secreting the lubricating slickness to move on as it goes.

There is a curve of pale-yellow crust—the remnant of a previous meal—on one of the plates Mah-Jabin takes out of the cupboard, on the china so intensely pigmented it seems to stain the air with each movement like a beetroot leaking colour: once it would have been Kaukab who noticed such a flaw in a chore assigned to the girl.

Her mother is getting old.

They sit together, eating side by side, Kaukab letting out a sigh of pleasure and touching Mah-Jabin every now and then. The girl bites off buttered chappati segments and jabs at the limp, endlessly compliant ampersands of the pepper-rings soaked with sunflower oil, the fork marking the sauce like bird-imprints on sepia mud.

"I wonder what that girl was doing on Omar Khayyám Road," Kaukab says. "Did you talk to her? Was she with someone—that Hindu boy, perhaps?"

Mah-Jabin has been fearing this question. She is unable to control the roughness of her reaction: "Oh Christ, what difference does it make who she was with?"

"You had been quiet for a while so I was just making conversation," Kaukab says as she pushes her plate away with her hands and her chair backwards with her calves, standing up violently. The three furrows deepen on her forehead; they've been there for as long as her children remember, Mah-Jabin wishing to—as a child—write her alphabet on these equally-spaced straight lines drawn on the brow as though in an exercise book. "And do not try to sound white by saying things like 'Oh Christ,' because you don't impress me. Do you hear me?" Her eyes narrow in a blank white glare. "I said do you hear me?"

"I'm sorry. It's not your fault," Mah-Jabin sighs. "I was just thinking about Uncle Jugnu."

She winces inwardly at what she has just said, feeling degraded, that already the death of the two loved people is being used in deceit because she does not wish to hurt this living person by her side, either that or because she is too cowardly to confront her: so will this terrible thing called life extract concessions out of her, teach her to compromise, and force her to become less than her best self, force her to reduce the amount of honour due the memory of her lost ones! One day she is going to wake up and not recognize herself.

They have talked about Jugnu and Chanda on the telephone several times since January, and again on her arrival today—and before January too, over the long anguished weeks and months when they disappeared like two raindrops in a lake, the months of disappearance that led to the brothers' arrest—and there is nothing more to be said about it: Kaukab is unshakeable that they have not been killed and that they will return one day, that to give up hope is a sin, that the brothers could not have murdered their own sister in cold blood. "I don't care how many people agree on what has happened to Jugnu and Chanda: a lie does not become truth just because ten people are telling it. And I won't lose faith in Allah's benevolence no matter how bleak things look: the sun never disappears, it's the earth that changes sides."

She has given the girl the news of the graffiti scrawled on Jugnu's house: *They lived the life of sin and died the death of sinners* and *They have been burning in the Fire now for over six months but remember that Eternity minus six months is still Eternity.*

Mah-Jabin clears the table in the steady golden light in the blue-skinned room, in the talkative silence of the stream that Kaukab, still angry, leaves behind when she takes her transparent-red rosary lying in a saucer like the circle of pollen grains in the middle of a flower and goes upstairs to say her prayers.

With a loose bulky knot Mah-Jabin shortens the length of the curtain covering the glass in the front door and carries a chair into the burning slice of sunlight, listening out for her mother's loud end-of-prayer Arabic, when she begins to mix hair-dye in the plastic lid of an old aerosol can, using a worn toothbrush which she identifies from the characteristic disfigurement of the bristles as having once been used by her father.

Kaukab comes down, the cranberry rosary swaying from her grip, the beads larger than those she used in her younger days when the fingertips were nimbler, more-sensitive, just as she needs a large-print copy of the Koran now because her eyes too are beginning to fumble amid words.

Even after the contact and consultation with Allah, her displeasure at the girl, and the sadness which the outburst had caused, is there in her: she approaches the sunlight wordlessly and takes the chair, bending her head forward.

Mah-Jabin—standing ready behind the chair—knows that being unable to dispel her anger before the prayer must have exacerbated her mother, that it must have interfered with the concentration required for the worship—like the intermittent annoyance of a hang-nail during daily chores. The only thing for Mah-Jabin now is to wade upstream and begin the journey anew, this time making sure that the bend leading to the vortex is avoided, but she cannot think of anything to say.

Gently—and in strategy—she wets a knuckle with her spit and touches Kaukab's earlobe with it: Kaukab sighs to empty herself and speaks at last, "Mah-Jabin, make sure you don't get any dye on my ears."

The girl smiles at her triumph. "Stop worrying. *There*—I've wiped it off."

Nevertheless, Kaukab asks her to keep within reach a rag that is an off-cut from a new *kameez* she has sewn for herself: "The rag in the drawer, a shade less blue than navy. Yes, I did say to myself when I was buying it that my Mah-Jabin would ooh and aah over this colour. Four pounds per yard. I still haven't stitched the hem of the new *kameez*." And, when Mah-Jabin tells her with a smile that she would be unable to help her in that task as she could never achieve those tiny invisible stitches, Kaukab asks her if she remembers the time she had sat with a new *kameez* on her lap—working on the hem all day—and discovered at the end that she had stitched it onto the one she was wearing! "I don't remember doing it but I can believe I did it," replies the girl. "There. Finished. My turn now. No, hold on. *There*. Finished *now*."

She spreads the blue cloth across Kaukab's knees and sits on the floor with her hair in her mother's lap.

The hair does not fill the lap anymore and Kaukab misses the weight; she draws the comb of her fingers along the length and when it ends suddenly—shockingly, as in the dream in which the dreamer stumbles off a kerb—her fingers groping the empty air are an illustration of what is now missing from her life, what was once so palpably there—so palpably *here*.

She begins to say something but remains silent, simply runs her fingers through what remains of the black locks just for the slippery slipping pleasure of it, how it slides off her fingers, the softest sensation in the world to her, and, once absent, impossible to summon at will.

"Are you comfortable propped up like a rag doll on the floor? Let me know and you can sit on the chair and I'll stand up." Kaukab works the wet henna into Mah-Jabin's hair, scoop by scoop of fingers. "Well, tell me anytime you get tired and I'll stand up. In Pakistan we used to squat in the toilet and when I came here I thought I'd never get used to the Western toilets. But now, after all these years, those others seem impossible: how did we manage to squat like that every day?"

"The body gets used to things."

"Even if the mind doesn't."

She packs the entire bowl of henna into the girl's hair, patting it on until the head appears as though coated with a fragrant mixture of mud and moss, tangy as tamarind, sweet as brown sugar; and the pulverised dark green leaf, through each pore and microscopic crack that the drying and the powdering had opened up, begins to release its red sap, diluted by water and made sticky by the lemon.

Kaukab holds the blue cloth firmly at the girl's shoulders and slides her chair back across the floor so that the cloth is pulled off the lap and rests like a little sailor cape at the girl's back, a barrier between the henna and the fabric of the girl's shirt. She takes the front-door key, attached—for want of pockets on her *kameez*—with a safety pin to her veil, and gives the pin to her to secure the blue cloth at the front.

The back of the house has been moving out of the sunlight at a snail's pace over the previous hours, and now—now that the sun has vaulted over the roof—it is in total shade, the sodium-yellow warmth directed at the front.

Mah-Jabin makes herself coffee, Kaukab peels an orange and places the segments curved like leaping dolphins onto a plate, and they both go outside to sit on the front step where the breeze turns the lilacs' pages in the little garden, the shadows beginning to stretch like chewing gum.

Light is gone from the back to appear here as rain soaks into the earth and flows away underground to emerge elsewhere as a spring.

The girl sits diagonally on the step, instinctively turned a little away from the house that joins theirs on the right, to keep it out of sight: Jugnu's house. But it is there nevertheless, she cannot ignore its presence: the soul has many eyes, is capable of seeing in every direction.

The woman next door on the left has taken advantage of the sunny afternoon and put out a rug to air that releases swinging plumes of fenugreek odour. "She must put fenugreek in everything," Kaukab says; she is consuming her orange in the Pakistani manner, dipping the blunt-nosed segments in salt first. "The smell penetrates. In Pakistan it gave no trouble because the houses there were—are—big and airy and nothing lingers. But here the rooms are small and closed up, and the smell refuses to shift."

"That's not the least of it: if I remember correctly from the few times you used fenugreek the damned thing gets into your sweat and urine after you've eaten it."

"Be quiet!"

"Sorry," Mah-Jabin laughs, for the first time in weeks, and touches her mother's knee with her own. The laughter dissolves in the sunlight, while, like a music-box left open beside her, the coffee steams in the dry air.

A voice bursts through like a ball landing in the little garden: "Mother and daughter are enjoying the sunlight, I see. And the daughter-empress wants to lighten the colour of her hair, does she?"

Mah-Jabin looks up: a vaguely remembered neighbourhood woman is struggling with the rusted screeching latch of the garden gate. Kaukab explains how to circumvent the eccentricities of the catch and the woman—acting on the advice—gains entry to advance towards them under the jewelled nets of the lilac branches.

Mah-Jabin—fearing that the woman has come to collect material for gossip—wishes to retreat inside, but the woman flags her down: "I won't take a seat, beautiful. I've just stopped by to remind your mother that Ateeka—the wife of Zafar-who-has-a-clothes-stall-in-Thursday-market and not the left-handed Zafar—is flying to Pakistan on Monday, so if there are any presents that have to be sent back home there is still room in the luggage."

Kaukab tells her that earlier the taxi-driver-Mahmood's wife had called her out to the garden gate in passing and given her the same message; Mah-Jabin can envisage the woman going along the street, one of the many who begin doing the rounds in late morning, all involved in that organized crime called arranged marriages.

Mah-Jabin dips a finger in the hot coffee until it begins to burn, pulling out just in time, as though she were teasing a pet bird, withdrawing the fingertip from the bars of the cage before the inevitable inflamed peck.

She looks at the roses to distract herself, the petals wrinkled like elastic-marks on skin, the blown heads lying in whole clumps under the bushes like bright droppings of fantastic creatures.

The grass is rising like knives, the green the colour of the butterfly fabric, and now Mah-Jabin remembers that this woman is the mother of the girl she'd seen earlier with her Hindu lover on Omar Khayyám Road. Mah-Jabin examines her with interest now.

The visitor slips a foot out of her shoe and rests the dry cracked sole on the bottom rung of the fence dividing this garden from the next. She has

not stopped speaking since she came: "Of course Ateeka's boys are growing up and eat everything they can lay their hands on, so all the fancy food
and the biscuits and cakes intended for the visitors who are coming to the
house to see off their mother must be hidden away. She thought that the
built-in space under the settee in the kitchen—where she stores her linen
and pillow-cases—was an ideal hiding place. And what do you think happened? This: the guests came last night and settled on that very settee!
Now the kettle is whistling and steaming, the milk has boiled and got cold
and been boiled again, the cups and plates are at the ready, but how to get
at those pastries, from Marks and Spencer no less? She says she just sat
and looked at the guests' faces, getting up now and then and pretending to
give the cutlery and crockery one last wipe with the dish cloth. 'I'm sure
they thought I was the cleanest woman on Allah's earth,' she told me just
now. 'Either that or the most forgetful and the most crazy.' It must have
been a spectacle to behold, Kaukab."

Mah-Jabin finds herself gripped by helpless laughter; all three are shaking with noisy delight, touching wrists to the rims of their eyes.

"I am telling you the truth, Kaukab. If it isn't true you can change my
name to Liar."

Kaukab soaks up on a tissue paper the line of red liquid that has broken
onto Mah-Jabin's forehead.

"Kaukab, what brand henna is it, Lotus- or Elephant-?" the woman
asks, but does not wait for the reply, continuing distractedly: "These last
few days have been very hard on Ateeka, though, because her sister in
America was fondled and handcuffed by police for wearing her head-to-
toe veil. It would soon be a hanging offence to be a Muslim anywhere in
the world, it seems. The police officers—"

"Whereabouts in America, auntie-ji? Wearing masks in public is illegal
in some states over there," Mah-Jabin explains. "The officers could've mistaken her face-veil for the hood of a Ku Klux Klan member."

"What? A *who* member?" the visitor is puzzled while Kaukab—breath
pulled in in disapproval—gives Mah-Jabin a look of reproof for interrupting and trying to enlighten a grown-up. "In Portsmouth, Virginia.
They stopped her as she walked towards the shops, and even though
she explained she was wearing Islamic dress they asked her to uncover

her face: when she refused they handcuffed and searched her while she screamed 'Stop touching me, stop touching me.' An *unmarried* girl: anything could have happened."

Yes: the girl could've damaged her hymen in the scuffle, Mah-Jabin thinks, with contempt. She had not been allowed to see a gynaecologist when she had hormonal problems at twelve, not even a female one; the neighbourhood is full of teenaged girls who are doughy and have chins coarse as cactus, bristly like their brothers.

But it is the tears that fill the visitor's eyes in sudden overflowing fullness that are occupying Kaukab: she quickly tells Mah-Jabin to go indoors and look at the post that has been waiting for her in her absence, upstairs in her room. The girl stands up, baffled, notices that the woman is on the verge of weeping, and edges open the door to enter the house quietly.

The woman takes the place vacated by her and Kaukab places her arm around her. "Kaukab, it has been such a terrible morning . . . I feel I can tell you everything, you are like a sister to me . . . My daughter refuses to behave properly with her husband . . ." She presses her veil to her eyes with both hands and begins to cry silently, freely.

Kaukab looks up at Mah-Jabin who has not moved an inch from the open door behind the two women, motionless with incomprehension.

The woman says from behind the veil, her voice weak, "Go in and look at your letters, beautiful, and leave me alone with your mother for a while. Go on . . . Did you know I am always telling Kaukab how beautiful her daughter is? People tell stories about faces such as yours . . . Go now . . . Has she gone? This morning I went to see the cleric-ji at the mosque and he says that in all probability my girl has been possessed by the djinns, that's why she's behaving erratically . . ."

Mah-Jabin withdraws, lest a comment from her now cause both women to turn on her. Djinns!

The Madonna lilies have been giving off fragrance as candles give out light, filling the house into which Mah-Jabin steps. She drifts upstairs. The two pieces of post are in the drawer directly below: a poll card for the general election; and a letter that bears a stamp portraying a tree ablaze with festive pink-white blossoms in the distance and in the foreground a sprig containing a ruffled orchid-like flower and a leaf resembling the imprint of a camel's foot: it is *Bauhinia variegata,* the wording informs along a vertical margin, and horizontally that the stamp is one of a series depicting the MEDICINAL PLANTS OF PAKISTAN. Mah-Jabin lowers herself onto a chair, having recognized the hand that had written out the address. Her husband has never attempted to communicate directly with her before and she wonders what is contained within the letter that bears the pretty flower of the tree that is valued for, amongst other things, its effectiveness against malarial fevers, the ability to regularize menstrual dysfunction, and as an antidote to snake poison.

She won't unseal the letter, as though it is a way of keeping his mouth shut. Touching her head to see if the henna is still wet, she discovers that the preparation has lost almost all of its moisture—clinging to her hair but crumbling like green sand on contact, having deposited the gluey dark-red sap onto the filaments. In the bathroom she becomes curious and opens the letter, but cannot bring herself to read it. She opens the narrow angular cupboard in the corner that houses the immersion heater swaddled in insulating pillows of shiny silver nylon. "Hello, spaceman." She switches it on and, just before closing the hatch of the rocket, tosses the crumpled letter and envelope in—toxic waste to be dumped into some distant black hole.

She taps out a tube from the box of tampons in her toilet bag and, later, throws the empty tube into the wicker basket but picks it up again, pressing it into a flat strip and putting it in her pocket to dispose of later, away from where Kaukab may come across it, she who had warned the twelve-year-old virgin against using these kind of napkins that have to be inserted into the body lest she be "ruined for life."

Just before she leaves the bathroom, and as though acting on a will and independent memory of their own, the fingers of her hand open the door to the immersion heater once again, reach around the belly of the quilted water-drum and grope in the darkness there: when they find what they are seeking she too remembers it suddenly, as though a jolting electric current has passed from the object to her brain.

The knitting needle she had dropped there nearly nine years ago, shortly after returning from Pakistan, is still there, undissolved by the passage of time and the lack of light. She sinks queasily to the edge of the bath, holding tightly against her breast the hand that had touched the slippery smooth solidness of the spike, as a mother might console and reassure a child by hugging it after it has witnessed something disturbing.

Equipped with that knitting needle she had shut herself in here after discovering herself pregnant—the smell of rust in her nostrils and the taste of iron behind her teeth and gums seeming to grow richer every second, as though chains to bind her were being forged within her—and had realized only then that she did not know how to proceed. How exactly was it done? In the end her courage had failed her and she had sat trembling. A legal termination at a clinic was an impossibility: her only source of money was her parents and they would not have allowed her to have an abortion, and would have used the pregnancy to renew their efforts to make her return to her husband.

In the end she had induced a miscarriage by taking quinine tablets for a fortnight, something a young mother of eight in Sohni Dharti had said she found effective whenever she needed to give her body a respite, her husband refusing to see reason and claiming the use of contraceptives would lead to the unborn children pointing to him on Judgement Day and saying to Allah, "That man is the one who did not allow us to be born and swell the numbers of the faithful!," with the result that once the woman had given birth in the January and December of the same year.

With surprising heat in her heart, she takes the flattened and curved tube of white cardboard from her pocket and tosses it—like the crescent moon come unstuck and spiralling down—into the rubbish before leaving the bathroom.

"Mother, what was the matter with auntie-ji?"

Kaukab is at the sink, washing the lunch dishes, Mah-Jabin's coffee cup, the plate that had held her own orange pieces, and the henna bowl. She doesn't answer the question immediately—once again concealing everything regarding the Pakistanis that the children might deem objectionable. She knows Mah-Jabin will ridicule the idea of djinns.

"Nothing. She was just a little tired."

Mah-Jabin had heard a few words of what the woman had said to Kaukab: the girl's husband is demanding to know why she hasn't conceived yet—either she is secretly taking contraceptives or she is barren. He called her a stony valley that had wasted all his seed. "She mentioned something about her daughter and her husband—"

"Every marriage has it ups and downs," Kaukab says abruptly, and then as abruptly: "What was in the letter?"

"I threw it away unopened," Mah-Jabin hears herself state flatly.

Kaukab nods; she still holds on to the hope that Mah-Jabin will return to her husband, if he'll take her back, that is, and if not that then perhaps another marriage could be arranged for her—which would be difficult because she is no longer a virgin, is used goods. She peers over her shoulder to meet her eye, "I forbid you to go to America." Her hands clench into fists. "A strange country full of strangers! I'm sure your father wouldn't approve either."

"How do you know I'm going to America?" Mah-Jabin is puzzled. "And well, I've been to a country full of my own kind of people and seen what that is like so I thought I'd try a strange country full of strangers this time." Trapped within the cage of permitted thinking, this woman—her mother—is the most dangerous animal she'll ever have to confront. "I'm just going to stay with some friends during the summer. Who told you about it? And may I add that I am not *afraid* of Father."

Oh your father will be angry, oh your father will be upset: Mah-Jabin had grown up hearing these sentences, Kaukab trying to obtain legitimacy for her own decisions by invoking his name. She *wanted* him to be angry, she *needed* him to be angry. She had cast him in the role of the head of the household and he had to act accordingly: there were times when he came in to inform the young teenagers that something they had asked from their mother earlier—the permission for an after-hours school disco, for example—was an impossibility, and it was obvious from the look on his face that he personally had no problem with what the children wanted. Sometimes Mah-Jabin wonders whether her mother knows Shamas at all. Shamas wouldn't object to her visiting America, she knows. And she says these things out loud now.

Kaukab smarts at the words. "How your tongue has lengthened in the past few years. Is this what they taught you at university, to talk like this, your precious university far away in London that you had to attend because you wanted an education? If education was what you wanted you would have gone to a university within commuting distance and lived at home like decent girls all over these streets. Freedom is what you wanted, not education; the freedom to do obscene things with white boys and lead a sin-smeared life."

Mah-Jabin's head not only hums like a wasp's nest but also feels as weightless as those oblongs of chewed-up paper glued together with spit. "I knew it was not the distance that worried you; you had after all sent me a thousand miles away at sixteen."

"We did what you asked us to do." Kaukab moves closer and stares at her as though pinning a dangerous animal to the ground with a lance.

"I was *sixteen:* in every other matter I was considered a child by you but why was that decision of mine taken to be that of an adult? Another parent would have given me time to think but you were thrilled that I wanted to go and live in your beloved country," Mah-Jabin screams. "And I *was* afraid as the time approached for us to leave, but I knew I couldn't have said no at that stage."

"No you couldn't. These things are not child's play. We had given our word, the wedding arrangements were ready over there, and, yes, I would've *tied* you up and taken you there had it come to that. And what's wrong with Pakistan? Many girls from here are sent back to marry and live there, and they are happy there. Only the other month, the matchmaker told me of a woman from here who has been divorced by her Pakistani husband by mistake, and she's *still* eager to go back and live with him there. That's what a good and dignified woman is like." She pauses for a moment and repeats her question: "What's wrong with Pakistan? I grew up there—"

"And look what happened to you, you fool!"

The hard open palm of Kaukab's hand lunges at Mah-Jabin and in striking her face takes away her breath. This is something Kaukab has longed to do whenever she has thought about the girl in her absence and really isn't a response to what she has just said: she simply happened to be within reach as the need overtook Kaukab and the moment chose itself.

The force of the impact knocks Mah-Jabin off the chair, while Kaukab's rosary—looped double at the back of the chair—snaps and the beads clatter to the floor. Kaukab's hand alights and grips the girl's soggy gritty hair like a claw and slams the head many times against the wall with all her strength, the red stain of henna growing richer and larger on the wall, Mah-Jabin crooking her elbow against the side of the head until Kaukab finally lets go and moves to the sink at the other side of the kitchen, washing the redness—sticky as blood—off her hands, her back turned towards the girl.

Mah-Jabin opens her eyes and slides herself upright against the wall, the pull causing the safety-pin at her throat to open up and the point to enter the soft hollow between her collarbones.

Sometimes the right question can be as difficult to come by as the right answer. Yes: Mah-Jabin has spent the last nine years, and most of the two years of her marriage before that, looking for the question that has come to her only just now. She remembers that Kaukab, on catching Jessye Norman on television once—singing a lyric Kaukab did not know the significance to, in a language she did not know—had risen to her feet slowly as though in homage to the grandeur of the heart-breakingly beautiful goddess standing proud as a mountain against the Paris sky, and afterwards had managed to articulate only a few words:

"I love people who accomplish great things."

The sentence had startled the girl; and there were other similar occasions. Sometimes an idea would seem to come to Kaukab and disappear immediately so that her face was dark once again but not as dark as before, this being the darkness left behind in the flight-path of a firefly, a darkness aflicker with the knowledge that something had happened here recently, some illumination, the brain cells vibrating in the lucid wake of an insight. She would sigh, and talk to her daughter wistfully for a while.

Mah-Jabin remembers Kaukab telling her she regretted not having been able to have had an education, that she had wished to own a bicycle as a girl but it was out of the question even within the confines of the courtyard because her mother feared she would fall off and break a limb and no one would marry the cripple, so that she had bought herself a tiny pendant in the shape of a bicycle and put it around her neck on a chain, just as real bicycles are secured to trees or pillars with real chains.

And yet this same woman who had allowed her daughter to leave school at sixteen, hadn't allowed her to ride a bicycle lest she be ruined for life. Why?

"Why don't you hit me harder, Mother? Like this . . ." Mah-Jabin strikes her own face as she walks towards Kaukab. "Like this . . . this . . . this . . . Hit me harder . . . harder . . ."

Kaukab takes the cutlery from lunch and the knife with which Mah-Jabin had prepared the red peppers and drops them into the soapy water, standing solid as stone while the girl shakes her violently from behind with both hands. "You must be a moral cripple if you think what you did to me wasn't wrong. Didn't you once tell me that a woman's life is hard because you have to run the house during the day and listen to your husband's demands in bed at night? So why didn't you make sure I avoided such a life? Answer me . . . Answer me . . . Why do you people keep doing the same things over and over again expecting a different result?"

Kaukab's hand searches for and finds the handle of the long steel knife inside the water covered with the lace of bubbles.

"What was it you said to me once, Mother, that the first two decades of marriage belong to the husband, the rest to the wife because she can turn her children against the husband while she's bringing them up, so when they are grown up they'll make him eat dirt while she reigns over them all for the rest of her days."

Kaukab stands immovably while the girl pulls at her shoulder to make her turn around, she the most intimate of her enemies.

"How fucking wise you are, Mother, such wisdom! Victory awaits all the beleaguered Pakistani women but what a price, Mother, two decades of your life wasted . . . What a waste when instead of conniving for all these years you could just walk away . . ."

Drops of water slide off the blade slowly as the knife rises vertically through the air. "Get away from me, you little bitch!"

The hungry steel slices an arc as Kaukab swings around and then Mah-Jabin stumbles backwards with one arm raised and the other across her stomach.

"How dare you throw questions at me like stones!"

Dazzle explodes on the blade—like blood spurting from a vein—when the weapon enters a beam of sunlight. The air itself seems to contract away from Kaukab as a school of fish twitches itself to safety at the approach of a predator. The bowl that had held henna falls to the floor, spinning on its edge like the silver cups that revolve around the lights on top of police cars to make them blink.

Eyes dilated as though lost in darkness, Kaukab lowers the knife, that diamond-hard tip that had very briefly become the sharp point of her despair and defeat.

Her own jewelled eyes flashing, Mah-Jabin throws back her head and laughs for the third time today, face tilted up to the ceiling.

"Here we have proof that Chanda was murdered by her brothers, that a family can kill one of its own. I wonder if this will stand up as evidence in court so that those two bastards can be put away for life. My god, for all of you she probably didn't die hard enough: you would like to dig her up piece by piece, put her back together, and kill her once more for going against your laws and codes, the so-called traditions that you have dragged into this country with you like shit on your shoes."

The knife falls from Kaukab's lifeless grip. "Oh God, Mah-Jabin . . . I didn't know I had the knife in my hand. I just tried to push you away with my *hand*."

"Please don't come near me, Mother. And you would love me to go back to Pakistan to my husband, wouldn't you, back to my 'earthly god'? Or find me someone new like they did for poor Chanda. How many times had she been married before she met Uncle Jugnu? Twice? Three times? Yes, if it doesn't work once, try again, because you are bound to hit the target eventually, as long as it's *you* who decides what to do: if the bitch decides to take matters into her own hands and finds someone herself then raise the fucking knives and cut her to pieces."

"Not everyone has the freedom to walk away from a way of life," Kaukab says quietly. "The fact that you have managed to do it easily has made you arrogant and heartless."

"It was not easy! It is still a torment. What hurts me is that you could have given me that freedom instead of delivering me into the same kind of life that you were delivered into. I want to go back into the past and tell that young girl who was me—and whom I love—what not to do, but no one can return to the past. But it was easier for you because I was there right next to you: if you loved me you would have prevented me from doing certain things—"

"I did not have the freedom to give you that freedom, don't you see?" Kaukab is pained and broken at the realization that someone as close to you as one of your children can make so many mistaken assumptions when they take it upon themselves to evaluate your life.

"Don't lie. You would have done it if you wanted to. You still want me married because you still believe a woman must have a husband. Please, don't come near me, I said."

But Kaukab walks by her and begins to pluck the rosary beads off the floor.

"Yes, I do want you to go back, because in the eyes of Allah you are still married to him. You may have divorced him under British law, but haven't done so in a Muslim court. My religion is not the British legal system, it's Islam." Snatches of sentences are coming to her from the past few timeless minutes like waves returning to a shore and she deals with them as they come. "When I said a woman's troubles are over within twenty years of marriage because now her grown-up children will defend her against the father and in-laws, I didn't mean you have to connive and tell your children certain things deliberately. You need someone to talk to, to tell your troubles to, and her children are the people closest to a woman. You don't connive to bring about that situation, it happens of its own accord." She is on her haunches, weeping, as she lifts the beads off the linoleum like picking shells off a beach. "And what is this talk about me taking a knife to you: do you really think I could harm you?" There is a sense of consolation to the activity her fingers are engaged in, almost as though contact is being made with the dead: as a child she had seen her mother and grandmothers, and the other women in the house, similarly bent over the myriad daily tasks of the day, and sometimes—but not today, not now—the feeling is close to celebration, a remembrance and a praising of those now dead and absent but still living in her mind, unsung elsewhere and otherwise. Gone so thoroughly it is as though she had dreamed them.

Mah-Jabin moves towards the stairs, on the floor coated with dried-up or drying henna that she had shaken loose when she hit herself, and from the powdered layer under her feet it is as though she is in a room in Pakistan after a dust storm has just passed through. "Don't worry." She pauses by the bottom step. "It's not the first beating I've taken from you. Your husband beats you and you beat your children in return."

"I cannot understand why you constantly pluck this one string. I wish to Allah I had never told you about him hitting me and I've told you a thousand times since that it only happened that one time and that I didn't speak to him for many months afterwards. He begged for my forgiveness and when that didn't work, he even moved out for nearly three years." Kaukab comes to the stairs, obstructing the flow of light into the well, and watches the girl's ascending back. "Have *you* never made a mistake? Remember if you ever go back in time, make sure you choose to fall in love with the right person at fourteen, so that when he marries someone else two years later you wouldn't have to ask your parents to arrange a marriage for you somewhere far-away—somewhere like Pakistan, for instance. We sent you to Pakistan because you wanted to go live in a place where you wouldn't have to witness that young man leading a happy life with another woman."

A moth pressed to a window-pane, Mah-Jabin stops on the staircase as though air has suddenly solidified ahead, but she doesn't turn around. She rubs the point of pain at the base of the neck where the safety-pin has broken the skin, rubs it until it is lost in the smudge of heat the friction creates, and then, when the light rises a tone higher to signify that Kaukab has returned to the kitchen, she continues up the stairs, breaking free of the chains that her mother's words had briefly become around her ankles, head bowed like a lily on a broken stem.

He, a stranger, had smiled at her for a few moments and held her eye. That's all it had taken. Over the next few days she re-imagined and revised those first moments. He had paid her a compliment by noticing her and she had fallen in love: it was that easy because she had never been an object of curiosity, a scrutiny other than the kind that was openly intrusive, always aggressive, usually hostile. But what was deadlier was that she believed he too was in love with her, that he contrived to run into her here and there. She imagined herself beside him as his lover, naked, her tresses parted in a two-panelled robe along the front of her body, playfully identifying on his person the thirty-two signs of excellence in a man: deep in three respects and broad in three as well; glowing a healthy red in seven;

fine in five and long in four; elevated in six, and shapely and short in four. He lay with his head in her lap, and she kept up a commentary as she ticked these off to him, both of them attempting to suppress their giggles, "It is said that it is a mark of excellence in men if the navel, voice and breath are deep, and the thighs, brow and face are broad; if feet and hands, the corners of the eyes, palate, tongue, lower lip and nails have a rich red hue; according to the ancients it augurs well if fingers and finger-joints, hair, skin and teeth are fine; in the rulers of the earth the jaw-line, eyes, arms, and the space between the breasts are long; happiness is said to be ensured if chest and shoulders, finger-and-toe nails, nose, chin and throat are raised and prominent; and if back and shanks and the male member are shapely and short—oh dear! Well, thirty-one out of thirty-two isn't bad. Alright, I agree that it should be thirty-one and a half because it *is* shapely."

Each day she found another justification for her obsessive belief. He didn't have to speak: she *felt*. He gave no sign but she thought he was being prudent because in this neighbourhood, and in the way they had been brought up, the things that were natural and instinctive to all humans were frowned upon, the people making you feel that it was you who was the odd one out. Everyone here was imprisoned in the cage of others' thoughts. She and he were born here in England and had grown up witnessing people taking pleasure in freedom, but that freedom, although within reach was of no use to them, as a lamp with a genie was of no use to a person whose tongue had been cut off, who could not form words to ask for the three wishes.

She had been brought up to be patient—because for every thirst there was a cloud—and so she had waited, waited for their wedding night when they would come together at last like the two halves of a deck of cards cut and pushed back into each other with a forced ease, merging with a hesitant avidity. And may that night be longer than all nights.

Girls frequently sighed with relief when they got married because the husbands were less strict than the mothers had been, with whom it was as though they'd been handcuffed to dangerous lunatics at the moment of birth. Mah-Jabin, however, learned that the women of the family in the vicarage—the women whom she had to win over to gain access to the man of her life—were at least as traditional in outlook as her own mother, and she covered her head so quickly it was as though she was standing under a bird-filled tree, stopped wearing the few Western clothes that Kaukab had allowed her, and prayed five times a day.

A year and a half passed in the hopeful torpor, the single-mindedness, and the apparent masochism that had to be made intelligible to her white schoolfriends, there being no need for explanations when it came to the Indian and Pakistani girls, most of whom were trapped helplessly in similar webs of their own.

And then one day Kaukab mentioned in passing that so-and-so's boy was getting married. Mah-Jabin ran upstairs before Kaukab finished speaking and bolted the door as though it could shut out that news from her life.

The boy had not been able to get into a medical college within commuting distance and would have to move away in the autumn: the parents suspected it was a conspiracy of the white people to get Pakistani children away from their culture, to make them have sex before marriage and every day as though it were a bodily function, and to eventually make them marry white people, it being a neighbourhood curse to say may your son marry a white woman; Mah-Jabin remembers being sent into her brothers' room by her mother to look for condoms, and addresses, photographs or phone numbers of white girls, and remembers being told about a family that was tragic because the father had cancer and the daughter had just married a white boy.

And so—after telephone lines had burned between England and Pakistan—it had been decided that before he left for medical school the boy would marry his cousin from Pakistan; the parents had made sure he was ambitious and a high achiever—if he gained 90 percent and stood first in class then that was fine, but if 95 percent meant only a second place then it was not good enough. And they were not about to lose their prize of a boy to some white girl who most probably wouldn't be a virgin.

The two doctors in the surgery at the end of the road—Dr. Lockwood and Dr. Varma—who had taken an interest in the boy after learning that he was applying to medical schools and wasn't just another young no-hoper from around here, warned him of the dangers of inbreeding, but the father had gone to the surgery and reminded the Englishman that Queen Victoria and Prince Albert were first cousins, and told the Hindu woman that before lecturing the Muslims on the dangers of genetic defects she might want to do something about her own gods, who had eyes in the middle of their foreheads and what about those six-armed goddesses that were more Swiss Army knives than deities.

Shamas warned Kaukab to be careful and not lay a hand on the girl, because otherwise tomorrow the local newspaper would be carrying the headline BRITISH-BORN DAUGHTER OF PAKISTANI MUSLIM COMMUNITY LEADER BEATEN OVER MATTER OF MARRIAGE, bringing into disrepute, in one fell swoop, Islam, Pakistan, the immigrant population here in England, and his place of work, which was—in the matters of race—the officially appointed conscience of the land.

"How will I bear it, Mother, seeing him with his arms around someone else?" They were in the bathroom and Kaukab was shaving off the hair at Mah-Jabin's groin while she stood in the tub with her legs spread: the girl had lost all sense of herself, but the religion demanded that pubic hair must not go beyond the length of an uncooked grain of rice. "I don't want to live here, here in this neighbourhood, this town. Let's move away."

Kaukab dried the girl's legs with a towel and looked for the box of sanitary pads: "We'll think of something, baby."

The wife of Shamas's elder brother had died recently in Sohni Dharti and the olive-green house was without a woman (a fate that may not befall even an enemy's home); Kaukab and Shamas had felt it their responsibility to somehow come to the aid of the devastated husband and son the dead woman had left behind: they asked Mah-Jabin if she would marry her cousin and move to Pakistan; she said yes. Life for her had become wandering from one dark room to another. As she was looking into a hand-mirror one day and had turned it around—to the side that gave a magnified image—she realized that she had been looking at the magnification of her face all along: she was wasting away.

She begged forgiveness from Allah for her charade of piety over the previous two years, and now, addressing Him in her prayers, said that she would put to rest all her doubts about His existence if He were to perform a miracle and make her his bride, see to it that she was rowed across these turbulent waters.

But miracles came from faith, not faith from miracles.

Kaukab had never lost faith that Allah would find a way of helping her widower brother-in-law—a man whom she loved and respected like a blood-brother, difficult though he was—and she was pleased when Mah-Jabin unexpectedly agreed to marry his son and settle in Sohni Dharti to run the house and look after her ageing, grief-stricken uncle. Things had worked out for everyone, and in the girl's silent fantasy of the past two years—her silent and extravagant fantasy, misguided, innocent and unbounded—Kaukab saw the proof of how Allah blinds His creatures when He needs to further the designs of destiny.

It's stopped raining so that out there everything that can sparkle is sparkling. Mah-Jabin lowers her ear to the opening of the conch shell that is a one-third open orchid or lily in bone, a stone vulva, a book warped and soaked double by rain, and listens to the sea that is not there with her eyes closed.

The henna has imparted a reddish darkness to her hair, a tone of black found on photographic negatives. Each night the stars seem a little further away. This house is almost not a building but an emotion; every last surface here bears scars of war. Through glass and water-beads she looks down at the front garden, the lilacs bathed clean, the roses newly shattered like china in the rain, the front gate where on arrival she had smelled a cloud of the perfume her mother always wears, the vapour of jasmine telling her that she was out here only moments ago—and now she knows how her mother found out about her planned trip to the US; she had told the taxi driver about it, and he must've called and told his wife, who had then stopped by to tell Kaukab that her daughter was on the way, calling her out to the gate. The Indian and Pakistani taxi drivers are known for spreading news to all corners of Dasht-e-Tanhaii through their radios—who was seen when and with whom and where—and she always avoids a conversation with them, letting them listen to their Hindi music or taped sermons of Muslim clerics, but today a song whose lyrics are meant to be misinterpreted had come on—

Choli ke pechay kya hai, choli ke pechay?
Chunri ke nechay kya hai, chunri ke nechay?

What are you hiding behind that blouse?
What is being kept covered under the veil?

The flustered driver had switched off the music to begin a conversation with Mah-Jabin, not allowing the singer's question to be answered by the other singer in the lilting duet—

Choli me dil hai mera,
Chunri me dil hai mera:
Yeh dil main doon gi mere yar ko, pyar ko.
The blouse contains my heart,
The veil conceals my heart:
The heart which I'll give to my lover, to my beloved.

She lowers the conch shell onto the table surface, and remains there, recalling how as a child she had wanted to fish in the sea that she heard surging within the red petrified folds and ruffles freckled with archipelagos of white stains, giddy at the thought of the fantastic creatures to be found down in the depths below the waves that weren't there, in the coves that edged its slow silver, the illusory sea that is the equivalent of the sky in a cupped-handful of water.

She leaves the room, her forehead burnt by the thoughts in her mind.

Outside, a male starling is carrying a flower in its beak to decorate the nest it has built for the female somewhere, and in the empty room the sea and all that it contains sloshes and echoes silently in the shell's red cone.

Like Being Born

Charag steps into the lake, naked, and scoops water onto his head, bending his neck to let the falling drops flatten his hair. The water reaches the scalp and begins to pour down the face, getting into the eyes where the rich brown irises are an arrangement of suede-splinters—like the gills of a mushroom. A good deal of the light from the moon seems to be reaching the earth but without first lighting up the intervening sky and air—the earth is as though glowing itself. It's half an hour or so to dawn, and in the predawn light the world appears as though newly formed, softer on the eye, as exalted as a vision. Leaves float around him as he swims in the lake, one or two curled at the tips as in botanical illustrations, the oaks lobed like pieces of a jigsaw puzzle. His clothes lie on the shore among the stones while he moves through the water that is a skin trying to contain a deep-blue light which seems to come to the surface from somewhere down below, the colour of the blue vein on the pale inside of his elbow.

He is still undecided about whether he will visit his parents. He has driven all night to be back in Dasht-e-Tanhaii but now isn't sure why he has come.

He was the elder son and, throughout his boyhood, was always accompanied by the sense that the family's betterment lay on his shoulders. Nothing was ever made verbal but this expectation had been inhaled by him with each breath he had taken during those early years. His parents wanted to return to Pakistan: he would become a doctor and go back with them—this was understood by him. They—all of them—would be free of England when he finished his studies. He was troubled by the guilt of truancy every time he did something he enjoyed, every time he picked up his

drawing pad. His art teacher came to the house one day when he was fourteen, to plead with the parents to let him continue with the subject. She
had secured a place for three of the paintings in the little art gallery above
the public library in the town centre, and his photograph had appeared in
The Afternoon. The art teacher's letters had been ignored at home—the
mischievous attempts of the whites to lead the boy astray, said Kaukab, an
attempt to prevent the Pakistanis from getting ahead in life, encouraging them to waste time on childish things instead of working towards a
position of influence. When the teacher came to the house Charag had
felt humiliated, screaming at her inside his head to go away, wondering whether the parents thought he had asked her to come, that he had
betrayed them somehow.

He had to concentrate on sciences, spending his time in the laborato-
ries where the microscopes slept like hawks under their dust covers. The
science teachers advised him to simplify the diagrams that accompanied
his essays, concerned that it would become a habit and he would lose
valuable time during exams. But the diagrams were the only sketching he
could do without furtiveness and guilt at home.

Everyone at home was, of course, aware of his talent. Kaukab sometimes brought him a bar of perfumed soap so he could sketch the vignette
indented at its centre for her to embroider it in rows on her own or Mah-
Jabin's *kameez*s. And she asked him to convert the vines and geometric
designs from the borders of the paper kitchen-towels so that they could be
traced on the hands in henna, reducing it to fit the fingers, enlarging it for
the palms. She saved the sketches in a folder that lived in her sewing ham-
per and they were often lent to other women around the neighbourhood.
Whenever she couldn't find her tailor's chalk she asked to borrow one of
his colouring pencils.

His grades at A-level were not high enough to get into medical school.
Putting aside the feeling of guilt and disgrace and failure, he told his parents he would not be retaking the exams next year to improve his grades
for medical school, nor would he go to university this year to read the
many other science subjects for which his grades were good enough.

He planned to go to art college.

But he changed his mind when from the dark staircase he heard his mother slap the thirteen-year-old Mah-Jabin in the kitchen and say, "Who would marry you now?"

The year he went back to repeat his A-levels was a year enclosed on all sides by loneliness. Everyone he knew had gone away to university. He sat alone on the bus on the way to the school that was a low long building among the hills, made of gleaming glass and greyness and as windy as a harmonica, and in the classrooms he found himself unwilling to make contact with the new batch of students. Things had changed at home also: his failure had been a cruel dashing of his parents' hopes, and a cloud of something anaesthetizing hung over his brother and sister who had witnessed his commitment to his studies all their lives—and, having failed despite all the hard work, he had made them afraid of their own books and schoolwork; the event had injured their confidence in their own abilities.

Early in October a pain opened in his back and legs, and the doctor—after checking his reflexes by trailing and wafting a tissue paper along his naked body—had wondered if he would like to be referred to a psychiatrist since there seemed no organic cause for the severe ache. His mother said it was out of the question: a young girl in the neighbourhood had been sent to a psychiatrist by the doctor and had within months rebelled against her parents and left home.

The months passed. He lost the pain somewhere along the way, working hard on his studies, but again did not make the required grades. He went away to university in London to do a BSc in Chemistry: there was one last path open to medical school still—if he managed to do well in his degree finals he could apply for entry then, in three years' time.

But during his second year in London, everything changed: one night, drunk, he found the courage to speak to Stella. "I am never wrong about colour," was one of the first things he said to her.

"Are you wearing contact lenses?" he shouted over the music. "No one with hair that colour has such blue eyes. I am never wrong about colour."

She looked at him. "My eyes are that colour naturally. How do you know my hair isn't dyed?" It fell onto her shoulders from beneath a large black hat the rim of which had been turned up above the face, the slice pinned to the crown with a pointy rose made of folded ribbon, also black.

His hands were shaking. During the year in which he had tried to improve his grades, he saw many Pakistani and Indian boys and girls—who had been waiting since the beginning of puberty to leave home and find lovers at university—make desperate, clumsy and foolish attempts to pair up now that freedom had been delayed by one more unbearable year. But he had kept his distance and reserve. And upon arrival in London, the sadness was of a different kind: there was no fear of discovery or repercussions here but he was inhibited by incompetence and inexperience, by a profound sense of shame regarding his virginal state.

"Well?" she had now turned her back squarely on the boy she had been talking to when he approached her, and—in the privacy which included him—made a quick male-masturbatory gesture with the looped thumb and first finger of her left hand, to convey to him what she thought of the boy. Shunned, the boy stood behind her for a while and then miserably walked away.

Her confidence filled him with terror. Would she dismiss and denounce him similarly upon meeting the next person? Her lips were red and syrupy like glacé cherries.

"Well, young man, how do you know my hair isn't dyed?"

"It just isn't. I would know if it were. As I said I am never wrong about colour."

She shrugged and smiled: "Hey, listen, I have seen you around the campus. And at the weekend you work at that bar in Soho, don't you. I have wanted to talk to you for weeks now."

"My name is Charag."

"I know. I am Stella."

"I know."

They had to lean very close to each other to be heard and as a result could hear each other's breath. They were in the cellar of a student house in Notting Hill, the space packed with people, and, softly, she took his hand and led him to the edge of the room, the walls that had been stencilled with giant capsules and pills in acidic colours, tumbling and floating, a brightly glowing mural celebrating their milieu's fetish. There was to be a performance by a band—some friends of the party-givers who had travelled down from Scotland—but the party dispersed when the police arrived, summoned by the neighbours whose extreme dislike of the students and the young they themselves were unable to comprehend, thinking their high-decibel drinking sprees and benders went unheard just as their intense internal storms of confusion did. Charag and Stella lost each other in the crowd that spilled onto the street like a nest of termites broken into.

She came to Soho the following Friday, then again the next night, and asked her friends to leave without her, waiting for the staff to finish the after-work duties. And just before dawn—when the red dots on her bed covers were juxtaposed on the windowpane as though berries hung on the tree outside—he left her room to go back to his own house, burning with longing and humiliation, kicking in murderous rage at the dry plane leaves that littered the footpaths.

He had watched the cigarette in her hands: tiny pink eyes opening and closing, breathing, where the paper burned and sent into the air a brown thread parallel to and distinct from the blue wisp of smoke rising out of the live tobacco.

The anxieties had been many. The sense passed on to him during his upbringing was that the differences between the whites and the Pakistanis were too many for interaction to successfully take place; many marriages ended. The cleric at the mosque had advised the boys to stay away from the "faeces-filled sacks" that were earthly women and wait for the houris of Paradise. He said the boys should handle their members with tissue paper when they urinated, that it was a disgusting appendage. And, of course, intercourse was so dirty that the body had to be made pure afterwards by bathing. Charag had once heard one of the women assembled in the blue kitchen tell the others about how she had had to lie when confronted with the inquisitive innocence of her young son that day because he had wondered why her hair was wet so early in the morning: "I said his little sister had urinated on the bed and I had to purify myself with a bath at dawn to say the dawn prayers." He heard the women laughing and offering variations of the incident as he sat naked from waist to knee in his room, stopping with an elbow the trembling slippery magazines from sliding off the bed. The jingle of the belt buckle had to be silenced in a fist when the trousers were pulled up afterwards. He had built up and discarded and built up again caches of girlie magazines during his adolescence, the pages crossed with white splintery creases where they had been folded double to keep a combination of favourite images before the eyes during the moment of orgasm. He threw them away in moments of self-disgust, timing this cleansing carefully with the bin men's visit, so that they may not lie outside the house for days. Each visit to the newsagent for the purpose of beginning again was a defeat: he was weak and corrupt.

The following weekend Stella decided to take matters into her own hands, and they became lovers. His mouth was winter-chapped and dry while hers was cared-for and soft: her tongue felt like a hand going through the ripped silk lining of a pocket and scraping against the coarse fabric beyond.

His hand deposited a glowing impression on her belly as the net of capillaries sank away from the cold. He erased it by licking, warmly coaxing the blood back to the surface.

Her breasts were flattened under their own weight as she lay beneath him, her nipples the colour of her pink lips—his own were the dark tawny colours of his own lips.

At the tip of the penis, the dot of starlit ache—which had to be kept in place and referred to periodically to maintain the erection, but was never to be dwelt on because then it would spread and lead to climax—was growing larger.

His mouth looked for the oiled berry. Her taste came and went tidally salt and sour in his mouth, as eloquent as weather.

When he fell through the sensation and opened his eyes he was surprised to find her there.

And he could not hold her close enough.

The smell of his armpits was on her shoulders—a flower depositing pollen on a hummingbird's forehead.

They detonated the remains of each other's orgasm with fingers and tongues, areas of their bodies sticking together with sweat that was like the weak glue that holds segments of an orange together.

And all through the Christmas break—in a distrust of memory which upon reunion proved itself unfounded and thereby intensified the pleasures of reunion—he thought he would not remember her face when they met again. The house in Dasht-e-Tanhaii was silent that winter. Icicles dripped outside like washing. The nights brought a chill from the lake that added to the cold and stayed all day in the air that did not move.

Mah-Jabin had married a few months earlier and gone to live in Pakistan, and Ujala had no one to quarrel with.

He could not have given Stella his phone number, and longed to talk to her, to touch her. A fear had been breathed into the house once when a girl from school had telephoned Charag about homework: he hardly ever left the house after school but his mother had suspected a girlfriend behind that *one* phone call. She didn't know (nor would he himself for a while yet) what it meant to have a girlfriend, that a relationship was replete with subtleties through which intimacy and commitment were demanded and demonstrated, that you were supposed to meet regularly, even daily, introduce each other to the parents. Kaukab extended what she knew of Pakistani women—who were drenched in patience, and were grateful that they had found a man no matter what his behaviour—to cover all women.

The magnifying glass through which he was kept in sight was burning him.

The hook of Stella's bracelet had given his penis a small wound: when it began to heal the scab rubbed against the fabric of his underpants and whispered her name.

Back in London in the new year, he burnt matchstick after matchstick into an ashtray as he told her about his wish to paint. She listened as the sticks continued to burn, each flame sucking the thickness out of the wood and growing fatter itself; they went off and bent and remained luminous at the tip, looking like streetlights. She was wearing the jacket of his pyjamas, he the bottom half.

She told him he had to abandon his Chemistry degree immediately. "Simple." How light the burden of one's life became in the hands of a lover! She told him what he had to do and made plans for contingencies, showing him he was several moves away from disaster—he who had always thought that he could make one wrong move and sink.

After Easter he went home more and more often, wishing to tell his parents he was no longer a student, but came back to London without having had the courage to tell them. He heard Kaukab say to Shamas that the boy is probably being bullied by racist thugs at university and is coming home to escape them.

He would reveal the truth to them several months later, at Christmas, the house smelling the way it always did in winter, of fabric conditioners and washing powder because the day's washing was drying in the kitchen.

"A painter is not a secure job. When we came to this country we lived in broken-down homes and hoped our children wouldn't have to," Kaukab said.

"Mother, I am struggling because I am young. That's all." The skin above her breasts sagged, a funnel of wrinkles narrowing to where the division between the two breasts must be—nothing like Stella's new precisely stretched silk. This evidence of his mother's frailty and helplessness made him want to reassure her. "Mother, please don't worry. I'll be fine."

"At least Allah is smiling on me as far as my daughter is concerned. Her husband loves her and she's happy." There was not an hour in the day when a letter was not in progress to Mah-Jabin from Kaukab, in blue aerogrammes or on loose sheets in fat envelopes that bore the stamps on the left corners—Kaukab always forgot that the stamps were fixed to the right-hand corner. Mah-Jabin's own letters were happy when not ecstatic.

Even though she was many thousands of miles away, Mah-Jabin was closer to Kaukab than Charag, who was only a train journey away. She could imagine Mah-Jabin's life, against a background she had thorough knowledge of; Charag's life, on the other hand, was beyond her imagining—he was lost to her.

Stella remained a secret from everyone at home until Jugnu came to London to visit him while he was at art college. Charag hadn't wanted to tell him because he knew Kaukab wouldn't forgive Jugnu if she ever discovered that Jugnu had known about Charag's "sinning" and kept it from her. He was sure that his father wouldn't have a problem with it either but he couldn't confide in him due to the same fear.

The sky is so blue it appeals to the sense of touch. Soon it will be blue and gold. He rounds one of those small reed-covered islands that drift about the lake's surface and now discovers that he has swum straight into another swimmer, also naked, badged with a small leaf above the left nipple, her hair floating in the water, curly and heavy-looking like seaweed.

Her breasts are supported high by the water as though being cupped by invisible hands. "My Allah," the woman whispers, and he can see that her pubis is shaved clean like a Muslim woman's is supposed to be. She cannot swim away and simultaneously conceal her breasts and groin with her hands, and so she splutters and goes under, her foot brushing his penis where there is a dab of aquamarine from when he had had to urinate whilst painting yesterday. In trying to assist her he loses the rhythm of his own stroke and now it is he who's underwater, amid the silt and rotting foliage, fingers tangled in her long tresses. All bubbles and olive-coloured skin, she manages to break away and swims off as he comes up and expels the water from his windpipe and nose, blinking away the grit in his eyes. He treads water as he watches her arrive at the shore in the distance: she stands up and turns to look in his direction, the sheath of liquid swinging off her arms and hips in long tassels, dripping brightly from the tips of the breasts.

He waits until she has run off into the trees before beginning his own journey to the shore. Going along a path more daisies than soil he begins to put on his clothes. He cannot see her anywhere. He shivers. From the car parked under a nearby street lamp, he takes a net of oranges, his sketch pad, and a dozen pastel-sticks held together by an old wristwatch like a comic-book time-bomb, and returns to the lake, sitting on a piece of driftwood that is heavy for its size the way a lobster is. He sketches the mist. In the dawn light the paper is a soft luminous blue, and his hands are soon covered with pastel dust, and it is also there on the ground where his blowing has carried it in sweeps beyond the edge of the paper; the fans of coloured dust on the ground are as though his breath petrified and preserved. White, and grey, green as a surgeon's gown, and the chalky-red of a school's cracked clay tennis court.

Consumed in succession, he notices, each new orange has a flavour subtly its own, different than the last. Putting away the pastel sticks and the drawings, he closes his eyes, feeling that all the stars have been sieved out of his bloodstream for now.

He knows that his art has become uninspired of late, needing new direction. It's the thing that he has invested in most passionately, and he knows that his dissatisfaction with it could lead to the profoundest crisis within his adult self.

"Forgive me, but I hadn't meant to startle you," the voice comes from behind him.

He turns and finds her standing a few yards away, fully clothed, a gauzy veil covering the wet hair and shoulders. Has she been watching him? He thought she had fled the vicinity. "Are you all right?" he says. "I was too engrossed in my thoughts to hear anyone else in the water."

"Me too."

The small daisies growing on the path beneath her feet look like a stretch of living stars—the narrow earthen path between tall grasses that leads to the entrance of the Urdu bookshop owned by his father's friend.

She waves away an insect, blinking those sleepy eyes.

To bring a car to this place at the height of summer would be to have Gypsy moths come out of the pine trees and lay eggs on the tyres.

He is not sure what to do or say—she's just standing there looking at him—and so he begins to collect his things.

"My name is Suraya," she says, and hesitantly takes a step towards him. "Did you find the water too cold?"

He shakes his head. He has never really known how to act in the company of an Asian woman: it's always been his understanding—the result of his upbringing—that reserve and aloofness is the best way to behave towards them.

She is perhaps in her late thirties, and extremely beautiful to him, Italian-looking, Spanish, Latin American; she says: "I used to swim in the lake when I was a child and couldn't resist going in an hour or so ago, thinking no one would see me. I returned from Pakistan at the beginning of the year, and have been waiting for the water to warm up ever since then. My patience ran out finally."

He stands up, clutching his things. "What were you doing in Pakistan?"

But she says, "The lake, I missed terribly, and the woods beyond it, in spring, full of bluebells—I longed for them both in Pakistan." She points to the sketches he's holding: "May I see those?" And while looking at them, standing beside him, their clothes almost touching, she says, quietly, "I was married to a man in Pakistan. I have a little son there. But my husband got drunk one night last year and divorced me." She is looking intently at the pages, avoiding his eyes, not willing to see the expression on his face. "He's repentant and we both want things to be the way they were, but according to Islamic law I cannot remarry him until I marry someone else first. The new man would have to divorce me soon after we marry and then I'd be free to marry the father of my son again." She's staring at a fixed point on the page in her hand. "Are you a Muslim by any chance? What's your name?"

Charag takes a step away from her.

"I miss them both so much." She's still not looking at him. "Are you married?" There is a faked nonchalance in the voice.

"Forgive me but I have to go," Charag says and extends his hand to take back his sketches. But she doesn't move. The neckline of her tunic is embroidered like the young gypsy's in the first version of Caravaggio's *The Fortune Teller*, her hand pointing to the girdle of Venus on the palm of her unsuspecting victim's hand while she gently removes the gold ring from his finger, having beguiled the innocent boy with her beauty. The subtle thief.

"If only I could find someone suitable. I meet with the matchmaker regularly but haven't been successful so far. As I said, it'll only be a temporary arrangement. And, of course, we wouldn't have to be compatible in age. The Prophet, peace be upon him, was nineteen when he married a woman of forty."

And he was in his sixties when he consummated his marriage with a nine-year-old, thinks Charag.

She asks him: "How old are you?"

"Thirty-two." But his voice doesn't come out. He stands dumb-founded, this encounter beyond anything he could have ever imagined for himself—or for anyone else, for that matter. He gently takes hold of the sketchbook. She lets go but not before a tear the size of a pear seed has slid off her cheek and fallen audibly onto the paper.

It was the first sound you heard upon coming into this world: women—screaming, cooing, reassuring, out of control, in charge, shout-ing in pain, in pleasure, laughing, sobbing. Charag sometimes feels that to come to this old neighbourhood of Dasht-e-Tanhaii, these Asian streets and lanes of his childhood, is like entering one large labour room, full of the voices of women expressing a spectrum of emotions. It is like being born.

He doesn't know what to do with the tear as it lies glistening on the paper. Should he brush it away or shake it off, but wouldn't that hurt her needlessly, be too graphic a rejection of her proposal?

He watches it soak into the paper.

"You are very talented." She looks at him at last and produces a large smile, her eyes raw and red. And she decides to make one last effort: "I'd like to see more of your work. Where do you live?"

He is seized by an embarrassment so acute it seems to be organic in its origins—a pain almost, arising from the very meat and membrane of him. Of course what's taking place can hardly be termed seduction, but he recognizes in her desperation something of his own earlier anxiety and amateurishness regarding contact with the opposite sex. The culture she shares with him is based on segregation, and on the denial and contempt of the human body, and in all probability this is the very first time she has "propositioned" someone.

And just as he is about to walk away, she becomes resigned:

"You are an artist," she says. "Tell me, can you paint this."

He knows that by "this" she means the humiliation she's just suffered, the despondent clumsiness to which her circumstances have reduced her, and the longing she must feel for her son and husband.

"Can you?" Her pain stares out of her eyes.

"I don't know," he says quietly. "I can try."

She nods, wipes her eyes with her veil, and slowly walks away from him.

He goes back to the car and sits there for a few minutes.

Soon the rays of the sun would go in through the windows and ignite consciousness in every house of Dasht-e-Tanhaii, the caterpillars climbing the milk bottles on the doorsteps to drink dew off the foil tops. He'll stay here, looking out at the sun on the lake for a while, and then go into the town centre for breakfast—before beginning the journey back to London.

THE MANY
COLOURS OF MILK

Shamas, on his way back from the town centre to fetch the Saturday papers, very soon after dawn, sees countless single threads of spider silk shining on the riverbank, sagging between tall reeds like lovers holding hands. They gleam and the eye wishes to return to them like favourite verses in a book of poems. A swarm of grey insects spins in the air, keeping to a funnel shape almost as if it believes itself to be trapped. He is crossing the bridge, and the river—down there—seems to drink the sunlight, sucking at its warmth. The grass is so rich there that it would creak underfoot. Down there was where the two lovers were looking for the place where the human heart was found: Kaukab says that the girl's mother is convinced that she has become possessed by the djinns—that is why she won't accept her new husband. Shamas has been careful not to tell Kaukab about his chance encounter with the girl and the Hindu boy—their secret trysts must remain a secret.

This river is a recent stream compared to the rivers of the Indian Subcontinent: the Indus, its far bank wedded to the horizon, is an ocean-wide stretch of water that remembers thousands of years of history. And the river of his childhood—the Chenab—could rise by several metres during the monsoon.

He built a small boat for himself during his early teens, naming it *Safeena*, which meant both a boat and—in archaic use—a notebook; and he would take it out to sit in the cattails and the *narkal* reeds and the pangrass of Chenab's shallower regions, reading, the sounds of the migratory waterfowl coming to him from the other side of the green curtain if it were winter, the flocks arriving from the Himalayas at the beginning of October in minute-long V formations.

This year's butterflies would soon begin to emerge—a season heaving with life, the air above the river slightly fragrant like a garment still carrying the odour of its vanished owner. And now a piece of red cloth with a silken sheen, giving off a pronounced honeysuckle scent as though it had been used to swab up spillage from the perfume flask, floats across his vision, about to fall into the water. Instinctively he reaches for it before it disappears, and as he's bending over the low wall towards it the newspapers slip from his grip and fall into the water below, changing colour instantly as the water soaks the paper. He's suddenly lighter, his muscles relieved, the fingers holding nothing but that scarf which has butterfly blue lozenges along its crenulated edges. He looks around. The sun laughing in her glass bangles, a young woman is looking at him from a few yards away. He holds out the scarf towards her.

"Thank you." She whispers quietly. "I am sorry about your newspapers." And immediately she turns and begins to move away from him, twisting the retrieved scarf and using it like a ribbon to collect and secure her hair in a loose ponytail at the base of the neck, her skin that pale rust-brown colour that white jasmine flowers take on at the end of the day.

Propriety dictates that he should not attempt to detain her but he hears himself say abandonedly, "It's a beautiful morning."

She stops—no doubt as staggered by his boldness as he himself is—and, turning around after a while to face him, nods her head which is a mass of curls, a few of which are already escaping the scarf and tumbling onto her shoulders. Small, fine-boned, she is perhaps in her late-thirties and is wearing a primrose *shalwar-kameez* with a wide length of see-through chiffon draped about the body to serve as a head veil when required. Her expression conveys a mark of consternation and she looks around, perhaps to make sure that this encounter is being observed by someone, that she is not too alone here with him, or perhaps to make sure that they are *not* being observed.

Feeling ashamed for having given her cause for concern and irresponsible for not keeping in mind the risks to her honour before addressing her, he raises his hand part way to his forehead to bid her farewell in the courteous Subcontinental Muslim manner and quickly turns around to go back into the town centre and get more newspapers.

"I was on my way to the lake. There is an Urdu bookshop there and I wanted to know the opening times," he hears her say. Her face awaits him with the polite hint of a smile when he stops and turns around, the face that only seconds ago was tortured by doubts and dark considerations. She takes the edge of the veil and covers her head in a gesture of infinite grace, handling the fine material gently—one of those actions that reveals a person's unspoken attitude to things; the thin sun-flecked fabric settles on her hair in a wonderfully slow yellow wave. "I think the shop is called the *Safeena*. It is, if I remember correctly, a poetic Urdu word for 'boat' and also for 'notebook.' "

Like a matchstick struck on the inside of his skull, spilling sparks, the ecstatic torpor of adolescent summers comes to him in a brief warm illumination, and he experiences a thrill which is very close to happiness. "It was the name I gave my rowboat during my boyhood on the banks of the Chenab. And the shop, the property of a friend, was named by me after my boat."

The bridge between them is made of glass and so he takes one very tentative step towards her.

She's considering him, as though thinking deeply. "My name is Suraya." She smiles, more openly than she had the first time, and a very pale apricot-brown mole (if it were surrounded by others like it, it would be called a freckle—it's *that* pale) on the side of her mouth gets pulled into a fold in the skin, vanishes into a laugh-line.

"The shop is open in the afternoons on Saturday and Sunday, if you would care to visit," he says. He is concerned for her safety: she shouldn't be seen talking to a stranger. A Pakistani man mounted the footpath and ran over his sister-in-law—repeatedly, in broad daylight—because he suspected she was cheating on his brother. *I only fear that by dying you will pollute the dead just as your life pollutes the living.* This was here in England and, according to the statistics, in one Pakistani province alone, a woman is murdered every thirty-eight hours solely because her virtue is in doubt. He should withdraw; and he bows slightly at the waist towards her: "Now, if you'll excuse me, I must leave."

Touching her scarf, she says, "Thank you for this. The wind kept it just out of my reach as I ran after it; but Allah had planted you in my path to help me. I nearly caught it once but it seemed to fly at the speed of thought. And I am sorry for the newspapers."

"I'll go into town again and get some more." He recriminates himself for vainly thinking that she's delaying him on purpose, that she wants his company. And yet she *is* looking at him intensely, and since he doesn't know what to say, is standing here silently, her eyes roam across his body as though searching for the slot to put coins into to make him operate. Suddenly self-conscious, he raises his hand and touches his hair to see that the breeze hasn't dishevelled it too much. With an agitated heart he turns and walks away, feeling suddenly very old, exhausted, leaving behind the pale gold English river, the glittering continuity of it, and those countless single threads of spider silk that are shining on the tall reeds, sagging in bright curves. It was there on the bridge that Chanda's mother had approached him a few weeks ago to tell him Jugnu had been spotted in Lahore; he shakes his head and frowns to dispel the memory. Before him the columns of the flowering horse chestnuts stretch either side of the road that climbs the hill; the town centre is situated at the top. The pale shadows of the horse chestnuts are combed across the road, a white butterfly again and again turning an iridescent bluish-pink as it flies across them.

In the town centre there are horses of stone. Lions guard the entrance to the library. A granite deer looks down from the top of the train station's façade.

The electric light inside the newspaper shop seems to be a continuation of the weak sun shining outside. He quickly explains that he has lost the newspapers to the river and asks for another batch. As always he doesn't wish to be engaged in a conversation because it might lead to talk about the murdered lovers. They have become a bloody Rorschach blot: different people see different things in what has happened.

And so he leaves as soon as possible, speaking no more than two or three sentences between arriving and departing, finding contentedness only in wordlessness these days.

As he turns around to leave, he is aware that his eyes, as always, are lifted slightly higher than need be, to catch a blurred glimpse of the magazines on the top shelf.

With the newspapers under his arm he begins the journey home, lingering outside the florist—called *La Primavera*—to look at the brush-like Australian flower-heads and sprays of eucalyptus like a flinging of coins; at the wide-open lilies possessing a thick chewiness of petals; the Germolene-pink roses; the gardenias; the carnations as red as bullet wounds, luxuriant with pain; the small flowers with petals the size of his grandson's fingernails; sunflowers that seem to be on fire; the edge of a leaning arum pressed flat against the glass like a soft marine creature in a tank; leaves of every shape, each as different in its serrated outline as the notches on different keys. There are roses in the window the colour of Suraya's clothing, he remarks to himself in passing . . .

He raises a hand in greeting at a plumber from Calcutta whose van bears the legend, *You've tried the cowboys, now try the Indian,* his heart full of anxiety that the man will stop the vehicle and come over to talk.

The breeze gives his face feathery touches.

Changeable like a cloud, a low flock of pigeons keeps flying by, the white wings taking on various tinges from the colours reflecting off the shop exteriors, and, as he watches, the flying birds form the faces of Chanda and Jugnu in the air just for an instant—two images undulating like pages on moving water. The lovers are everywhere, lying in ambush.

He can never be certain about Chanda's father but he is sure the mother knows nothing about what happened to her daughter and Jugnu. According to the Home Office statistics 116 men were convicted of murder last year as opposed to just 11 women. Women are usually at the receiving end.

A few days after the couple went missing, the girl's father had visited Shamas to say that he was aware of the rumours implicating his family in Jugnu's disappearance. He sat in the blue kitchen, drinking the tea Kaukab had made, and insisted that neither he nor his wife and sons knew anything about what had happened to Jugnu. It was strange. The fact that Chanda too remained unaccounted for didn't seem to enter the man's mind—or if it did it didn't seem to concern him, and he didn't see why it should concern anyone else either. The only crime he and his wife and sons could be accused of was the possible one against Jugnu; the girl—the daughter of the parents, the sister of the brothers—belonged to him, to them, to do with as they pleased. Is that it? Would he, would they, expect a pardon if Jugnu were to turn up tomorrow, unharmed, but the girl were to remain missing?

And then he had felt ashamed at these thoughts: he knows that it is a matter of great distress for a parent from the Subcontinent—for the majority of parents on this imperfect and shackled planet, in fact—that their daughter is living with someone out of wedlock. It is likely that Chanda's father could not bring himself to mention his daughter's name because of the shame he felt, not wishing to see the girl coupled with Jugnu in his own speech, not having the strength to see them together even in language.

Now Shamas briefly pictures the two names merged and intertwined with each other: C J h u a g n n d u a

Despite understanding his discomfort, there are, however, times when Shamas imagines Chanda's father physically preventing his wife from revealing some important bit of evidence. He imagines violence. *Keep your mouth shut! This woman is a complete* haramzadi! *The* kanjri *woman didn't say anything when it was time for her to speak and raise her* badmash kutia *daughter properly and now she cannot hold her tongue!* It is a possibility, however grotesque; it happens in millions of homes throughout the world every day, from hamlet to metropolis. Hadn't he himself slapped Kaukab one day all those years ago? He had torn her shirt with both hands and dragged her across the room with all his strength, one of her breasts exposed and bloody from his fingernail.

It happened in 1974, the year the younger boy, Ujala, was born. Kaukab returned home from the maternity ward on a bright April day with the sun lying like a new coat of metallic paint on the street. The two other children—all toffee-sticky fingertips and grime-covered toes in their mother's absence—examined the baby and declared he looked like a tortoise because his upper lip was pointed in the middle, that he was the colour of tangerines, and his always-clenched fists made them think he was tightly holding on to coins.

Within hours the house was heavy with the intimately lush smell of recent birth that the mother and child gave off—it was like heat clinging to footpaths long after the sun has gone. Ujala was born in the middle of April just a few days before the Muslim month of Ramadan began. Dozens of people came to see the baby because the word immediately spread that he was a blessed child destined to be an especially pious Muslim: he was one of those rare boys who are born without a foreskin, the Muslims believing that such children have been marked by Allah for an exemplary virtuous existence in the world.

For Shamas the visits and the visitors were a headache. Kaukab, on the other hand, felt several stories high after the baby Ujala was born.

"Who else but a cleric's daughter would have been blessed by such an event!" said one visitor, the matchmaker, in tones of wonderment and awe. "I knew someone in Peshawar who was born like that. I remember the lullaby his mother used to sing to him—*O nurses with milk too white and sweet: wean him soon as can be, for the black hearts of infidel kings will be his meat.* The boy had learned the entire Koran by heart by the time he was three years old, and he was teaching Arabic to the djinns by the time he was five. A number of profligate djinns converted to Islam at his hand."

But the angels, it seemed, forgot about the baby after the birth because his health began to deteriorate after about a week: he became increasingly irresponsive to noise and other sensations, and seemed deficient in strength, so much so that eventually even the act of crying seemed to defeat him. As the days passed he lost weight despite regular breast-feeds and the minor infections he had developed began to give the doctors cause for concern despite the medicines prescribed. One afternoon, after he had been fed, Kaukab brought him to lie next to Shamas and he had leaned over the small soft heap and stroked the head, the nap of short hair on the pate like some kind of moss under the touch. Shamas's little finger hovered closed to the baby's lips and when the tiny mouth moved to take in the tip of the digit and began sucking at it forcefully, everything suddenly became clear. His legs shook as he went into the next room, the kitchen. She was cooking the children's lunch, pale steam rising from the pan like morning mist from a pond.

"He is still hungry, Kaukab."

"That's very strange. I've just fed him."

"Perhaps you should feed him again. He suckled my finger: you should've seen how he reacted when the finger got near his mouth. He was electrified."

"I am empty and raw. I've just fed him."

"Have you remembered to give him his medicine?" For a moment he thought he was going to black out.

"Of course I have."

He was clenching and unclenching his fists, the palms feeling cold. "I just thought you might have forgotten: you are after all fasting, and people become forgetful when they fast. Or are you making the baby fast too? Not giving him anything—milk or water or his medicine—from dusk till dawn?"

"I don't know what you mean. And don't raise your voice, please."

"What I mean is that I think you have been making the baby—your *holy* baby!—observe Ramadan. You have been starving him during the daylight hours."

"If it's true—which it isn't—then it's because he *himself* insists on it. He refuses to let anything pass his lips during the daylight hours. And don't make light of my beliefs: he *is* an exalted infant. Must you talk like a heretic in this house? I blame father-ji for marrying me to a Communist."

"Get your head out of the clouds and come give him milk right now." He was trying to speak quietly because he could sense the other two children—the nine-year-old Charag and the four-year-old Mah-Jabin—on the staircase next to the kitchen. A few moments ago a yellow-and-green striped sweet the size of a sparrow's egg—slipped from the hands of one of the children—had fallen and landed at the bottom of the staircase, alerting him to their presence. They must've been up there, listening, and now he could hear the small movements they were making.

"No I won't come. It's my milk. He and I will break our fast at sunset. It's just a matter of changing the routine: I give him everything he needs during the night."

"Has someone stolen your ears? I said come now." The world had become stark, the colours harsh in his eyes.

"No. I have just fed him and have nothing left."

"Show me." They stared at each other until neither of them knew who the other one was. By grabbing hold of the neckline he tore open her *kameez* with both hands to reveal a soaked brassiere which he pulled at here and there until one of the cups ripped and spilled its load like weights in a sling. She had resisted and he had dragged her across the floor, her exposed breast bloody from his fingernail. In the next room he lifted the baby in its sail-white blanket and placed it in her lap where she sat on the floor, milk beading bluishly at the tip of the chocolate-coloured nipple. Inert and apparently insensible, she hadn't moved to connect the baby to the breast and he had slapped her face:

"Feed him, you *haramzadi*!"

The pale steam that had been rising from the pan in the kitchen had become black smoke as the unstirred food had begun to burn, the dark tendrils choking the house. He went and turned off the gas. The acrid smell had replaced the lime-and-rosehip perfume that the geraniums in the kitchen had released when the two of them had stumbled against them in their struggle. As he turned off the gas he was aghast to see her step into the kitchen, her wide open eyes the size of rose leaves, the baby screaming in the other room. His disbelief and desperation grew fuller, becoming its own organism, out of control. He was he but less and less with each passing moment. With one jerk she freed her wrist from his grip when he grabbed hold of her to take her back. As though she were walking in a howling storm, she staggered to the sink and washed her hands:

She had been cutting up chillies earlier and didn't want to touch her baby with those hands.

With safe hands she picked up the baby and nursed him, despoiling his fast, wincing at the pain breast-feeding had always caused her.

They didn't speak to each other for the next six or seven months. One day he decided that he should talk to her: she listened to his apology, listened as he hinted that an apology from her too was required—and later, to convey to him that she hadn't forgiven him, and had no intention herself of asking for forgiveness, she burnt the wedding dress on to which she had embroidered his verses years ago.

He moved out of the house within the week, having rented a small room two bus-rides away on the other side of town. Each month he posted most of his wages into the house through the letterbox. One year passed, and then two; two-and-a-half. He lived in squalid conditions and days would at times go by without him having talked to anyone. His world was so reduced that half an eggshell would have served as sky.

He met her and the children only a handful of times, either by chance or very reluctantly. When he saw her coming up the stairs one day he locked the door from the inside and pretended to be out: she banged to be let in, aware of his presence perhaps, and was eventually forced to say out loud through her tears that she was bringing him the news of his mother's death back in Sohni Dharti.

Although they both wept in each other's arms for over an hour, and although he sent her back with the reassurance that he would be there in the house with her and the children before the week was out, he was still not there months later. One day in the snow-buried March of 1978 he came to leave his wages for her at the little seafood shop where she had started work not long ago; he had made sure that it was an hour when she would not be there—the other shop assistants would pass the money on to her. There was no one at the counter and he sat down to wait in the warmth. Outside, the day was as white as a new page, and there were icicles as long as spears. As he dozed and half-dreamed, the shop turned into a kaleidoscope brightly filled with black-and-cobalt-blue fragments whose reflections produced changing patterns on everything, including himself.

The winkles had escaped from their tank.

They were roaming because the urge was on them: on the coastline a hundred miles away the tide had come in, and things of all kinds were emerging from the sand to feed on what the sea had brought in. The small shelled creatures in the seafood shop had not been away from the beach long enough for their internal rhythms to adjust yet, and they had begun to explore, having lain motionless till now as they would on the beach— retreating underground and sealing the entrances to the burrows as though holding their noses shut at the low-tide stink.

The other life of the planet had broken through into the one being lived by the human beings, that immeasurably vast life for which the humans were mostly an irrelevance.

Shamas watched the nightsky-blue creatures surrounding him. The tide had come in far away but the sea had flooded the interior here. He let the beautiful lapis lazuli creatures leave the tank and make their magne- tized way up the walls, explore the windowpanes like a child's eye losing concentration and beginning to roam the page of the textbook, paint wet trails on the foliage of the plants like a tongue on a lover's skin, and climb onto the tables to go on slow voyages.

The shop assistant came out from the back and said she hadn't remembered to secure the lid of the tank in time for the tide.

She gave him a letter which Kaukab had left for him, and, as she hurried from corner to corner to pick up the blue shells, she asked Shamas to hand over the money but he said there was no need because he had just decided to go home to Kaukab for good.

He picked off the shells from the chilled glass panes of the window. Shamas helped contain the homesick beach-creatures and afterwards glanced at the letter: it was from Jugnu; he wrote that he was thinking of leaving America and coming to live in England, that he could be there with them by early summer. Shamas reached in through his coat and placed it in the warm breast pocket of his faded rose-red shirt and began walking through the wet sugar-and-salt of the snow, back towards Kaukab and Charag and Mah-Jabin and Ujala. Following ghosts of buried roads.

He's back on the bridge, on his way back home this time with the new set of Saturday newspapers. He's in solitude's bower, looking down at the water. The sunrise is the colour of the insides of fruit, bright and wet-looking. And the morning air is looser on his face, unstill and the opposite of heavy, as before a storm.

This was where he met Suraya. He lifts his fingers to his nose to see if they retain the scent of her scarf but all he can smell is the newspapers. Would she really come to the *Safeena* this afternoon?

The river flows. Poorab-ji, from the Ram and Sita temple down there on the bank, has come to see him twice since that morning back in January. A good, kind friend and man, he had puzzled Shamas nevertheless when they happened to meet right here on this bridge at dawn some years ago. It was Sunday and a small group of Saturday-night revellers—young white men and women—had come down the road, smelling of alcohol, hair and clothing awry, on their way back to their homes from some late party. Laughing, the still-drunk boys had chased the loud girls and they had let out shrieks and shouts as they all went on their merry way. The look of distaste—revulsion—on Poorab-ji's face had surprised and disappointed Shamas. No doubt Poorab-ji had just seen sordid promiscuity on display, debauchery, lewdness, whereas for Shamas there was hardly anything more beautiful than those young people, fumbling their way through life, full of new doubts and certainties, finding comfort in their own and others' bodies.

And more wonderful still the single sheet
over two lovers on a bed.

When he gets back home he can see that Kaukab is up because on the tabletop there is a wet ring made by the base of a teacup, shining in the morning light. The sun had picked out the course of tears on Chanda's mother's face in this manner that day she approached him on the bridge.

He goes to the dresser and looks in its drawer to see that Kaukab has taken her pills and tablets: after Chanda and Jugnu had disappeared Chanda's mother was said to have "just given up," neglecting to eat and refusing to take medicine; and he sometimes fears Kaukab will begin to behave in a similar way, neglecting her knee and blood complaint. Satisfied, he replaces the bottles of tablets without making them rattle.

She now enters the kitchen, rosary in hand, the beads the size of pills—her own medicine. "I thought I heard someone. Doors have taken on a new meaning now: any one of them could open any time to reveal Chanda and Jugnu. Don't you agree?"

For Kaukab to think of Jugnu is to always see a moth or a butterfly around him, somewhere towards the edges, the way Charag—her artist son—scores his name in the corner of his canvases, in the wet layers of paint.

"A cup slipped from my hands and broke earlier," Shamas tells her. "I think I managed to get most of the shards off the floor but you'd better not walk barefoot, especially . . . here, and also . . . over here."

"It was the last of the set I bought all those years ago." She lifts the lid of the bin to briefly look at the porcelain pieces. "I remember it hurt me to buy it because I thought we would have to leave it behind in England when we moved back to our own country. It seemed like a waste of money. I was reluctant to buy anything because our time here was only meant to be temporary. But things didn't turn out the way we thought they would. Decades have passed and we are still here. Hazrat Ali, may he forever be sprinkled by Allah's mercy, used to say that I recognized Allah by the ruins that were my vain plans for my life."

Shamas shudders. And then he says, "I think last night I dreamt I was crossing the Chenab towards Sohni Dharti."

"For the past three days I've dreamt that I am travelling towards Mecca but, even though I can see the city on the desert horizon, it never comes any closer. I always wake up before reaching it." Her voice breaks in her throat. "Each night I've gone to bed asking Him to let me sleep until I get to the sacred city but to no avail."

"Have you given any more thought to a visit to Pakistan?"

"We'll go for a visit of course, but I refuse to settle there permanently even though there is nothing I would like better. There is nothing on this planet that I loathe more than this country, but I won't go to live in Pakistan as long as my children are here. This accursed land has taken my children away from me. My Charag, my Mah-Jabin, my Ujala. Each time they went out they returned with a new layer of stranger-ness on them until finally I didn't recognize them anymore. Sons and daughters, on hearing that their mother is dying, are supposed to come to her side immediately to ask her to cancel their debt, the debt they incurred by drinking her milk. It is her privilege and her right. There is nothing more frightening for a person whose mother has just died in his absence than to learn that no one had asked her whether she released him from the debt of milk; you are supposed to beg her to lift that mountainous weight from your soul. I can't see any of my children doing that when my time is near. Perhaps Allah is punishing us for leaving behind our own parents in Pakistan and moving to England all those years ago." She shakes her head and says after a silence: "Weren't you a little too long with the newspapers? Was the shop not open yet for some reason or did you wander off on one of your walks?"

He panics as though he's been caught stealing. "Yes, the shop wasn't open yet," he tells her abruptly. *I look forward to seeing you this afternoon at the shop*—she, Suraya, had said just before they parted.

No, he won't go to the shop today. He cannot believe he has just lied to Kaukab, and he doesn't understand *why* he has done it.

Kaukab moves towards the stairs. "I won't move to Pakistan. What would my life be then? My children in England, me in Pakistan, my soul in Arabia, and my heart—" She pauses and then says: "And my heart wherever Jugnu and Chanda are." Her eyes fill up with tears as she declares this last, knowing the look on Shamas's face is saying "Really?" She knows no one will believe that she misses Jugnu and prays for his safe return constantly; she would have been overjoyed had he made his union with that girl Chanda legitimate in the eyes of Allah and His people. The only way, it seems, she can convince the others of her loss regarding Jugnu is by renouncing Allah and His injunctions, by saying that what Chanda and Jugnu were doing next door was *not* a sin. But how can she renounce Allah?

She goes upstairs, and Shamas lowers himself into a chair. He tries to bring Suraya's face before his eyes. Doesn't she look a little like a younger Kaukab, the Kaukab he married when he himself was that young poet in Lahore? He wonders whether he had given her his name after she had introduced herself. And now he feels ashamed at this absurd train of thought. This is madness. But it was as though she herself had wanted his company. He sees other women, other women he finds attractive, during the course of his daily life, the way all men do, but, after he has registered that fact, remarked on their beauty, nothing comes of it because nothing can—they are not interested in him. Why would they be? He would have ignored this morning's encounter similarly, but *she* seemed to want to be near him. He wishes he had shaved before going out this morning. No, no, this is insanity. Surely this is how teenage infatuations are born—he must act his age. She is much younger than him, by twenty-five or so years at least—she was probably born around the time when he was in his mid-twenties, writing those love poems. He takes a deep breath and tells himself to pull himself together. No, he won't go to the *Safeena* this afternoon.

Relieved at the decision he's just made, he lets out a small laugh at the madness of what he has just been thinking, and the weight of the world is suddenly off his shoulders. In one of Jugnu's butterfly books, he had last year secreted a prostitute's telephone number copied from the classified columns of *The Afternoon;* he gets up and finds it now, but then, filled with wretchedness, tears it up. He flicks through the book for possible distraction and comfort. *There is a butterfly called Sleepy Orange . . . In the woods of Siberia and the Himalayas there is a Map butterfly, and an Atlas moth in the islands of south-east Asia . . .* And other names, even stranger: *Figure of Eight. Figure of Eighty . . . One of the rarest gems on the planet, there is a butterfly in the wooded hills around Sikkim called Kaiser-e-Hind—the Caesar of India . . .* The thought of the magazines glimpsed in the newsagent comes to him, and he wonders whether he should take a bus to a shop in a faraway area and buy a few. If Kaukab ever discovers them he'll say they must have been lying hidden since the time when the boys were growing up. But what if she checks the dates on the cover? And he burns with shame as he remembers that two or so years ago, his flesh aching with eager longing, he had found himself going through the things his teenaged sons had left behind in their rooms, lifting up the carpet, feeling for a loose floorboard, sending an arm out under the mattresses, hoping one of them had forgotten to throw away a magazine.

Hiraman the
Rose-Ringed Parakeet

The lake has the subdued glow of antique satin. Suraya stands on the xylophone jetty and looks at the names and initials lovers have carved on the wood in Urdu, Hindi and Bengali as well as English. The gouged dots and full-stops are the size of dimples on a doll's knuckles. The wood is so skin-smooth that as she touches it she has a feeling of being stroked by it in return.

A wet late-spring dawn, Sunday, an emerald-and-grey hour, and nature is at its most creative. She should have come here yesterday afternoon, to visit the *Safeena,* as she promised that man on the bridge; but in the end a feeling of wretchedness had overpowered her. She is ashamed still of how she had approached the young artist here a few weeks ago. It had been her young son's birthday the previous day, over there in Pakistan, and she had become desperate to change her situation, to fly and be with her son and husband. She had wept through the night, overcome by fear, doubts, and self-pity, with short nightmare-filled bouts of sleep, and just before dawn had entered the chilled waters of the lake.

The scent from the pine trees saturates the web-soft air. The solid world seems to have dissolved, leaving behind only light and atmosphere—a world made from almost nothing.

She walks over to where she had forced the young man to have a conversation with her. There are bits of his orange peel, nearly dried up and curling, on the shore, their brightness muted for now. Colours have long and slow births on such spring dawns.

The matchmaker has shown her no one she finds suitable. A number of them are illegal immigrants or asylum seekers who want to marry her to get official residential status in Britain. And amongst the legitimate citizens, not many are willing to go through a temporary marriage; and those who do, almost salivate when they see her, happy that they would be allowed to paw at her soon like a prostitute bought for a short while.

The matchmaker tells her not to lose heart: "Have you seen the way men look at you? Indian, Pakistani, *and* whites, and the *blacks*—ha, *they* can dream. They all cannot resist a second glance. And, no, you are not too old. Some white women of your age aren't even married for the first time yet."

She approaches the water and washes her hands. She has just been to her mother's grave with a bag of potting soil and two dozen tulips. Her mother had contracted meningitis last autumn during the pilgrimage to Saudi Arabia and Suraya had left Pakistan to come and nurse her. The divorce was still weeks old then, and her husband had decided that she should stay on in England after the mother's death: "Marry and divorce someone there, and then come back. I'd feel humiliated if you married someone here, because I don't want to see another man touch my wife, the woman I love." She had resisted the idea because she had missed her son, but in the end she had relented. She lives in the house she inherited from her mother.

Allah has decreed that a man can marry any woman who is not his close blood relation. And so under Islamic law, the punishment Suraya's husband must receive—for getting drunk and for not taking the matter of divorce seriously enough—is that he can have any woman *except* one. One woman is barred to him, as she is not to other men—that's his torment. But—such is Allah's compassion towards his creatures!—she is not barred to him permanently: if the woman who has been recklessly divorced can fulfill the requirement that Suraya is having to fulfill, then the original husband can possess her again. Limitless is Allah's kindness towards his creation. *Allah is not being equally compassionate towards the poor woman who is having to go through another marriage through no fault of her own* is a thought that has occasionally crossed Suraya's mind, along with *It's as though Allah forgot there were women in the world when he made some of his laws, thinking only of men*—but she has banished these thoughts as all good Muslims must.

She wonders when the tulips will bloom. It was her mother's wish to have tulips on her resting place: she did tell Suraya the reason for the request but it seems to have slipped her mind completely. She planted all but one of the bulbs in perfect rows because her mother used to say that only Allah is perfect and that we should acknowledge that fact when performing a task, that we should introduce a tiny hidden flaw into every object we make. "The Emperor Shah Jahan had made sure that there was a built-in imperfection in the Taj Mahal—the minarets lean out by three degrees," she said.

When she set out at first light, there was an insubstantial rain—it was more a misty drizzle and there was no patter on the drumskin-tight nylon of the umbrella—but now even that has diminished; were she to look up, only one of her eyes would receive a droplet. The lake is girdled by concentric bands of many-coloured sands, pebbles, and, higher up the shore, pine needles; and the water's edge is softly gnawing at them. She turns and moves towards the hut that stands surrounded by maple trees. Across a part of its side, ivy grows in every direction as though a large can of green paint has been splashed on the wall. This is the Urdu bookshop. She looks in through the window. What was the name of the man she met on the bridge yesterday? Was he a Muslim? The sign above the door is painted in a red as deep as dolphin blood: it depicts a small boat with a pair of oars lying next to each other inside it like man and wife.

She mustn't despair at her predicament, she tells herself; this is not the end of her life: it's a chapter.

Shamas is walking towards the *Safeena*. The drizzle has stopped completely. There is a small clump of reeds on the edge of the lake, and caught in this wet light the blades give out a diffused green gleam: each blade is a giant grasshopper wing. The bookshop is painted a rich brown, the colour of warm spices. In the early days—twenty years ago—it consisted of nothing more than a few boxes of books. It was all spiders and exposed wiring but then it was slowly cleaned up and a wallpaper that was a jungle of flame-of-the-forest sprigs and pairs of deer with powder-puff tails was put up. The walls had had holes in them before that and brightly dusty wedges of sunlight would be found in the interior in the afternoons as though someone had strung geometric paper lanterns everywhere. The roof leaked like a sponge sometimes.

But the owner was passionate about books and people would joke that given enough time he would track down even a signed first-edition of the Koran for you.

He looks up at the sky. Today will be one of those late English spring days that have no independent temperature: it will be hot out under the sun but the body will feel cold if taken indoors.

The owner of the *Safeena* went to Pakistan at the end of last year to untangle various financial matters concerning the money he had been sending his nephews for over a decade to buy land and property, and he died there, the relatives telephoning the widow here in England with the news three days after burying him. There is a possibility that he had been poisoned: there have been a number of cases recently where a person who had gone from Britain to sort out financial affairs had been murdered and buried by family members and business partners who had been mis-appropriating, siphoning off, or embezzling the money they were being sent.

The widow gave Shamas the keys to the *Safeena* when he said he would open the shop for a few hours each weekend until the existing stock sold out; she could then sell the hut. She had waved her hand resignedly, "All I need, brother-ji, is a place to spread my prayer-mat."

The sun is pale, dripping silver. Fuses lit at random, the lemon-yellow dandelion flowers will be everywhere within the hour. The air smells of morning, of moist sunlight. He approaches the *Safeena* and stops. Someone—Suraya—is looking in through the windows, that red scarf still holding her hair in a bunch, the blue lozenges along its edge glittering in the morning air like unpurchasable gems, alive with reverberating pigment.

"I am sorry I couldn't come yesterday, Mr. . . . . Mr. . . . ." She must try to find out his name, in order to be able to tell what religion he is.

"I am Shamas."

Muslim. She looks at the marriage finger: there is no ring, but that is no proof because the wearing of marriage rings isn't really a strict custom in the Subcontinent.

She must try to keep him here, to find out more about him. "Tell me, do you think it was here that the police found a human heart some weeks ago? I overheard some little girls in a shop saying that when the children who chanced upon it had poked it with a stick it had given a few beats. What imagination the children have!" Perhaps he will now make a comment about his own children?

"No, it was closer to another shore, closer to the river where we met, nearer the area where there is a beekeeper from whom the Sultan of Oman bought forty queen bees, chartering a plane to fly them home. He had tasted their honey in a London hotel."

She nods. The dawn surrounds them both with its green-and-blue, the deep sky above and the almost-luminous new growth of leaves below it. He is surely too aloof and dignified to be interested in her. He is obviously not a factory worker or taxi driver because his hands are soft-looking and almost pink.

"Yes," he is continuing, "the heart was found in the other direction. A young white man was responsible. It was his dead mother's and he stole it from the hospital just because he didn't want it to be transplanted into a black man's body."

The information is shocking, and Suraya feels it as such, but she is aware that for several months now she is a little numb to the world, the news about it—no matter how monumental or significant—coming muffled by her own difficulties. Nor can she remember the last time she felt pleasure, genuine gladness that plumbs the soul, as she did when she embraced her son, pressing her nose and mouth into his soft neck, or when she tussled with him on the floor, glad that he was not a girl because you couldn't be that rough with girls: she remembers her mother stopping in her tracks and sharply telling her father not to play too enthusiastically with his little daughter lest he cause "irreparable physical damage to her private areas," having warned him many times before that, "If a flower loses a petal it doesn't grow back!"

She is thankful to Allah that she doesn't have any daughters.

Her longing for her boy is so great that last month while swimming in the lake, in the predawn darkness, she had had the urge at one point to just let go and sink to the bottom, let the water suck the life out of her while the bright moon watched above. If something doesn't happen soon, she thinks now, I might still do that: float lifeless above the X-shaped giant's still-beating heart. She remembers hearing from women in her childhood that this lake requires a sacrifice every six years, and she wonders how many years it has been since the last drowning.

"My daughter"—the man has begun another sentence—"thought it was the heart of her murdered uncle."

It takes her a moment or two to register what he's just told her. The force of it causes her to raise her hands to her breasts—it's almost a blow to the heart. "Allah!"

"I am sorry," he says, looking stunned. "I didn't mean to shock you, forgive me."

"When did it happen? Recently?"

"Yes. Please forgive me. I don't know why I mentioned it."

Recently. The poor man is living through the death of his brother, grieving, and there she was, planning, working out strategies, wondering whether she sensed in him an attraction towards her! Her eyes fill up with tears because of the disappointment of realizing that he is probably not interested in her—she'll have to keep looking for someone else. She feels exhausted. And yet there is also a surge of shame, because with a part of her brain she's also wondering whether it wouldn't be easy for her to use his grief to her own advantage. She'll offer him comfort and then he will become grateful to her—yes? She's filled with self-disgust, her eyes brimming with water. What has she turned into and who is responsible for doing this to her?

"I am sorry, I shouldn't have told you that. Are you all right?"

"Yes, thank you." She raises her veil to her face and realizes she's been holding a piece of the desiccated peel from the oranges the young artist had been eating last month: she must have picked up the cardboard-like fragment from the shore earlier. She lets it drop, and turns to leave.

. . .

"I'll open the *Safeena* this afternoon if you'd care to come," Shamas tells her, attempting to delay her departure. "I was out on just a walk now." Though of course it's all futile: he didn't come to the bookshop yesterday because he was afraid of himself, but she hadn't come either. She had said she would—but she obviously has a rich and full life already, friends, family, lovers. She stops at his words, eyes still swimming. She is obviously very sensitive: the mere mention of Jugnu's death had produced tears. He can tell her other things too. He envisages a friendship. He'll tell her how much he regrets never having continued with his poetry, and that he would like to go back to Pakistan now that he's about to retire, go back and see if he can do something for the betterment of his country. He'll tell her that he heard about the discovery of the human heart from two clan-destine lovers—a Hindu boy, and a Muslim girl whose mother is con-vinced that she's possessed by the djinn and is asking around for a holy man who'd perform an exorcism.

"I'll come, yes. When I was a girl, my father, may he rest in peace, brought me here to a reading by the Pakistani poet Wamaq Saleem."

Shamas is delighted. "I was among the organizers for that reading." They were the years of Wamaq Saleem's exile—the monstrous military regime had succeeded in forcing him out of Pakistan. His books of verses sold by the hundred-thousand in Pakistan and India, and about a hun-dred people had arrived at the lakeside hut to hear him recite that after-noon despite the fact that the autumn sky was breathing a chilly wind.

"It has been said that Wamaq Saleem did for Pakistan what Homer did for the Mediterranean and what the Bible did for Jerusalem."

Suraya says, "I remember the women listeners had brought him flow-ers, containers of perfume, and jars of honey, because just like the Prophet, peace be upon him, it was his favourite food. And men presented him with bottles of whisky and gin. My father had brought an embroi-dered shawl, and I presented it to him."

Shamas realizes he's smiling, feeling light if not lightheaded.

She seems to be one of those people to meet whom is to meet oneself.

She is wearing a short woollen jacket, yellow with white embroidered paisleys, and, lightly gripping it between fingertips, she says: "This was once a Kashmiri shawl, identical to the one we gave to Wamaq Saleem. It was my late mother's—may she rest in peace—but moths chewed up a part of it. I couldn't bear to throw it away so I cut it up to make a jacket."

He wants her to stay but senses that her wish for his company is vanishing like dew by the second, and, as though about to take her leave, she touches the cherry-red scarf at the nape of her neck and says, "Thank you once again for this." She smiles at him. That mole. Every moment he has spent talking to her has been of great value and worth: an image comes to him of an hourglass filled not with the usual sand but little diamonds. He would like to converse for a while longer but he must go now, fettered by his conscience—that self-arresting chain—because although it has been exhilarating to be in her presence he won't be able to forgive himself if he becomes a cause of dishonour or harm for her. Someone returning from the mosque after his dawn prayers could notice them together and by midmorning the entire neighbourhood would know, and by the afternoon the whole town due to the communication radios in taxis. And, just as numerous other places and roads have been given Indian and Pakistani and Bangladeshi names to give the map of this English town a semblance of belonging—amassing a claim on the place bit by bit—this lakeside location would then be named Scandal Point, after the prime rendezvous spot in Shimla, so called because fifty years ago an Indian prince and the beautiful daughter of a senior British official had met there for a long ride together on their horses, their subsequent absence over the following few days scandalizing the town's white population.

"So, yes, come to the shop this afternoon, if you'd like to look over the books," he hears himself tell her again, desperately, before walking away. The moment of parting leaves in him an inarticulate ache. He is embarrassed by the kind of impression he must have made on her—someone comically desperate for company. He hasn't had a conversation with someone about the matters that interest him for a very long time. Talking with Kaukab is, for both of them, frequently another way of being alone, the conversation highlighting the separate loneliness of each.

He has also lost most of his friends from the Communist Party: he used to feel enlivened at the meetings, but almost everyone in the Party thinks the break-up of the Soviet Union would result in a better world, while he himself thinks that one of the greatest tragedies of the twentieth century is that the Soviet Union disgraced itself, that we danced on Communism's grave, and so he no longer attends the Party meetings. Additionally, of course, the death of Chanda and Jugnu has made him reluctant to talk to anyone.

Suraya watches Shamas leave. She wonders how bold she should be when dealing with him. Her aim after all isn't to just interest him in herself—it is to eventually get him to marry her. And while men are happy to consort with women who are forthcoming and assertive, they will judge that trait objectionable in a potential wife.

She has been told that she can be vividly bold; and she herself had read that component of her personality as courageous, but now she thinks of it as adventurousness, perhaps even recklessness, because it is this very trait that has landed her in the trouble she is in. She'd been sent to a Pakistani village to marry a man she had never met, and she admits that she had occasionally behaved in a spirited manner because she knew that her in-laws—and her handsome and loving husband—were in awe of the fact that she was "from England." Her husband's behaviour was loving towards her at the start anyway, before his secret drinking got out of control—though she was, even early on in the marriage, frightened by his acts and rough demands when he got drunk, behaviour he had no knowledge of when he sobered up and became gentle towards her once again as though she was a porcelain doll.

Yes, a delicate doll: she exaggerated the shock she felt at the primitive and coarse nature of village life, because it made her husband think she was something special, made of finer clay. She pretended not to understand the codes and mores which governed the daily conduct of the people around her, saying, for example, that she found the decades-old feud with a nearby family ludicrous. Her wide-eyed innocence was found endearing and laughed off, but one day she had gone too far. She discovered that a man—one of the men from the family with which her in-laws had the decades-long feud—had been raping his niece for the past few months and that the matter had come to light only now because the fourteen-year-old girl had fallen pregnant. The entire family accused the girl of having relations with someone and thereby bringing dishonour on the bloodline. She was unmarried but not a virgin! Terrorized by the uncle, she refused to tell who the perpetrator really was. The matter hadn't yet reached the ears of the world outside the house because the girl hadn't yet begun to show, but Suraya had been told about it by her servant girl who worked at that house too. Suraya feared the pregnant girl would be murdered any day for disgracing the family. She couldn't go to the police because, under Pakistan's Islamic law, rape had to have male witnesses who confirmed that it was indeed rape and not consensual intercourse; the girl did not have witnesses and therefore would be found guilty of sex outside marriage, sentenced to flogging, and sent to prison, marked an abominable sinner from then on, a fallen woman and a prostitute for the rest of her life.

The confidence of her English life still clinging to her, Suraya decided to go to the house of the feuding family to reveal the real truth to them and ask them to be compassionate. She was walking into a conflict decades in the making but she thought she could be persuasive.

She realized her mistake very soon after she walked into the enemy courtyard. She remembers every detail, the time slowing down. The men of the house clustered around her and barred her way when she attempted to leave. People were always losing their way in the thick winter fogs and she pretended she had entered the house by mistake, putting aside her fears about the pregnant niece, her own survival now at stake. Eventually she was allowed to leave the house with her virtue intact; the men did, however, tell her that they were going to let everyone know that they *had* raped her because it would cast a mark on their honour and their name and their manhood if people thought they had had a woman from the other side of the battle-line in their midst and hadn't taken full and appropriate advantage of the opportunity.

As it turned out it was as bad as if they had raped her. What mattered was not what you yourself knew to have actually happened, but what other people thought had happened. Her husband and in-laws believed her completely when she said that she was still pure, that nothing irrevocable had occurred in the house of the enemy, but in the end that fact was worthless.

All this pushed her husband over the edge. More and more he began to seek solace in alcohol, saying he needed it to breathe, often coming home knee-walkingly drunk, taking off his cap and waistcoat and attempting to hang them on the *shadow* of the hat-stand on the wall, his behaviour becoming increasingly volatile so that eventually she was afraid to even let her bangles make a sound, not knowing what would provoke him, though he was always remorseful after his outbursts, telling her how much he loved her, that he just couldn't get the barbed comments of people out of his head.

There were days when, in his shame, he didn't want to see anyone: not even himself—he draped the mirror with a cloth. But then there was disgust and rage in him as he handled the veils that came into the house to be dyed because her father-in-law was a dyer: "They are getting shorter and shorter. The women of today are increasingly shameless."

She could always tell by the sound of the knock on the door at night that he had been drinking and also how much he had had; his language was coarse when he addressed her on these nights, as though he wouldn't get the full worth of the money he had paid the alcohol-seller if he didn't call her abusive names.

She tried to resort to her earlier spiritedness, trying to remind him of happier times, but that behaviour now seemed to enrage rather than enchant him, a sign of Western decadence.

One day he slapped her with his coarse rectangular hand. The next day he began to shake her violently: "I *know* what you did in that house. Admit the truth at once if you don't want my fist to aid your memory." He did beat her the next day. And the day after that he waved a knife and shouted, "Your death is hidden in this dagger . . . The role of a woman is to give life, the role of a man is to take it . . ." The next day he took the final step:

He said the word *talaaq* three times: I divorce thee, I divorce thee, I divorce thee.

And he pushed her away with his foot. In the morning he claimed he didn't remember uttering the deadly word in triplicate; and even if he did say it, he certainly hadn't meant it—but what had been done could not be undone now. The husband—who was the only one in a Muslim marriage with the right to divorce—had uttered the word three times and according to Islam they were now divorced.

There were no witnesses but even then they couldn't ignore what had happened: Allah had witnessed.

Many drunks were repentant in the mornings when they woke up to find the wife and children weeping at the ruin their life had become a few hours earlier: the husband, intoxicated, had probably had his hands pushed away in the darkness by the wife who was revolted by the smell of alcohol and he had said the word three times in rage. *Talaaq. Talaaq. Talaaq.* It was as simple as that.

Every day the clerics of the mosques all across the Subcontinent were visited by thousands of distraught couples, and every day the Muslim newspapers—here in England, and there in India, Pakistan and Bangladesh—received letters from men who said they loved their wives and children dearly, and that they wanted to keep their family together, that the word *talaaq* was uttered by them only in anger—but Allah's law was Allah's law and nothing could be done.

Nothing except the path Suraya has already embarked upon.

The man—her husband—doesn't have to marry another woman before he can marry her again. Allah's law is Allah's law and cannot be questioned.

Shamas sits in one of the yellow chairs with the newspaper and listens to Kaukab. Having just returned from the neighbourhood shops, she is telling him about the various things she has heard from the women out there as she prepares food in the blue kitchen, keeping up a monologue as she moves from cupboard to dresser to counter to oven. On a tablecloth as white as canvas, she arranges the still life of their lunch. A spring or summer meal is nothing without the freshly beaten coriander-chilli-and-mint chutney, so she had gone to the shops to pick up the mint and the coriander—bushels of the freshest imaginable green secured by stationery-shop rubber bands—and the chillies in polythene bags so finely thin they failed to rustle. She also brought limes that had scars on the peel, made by the sampling pecks of birds, indicating that the fruit had grown on the outside of the tree crown and had therefore been exposed to more sunlight than the ones that had grown concealed within the canopy, the ones with undamaged skins. She halved a lime and rubbed one piece on the plates they would eat out of, to impart a note of zest into each mouthful, and squeezed the other half over the salad of sliced onions and then coated each slice with fiery black pepper so that every curving piece would become as lethal as a sword in the hand of a drunkard.

Mangoes the colour of copper pots have arrived in the shop, she says, £3.60 for a box of five, as have guavas whose flashing pink insides are like a burst of poetry and the red pears which everyone is always reluctant to peel because you want to eat that *colour*, wishing eyes had tastebuds.

A woman in the neighbourhood has received a letter from the wife of the Bengali family who used to live in the house next door—before Jugnu bought it because the family had decided to go back after their son had been beaten to death in a racial attack by the whites—and in the letter she says that she was totally devastated to hear that her old neighbours' daughter Mah-Jabin has cut short her lovely long hair.

The Indian and Pakistani mothers of growing daughters are asking the shopkeeper to stop importing a certain English-language women's magazine published in Bombay. They deem it vulgar and pornographic because in this month's issue a young Delhi wife had written in to say that she had recently given birth to her first baby and that her husband, saying that her vagina was too loose now, had taken to entering her where she was tighter; the letter was to the medical-advice page and the woman had wanted to know if there was any way she could tighten her vagina, or failing that, perhaps some way could be suggested to make what her husband now does to her not hurt as much.

The parents of a seven-year-old Muslim child—who had recently begun to be educated, at home and at the mosque, about various sins and their punishments—had been summoned to the headmistress's office yesterday and informed that the boy had been telling his white schoolmates that they were all going to be skinned alive in Hell for eating pork and that their mummies and daddies would be set on fire and made to drink boiling hot water because they drank alcohol and did not believe in Allah and Muhammad, peace be upon him.

Someone has heard someone else say that Chanda was pregnant at the time of her murder and that, like Jugnu's, the foetus's hands were luminous, that they could be seen glowing through Chanda's stomach and clothing.

Music and talk from the radio tuned to the Asian station accompanies the two of them as they clear the table after lunch. There's a phone-in about the problems of life in England: ... *Are you tired of being treated like a coolie by the whites? Give us a call. We would also like our younger listeners to contact us. Are you in a rage, one of those unemployed, newly bearded, mosque-going misanthropes they are writing about in the newspapers; the kind of guy who is either still a virgin or married to a non-English-speaking first cousin brought over from a village in Pakistan or Bangladesh, the guy who lives with his parents, hides outside his sister's school to see if she's talking to boys, and thinks she shouldn't be allowed to go to university. Give us a call on ...*

He settles down after lunch to look at a local health authority pamphlet that has to be translated into Hindi, Urdu, Bengali and Gujarati—he will do the Urdu. Tuberculosis was thought to have been eradicated in the 1960s and all medical research into it was stopped in the West while it continued to rage elsewhere in the world, but now it is resurfacing in the poorer neighbourhoods (those pockets of the Third World within the First) of London, Liverpool, Glasgow, New York and San Francisco. He remembers the mobile radiography units parked outside mills and factories and the Employment Exchange thirty years ago. The rate of infection was above average in the migrant workers because they had poor nutrition and lived in over-crowded lodgings, one inhaling the germs coughed up by the other. Many of them live in similar conditions even today—over half the houses in this neighbourhood were declared unfit for habitation seven years ago—and they must be warned about the dangers of infection. And the regular trips back to the Subcontinent also expose them and their children to a greater risk.

He works for most of the afternoon, and then walks through a lace of insects to open the bookshop soon after three o'clock, under a sky filled with widely separated white clouds shaped like forest animals. On a wall the graffitied initials of the National Front have been modified by Asian youths so that they now read: NFAK RULES—Nusrat Fateh Ali Khan being the world-renowned Pakistani singer of Sufi devotional lyrics.

Beside the path that will convey him to the lake, a day-flying Cinnabar moth flutters away to safety inside the Oxford ragworts. He cannot see the lake yet but the white-paper scraps of the fluttering gulls hint at where it lies ahead.

The thought of Suraya has been with him constantly during the previous hours. As he walks under the blue-and-white forest of the sky, he realizes that he has been standing on knife-blades of impatience all day, waiting for this hour to arrive, even when he was a thousand leagues under concentration, doing the translation an hour earlier. He has been thinking of her, yes, but there has also been the fear that someone had seen her talking to him and that she is even now—somewhere—being harmed for it. This terror has been hurtling around inside him like a grenade with the pin pulled out. From time to time his breast narrows and his strength diminishes.

He unlocks the shop and goes in. The eyes of the deer on the wallpaper shine like little lamps draped with blue veils. The small creatures sit two by two, surrounded by branches of the flame-of-the-forest, the petals curving like the beaks of parakeets.

As he waits for her to walk out of the deserted spaces of the afternoon, the sun striking the lake's silver at an angle, a part of him hopes she won't come. He had drawn pleasure by talking to her, and she too had seemed animated several times, but he is too aware of the dangers. He is reminded of an Urdu saying which advocates caution when in the presence of something beautiful or pleasurable: Don't forget that serpents haunt sandalwood trees.

From the door of the *Safeena,* he sees her arriving, and as she reaches Scandal Point and moves towards him he wishes he hadn't opened the shop this afternoon too: he is relieved to see that she is safe, but he now suspects that someone (a husband or brother or—after an inch-long story in the inner pages of the Urdu newspaper which said that a middle-aged woman was found with her neck broken in a village outside Lahore—a young nephew) has followed her and is hiding nearby to confirm his suspicions about her.

"I went to the door because I heard a strange musical noise," he explains to her. "I have heard it all day. Either it is a strange bird or a shop around here has recently stocked a new kind of whistle that is proving very popular with children." She is wearing a fresh set of *shalwar-kameez* and the same paisley jacket cropped at the waist. He raises his hands to indicate the shelves: "Fiction there. Non-fiction from here to here. Poetry there. And the few books on art there." And he tells himself to remain silent from now on so she can look around and leave as soon as possible—for her own safety. They say it's hard to kill a fellow human being. *Don't aim at the victim: aim at something* on *the victim—the knot of a tie, a flower printed on the dress.* Would they aim at one of the paisleys, with its tiny ruby centre, before pulling the trigger, they who had watched her talking to him this morning and have followed her here this afternoon, they who are hiding just outside now?

She picks up the large mustard-yellow *Muraqqa-e-Chughtai* from the shelf—a volume of the Mughul Urdu poet Ghalib's verse illustrated with paintings by Abdur Rahman Chughtai—and says quietly, "Oh, you have this."

"Yes. Originally published in 19 . . . 28. There is *Naqsh-e-Chughtai* beside it—same text but different paintings, from 19 . . . 34." He remains in his chair, telling himself not to draw close to her: between them lies a fragile bridge of glass. "Can you see it? The dust-jacket is grey and shows a deer sitting beside a small cypress tree growing out of a jewel." He must try to remain quiet and not point out any more books to her. She moves along the shelves of Urdu and Persian poetry, opening and closing the volumes, and after a while says to him,

"A lot of Persian poems are about flowers and spring."

"Yes. My younger brother visited Iran some years ago, and he said that the abundantly flowered arrival of spring in that country cannot fail to inspire even a casual observer. I personally think that it would be difficult to find more rapturous descriptions of spring than those in the poetry of Qani."

"Is that the brother who . . . was . . . murdered?" She looks down at the floor.

"Yes, and I am sorry once again for revealing that to you so clumsily earlier."

"Please think nothing of it. May I ask how it happened?"

He doesn't want to distress her. "I'd rather not talk about it."

"I understand." She turns to the shelf and gives herself over to the books.

He looks at the afternoon. "I think I saw the butterfly I have been chasing fly in here," Jugnu said—once, when both he and the bookshop's owner were still here. Out of breath, he'd come into the *Safeena* holding his green long-handled butterfly net like a flag. Shamas had pointed to the Urdu translation of *Madame Bovary* on the shelf and said: "The only butterflies in here are the ones in there." Jugnu went out to continue his search, but he returned to the *Safeena* later and picked up *Madame Bovary*: "Now. I do remember that there are butterflies in here. Three, I think—the first black, the second yellow and the third white." And five minutes of turning the pages later he announced: "Yes, they are still here."

Shamas turns his attention to Suraya again. He feels she may have taken his last comment as a rebuke, but he cannot think of how to make amends: she's perusing the books, head bowed, her back turned to him determinedly. Shamas shifts his gaze and fixes it on her so that their eyes would have to meet even if she slightly alters the position of her head. He smiles at her when that happens—as though making up with a lover after a fight—and nonchalantly points to her Kashmiri jacket:

"Do you know why paisley is so linked with Kashmir? No? Imagine two lovers quarrelling in that region. Her footsteps formed paisleys when she hurried away from him in distress. He searched for her forlornly in the forest glades where luminous orchids arose from the"—it is too late for him to stop—"spilled semen of mating animals and birds, where the urge for existence forced creepers and vines towards faraway chinks of sunlight, where the branches quivered with living songs and at sunset the sky turned red as though the departing sun had heaped rubies on the day's shroud. And it was the paisleys imprinted amid the low flowers that eventually led him to her. He was the god Shiva, she the goddess Parvati, and when he found her he commemorated their union by carving the Jehlum river as it flowed—and still flows—through the valley of Kashmir in the shape of a paisley."

"Thank you," her eyes dance as she smiles. "That is beautiful."

And, buoyed by her smile, he indicates the Chughtai books in her hand and says: "Chughtai drew the jacket design for my book of poems, back in the 1950s."

"You published a book?" She's electrified and almost gasps. "And *Chughtai?*"

"He was a great friend to the Lahore publishing world." He looks at her. "And as for my book: it was ready for publication but nothing came of it."

"Why? Do you have the poems in a notebook, perhaps? I'd like to read them."

"No, there is no copy of the manuscript. My wife had the only copy but that was . . . destroyed. And I am not sure whether I remember them accurately myself anymore." He pictures himself laying out Kaukab's wedding dress and writing out the verses in a notebook—in a *safeena!*—for Suraya to read; but, of course the wedding dress was reduced to ashes all those years ago.

"You must try to remember them," she says, and adds with a smile: "Some day I'll come to the *Safeena* and ask you to recite for me, like Wamaq Saleem. The only difference being that ours would be a private reading, for one." She approaches him with the two volumes by Chughtai, holding them in the crook of her arm like a college girl. "I'll take these. I looked for them in Pakistan but the village where I was didn't have a very well-stocked bookshop, as you can imagine."

"What were you doing in Pakistan?" Her hair is secured by the length of silk he had retrieved for her yesterday: at lunch the red insides of a Moroccan blood orange—one of those fruits that always produce intensely scented urine—had reminded him of the colour of the scarf.

So he has a wife, she who had the only copy of his book of poems. But he could still marry her because a Muslim man is allowed four wives.

Suraya had wondered, before coming to the *Safeena,* and has wondered during her visit here too, about how much she should reveal to him. Should she tell him everything about her situation—I am looking for someone to marry temporarily . . . But that would frighten him.

Should she wait until they are better acquainted—until she has "a better hold on him"? And how will she get him to divorce her eventually? At home she had burst into tears at that. *Dear Allah, why can't I understand the reasons behind your laws?* It's the *man* who deserves to be punished if he has uttered the word "divorce" as idle threat, in anger or while intoxicated, and, yes, the punishment for him is that he has to see his wife briefly become another man's property, being *used* by him. But why must the divorced wife be punished? Nothing is more abhorrent to a Muslim woman than the thought of being touched by a man other than her husband. She hides her body like a treasure. But if she wants her husband back she has to let another man touch her. This is her punishment: a punishment she deserves, perhaps, because she did not know how to teach her husband to be a good man, how to teach him to control his anger and be a good Muslim, stay away from alcohol?

But Suraya knows she'll be able to go through with every humiliation and degradation eventually, that she'll let another man—Shamas, for instance—touch her because she doesn't want to go through life without her son and husband: she'll be one person's friend, another's confidante, someone else's mistress—but she is their *everything*.

"I was married to someone there. I am now divorced," she hears herself tell Shamas now, in answer to his question. "I have an eight-year-old son who is with his father." That's it for now. She feels drained. "I don't know when or if I'll go back to Pakistan. As things stand I have no one and no plans." She pays for the two books but she cannot leave without first arranging their next meeting. She has been thinking quickly for the past few minutes, but nothing has come to her. She tries to find a way to prolong her presence here while thinking.

And, of course, she mustn't let him think that the next meeting is her idea—it's possible that he's the kind of man who likes to be in control (and most men are; women just have to orchestrate the events to let men *think* they are in charge).

"It's just occurred to me that the noise you heard earlier could actually be a bird and not a child's whistle." And she tells him how a flock of Subcontinental rose-ringed parakeets is causing havoc in the gardens and orchards on the outskirts of Dasht-e-Tanhaii. She saw them herself last week. About thirty in number, they are the descendants of a pair of Indian rose-ringed parakeets that had escaped from their cage some years ago.

"I am very fond of those birds," he tells her, "but I haven't seen one for decades now."

"I wouldn't mind taking you to where the flock is," she says (perhaps a little too abruptly?).

"I would like that, yes. We'll look for the birds the way my brother used to look for butterflies. His name was Jugnu by the way—"

"Please don't feel you have to tell me things you'd rather not."

"No, I want to. I'd like to." He looks straight into her eyes and says: "So how shall we arrange to meet again?"

As he watches her leave along the path lined with tall grasses, he wants to run after her and tell her why he is fond of parakeets. But he stops himself, deciding he'll tell her the next time they meet. *"Do you know the story of Hiraman the rose-ringed parakeet and princess Padma-vati?"* Hiraman, the talking rose-ringed parakeet, found fault with every beautiful maiden that Rajah Ratan Sen thought about marrying. He said to Rajah Ratan Sen, "One mustn't settle for the ordinary. Across a distance of seven seas from your majesty's palace, there is a land called Serendip, ruled by Rajah Gandhrap Sen. And the name of the Rajah's daughter is Padmavati. Delicate as a lotus. Radiant as the morning star. Her scented locks a monsoon cloud and the parting in them, leading to her brow, is the path to heaven itself. That brow: as spotless as the moon on the second night of a month, shining through nine regions and three worlds. Eyes like two fish playing face to face. Her glances: like two wagtails fighting on the wing. Her hips wide as an elephant's brow. All forms of beauty are determined to cling to her the way a green pigeon grasps a twig as it leans down to drink water from a stream, for it thinks everything on earth unworthy of contact, continuing to hang upside down from branches even when killed." Padmavati's attributes and virtues so captured Rajah Ratan Sen's imagination that he eventually lost his entire being to her description and set out to look for her . . .

. . .

Shamas walks around the *Safeena*, thinking of their next meeting, how he would tell her that—to his mind—Hiraman the parakeet represents an artist, they who tell us what we should aim for, they who reveal the ideal to us, telling us what's truly worth living for, and dying for, in life.

Now and then he opens a book he had seen her look into earlier.

Тhe Oldest Acquaintanceship
in тhe World

Having got off the bus, Chanda's mother stands under the cherry tree by the side of the road, on the outskirts of Dasht-e-Tanhaii, surrounded by the green slopes of the hills, while a flock of rose-ringed parakeets knives by overhead. Her husband—who had alighted with her—has gone somewhere beyond the curve of the deserted road through the hills. The grass at her feet is clogged with the faded drifts of pale-pink cherry petals. She looks at her shoes: they bought these shoes together, mother and daughter, two years ago.

She can see her husband coming along the bend in the road, muttering to himself, shaking his head, looking pallid in the lavender shadow of the hill's green shoulder. The couple have just been to visit their sons who are being held at a prison an hour's bus ride away. They had got off the bus at this remote location because Chanda's father thought he saw someone disappear around a tree—giving chase to a butterfly. Jugnu? They had broken their journey home and hurriedly disembarked at the next stop. She had remained under the cherry tree and he had rushed back up the road, towards where he had caught the fleeting glimpse of the butterfly hunter. In his long absence she has let herself cry out loudly into the air, letting out the sorrow she had felt during the visit they have just paid to the prison: one of their sons was beaten up yesterday by white inmates—his left arm and jawbone are broken, and his face is bruised beyond recognition. He can't tell on the people who did that to him and has told the prison authorities he had a fall.

She smiles to hide the traces of her grief from her husband, so as not to upset him.

"It was just a boy," he says, drawing up to her, "with a paper aeroplane." He looks around as though he has found himself in the middle of an ocean, searching for the shore. "But I did see someone else. Shamas, standing beside a stream. And I think there was a woman with him. Or at least I think they were together. She was standing a little distance away."

"Allah! Are you sure?"

"I don't know. No, I am not sure. Has another bus passed since?"

"Yes, but it was one of those that turn into Annemarie Schimmel Road, going towards Muridke, instead of carrying on towards the Saddam Hussein bus station." She takes out a handkerchief from her handbag red as a lobster shell and passes it to him—the exertion has brought out a bath of sweat. "Was the woman with Shamas white?"

He shakes his head. "It's probably nothing. Isn't it from Muridke that a holy man has been summoned by that family on Faiz Street, to come and exorcise their daughter of the djinns?"

"Yes. He'll come soon," she replies. "She's not behaving appropriately towards her family and husband. Last night I found myself wondering whether that was what was wrong with our own daughter—the djinns possessed her and caused her to rebel."

He wipes his face with the handkerchief, his breath steadying slowly. He seems to have found his bearing now that he is close to her: her side always welcomes him back from being just one of the many to being the lead in the play of their life, even though certain areas of her mind are not the right shape to accommodate him. When he is not with her he is alone even if surrounded by people. Whilst sticking price-labels onto the packets of spices he would shout from behind a row of shelves,

"Chanda's mother, how much for the packets of fennel?"

"Twenty-nine p for the small ones, 51p for the larger," she would answer from the counter, "and must you ask me every time?"

"It's just an excuse to hear your voice, my beloved." He would stand up and wink at her from across the tops of the shelves, or from around the white-and-blue pyramid of sugar bags. She would quickly conceal her pleasure behind her veil; oh, what was she to do with this husband of hers! She would reprimand: they were adults, parents of three children, but he persisted in acting like a teenager at his age and insisted she behave as though the world was her bridal chamber and every day her wedding night. Many summers ago, after she had got carried away with the nail-clipper the day before (as everyone does from time to time), she had asked him to peel an orange for her, her own fingertips slightly raw, and he had taken that to be a cue for the establishing a ritual: from then on, the moment new oranges arrived in summer, he peeled one of them and left the fleshy star in a plate with a pinch of salt on the cash till beside her, the segments arranged and the plate chosen with care because the first bite is always with the eye. The customers would elbow each other, smiling, as he selected the heaviest and darkest fruit from the boxes, but it was as though she was the only one who noticed their mirth.

But there is scarcely any laughter in their life anymore.

Now he says, "I was so sure it was a butterfly collector: it looked just like a butterfly from the bus, and the boy was tall enough to be mistaken for a grown man." He indicates the direction he has come from: "There is a group of them—young boys. Some are fishing, using rods and reels. Some swimming."

Standing under the cherry tree, she wonders whether she should broach the subject of the two boys, and then says, "I couldn't bear to see him all stitched up—those black knots were like spiders poking out of his face. All those bandages and that arm in the sling."

"Even the other one looked thinner." He nods after a while.

"He said, 'The year is getting hotter and I can *smell* the mangoes ripening over there in Pakistan—even from behind all these doors, each with a padlock on it weighing a kilogram.' "

"They miss your cooking. 'You should have this recipe printed in a newspaper,' they'd say after every other meal." He touches her gently on the arm. "They'll regain their health once they are acquitted in December and we bring them home."

She raises her bowed head, looks him squarely in the face for a moment, and then looks away in the direction the bus will come. After a silence she says, "On the bus, just before you told me about the person chasing the tangerine butterfly, I saw a tree with only one long branch in flower. The rest of the crown was dry, leafless. And I remember being told once about the grave of a pious man, how the branches of the tree directly above it continued to flourish, supplying it with shade, even though the rest of the tree had withered and was tinder dry. On seeing the tree from the bus I had the urge to get off and open the earth under that flowering branch, to see if . . . if . . ."

"You mustn't think like that." He looks at his golden wristwatch, comes out from under the cherry tree and moves closer to the edge of the road, where the pillar designating this point a bus-stop is planted.

"It's hard to know what to think. A person can go insane at times. I haven't told you this but when that woman from Bihzad Lane returned from Pakistan and said Jugnu was seen in Lahore, I madly approached Shamas to tell him that."

"When?" he is astonished. "Why?"

"Don't be angry. At dawn one day."

"That was just a rumour, people gossiping. What did he say, and what did you hope to accomplish?"

"I have admitted that I acted madly, and I have asked you not to be angry—so don't give me that look. I wanted my sons out of jail—and with good reason too: look what has happened to one of them! The day before I approached Shamas I'd heard that there were 1500 suicides in prison last year, and I had panicked, my mind in turmoil. I thought Chanda and Jugnu had sold their passports to another couple and decided to stay behind in Pakistan. It was all staged: that other couple came to England and left the luggage and passports in the house and then disappeared. I lie awake at night and the night makes you think up strange things. I set out of the house at dawn one day to look for Shamas, knowing he goes to town to get the newspapers."

"He must think our whole family is unhinged." He throws up his hands, too amazed by where the story leads.

"I *said* I didn't know what I was thinking." Her voice carries the hint of a sob.

He looks at her with a kind smile after a few moments. "I'm sorry. It's hard to know what to think. Earlier, I thought I heard a parakeet's cry!"

"You did," she replies after a while. "I heard it too. They say there's a flock of them out here. And it's thriving. There is a fear that they'll soon be everywhere. Such a harsh voice." She joins him at the edge of the road for a while and then they both return to the cherry tree, to its dead litter of pink-brown petals.

"If only she had a grave, I'd plant tulips all around her," she says quietly.

"Tulips are blessed. Their Urdu and Persian name—*lalah*—has exactly the same letters as His name—Allah."

She looks at him and sees the tears in his eyes.

"Why are you . . . ? No, don't . . . ," she manages to say.

He covers his eyes with his wrist.

"Don't cry." They have both deteriorated over the past years, as though the leavers had taken something of their life with them when they left.

"You think I have a heart of stone, that I wasn't terrified when I saw the extent of his injuries. And I couldn't believe what you said to them, that they must tell you the truth about what happened to Chanda and Jugnu. 'Your father won't tell me the truth so you must.' " He shakes his head. "I know you think I've hidden something from you, that I know what happened to Chanda."

"I don't think that," she says quietly, from the other side of a dark forest of suspicion that lies between them.

"What has happened to you has happened to me too. I swear to you on my salvation and the verity of Islam . . . I want my daughter back, and I want my sons back."

"I don't know what to think, but I don't doubt you. I won't doubt you if that's what you're asking me to do."

"You mean, if I didn't ask you to, you would think me capable of deceiving you? So up until a moment ago I was . . . in your eyes . . . *involved* in whatever it was that happened? The only thing I have kept from you is my grief so as not to upset you." He looks up at her with eyes that are round as sea pebbles. He presses the handkerchief to them and gives a little laugh: "Scoundrel tears! We'd heard the English were courageous Empire-builders, but even some of them burst into tears when they lost the World Cup five years ago. Smith did, and I think Stewart also. And the Pakistani players cried because they had won."

"No, I don't know what to think anymore," she says quietly. "May Allah forgive me, but I've even caught myself thinking it was unimportant that they were living in sin, so what if it goes against His law, that if I could do it all again I wouldn't break all ties with her over this matter. As I was passing by the marriage registry office one day last year I looked at the list of upcoming weddings on the notice-board and saw that one Pakistani girl was going to marry a white boy, and just for a moment I said to myself our girls are doing all sorts of things these days, so what if my Chanda was living in sin." Her face pale, she is shaking rigidly, a dead light in her grey-and-caramel eyes. "How do I know they will be safe in prison from now on?" A Pakistani teenager, twelve hours away from having completed a three-month sentence, was found dead in his cell last week: a white inmate has been charged with his murder. His parents were given the news of the death as they planned a welcome-home party. "Twenty black people died in police custody last year."

"Another bus should have come along by now." He is suddenly aware that they are on the outskirts of the town, alone and exposed, in an unfamiliar place—away from their neighbourhood. Women walk close to their men in other parts of Dasht-e-Tanhaii but allow themselves to dawdle on entering the familiar streets of their own neighbourhoods, falling behind without care. Although even there he had witnessed—just two days ago—two white men shout loudly and repeatedly, *Sieg Heil!* as they walked by a group of women and children outside the shop. He looks at her: "How do you know about the number of black deaths in police custody?"

"I happened to hear it on the radio."

They fall silent, both of them entangled in the same fear. But then she is suddenly visited by inspiration: "We should have them transferred to another prison. We'll ask Shamas-brother-ji to help arrange it."

He shakes his head, astonished.

"Yes. He's a good man. He'll help us. I'll talk to him myself," she says animatedly, and looks in the direction where her husband had seen Shamas earlier: "I'll talk to him right now! I won't let my sons be in danger longer than they have to."

She looks as though she's about to set out to look for Shamas. He grabs her by the upper arm. "No."

"He'll tell us which forms to fill, where to go, who to see. We don't understand the procedures, and with our lack of proper English we'll probably make mistakes filling up the forms, causing useless delays."

"No. I know we have to find a way to ensure their safety—I am not blind, I saw how badly beaten up he was. But you are not approaching Shamas again. Just *think* about what you are saying!"

She nods, defeated, so that he releases her arm. She inhales deeply to compose herself. "I wanted to ask my sons so many things today but my English isn't very good. That prison guard kept telling me not to talk to them in 'Paki language' each time I felt like saying what I truly feel. 'Speak English or shut up,' he said."

"Your English is better than mine," he says.

She waves a hand dismissively. Dressed in blue, she stands under the cherry tree with him beside her: the immortal rocks and boulders watch them from across the road.

She smiles. "Yes, in a month, when the mangoes begin arriving, we'll see if we are allowed to take some to them. Brazilian mangoes are available now but I don't get any music out of them." Plum-stone, peach-stone, apricot-, mango-, cherry-: when the children were younger, each year at the beginning of autumn when she cut back the rosebush that grew in the corner under that window she found a heap of soft-fruit stones they had dropped there from above during the summer, the earth directly below the two boys' bedroom.

Seeing that he hasn't said anything in response, she places her hand on his shoulder. "You mustn't let your heart ache too much. Let's trust Him to help us out of this predicament."

Where are you? You don't even have the safety of a grave, lying somewhere exposed to the wind and the rain and the sun and snow.

The sons say they didn't do it but they are certainly said to have boasted of it. One said, "I'll admit to anyone that I did it while wearing a T-shirt saying I did it with a picture showing me doing it." And the other that, "They were sinners and Allah used me as a sword against them." Chanda's mother wants to go into their souls with a lighted lamp to look for the truth. People say they admitted to having done it, but people also say a lot of other things.

"The bus is here."

Though the sky here is a taut blue now, it must be raining some-where in that direction because the vehicle is wet. Climbing aboard, they exchange greetings with the Pakistani driver, pay, and take their seats. The group of boys that had been fishing on the riverbank up the road are occupying the back seats, giggling and talking noisily in a huddle, smelling of grass and mud and moss, rods and hoop-nets leaning at various angles between them. Chanda's father knows the reason for their noise and the laughter they are trying to suppress but failing to, the shoulders shuddering like someone operating a road drill: they are looking at the torn pages of a pornographic magazine they had found scattered on the bank, assembling or rotating the pages, tilting their heads. They were looking at them earlier when he had walked up to them, and what he had mistaken for a butterfly was not a paper aeroplane—as he had claimed to his wife on returning to her, having backed away from the boys in shock and embarrassment—but a coloured scrap from a page that the wind had snatched from a hand.

The bus driver lives not far from the shop; his wife had told Chanda's mother that Chanda's father had said to him his daughter had died for him the day she moved in with Jugnu, that he would allow no sinner near him were she hundred-fold his daughter, that she—shameless baggage—may have gone missing but she was not missing from *his* home, and that he was proud of his boys for what they had done. She has not confronted him with this. The neighbourhood is a place of Byzantine intrigue and emotional espionage, where when two people stop to talk on the street their tongues are like the two halves of a scissor coming together, cutting reputations and good names to shreds. And so it is possible that the bus driver had lied, that his wife had, and also that Chanda's father had actually said those words or something similar, helplessly, to save face in judgemental or belligerent company, implied these words with expressions or uttered them explicitly with the tongue, feeling himself encircled; "Yes, yes, what had to be done was done. Now leave me in peace."

There are times in this life when a person must do or say things he doesn't want to. Human beings and chains, it is the oldest acquaintanceship in the world.

She rubs the glass of the window, and it seems to him that she is trying to erase the outside world. He begins to read the Urdu newspaper, and therefore they are both occupied when the bus stops and two new passengers come on board and begin to make their way to the upper deck.

"That was Shamas!" Chanda's mother whispers, tugging at her husband's sleeve. "And there *was* a woman with him!"

He lowers the paper. "Where? Do you think it could be one of his secretaries. A white woman?"

"No: one of ours. The very one you must've seen. What would he be doing out here with his secretary? They've gone upstairs. She was wearing a Kashmiri jacket, and he was holding a green feather. Looked like a parakeet's."

"Are all the sons of that family like that—defying conventions, doing what they please?" Chanda's father says with quiet indignation. "They can do what they like with white women—we all know the morals *they* have—but at least leave our own women alone. You would think it was their mission to corrupt every Pakistani woman they come across." And he adds decisively, "In my opinion they are still infected with their father's Hinduism. *Lord* Krishna and his thousand girlfriends, indeed! And they jeer at our Prophet, peace be upon him, for having just nine wives!"

She sighs: "Maybe we are both mistaken. May Allah forgive me for thinking badly of others. Perhaps they were not together. I didn't see any contact between them; did you, earlier?"

He shakes his head in a quick no, because he is still angry: "I am not sure I would accept his help even if he offered it. His brother corrupted my daughter! All this mess—it's their fault."

The bus stops after twenty minutes and the driver, leaning out of his seat, asks the young anglers at the back to disembark. The amount they paid on boarding doesn't buy them the distance beyond this stop.

Every other passenger looks back briefly, including the man who had got up to leave at this stop.

With their riverbank-odour of moss, soil, young leaves, and the smell of the river water in which two of them had been swimming earlier, all five of the children have fallen silent and are frozen in the attitudes in which they had been caught by the driver's demand.

The driver unbolts the little metal door next to his seat and comes out into the aisle that is littered with used tickets bearing marks of footprints, like cancelled stamps on a letter. "Get out, please, or give more money if you want to go more. I remember how much you paid."

The boys, their clothes a fruit-bowl of colours, protest ecstatically and state their destination. They are testing life to see what they can get away with, and how.

"Show tickets, please." He walks past the man standing before the open door and goes down the aisle towards them, their voices becoming louder. The stationary vehicle is slashed by the sun's rays and it is like being inside a diamond.

The tickets are produced and he is right: "Please give 25p more, each. *Haram-khor!* No, no, then out please! You make trouble for me. Or 25p more, each. I ask nicely. *Behen chod.*" All six are speaking at once and it is an equally matched quarrel: each side finding a fitting arrow to return to the other's accusation.

"Oi!" The man standing at the front of the bus shouts, startling everyone. "Oi, Gupta, or whatever it is you call yourself, Abdul-Patel. Mr. Illegal Immigrant–Asylum Seeker! Get back into your seat."

The driver looks back, stunned. The boys' protests fall to a murmur, their exuberance sinking like suds.

"Get back now. Come on, quickly," he points to the driver's seat and jerks his finger as when an adult orders a child. "Stop wasting everyone's time."

"But, please, I lose my job if inspector comes suddenly now . . . ," he wheedles. "Each need to pay 25p more after this stop . . . please . . ."

"Come here."

Whipped, the driver takes a few steps. "I lose my job . . . They make trouble for me . . ."

They look at each other, a border lying between them.

"*I'*ll pay you—here—how much?" He opens his wallet. "Come here, I said."

The driver returns to his seat without another word, is paid, and the man gets out ostentatiously after saying, "Show us some respect. This is our country, not yours."

The white passengers continue to look out of the windows. Chanda's mother's heart bangs hard and painfully against her chest. Her face and, inside her clothing, her body is burning, her blood flooded with heat.

"I hope the driver won't take his humiliation out at home later today," says Chanda's mother as the bus moves on, "lashing out at his *own* children, and the wife." But the bus suddenly halts now on the side of the road and the driver comes out once again into the aisle, avoiding the eyes of the passengers. He opens the door and goes out. One minute, two, three, four and then five pass, the passengers becoming restless, and then a few of them get up to go to the front and notice that the man is sitting by the roadside, on a rock beside a flowering shrub, with his head in his hands. There are several quiet "Excuse me"s to attract his attention but he won't look up.

No one knows what to do. "Please come in, dear," a white woman tentatively sticks her head out of the door and says, but he does not respond. She stands with her hand pressed to her mouth, and then Chanda's parents watch as Shamas comes downstairs with a puzzled look on his face, still holding that bright green feather. He goes out and they watch him talk to the driver and a few minutes later the man comes back in. "There *is* something you can do about it. Report it to your superiors," he tells the driver in Punjabi. "Report it and then ask them to begin a record of racial incidents on the buses, racial abuse towards drivers. Come to my office tomorrow. We'll also take up the matter with them." The man nods and gets back behind the wheel.

Shamas glances at the other passengers and then he goes back upstairs.

"Do you think he saw us?" Chanda's mother asks.

"That woman in the paisley jacket was standing in the stairs, waiting for him. But it could be just another anxious passenger. No?"

She assents with a nod, "I suppose." The bus resumes its journey. Neither says anything during the many minutes it takes for the bus to arrive at the ring road around the town centre, the vehicle's turnings and movements jolting the passengers lightly like bottles in a crate. The little anglers at the back begin to collect their nets and baskets and harp-stringed rods, and it is suddenly discovered amid much merry howling that the bait tin had been left half open.

It is the pearl hour of late afternoon, mildly radiant, and the bus passes the roads lined with shops on either side. The boys scented with the green-leafed world are walking on their haunches in the aisle, looking for the maggots between the passengers' shoes, grinning widely as though each holds a slice of melon before his face. Chanda's mother lifts her feet up with great anxiety, holding them away from the carrion-eating worms, kin to those who have fed on her dead daughter.

"I can't help wondering if something *is* going on upstairs," Chanda's father points up towards the metal ceiling.

"Don't," she shakes her head. "He's a good man. See how helpful he was to the driver? And I remember how polite he was towards me when I approached him with that harebrained idea that dawn." She looks at him. "Don't frown—I give you my word that I won't approach him again."

Chanda's father *is* frowning, has grown more thoughtful: *I thought Chanda and Jugnu had sold their passports to another couple and decided to stay behind in Pakistan . . .* But why couldn't it have happened? Why can't they persuade a couple to go to the police and say they entered Britain on Chanda and Jugnu's passports? But: he shakes his head—who would agree to do such a thing?

As he sits there the first few details of the subterfuge begin to fall into place: "*Oi, Gupta, or whatever it is you call yourself, Abdul-Patel. Mr. Illegal Immigrant–Asylum Seeker! Get back into your seat . . .*" Illegal immigrants! Couldn't they get a couple of illegal immigrants and pay them to go to the police with this story?

He turns to his wife: "You just said it was all a stupid idea about a fake Chanda and Jugnu coming to England and all that, but I don't think it is. Not really." Uncharacteristically demonstrative, he leans in closer to her. "I have been thinking. Why *can't* it have happened? Who's to say it didn't?"

"My Allah! Are you saying Jugnu and my Chanda are alive?"

"I don't know. But why can't we get a man and a woman to go to the police and say they entered Britain on the passports they had been sold by Chanda and Jugnu in Pakistan? No one at the airports checks to see that the photographs match."

"That is exactly what I said to Shamas."

"I think we can do this."

"Are you being serious?"

"Yes, of course."

"Who will agree to go to the police and say such a thing?"

"The country is full of illegal immigrants. We'll find a couple and pay them to do it." He is talking and thinking fast, the adrenaline coursing the veins. "The police would deport the couple, obviously, but I think they will be happy to go back to Pakistan if we pay them. We'll pretend we have other candidates available for the two vacancies so they won't ask too high a sum."

"That still doesn't explain where Chanda and Jugnu are."

"But the story proves that they were not killed by anyone in our family.

Why should Chanda's brothers be in jail if she cannot be located? It's not *their* fault."

Chanda's mother shakes her head. "It won't work. There are too many inconsistencies."

"Name one."

"Allah, you are being serious about this?" she says, aghast.

"Deadly serious."

"Chanda's ghost will never forgive us."

"Let's take care of the living first."

"Such heartlessness!" She bursts into tears. "Men! How can you say that about your daughter?"

He doesn't respond immediately, waits until she's exhausted her tears, her breathing beginning at last to stretch deeper. "I do have a heart," he says quietly. "I saw the wounds and the bandages on my son earlier today, and you yourself said we have to do something to ensure their safety, didn't you? I won't ask Shamas. So we have to do something ourselves."

She doesn't reply immediately, "They are my sons too." She sighs and then asks, "What if the fake couple agree to go to the police, and do go, but then later decide to tell the police that we had put them up to it? We could all go to jail. Conspiracy to pervert the course of justice."

He considers this for a few beats and then shakes his head: "We'll just deny it. It's their word against ours." He thinks about it and adds: "We'll pay only part of the sum to the couple to begin with. We'll give the rest only after they have done their work and are about to be deported."

"Or we could say they'll get the remainder of the money only in Pakistan—only once they have been sent back there."

He nods. "That's even better."

He has enough money in bundles of banknotes. The boys had been part of a group that had managed to smuggle in heroin from Pakistan some years ago, hidden in fruit and vegetables. No one in the family knew and when they had told him about it he had made them promise never to do it again. The boys' friends—one of whom owned a curry house—had set up a dummy company, importing seventy-four boxes of guavas and loquats and *jamun* and *shaftalu* and mulberries and *falsa* on one occasion, and forty-six on two others. Heroin with the street value of about £750,000 had been brought into the country but the boys had participated only on the first occasion—their job was to go to a motorway car-park, meet the man who had collected the boxes from the airport, and bring the boxes to Dasht-e-Tanhaii in their own van.

He says, "Just the other day a young man came to the mosque, saying he was an illegal immigrant from Pakistan and that he was looking for his brother who had come to England some years ago and hasn't been heard from since."

"Did he leave an address where he could be contacted?"

"No. He said the missing brother has a single hair of real gold amid the normal black ones on his head. But, no, he didn't leave an address. In any case, there are many others like him. We'll have to keep our eyes and ears open for similar people."

The vanilla-yellow and apple-green bus lurches and winds its way through the town centre towards its destination, stopping every now and again at the piano keys of a zebra crossing, its reflection passing across the glass of shop windows the size of cinema screens, and they sit wordlessly side by side, their faint reflections out there making them feel they lack the quality of presence.

She places her sun-sheathed hand on top of his, very tenderly, and rests it there for a while. Whatever has happened to her has happened to him too.

When the passengers begin to disembark at the station, they both remain seated as though dazed. "Her soul will never forgive us," she says quietly. And then they watch as Shamas comes down, on his own, followed by three other passengers. "We were obviously mistaken," Chanda's mother says. "He and the woman were not together." The woman is the last passenger to come down from the upper deck.

"Did you see how beautiful she was," Chanda's mother whispers as she gets up to leave. "Allah, she was like a houri."

Lost in their own thoughts, neither of them had noticed that at the end of the journey it was *Suraya* who was holding the bright-green parakeet feather.

The Dance of the Wounded

It's the task of insects to pollinate flowers. But Shamas remembers being told about a rare plant that is found only on a remote hilly island, and how soft paintbrushes are employed to collect and transfer its pollen from flower to flower: the insect that had performed that function until quite recently has become extinct—an insect unknown to man. It is agreed that the plant couldn't have survived through the ages without the now-missing insect. No one knows what it was. The flowers are the only indicator that it must have existed until quite recently.

They are like flowers placed on a grave, mourning an absence.

As the late-May evening darkens towards night, he, walking towards the lake, takes in the rich fragrance hanging about the roaming inflorescences of a buddleia, the whir of a moth reaching him from somewhere inside the grey-green foliage like a burst from a sewing machine.

The hazy perfume decides to accompany him for a few steps while, above, the moon drifts companionless. Since meeting her at the *Safeena* that afternoon in early May he has seen and talked to Suraya a further five times, never arranging the next occasion too definitely or firmly, and never knowing if she would come but always expecting that she would.

They have remained formal, almost shy, and there hasn't been even an instant's physical contact, because between them lies a glass bridge. So far there have been no consequences and therefore, at times, he finds it difficult to believe in the reality of the entire matter. He has read somewhere that, although the constant stimuli of daytime experience keep us from noticing it, we are dreaming at low levels all the time.

Each time he has met Suraya his sense of betrayal towards Kaukab has been stronger than before. *It is not as though I am leaving her:* he had tried to reason with himself early on; but he is too old to be deceived by an argument as feeble as that: he *is* leaving her—he's just not moving out of the house. Each journey towards Suraya has required a lion's heart, and he has tried not to think about Kaukab's reaction if she ever finds out.

The moon is still quite low and the junk shop is stuffed to capacity with its dusty reflections, one hanging in each peeling mildewed mirror. Stars and a number of constellations are visible in the darker parts of the sky, and looking up he remembers that the powdery galaxies are supposed to be the dust raised by Muhammad's winged mount as it carried him to the heavens for an audience with Allah on his Night Journey. He steps over the crooked transparent vein of a small stream. He is walking towards the cluster of large and costly lakeside houses where flowers bloom by the hundred and the unopened frond tips of the giant ferns look like fists of red-haired gorillas.

The family in one of the houses is descended from a holy man in the Faisalabad region of Pakistan. Among the followers of the revered ancestor of the lakeside family had been the forefathers of the devotional singer Nusrat Fateh Ali Khan—the man referred to by one London critic as *the best and most-powerful singer in the world today,* and by another as *one of the three or four truly sublime voices of the twentieth century—up there with Maria Callas and Umm-e Kulsum.*

Whenever he can, Nusrat attends the annual *urs* celebrations at the shrine near Faisalabad to humble himself before the ancient saint. The saint must have shown some kindness towards his ancestor, all those centuries ago, but no one can tell exactly what it was; nor is this specific detail relevant to Nusrat—you don't recall the taste of your mother's milk but that doesn't mean you didn't need or drink it at one time. It is also his way of honouring his own ancestors: if they thought the saint was worth venerating then their descendent is willing to trust them.

Nusrat's growing fame in the world has meant that he is in England this month, performing a number of concerts before flying to Los Angeles to record the soundtrack of a Hollywood movie. Immediately before that he was in Japan, filming a television special; this had coincided with the annual Faisalabad *urs* and, regretting that he could not attend the shrine this year, he has instead decided to visit the descendants of the saint during his stay in England.

Tonight—while the aspidistras in the dark gardens open their flowers so that they can be pollinated by snails and slugs—the awe-inspiring voice will perform its ecstatic songs in a white moonlit marquee behind the lakeside house, to an audience of all-comers. Suraya will be attending. And Kaukab.

He told Suraya about the concert during a brief encounter earlier today: the girl whom Shamas saw on the riverbank with her secret Hindu lover a few weeks ago—the young couple looking for the place where the disembodied human heart was found—has been beaten to death by the holy man brought in to rid her of djinns. While Shamas was at the house of the dead girl's parents earlier today, a house filled with mourners and people come to pay condolences, he had found himself alone in a room with Suraya for a few moments. Like everyone else she was dressed in the palest possible colours so as not to offend the dead and the bereaved with reminders of the joys of life, the joys the dead girl and those whom she has left behind will never now experience themselves. Suraya was looking for the roses and the jasmine blossoms. "They are to be added to the water to wash the body," she explained, and he had handed her the canvas bag full of crimson and white blossoms lying in a corner of the room, blossoms as bright as bee-eating birds. Here and there a small frail-winged insect clung to a petal with its gold-coloured legs. "I saw children picking them earlier from our front garden, blowing away the aphids, carefully picking up any petal or blossom they dropped on the ground," he said to her, "and I couldn't understand at first who had sent them or why." And then he had found himself telling her about Nusrat's recital tonight—his way of asking her whether she would come. She hurried out of the room, leaving him wondering whether the subject of songs and singing wasn't deemed inappropriate by her in the house where a funeral was being arranged. But he was anxious to see her again and hadn't meant any disrespect to the helpless girl who had died so brutally. She was killed during the exorcism arranged by the parents with her husband's approval. The holy man reassured the family that if reasonable force was used the girl would not be affected, only the djinn, and that there was no other way to drive out the malevolent spirit than by beating the body it had entered. The girl was taken into the cellar and the beatings lasted several days with the mother and father in the room directly above reading the Koran out loud. She was not fed or given water for the duration and wasn't allowed to fall asleep even for five minutes, and when she soiled herself she was taken upstairs to the bathroom by her mother to be cleaned and brought back down for the beating to continue. The holy man heated a metal tray until it was red hot and forced her to stand on it. It was obvious that she *was* possessed because she began to speak in Punjabi, her mother-tongue, which she had never spoken with her parents, the cunning djinn inside her realizing that the holy man could not speak English and could only be reasoned with in Punjabi, pleading for mercy.

According to the report in *The Afternoon* the coroner found the arms and legs broken by a cricket bat. The front of the chest had caved in as though she had been jumped on repeatedly.

His beard large enough for peacocks to nest in, the holy man has been arrested and will probably be sentenced to life imprisonment for murder, and the mother and father would perhaps receive a decade or so each for being accessory to the killing.

In the neighbourhood there are as many opinions about the death as there are mouths:

Amid the young: "I went to school with her and she was fine with us, her friends. She must've acted strangely only at home. And I too wouldn't be caught dead speaking my parents' language—even though I can."

Amid the old: "What kind of mother is she, hmm? What kind? How could she eat herself when the girl was going hungry? He beat her with a bicycle chain."

Amid those in the middle years: "These holy men are crooks, the kind who are aiding the white people to blacken Islam's name. I myself was exorcised and it was successful. Look how healthy I am now, while before I used to have terrible stomach pains and used to black out all the time."

Some of these Shamas heard today at the girl's house and during the burial, and some were told to him by Kaukab. Shamas has been careful to control his rage and grief when talking to her about the killing because he knows that Islam requires her to believe in djinns, in witchcraft, in spirits. She too has quietly preempted his objections, saying to herself earlier today but within his hearing, "*This* holy man was a charlatan or incompetent, and the diagnosis that the poor girl was possessed could have been wrong—but that doesn't mean there are no djinns. Allah created them out of fire—it's stated plainly in the Koran." Almost everyone in the neighbourhood believes in such things. Only today Kaukab said that, while she was at the shop buying hibiscus-flower oil for her hair, a woman had nervously approached her and, having casually opened the conversation by asking her if she knew a way of getting out eye-kohl stain from white linen, had asked whether her husband's name was Shamas: "The children are going around saying that in the lakeside woods a pair of sad ghosts wanders, luminous, like figures stepped down from a cinema screen, a man and woman, his hands and her stomach glowing more than the rest of their bodies." Kaukab and Shamas both know about this rumour, but now there is a new detail: "And they call out repeatedly and quietly to someone called Shamas without moving their lips."

The air is filled with the perfumed longueurs of an Urdu lyric as Suraya arrives at Nusrat Fateh Ali Khan's performance. Troubled and tender, Nusrat's voice is singing its moon song inside the glowing white-canvas enclosure on which the blue foliage moving in the warm breeze has draped its slurred shadow. Faces, alike as coins in their attentiveness, are turned towards him, the arena lit intimately with pale paper lanterns containing electric light-bulbs.

Suraya was getting ready to come here when her husband and son telephoned. While she was speaking to her boy he said, "You are wearing your gold earrings, aren't you, the ones Father says look good on you? I can hear them jingle." Yes, she was, and after telling him that he was a clever young man, she had taken them off, feeling she was betraying her husband by ornamenting herself for another man. But after the shocking news her husband gave her a few minutes later, she had decided to put them back on. Her mother-in-law is planning to find another bride for her husband. Suraya had almost screamed out in pain but then the old woman had come on the phone to tell her that a man needs a wife: "How long is he supposed to wait for you?"

The pendant earrings tinkle gently on her ears: she needs them, has adorned herself for Shamas. Apart from the encounter at the dead girl's house earlier today, the two of them have met several times since going out to see the flock of rose-ringed parakeets, and she has even persuaded him to recite fragments of his poetry, has brought her mother's old car back into use to be able to get to him more conveniently, and they have even had a small argument (about his irreverence towards Islam: "Whenever I said something that my mother perceived as contrary to Islam," she had told him, deeply shocked by his words, "she would respond: 'Speak softly! My Allah lives in my heart and He will hear you.' " And when he persisted with his reasonings she had snapped at him, deeply offended, telling him that the limited proofs and illusory understanding of this world couldn't cast a veil upon Allah: "The water's surface does not stop a plunge.") But she has been unable to decide what her next step should be.

Nusrat and his party of eight musicians are on a slightly raised dais at the front, the bright Persian carpet under them as intricately patterned as the foil around Easter eggs, the wool flashing its sapphire and lapis lazuli. The complexity of this music requires years of dedicated training and absolute coordination within the party as a whole, but the resulting melodies and rhythms are so immediately appealing that they are loved and memorized even by children—like Suraya's own son; and since children are always included in family outings and occasions in the Subcontinent—the concept of babysitters being alien—there are several of Nusrat's younger admirers here tonight, a four-year-old recognizing him upon entering the marquee and shouting to his mother, "Mummy: Nusrat! Look, there!"

Suraya's mother-in-law said: "He'll marry another woman now and when you are finally through your own difficulties he can marry you too. Islam allows him four wives."

"I won't tolerate another woman as a rival wife," Suraya had roared down the telephone. "As Allah is my witness, I'll kill her."

But isn't that what she will be asking Shamas's wife to do—share him with her, even if briefly?

Her hands shaking, she steels herself as she listens to Nusrat who is singing a love lyric, and when he comes to the word "you"—denoting the earthly beloved—he points to the sky with his index finger to indicate and include Allah in the love being felt and celebrated—a lover looking for the beloved represents the human soul looking for salvation.

Time is running out for her. She turns and searches for Shamas in the crowd: something (what?) must happen soon. Tonight.

What have you written under my name in the Book of Fates, my Allah?

Shamas locates Kaukab from where he stands at the back—she has made her own way here with a group of neighbourhood women—and then, with the same glance, he spots Suraya, shadowy in olive-green silk, poised as a cypress, the moonlight smiling in her glass bangles.

Nusrat is in the Thal desert of Southern Pakistan, a sandstorm raging about him, many centuries ago: he is the beautiful Sassi, the young woman who was born to a Brahmin priest but had been placed in a sandalwood box and floated down the Indus because the horoscope predicted she would bring disgrace to the family by marrying a Muslim; she was found by a Muslim washerwoman and raised as her daughter. Now, grown up, and become lost in the burning dimensionless Thal, she cries out to her beloved Punnu, looking for any sign of him as the howling gusts tear at her clothes. Punnu had mysteriously disappeared from her side during the night and she had set out to look for him . . .

The tips of the tabla-player's fingers are moving on the skin of his drum very fast like a skilled typist's on a keyboard.

The birth horoscope of Sassi had also said that her story would be told for many centuries to come.

She will die in the desert, but not before a single footprint left by Punnu's camel has provided some hope, the last sign of her beloved:

She pressed it to her breast.
Too often though, she feared to touch it
Lest it disappear.

She dies with her head resting on the crescent shape.

A girl in the audience, moved to tears, is weeping to herself as Nusrat sings in a pain-filled voice. Shamas recognizes her: according to Kaukab, she is married to a first cousin brought over from Pakistan, and their first child was born with one lung smaller than the other, while the second child has no diaphragm in his torso, and, in the sixth month of her third pregnancy, she has recently learnt that the foetus has failed to develop ears; she has to have a scan every day. As she weeps now she is, no doubt, asking the soul of the pious and ancient poet-saint—whose verses are being sung by Nusrat—to tell Allah to lessen her burden. *I speak to you, my brother in far generations . . .* The women hold her, striving to console, their faces on the whole more still and troubled than the men's.

Shamas can see Chanda's parents in the group of listeners, near the white globe of a lantern that is being circled by a yellow-bodied Large Emerald moth. He must avoid eye contact with them. The Large Emerald alights and begins to skim scuff flutter along the upper slope of the white sphere, and, coming to the round opening at the top, it drops down into the lantern like someone throwing himself into the mouth of a volcano. Shamas has heard that one of Chanda and Jugnu's murderers has been attacked in the prison; and for some days now he has been expecting Chanda's parents to approach him, needing help to have their son moved to another prison. They cannot speak English themselves and are among the many people who require Shamas's help and advice every day in negotiating a path through their life in England. At his office he and his staff have to explain various procedures to men and women who are unemployable in two languages, loathed in several, who know no English or are too intimidated to walk up to someone white-skinned for help.

But they haven't approached him yet. Perhaps their daughter-in-law is an English speaker and has taken charge of matters? Nevertheless, he must let it be known, through Kaukab, that Chanda's family are welcome at the office any time they need assistance. A curl of smoke is issuing from within the lantern where the yellow-bodied moth has obviously been incinerated by the burning bulb. He needs to sit down—the idea that he has to help the two murderers! But he must: he must let Chanda's parents know that they shouldn't hesitate before asking for help. Nor is there any need to approach him directly if they don't want to. He doesn't *own* the office, he just works there.

There are flames in his breast. Like a jet of air from a bellows, each breath he takes fans the fire inside him. He needs comfort and looks around. He doesn't want to have to think about Chanda's brothers—

terror in his heart as he imagines the two lovers' last moments on earth. Earlier today, at the burial of the girl, he was told by someone that human remains were found outside the church in the town centre by road-digging labourers yesterday. The news was to Shamas's skull as axe to wood. But he has since learned that it was probably a very old grave. If the bones are less than seventy years old the police are required by law to investigate how the person died.

He stands listening to the music. People are jubilantly throwing double handfuls of banknotes at Nusrat as he sings. A young woman gets up and, dancing there and back, goes to place a rose in Nusrat's lap; her open movements of pleasure are seen by some as a lack of womanly restraint and they win her disapproving looks from a number of people in the audience, male and female.

Shamas's gaze—running past three teenaged boys whirling slowly in one corner, their arms entangled in the soft antlers of smoke rising from incense sticks, their mirrored caps glittering in the pale light—finds Suraya in the seated crowd of women. He notices with consternation that a number of other men are looking at her every few moments, taken by her beauty.

Suddenly the amount of light in the place increases, as when lightning flashes during the day: she turns around to meet his eye briefly.

Nusrat's voice has now become the fabled Heer. Given in marriage to a man she doesn't love, she is inexplicably feeling drawn to the wandering ash-smeared mendicant who has appeared at the door asking for alms. She doesn't yet know that it's her beloved Ranjha, the flute-playing cowherd. *Don't anybody call me Heer,* says Nusrat-Heer in a pining tone, *call me Ranjha, for I have spoken his name so many times during this separation that I am become him . . .* Her brothers—in collusion with the rest of the family, and the corrupt holy man of the mosque—are going to poison her eventually for abandoning her husband for Ranjha. She would condemn them with her last breaths, the poet-saints of Islam expressing their loathing of power and injustice always through female protagonists in their verse romances: Heer didn't consent to her marriage to the man she didn't love—refused to say "yes, I do"—but the mullah conducting the ceremony had been bribed by her family and he said that he had seen her give a nod, and that that was sufficient as a sign of her consent. In their turn these verses of the saints—because they advocated a direct commu-nion with Allah, bypassing the mosques—were denounced by the ortho-dox clerics, so much so that when the poet Bulleh Shah died the clerics refused to give him a burial, leaving the body out in the blazing sun until hundreds of his enraged admirers pushed the holy men aside and buried him themselves. Even today the Sufis are referred to as "the opposition party of Islam." And always always it was the vulnerability of women that was used by the poet-saints to portray the intolerance and oppression of their times: in their verses the women rebel and try bravely to face all opposition. They—more than the men—attempt to make a new world. And, in every poem and every story, they fail. But by striving they become part of the universal story of human hope—Sassi succumbed to the piti-less desert but died with her face pressed to the last sign of her lover.

Shamas watches as three women in the audience—one of them carry-ing a half-asleep child holding a doll with a moustache drawn on in biro—get up and leave the gathering: they belong to a sect that forbids this music and devotional singing, but since their disapproving husbands are restaurant waiters and wouldn't have been home until after two a.m. they had decided to come to see Nusrat; they have obviously lost their nerve and are returning early.

Kaukab had arrived with the three women in their car, and, with a glance and a raised hand towards Shamas, is leaving with them. He catches up to her—out in the narrow street with its cattle-like crowding of parked cars—to say that if she wishes to stay she should, that he will arrange for someone to take her home later, but she says she would prefer to leave with her friends; the strong perfume of the incense has given her a headache.

He needs to be with her, agitated and forlorn after his thoughts of death. As Kaukab stands next to him, her face partly averted, her demeanour guarded, he can tell she doesn't wish to be polluted by his breath: she tolerates, with melancholy weariness and faintly visible dis-gust, the glass of whisky he allows himself a few times a month.

He's alone as Kaukab drives away, alone under the stars that are nuclear explosions billions of miles above him. He watches as a shooting star tra-verses the night sky, reflected like the sweep of a razor in the paintwork of several metal roofs. According to Islam, when something important—

favourable or disastrous—is about to happen in the world, and Allah is arranging the final important details with the angels, Satan moves closer to the sky to eavesdrop: shooting stars are flaming rocks that are thrown at him to drive him away; and they therefore should be read as the imminence of a momentous occasion.

Inside, in the enclosure lit with parchment moons, Shamas positions himself for the first time tonight to bring Suraya into clear view, but—after their eyes have met and he has felt himself turning red as though fanned into flame by her presence, a smile beginning on his lips—he moves farther away: this is too exposed and public a place for them to get together. He imagines what any scandal would do to Kaukab. What the ideas of honour and shame and good reputation mean to the people of India, Pakistan and Bangladesh can be summed up by a Pakistani saying: He whom a taunt or jeer doesn't kill is probably immune to even swords.

Shamas feels a crushing loneliness—he feels old. Sixty-five this year, the grey hair on his head has outnumbered the black for nearly two decades now. And lately whenever he has awakened in the middle of the night and has lain there, awake and alone (Kaukab has slept in a separate bed for some years now), his whole being has filled up with a clean and intense pain: wrapped in private terror, he feels afraid at what's to come—the inevitable black abyss. Five years? Ten? His heart fragments at the thought. The headboard of the bed feels like a headstone at that hour and he doesn't know where he is except that he stands far from any friend. His eyes travail until his sight is sore and strained: his vision fails and he sees no new world in the vasts of the darkness. He knows humans are mere shadows across the face of time, stuff to fill graves. He feels he's walking along life's road with a thumb extended to hitch a ride on a hearse. And no one has ever reported looking into a grave and seeing a door to another world in one of its sides; in any case, if it exists nobody living may be said to have the key to it.

While the girl was being buried today, someone's raised voice had brought to a halt the shovelfuls of earth that were being thrown on top of the white-shrouded form lying in the pit: the news had been brought that the dead girl's fourteen-year-old sister had placed a letter within the folds of the shroud, a message of love for her departed elder sister to take into the next world. Since Islam forbade such a practice—nothing may be buried with the body—Shamas had watched with terror as the men climbed down into the grave and pushed aside the earth to uncover the body. They exposed the soiled shroud to the haze of the afternoon, while the air flowed a sad amber and the bees hovered noisily around the bouquets and wreaths of flowers that were lying around waiting to be placed on the filled grave. The funeral resumed only when the letter had been discovered. "Minions of Satan!" said some of the men through clenched teeth when everyone was walking away from the grave later: the letter wasn't from the dead girl's sister—it was from her secret infidel Hindu lover, who had persuaded one of the women who had bathed and prepared the corpse to secrete it into the shroud. "Women and infidels: minions of Satan both!" The letter was passed around, a whole page filled with neat handwriting: "Such filth—what would the angels have thought had they found this upon her person in the grave?"

> You, who have gone gathering the flowers of death,
> My heart's not I, I cannot teach my heart:
> It cries when I forget.

Shamas caught sight of these words before one of the grave robbers tore up the letter into several pieces and threw it into the lake like a handful of white blossoms—a garland stolen from the dead.

He must stop thinking about death. He needs to touch Suraya, her youth, the life in her, feel her living breath on his face. His eyes search for her now among the members of the audience, but he cannot locate her. Oh, cut off the beak of this bird that says . . . *beloved* . . . *beloved* . . . She is a believer and must feel that it's wrong for her to meet him: occasionally during their meetings he has seen a war raging in her expression, a wild internal disorder, the dinful strife of faith and disbelief.

He changes his position several times within the enclosure but has definitely lost her.

Outside, as he walks out of the marquee, past the roses' stare, the dark-blue night air is stroking the lake's surface, the ripples washed with moon's pale silver light. At dawn the reflections of the sunlit ripples would be projected on to the bellies of the birds that would fly above the lake. Where is she? He is walking away, along the moonlight and glinting water of the shore, Nusrat's voice becoming dimmer with each step, singing of wounded lovers, dancing proudly in the face of death and ruin. No clear path is available to him in the darkness and the trees creak like ships' masts around him. His knees touch past tall wild flowers and grasses as he walks on. Where did she go? Only occasionally does he find a curved path that lies like a dismembered limb almost concealed by the tender cirri and tendrils of growth. Like hurrying skateboarders all around him, gusts of wind arrive occasionally, swerving, landing, gambolling and taking off here and there, all weave and waver. He has arrived at the edge of the cemetery, the graves outlined by foot-high fences, scrolling delicately like musical stands. Isn't it in one of these dreaming clusters of trees that the two ghosts roam, calling out to him without opening their mouths?

He stops because there is movement nearby, and he hears his name being spoken.

"Shamas-uncle-ji."

The dead girl's lover steps out of the shadows ahead of him. "Uncle-ji, I am lost. Could you please guide me to her . . . to her . . . grave . . . her resting place." He's holding a bunch of orchids in his hands. "I'd like to give her these." He speaks softly in a voice that is wearing mourning clothes.

"I think I remember where it . . . she . . . is," Shamas says, having recovered. "Come this way."

"I watched the funeral from the trees so I thought I'd remember the location," the boy says, looking down at the flowers as he walks. "There are almost a thousand graves here but I knew how to find her when I came in the evening, thinking the funeral was over and there would be no one here, but a lot of women were visiting her at that time. I went away and now I am lost in the darkness."

Shamas nods. Women aren't allowed to be present at the burial, and must come to the cemetery later. The dead girl's sister had wanted to watch her being buried but she had been told that it was an impossibility. In her grief she would have rebelled—it was her first direct experience of death so she wasn't familiar with the rules that must be observed, and she would have thought that her great loss entitled her to break Allah's law—but it turned out that she was having her period: so they informed her that she couldn't go anyway because of that reason, because she was in an unclean state. Forbidden to touch the Koran, enter a mosque, pray, even prepare food according to certain sects—that she was impure and polluted during menstruation was something she had known for some time, something she had come to accept by now, her arguments against it fully exhausted. And so she had acquiesced, agreeing to visit the grave later.

"It's there," Shamas points to the mound where the wreaths and garlands are dying, furred with shadows. The boy takes a step towards it but stops. In the moonlit darkness his skin looks blue as Shamas's own must appear to him: the colour of Krishna, the god who multiplied himself a thousand times so he could be with the thousand maidens simultaneously in the night forest—and so all lovers are one. The boy shakes his head: "I don't really know which rules to observe at a Muslim grave-site. Earlier I thought Muslims burned candles on their graves because I saw a light flickering on her resting place but then it disappeared—it must be one of those fireflies that have been discovered hereabouts."

Muslims do burn lamps on graves and the moths they attract are said by some to be angels, the spirits of the departed by others, or lovers in disguise come to say prayers for their beloveds' souls. "Fireflies, here in England?"

The boy takes another tentative few steps, fearful of protocol. "Yes, there have always been rumours of their sighting in Dasht-e-Tanhaii, but last week they were confirmed."

Shamas waits until the boy has reached her and kneeled down, and then he withdraws. In Shamas's thoughts, the girl—during her last few days on earth—appears as the moon threatened by the dragons of the eclipse—surrounded by her criminally stupid parents and that monstrous holy man. He goes back the way he had come, and when he arrives back at where he'd met the boy he sees that there is a heart lying in his path, there, in a patch of moonlight falling from the foliage above, a heart sliced neatly into two halves: the two pieces are lying next to each other—the inner chambers are exposed in cross-section, curved and muscular. Shamas backs away when the two halves are suddenly and weakly illuminated as though from within. The red light colours the ground and only then does he see that they are two orchids fallen from the cluster the boy had been carrying. The firefly that had alighted on them has just given a pulse of light—it arcs into the air and vanishes, leaving behind a blinding smear on Shamas's retina, a long trail slow to fade. He picks up the two blossoms, looking around for other fireflies, remembering how he captured those luminous insects in his childhood and kept them in glass bottles topped with perforated caps to make lanterns that quivered like liquid. A mass of them moving in the distance after a monsoon shower: the points of light opened and slowly closed like mouths of fishes. The air would be alive with responsiveness, and he could see them even with his eyes closed: in the darkness they conferred a facial vision that the blind are said to possess—a trembling warm sense of something there, nearby.

Could the presence of fireflies be the origin of the stories about the two ghosts wandering in the lakeside woods? He sets out again carrying the blood-coloured orchids. And now he remembers how a few days after his father's death, all those years ago, he had one night found himself walking towards the Hindu temple where his father had set himself on fire. He remembers seeing a cluster of fireflies in the distance, there near the temple: the edges of leaves, or various sections of the insects' own wing beats, could be seen by the light, faintly. But then something made him frown—the creatures were standing still, unmoving, as though a spell had been cast over them. When he drew close and saw the cause of that stillness, the fright had sent him—a grown man—running through the darkness. He remembers the sight to this day: each of the hundred or so insects had been pierced onto the thorns of the tree that was home to the birds known as the "butcher birds" because they impaled their victims on to spikes to kill them or to eat later. The speared fireflies had been alive, in the process of dying.

No, no, he must resist these thoughts of death! He speeds up madly to make a way out of the cemetery, going along the paved paths between the graves, getting lost, needing a map of this labyrinth, a flaw in the net to burst through, this net made up of almost a thousand knots. He needs Suraya. His teeth are bared and ache with dryness as does his epiglottis. The faster he runs the louder the noise inside his chest as though being produced by a dynamo attached to his legs. The tips of thorns of various bushes break and become lodged in the weave of his clothing as he thrashes his way forward. Where has Suraya gone? He's back on the lake's edge where the sand-grains glitter because all impurities have been washed out of them by the waves' motion. The beautiful radiant-skinned girl is no more and the boy was wearing black clothes, black as the wisp of smoke that remains when a flame is snuffed out. And now suddenly he knows where Suraya is: his search has stopped being a search and become a journey. Taking the moon with him like a balloon on a string he is walking towards the *Safeena*, towards Scandal Point, a mile and a half away. He feels he's moving further and further away from death with each step he takes towards her, holding a broken heart in his hands, pushing aside the blue brocade-and-velvet of the foliage as he shortcuts through the trees and grasses, the wetness on his fingers and palms making him think that a bunch of overripe cherries must have burst in his hand when he gripped a low branch for balance in the darkness, but then he remembers that it's only May and that the fruit won't appear till August, and he realizes that the wetness on his palms and fingers must be the sap that the two flowers are releasing, and he continues, the passage through the vegetation now narrowing like the neck of a bottle, now widening to bring him at last to the stir-less vicinity of the *Safeena*. He can see no one.

The night awakens at the sound of her earrings.

She is here as he somehow knew she would be, waiting for him. Going past the reeds' thicket of knives, he walks into the black lozenge-shaped moon-shadow thrown by the *Safeena* and lets it close over him like water. In the darkness he gently wraps his left arm around her neck and lowers his mouth onto hers, his other hand letting go of the orchids so that they fall at her feet, and then this free hand sinks up to the wrist in the curls of her head, her skin giving off the scent of birch bark and almonds. Bright gnats of static electricity dance in her hair and he tries to prevent the pulsing world of fireflies from invading his mind. She struggles at first but then kisses him back and he leads her to the *Safeena*. She's life. The angel of mercy. A clock-tower strikes one somewhere far away and the fragrance she's wearing is an olfactory smear in the hot dry air. He is aware of the noisiness from her lungs and of the difficulty she is having breathing in an orderly manner. When Zeus came to lie with Alcmena he stretched the night to three times its length; and so he too now wishes for dawn not to arrive at the appointed time.

. . .

Up to her waist in the water, swaying with the coming and going of the buried giant's heartbeat, Suraya washes herself in the darkness. The reeds lick her skin as she weeps quietly, desperately cleaning herself between the legs, on her breasts. "My Allah, please forgive me for what I have done. O Compassionate and Merciful One, forgive my sins." She scoops up water and rubs her body hard and fast, recalling the details of her debauchery. From outside the *Safeena* had come the buzz of a night-flying bee while he touched her everywhere, sowing little fires on her skin, small detonations, and from the wallpaper the pairs of deer in their red flame-of-the-forest bowers turned their necks to look at them, their noses depicted by black heart shapes. On the snakes-and-ladders squares of a Sindhi rug, he kissed off the pale red orchid-sap that his hands had smeared on various places of her body when he helped her undress—the saliva a magical liquid erasing bruises from her body. He whispered, saying he was surprised that he was already familiar with her breathing when he placed his face against her body. "This small shadow that your earlobe casts on the side of your neck is also known to me." They lay side by side, adrift in a boat, borne along by their story. "I should open the window a little so that the three butterflies of *Madame Bovary* can fly out at dawn to feed on the nectar outside." "What?"

She weeps among the reeds, scrubbing herself, while he is asleep indoors. She told her husband over the telephone that she has a most-suitable candidate and that he and his mother should give her a few more weeks before deciding on a new marriage for him.

She has the urge to lie down in the black water and stop breathing but the prospect of her son—soon to be on the mercy of a stepmother?—gives her courage to remain living. She has asked her husband to let the boy come to England for a few weeks but he says he fears she won't let him return to Pakistan. "The laws in the West are favourable to women: the authorities will side with you and I won't be able to do anything." And Suraya knows that his suspicions have some basis in truth: if she could have possession of her boy, she would gladly live with the wound of having lost her husband. "Why don't you *both* come for a visit," she'd suggested not long ago. But he had developed an intense dislike of England during the two years he had spent here after their marriage. She had been lonely in Pakistan and had persuaded him to come and settle here. "This country may be rich but it is too different from ours," he'd declared finally. "We have to go back. A person can't do anything here that he can freely over there. A dog was asked by another why he was fleeing a rich household where they fed him meat every day. 'They feed me meat, yes, but I am not allowed to bark.' "

She pleads with Allah as she purifies herself. One day when she was a little girl, she had gone home from the mosque in tears, having just learned that the Prophet, peace be upon him, had said there would be more women in Hell than men. The girls had been chattering during the lesson and the cleric had threatened them with that information. Weeping, she told her mother that she no longer wished to be a Muslim. She consoled her and explained that the Prophet, peace be upon him, had indeed made that statement but that it had been made good humouredly: in a mosque, when the collections were being made, he had joked with the women who weren't giving up their jewels to feed the poor and finance the jihad against unbelievers. The moment he made that statement the women stood up and argued with him merrily. But now, amid the reeds, Suraya wonders whether her childhood cleric might not have been right all along: *We women are wicked.* She had resisted having to do what she had done with Shamas last night, but had she resisted hard enough? Perhaps she should have tried to find another way of resolving her difficulties rather than sinning? But there *is* no other way.

She shivers with terror as she weeps. The moon's age-old eye watches her from above, the midges flickering firmly in perfect silhouettes against it—the orbits are strong enough to not let the breeze blow the insects away. She washes her face and wonders if her crying had been heard in there. Shamas said last night that occasionally when she speaks the songbirds in her throat awaken and he can hear the voice that as a girl had sang the poetry of Wamaq Saleem, accompanying itself with a guitar and a peacock-feather plectrum. She can hear those songbirds when she cries now. She gathers up her hair, pulling off the damp locks that are gently pasted onto her shoulders, each leaving behind an impression of itself in cool skin, a sensory shadow in low temperature. The gusts and ripples of breeze can be heard murmuring in the night foliage around the jetty's xylophone.

There must be a jasmine creeper somewhere nearby because it has shed some flowers into the lake—with outspread fingers she sieves a few out of the water and only now sees that they are in fact small pieces of paper, covered on one side with writing that she is unable to read due to the lack of light. Someone's torn letter, perhaps.

She sits in the darkness and wonders what her next step should be. Tonight she gave him what he wanted and now she has to ask for something in return. He turned out to be a great sensualist, probing her gently with his tongue and hands so that she moaned in shame and humiliation (and once with pleasure). He was gentler than her husband, whose member had been so large that she frequently suffered from cystitis. Afterwards, as they lay beside each other, he slid his hand out from under her head and gave her a book of henna patterns to rest her head on: "Quite appropriate. Pillows filled with henna blossom are used to induce restful sleep."

She has taken the first step back towards her son, he who made her feel she was at the place that was the planet's navel whenever she was near him or with him, the place where the earth was connected to the sky, he who said last month that no one makes *zarda* the way he likes it, "the way you used to make it, Mother. Grandmother always puts too much raisins in and it's too gooey." She could see him waving his hand in indignation, his small faintly hairy forehead creased furiously. Suraya had tried not to laugh out loud. In order to pass on the correct recipe, she'd had her mother-in-law brought to the phone, that woman who perhaps even then was planning to find another "mother" for Suraya's boy. How she would like to cut off her grey rat's tail of a braid! She has always resented Suraya, that woman, jealous (perhaps like all mothers) because the wife can give her son the *only* thing she herself can't, is not allowed to give by law and by nature. How shocked she was when the day after the wedding she caught sight of Suraya's back: Suraya had had a flowering vine painted with henna along her spine for the wedding night, from the small of her back up to the spot between her shoulder-blades. Her strong and handsome husband had become excited beyond measure by the surprising detail during the night, but the old woman read it as a sign of decadence.

How many more times should she let Shamas touch her before revealing everything to him. Perhaps last night is already enough? He has told her about his brother and his girlfriend. Chanda too could not marry

Jugnu due to the laws about Islamic divorce and women. She wonders whether she should exploit that similarity: would it help her gain his sympathy more readily?

Of course, she was shocked that Chanda and Jugnu's life ended in murder, but she had been appalled when she heard that they had set up home outside wedlock, sinning openly—but she had hidden her real reaction from Shamas, not wishing to alienate or contradict him. She had kept only the thought of reuniting with her son in mind and let Shamas talk as he pleased, not that the thought of her boy is ever far from her, making life difficult for her. That first time at the *Safeena* when she was half-looking, half-pretending-to-look at the books of poetry she had come across a line of Kalidasa and had almost had the wind taken from her lungs. In the forest a doe was walking

Slowed by her suckling fawn.

The need to be with her son had resulted in the dazed brevity of the previous days when she cultivated Shamas's acquaintanceship, ignoring the shudder of doubt and dread, relying on a boldness that has resulted in her committing tonight's sin. Now, all her bravery has evaporated and nothing remains but guilt and shame, a feeling compounded by the night's darkness around her, a sense of disaster and doom.

Her head feels heavy as a jar full of pennies due to stress and lack of sleep as she looks out over the dark lake, the surface of the water moving placidly like a sheet of very heavy silk to the left of her. She can smell the wild flowers that grow nearby, the bee- and beetle-filled wild-rosebushes the petals of whose flowers she as a small young girl would stick onto her finger-nails with spittle on the way to school to briefly give herself grown-up fingers. Earrings, necklaces, ribbons, perfume, lipstick. The young girls were learning to be women, to be false, teaching themselves to become the figures in men's dreams and fantasies. Now she realizes how lost she is at times because a dreamer isn't there. Well, they can all go to Hell. The only love worth striving for is her child's, her son's.

With a riot in every vein, she walks up to the *Safeena* and watches Shamas sleeping on the floor; the two orchids he'd been carrying when he arrived—a gift for her, obviously—are set beside his head, their ruffled edges aglow: he had dropped them outside but had gone out an hour later to retrieve them, one miniature reflection of them shining in each of his eyes. There are beet-coloured almost-black marks on one of the orchids—injuries suffered by the petals when they were dropped, or when the fingers pressed too deeply on to the thin succulence.

He has told her that his father was a Hindu and the terrible persecution he suffered in Pakistan; and so she wonders whether, to gain his sympathy, she should tell him that at school she herself had fallen in love with a boy of another religion—a Sikh—and that her mother had taken her out of school. But now suddenly she is ashamed: *Such cold-blooded shrewdness, Suraya! What would Allah think?*—and she lets out a whimper in desperation. *But what am I supposed to do: become nothing more than his sex slave, and then when he tires of me, go and find another man so that* he *can pasture the black scorpions of his eyes on my nakedness?* But, no, no, she won't allow herself to exploit the horrific death of Shamas's father. He has mentioned something about his wife's brother wanting to marry a Sikh woman back in the 1950s, and it was obvious that his sympathies lay with the two lovers (she herself had, of course, approved of the actions taken by the young man's family: imagine, marrying a non-Muslim!); and so she decides that she should tell him about her own young Sikh love, and that her disgusted mother had taken her out of school and enrolled her into a girls-only Muslim school, the segregated school where daughters could be taught traditional values like modesty and submission. The headmistress—and founder—of the Muslim school lived in the outlying suburbs and drove to the poor neighbourhood every morning, having dropped off her own daughter at a private co-education school; the Muslim school wouldn't do for her girl but was good enough for "these" people. While her own daughter sang about the pussy cat that went to London to see the Queen, the girls at the Muslim school sang, *Fatima, Fatima, where have you been? I've been to the mosque with Nur-ud-Deen.*

Suraya had resented being sent to the Muslim girls' school, but that was just a young person's petulance, she knows now. She is glad her mother took her out of the co-education school and sent her to a place where they taught her to fear and love Allah, made her think of the afterlife—saved her soul.

Yes, she will tell him about the Sikh boy: it would be another layer of sympathy for Shamas to view her through. But, of course, she can always use the girl who was buried today: Shamas has told her how he had seen her in the company of a Hindu boy—a conversation about those two secret lovers can be easily steered towards Suraya's own forbidden love. And now once again she is ashamed and distressed at how she is having to exploit the dead to free herself from her predicament. She holds her head in her hands as she remembers that the exorcist had made the poor girl urinate on to an electric heater so that she fainted from the shock she received.

She realizes that a wet scrap of paper—obviously part of the torn letter she found bobbing on the water earlier—has been sticking to the side of her neck from when she washed herself in the lake: on the piece a whole sentence is legible, undissolved—

They say that the heart is the first organ to form and the last to die.

A clock's three strikes spread across the lake's surface like ripples. She should awaken him and drive him home. This much time away from home can just be explained—*a group of us men got together and ended up talking after Nusrat's performance*—but he cannot be away from home all night. She remembers how she used to lie awake at night when her husband went out drinking, every sound in the night making her think a ghost was about, that the djinns were abroad, or that he had arrived home intoxicated at last, each thought filling her with more dread than the last.

SUMMER

The Sunbird
and the Vine

"Jugnu?" was Kaukab's first thought when the telephone rang in the middle of the night, two nights ago, making her sit up in bed and feel for her slippers so she could go down into the pink room and pick up the receiver. She was already halfway down the stairs before Shamas could emerge groggily from the room he sleeps in. But there was nothing on the line except static, as though the call was from somewhere far away. She recognized it from the telephone calls to Pakistan. She insisted on staying by the phone—and kept Shamas with her too—in case it rang again, but it didn't.

But there it was again yesterday, in the afternoon this time, with Shamas at work and she on her own in the house. The first time there was that dry sand-like static for several seconds before the line went dead but the second time someone spoke, a man, saying incoherently—shouting almost—that, "I want you to stay away from my wife!" and "We may be divorced but she's still mine, you *behan chod*!" The man sounded drunk and so Kaukab had hung up. She was reluctant to enter the pink room when the telephone rang again about an hour later, but she had been unable to help herself eventually—*what if it's Jugnu? Ujala?* "Listen," the man sounded a little calmer now, "just marry her and divorce her as per her plan, but don't touch her, don't you dare lay a hand on her body. I know according to Islam she must properly perform her duties and obligations to her new husband before he divorces her, but you won't ask her to do that, will you?" Soon he worked himself into a rage again: "Don't even think about asking her to do her wifely duty before divorcing her.

211

Leave her honour intact. Make no mistake: I lived in England and have friends there and so I can easily have your bones broken, you *dalla*."

It was obviously a wrong number and she presented it to Shamas as that when he came home in the evening—he had made vague noises as he always does when she tells him about her day. She didn't tell him what the man said or that he was definitely drunk because she'd rather not admit to him that alcohol can be bought in a land as pure as Pakistan, that people there drink it too. He might see it as encouragement.

But it was he who answered the phone in the middle of the night last night and when she came down she found his face pale. He seemed as though he was about to pass out. He said, "It was nothing. Go back to sleep," when she asked him who it was, and so she had assumed it was white racists who sometimes ring up at odd hours to threaten Shamas because he works for the Community Relations Council and the Commission for Racial Equality.

Now Kaukab is walking towards Chanda's parents' shop. Could the call she received have been made by one of Chanda's former husbands, who—unaware that the couple has disappeared—is angry that Jugnu has become her lover? He made the call to Shamas and Kaukab's house because he thinks Jugnu still lives with his brother?

She'll have to ask Chanda's mother if one of her daughter's former husbands is still in love with her.

But what was all that about marrying and divorcing? And how did he get their telephone number?

She cannot remember the last time she had the courage to walk into Chanda Food & Convenience Store, and now too her determination dissolves, her steps growing slower as she nears the front door, and then she continues on along the road. She has heard about how one of the family's sons has been battered beyond recognition in jail—all thanks to her own brother-in-law—and she fears abuse if she goes into the shop now. But she also knows that earlier in the year Chanda's mother had approached Shamas to tell him of a possible sighting of Jugnu in Lahore: that encounter was perfectly civil, she reminds herself, so she needn't fear rudeness if she enters the shop. And of course Chanda's mother had greeted her politely five weeks ago when they found themselves standing next to each other at Nusrat's performance: they had remained there for a few moments—a little awkward, yes, but still—and Chanda's mother had told Kaukab that she and her husband had seen Shamas in the outlying hills not long ago, holding what looked like a rose-ringed parakeet feather. "Parakeets, here?" a woman within earshot had said, "Allah, how I miss those birds!" and Kaukab had seized on the opportunity to move away.

She remembered the comment four or five days later and asked Shamas about the feather but he said that Chanda's mother must be mistaken. Kaukab had agreed: "Her daughter's death has hit her very hard. I fear for her sanity at times." There are words to describe all kinds of bereaved people—widows, widowers, orphans—but none for a parent that has lost a child: it's a fate too terrible for even language to contemplate.

She builds up her resolve after twenty yards and begins to walk back. Should she go in?

Suraya, on her way to see Shamas, brings the car to a halt when she realizes that the shop she's approaching on her right is owned by the parents of Jugnu's dead girlfriend. Her curiosity roused, she sits in the parked car wondering whether she should go in. There is still enough time before her meeting with Shamas, who had called her unexpectedly this morning asking to see her.

She looks at the coming and going outside the shop. She has had to be intimate with Shamas a further six times since that night at the *Safeena* after Nusrat's performance. But she is becoming surer of the dividends. Two days ago she even told her husband the name of "the very promising candidate" she had earlier mentioned to him and his mother. He got her to give him the man's address so he could have him scrutinized by the people he used to know when he was in England. She hadn't wanted to give him that information but had relented after he asked for it repeatedly because she didn't want him to think she was being contrary or disobedient, lest he refuse to marry her again, or go ahead and marry some other woman that that mother of his is no doubt searching for even now.

She cranes towards the mirror to check her appearance. Belonging to a hairy race, she had her entire body waxed last week, and has also had electrolysis on her face; all this she had somewhat neglected over the past few months. Shamas says he finds talking to her a comfort and a delight, that beauty isn't what he wants in a woman; but, like all men, he is as muddle-headed as a child: what he means is that beauty *alone* is not what he wants—a woman must be intelligent *as well as* beautiful. An intelligent but plain woman won't do. And so Suraya has started to pay attention to her physical appearance. And, yes, it must be admitted that there are times when she enjoys his compliments concerning her beauty, a sense of well-being spreading over her for a while, before she is reminded of her adversity, of her husband, her son, her Allah.

A woman goes by her car for the second time in five minutes. Her hair is clumsily dyed at home and the parting in the middle shows the stains on the scalp.

The tumble of Suraya's own hair is gathered up at the nape of the neck by the narrow red-silk scarf that she dislikes; but she has it upon her each time she sees Shamas because it must remind him pleasantly of the first time they met, "the cares of all the world falling out of my hands," he'd joked during their last meeting, referring to the newspapers.

The interior of the car is filled with the heated scent that she has sprayed on her clothing and blue-purple veil, the colour of bluebells. She knows Shamas's daughter Mah-Jabin was sent to Pakistan to get married: she must have missed things about England when she was there, just as she, Suraya, had when she was in Pakistan; and so this afternoon she plans to use the colour of her veil as a segue into talking about her homesickness in Pakistan—aligning herself with his daughter in an effort to deepen his fondness. She had looked through her wardrobe carefully to find something that was the colour of bluebells, something that would lead to the necessary transition in the conversation.

She watches the women and children go in and out of the shop, the July sun burning. She knows by now how good a heart Shamas possesses. Not long ago, while talking about the neighbourhood, he seemed to shock himself by the desperation of most people's lives here, family life frequently reduced to nothing more than legalized brutality. He counted nineteen mentally ill people in his own street, the street book-ended on one side by a house where lives a middle-aged Sikh woman whose husband left her and their twenty-year-old Down's syndrome daughter and went back to Amritsar to marry a young woman of twenty-five, the wife saying, constantly, "May God keep the coffers of Queen Elizabeth filled to the brim, for she provides me and my daughter with food and housing. I don't care if she is holding on to our Koh-i-Noor diamond so tightly her knuckles are white!"; and on the other end, by the house occupied by the Sylhet family, whose mentally ill father has been missing for several years, and the once-proud factory-working mother is now devastated because the young son has walked out of university where he was training to be a doctor and has taken up radical Islam, grown a beard and proclaimed everything from democracy to shaving cream unIslamic.

Of course the matter of Chanda and Jugnu has filled Shamas's own house and his own life with grief.

He said—and she was filled with an immense love for him at that moment, fantasizing for a moment about being his wife forever—he said, "Did I do all I could to make sure those around me didn't come to any harm? Has there been a time when I failed to condemn the pernicious excesses of the wicked, the unjust, the exploiters, robustly enough in the past? Was I unaware of their lethal nature because I myself had not been unduly affected by them yet, the way I am now that Chanda and Jugnu have been murdered?" He read a line of Syed Aabid Ali Aabid,

Chaman tak aa gaee dewar-e-zindan, hum na kehtay thay.

I did *warn: the prison out there has been expanding slowly, and now its walls have almost reached your own garden.*

His melancholy voice singed her heart. And this is the good man around whom she has been made to weave her web of insincerity and chicanery?

Overcome by remorse, she sits in the car and wonders if she should get out—but now she thinks of her son, and, her resolve and conviction strengthened, decides that she probably *should* go in and walk around the shop, perhaps buy some material for a couple of new *shalwar-kameez*s. Surely from amid the bazaar-like hustle-and-bustle she could glean some information that she might be able to use?

.   .   .

After the *ting!* of the bell above the door has announced a customer's departure, Chanda's sister-in-law is alone in the shop. She looks out onto the street, watching as Shamas's wife goes by, surely for the third time this afternoon, but perhaps she's mistaken. The shop is as wide as it is deep, is the converted ground-floor of the house in the upper rooms of which the family lives. She can hear footsteps in the ceiling—her little daughters, and parents-in-law. The shop front—behind her—is almost all glass, and she casts an occasional glance over each shoulder to keep an eye on Kaukab. *If Allah let the dwellers of Paradise engage in trade, I should choose to trade in fabrics, for that was Abu Bakar the Sincere's profession*—reads the sign nailed to the wall above that fabric counter to the left of the sister-in-law, a saying of the Prophet Muhammad, peace be upon him. Here there are shelves loaded with bolts of cloth with a long counter under them and the floor is littered with sequins and glitter-dust that have come off the fabrics, swept by the feet into galaxies and milky ways. Colours and prints go in and out like the seasons in this part of the shop. Two scissors hang from strings like a pair of dead birds, upside-down, drained of blood. Rolls of cloth—each forty-five inches tall—lean against the counter, the loose edges of the materials trailing, like a queue of very thin and very tolerant women wearing saris.

The sister-in-law goes to the stairs and shouts up that it's time for the girls to have their lunch and get ready for the Koranic lesson at the mosque. "And don't forget you have been asked to bring £1 each for the fund for the Bosnian refugees." She returns to the counter, coming past the two waist-high freezers for packets of frozen foodstuffs, topped with Perspex roofs that slide open like the glass coffins of fairytales. Her parents-in-law have told her about the scheme to send a fake Chanda and Jugnu to the police in order to have the charges against Chanda's brothers dropped—and she is fully on board. When her father-in-law told her about his idea, the afternoon he and his wife returned from the visit to the prison, he mentioned that not long ago he had met a young man at the mosque who was going around looking for his brother, a boy with a strand of gold growing amid the hair on his head. "The last message the family got from the missing boy with the gold hair was from here in Dasht-e-Tanhaii, so this is where he is searching. If only I could bump into that young man again—he would be perfect," said Chanda's father that afternoon; and then, luckily, on the night of Nusrat Fateh Ali Khan's performance, they found him in the crowd, drunk, in despair because it's unlikely he'll ever find his brother. When Chanda's father approached him, he said, "Whenever the exiles talk of their homeland, tears well up in the morning's eye—that's what dewdrops are. It's a line, uncle-ji, from a song by Nusrat Fateh Ali Khan, a poem by Wamaq Saleem which Nusrat set to music." His pupils dilated, he was in no condition to talk, and so Chanda's father has asked for his address and gone to talk to him the following day. He has agreed to help Chanda's family with their subterfuge—being deported back to Pakistan by the police for being an illegal immigrant, but happy with the money the family will pay him. They have to be careful: no one must see him in their company—no one must think they have anything to do with the tale.

Once the family has found a girl they'll send them both to the police station. Finding a girl is proving more difficult. It's usually men who leave for other countries, being stronger, bolder, the world being slightly easier for them to negotiate than it is for women.

The shop's door opens. The child standing in front of the shop door, munching a just-bought bar of chocolate, his mouth and gums coated with sweet mud, is brushed aside by a group of women. "Who are you, the door man?" one says, and enters the shop without waiting to hear his "I am just waiting for that tower block on that hill in the distance to fall down—it's derelict and empty and is gonna be blown up this afternoon." The women are outraged that he has failed to apologize for obstructing them. But they dismiss him and enter, because: Children? Who is happy with their children? Who? A hand is waved in the air to challenge the others to produce an example from the whole world. "No one. That's who. Look at the poor Queen and what her children are doing to her."

"Dragging her through dirt is what they are doing to her, sister-ji."

"Dragging her by her *feet*."

"By her hair."

"Through dirt and through mud. And she a woman who rules the *country*."

"Making her a laughingstock."

There follows a few minutes of silence in which the flowers on the fabrics fume hot and angry at the irresponsibility of the young. And then the women spread out across the shop, between the rows of free-standing shelves that fill up the floor space, stopping instinctively to tidy up a row of fruitcakes that are yellow and full of dark raisins and sultanas which make them look like blocks cut out of leopards. Here and there, there are baskets of fruits and vegetables, apples with the red cheeks of Japanese babies, mangoes, guavas, foot-long sections of sugarcane imported from Pakistan, the few sticks perfuming this enclosed air the way the cane crop can perfume the air of an entire village when it ripens. Eggs are usually here, next to the fruit, but in summer they are moved elsewhere because otherwise the customers say their omelettes turn out to be papaya- and pineapple- and melon-flavoured.

Over the next half hour the shop becomes so busy—women arrive to be served at the fabric counter too—that Chanda's sister-in-law has to call her mother-in-law down for assistance, the customers asking each other about whether this deep red linen would suit my dark complexion, whether this shop stocks the print they saw Shamas's wife, Kaukab, wearing last week, whether this stripe-covered georgette was the same as the one they saw hanging on the washing line on Jinnah Road . . .

Suraya, examining a packet of Multani clay to be used as a face mask, looks up on hearing Shamas and Kaukab's names, and looks towards the fabric counter. The clay, from the Pakistani city of Multan, is also used to clean the marble façade of the Taj Mahal; she replaces it on the shelf and crosses over to the fabric counter and—while wondering why the woman behind it gives her a second glance as though she's trying to recognize or place her—points to the material that apparently Kaukab wears. She remembers being a girl and becoming extremely fond of a teacher at the Muslim school just because she saw her wearing the same print as her mother. Now she wonders whether at some deep level Shamas's affections would be roused on seeing her in the same material as his wife.

His wife when she was younger.

But couldn't it also remind him of Kaukab in another way: renewing his love and sending him back to her, repentant of his infidelity.

She looks at the fabric indecisively. He has told her about the sometimes-vague sometimes-sharp antagonisms within his marriage to Kaukab, and she hasn't let on that she's more on her side than his. She sounds like an Allah-fearing woman, and Suraya has begun to wonder whether she would eventually be able to appeal directly to her, reminding her that the Prophet, peace be upon him, had had more than one wife.

"It would look beautiful on your skin tone," the woman behind the counter—Chanda's mother?—says as she asks her to measure enough material for a *shalwar-kameez*.

"Thank you," she says as she takes her package and turns away, the shop suddenly noisy with children's toy spaceguns. These are imported from the East and their *bleeps* and *peows* are much louder than the ones that are manufactured here in England, deafeningly so.

A group of middle-aged women are already on to the life-intoxicated boys who are pulling the triggers of the spaceguns—and suddenly everything is markedly silent. Wearing wronged and martyred expressions, the boys are now brought to the relevant mother and made to stand still with threats and pinched looks.

She smiles. She'll tell Shamas about these boys this afternoon. She has noticed that he loves talking about his children's childhood, the things they did and said. He won't be drawn on the subject of them as young adults, or much on what they are doing now. It is clear to her that their growing up was a time of strain and tension for him: there must have been arguments with Kaukab about how they should be raised, so that now he prefers to think of them as young children.

When he mentioned that his elder son, Charag, was an artist, she had wondered whether he could be the same young man she had met beside the lake back in spring, but then he said that Charag doesn't live in Dasht-e-Tanhaii, and hasn't visited this year.

She moves among the shelves, elated by the sights and the smells, picking up small boxes and jars, mesmerized by the pink, the blue, the red, the green, the orange, the yellow, the silver, the gold, unscrewing and sniffing the small roll-on vials of perfume, sandalwood, saffron, jasmine, rose. It's like being a young girl again.

She suddenly wishes she had a little daughter—to dress up, to buy beads and dolls for.

In a state as close to bliss as she has been able to capture during the past few months, listening to the women's voices all around her, she finds herself melting into a sweet lethargy. One of the things she misses most about being in Pakistan is the company of her women friends and acquaintances, lying on the veranda under the ceiling fans and talking about inconsequential matters, laughing, trying on bangles from the dozens arrayed on the floor between them like the Olympics logo for a planet that has more continents than Earth does, contradicting each other (and their own selves too, saying, "My Allah, do we women ever know what we want!"), shrieking at double entendres and innuendoes, and making lewd remarks about husbands (how often, and how fast, and, praise be to Allah, how slow?) and fiancés and about other men of the area too (having caught glimpses of them walking by in the street, she remembers whispering to her friends about the breathtaking beauty of the men of the family with which her in-laws had the feud; the women had agreed and then, dying with laughter, someone said she'd heard one of those handsome god-like men urinate in an alley while she was nearby, and—Allah!—the sound had startled her: "After he was gone, I couldn't resist looking and saw that he'd made an enormous crater in the ground the way horses do").

Smiling, she looks around but is suddenly reminded of the fact that her mother-in-law—a woman not unlike these very ones—is scheming to destroy her life even now, the witch who had said on the phone that, "You didn't even produce a child until you were in your late twenties, and even then after thousands of rupees' worth of hormones and injections that we had to pay for, my poor son having to visit you in the hospital morning-noon-and-night after you had miscarriage after miscarriage." Suraya had wanted to shout, "I wasn't lounging about on the hospital bed just to spite you and your son, you crone. I had needles stuck in my arms every waking hour, and my groin was all bloody and butchered after the operations." But she had kept quiet lest the witch double her efforts to find a new wife for Suraya's husband.

"I'd heard England was a cold country but it's so hot today," says a young woman who's standing next to Suraya. She moves her bangles up her arm to scratch her wrist. She's wearing one of those lockets which contain miniature Korans a third the size of a matchbox.

Suraya smiles politely and makes a non-committal sound.

"It's my first summer here. I came from Pakistan last November."

"A cousin born here in England went back to get married to you?"

The young woman replaces on the shelf the tub of cream she's been examining. "I am not married. I came to England on my own." She lowers her voice. "I am an illegal immigrant."

Suraya nods.

"I need somewhere to live for a while. You don't know any place, do you?" The girl points over her shoulder, through the shop's glass front. "Do you see that tall tower block in the distance? It's completely empty so me and a friend broke in last night and are staying there. He's nineteen and is almost like a brother to me, reminds me of my own, in fact." Her eyes begin to smile at the mention of the boy. "And that impression has got stronger over the past few days because he has been very ill of late and I have to take care of him, the way I used to take care of my brother when my mother and me were trying to wean him off heroin."

Suraya looks at the distant tower—no bigger than the locket around the woman's neck—and nods.

"He was in pain all night and nodded off at dawn. I think it's TB. When I left he was fast asleep. I'll take home some fruit for him this evening." She turns and looks at the tower. The smile escapes from her eyes and settles on her lips like a butterfly.

Suraya says, "You could say that you are keeping an eye on him even from here."

The girl gives a small laugh. She opens the locket with its hinged lid and shows it to Suraya: hollow inside, it contains—instead of the usual Koran—four strands of gold. "The boy has a single gold hair amid the black ones on his head. He plucks it every other month and I collect it in the locket for safekeeping. It's real gold. We'll sell it when we have enough."

Suraya looks at her wristwatch. "I am afraid I have to go. You should ask the shopkeeper for help in finding you new accommodation."

She goes out to her car, towards her meeting with Shamas at the *Safeena*. She should try to remember a story about her son to tell to Shamas, some clever observation or humorous comment of his, to make sure it would endear him to Shamas, with the result that, when the time comes, he would feel sympathy and pity for him and then he would want to do anything he can to unite the child with his mother. Yes: this would do—last week he said that snails look like jelly that has come alive in its mould and is trying to escape.

She's hoping to take the servant girl in the house in Pakistan into her confidence, in order to ask her what her mother-in-law and husband are planning. Turn her into a spy. She should try to coax her on to the line the next time, promising her a gift or two from England, a pink cardigan with golden buttons, perhaps; or bright hair-grips shaped like strawberries, butterflies, daffodils, tartan bows; or high-heeled sandals with rhinestones on the straps.

She must protect her son (and herself) whichever way she can.

Chanda's sister-in-law puts into a plastic bag the tube of beauty lotion that a woman is buying—a Pakistani import. The lines on a man's hand foretell how many wives he will have—one, two, three or four—but according to the slogan on the tube, *It's not the lines on the palm of your husband's hand that indicate a second wife—it's the lines on your face.* The woman departs, counting the change she's been given.

"Are you going to sell those strawberries to me at a cheaper rate, sister-ji?" says a young girl approaching the counter, a beam of light from the window striking the locket around her neck to produce a prismatic flash. Chanda's sister-in-law is about to refuse politely when the girl continues in a low tone: "I am a poor illegal immigrant, sister-ji, and Allah will reward you for helping me."

Chanda's sister-in-law immediately smiles at the girl, but looks around too, because she mustn't be seen in the company of this young woman—she could prove suitable and their plan won't work if someone has witnessed them together. Luckily they are alone in the shop. "Help yourself." She points to the strawberries. "It's my duty to help you."

"Me and a man from Pakistan came and said to the people at the port in Dover that we were lovers and that our families wanted to kill us, because I had disgraced them by falling in love with him. We said we wanted asylum. They let us stay while our application was being processed. I ran away from the holding centre and have ended up here."

"What about your lover?" Chanda's sister-in-law's heart is beating fast—she might not want to go back to Pakistan without him.

The girl shakes her head. "Sister-ji! He wasn't my *lover*. I am a good Muslim. No matter what kind of predicament Allah has placed me in, I'll never compromise my honour. He was nothing to me: Love was a fiction the agent in Pakistan told us to tell the English authorities. He is still in the holding centre probably. I told him I was leaving—I left Pakistan to make money, not languish in a locked building. Here in England, I'll be able to make in ten years what it would have taken me forty years to make over there."

Chanda's sister nods. "Where are you living at the moment?"

The girls points out the tower through the glass window, the other hand playing with the locket around her neck.

Chanda's sister-in-law turns around but, on seeing that a customer is approaching the shop, quickly tells the girl to go to the fruit section. A whirlwind of plaits and scarves and balloons with *Freedom for Kashmir* printed on them, her daughters come down from upstairs, ready for the mosque.

She serves the customers, keeping an eye on the girl with the locket, and when the shop is empty again after five minutes she goes over to her, beside the basket of strawberries, a hairy leaf sticking out of the brilliant baubles here and there.

"You should not have left your country," she says to the girl, who raises her eyes briefly at her, chewing the corner of her mouth, but doesn't say anything. "Don't you miss it?"

The girl stops what she's doing, all life gone from her hands which she rests on the fruit, and then decides to speak her mind. "I shouldn't have left?" she says angrily. "You lot who have legal status in a rich country don't know how lucky you are!"

Chanda's sister-in-law is taken aback. "I am sorry, I just wondered whether you wanted to go back after making some money."

But the girl doesn't seem to be listening. She looks at Chanda's sister-in-law with fury. "You don't understand what things are like back there for most of us." One balloon had slipped from the hands of the little girls and is floating against the ceiling above them, slowly drifting. She gives it a contemptuous glance. "Freedom for Kashmir, indeed. Pakistan can't afford to feed the people it already has within its borders, and yet it wants more people, a bigger territory. The same goes for India of course."

"Someone was just handing those balloons out on the street," says Chanda's sister-in-law, trying to placate her. "And I didn't mean to offend you by what I said." She knows she must give the impression of agreeing with the girl's opinions. "Every other day there is news of a group of illegal immigrants meeting a disastrous end. Those bastard prime ministers and presidents and generals—both Indian and Pakistani—they should see what people have to go through to reach a place where they can earn a decent living. They should ask those people whether they want freedom in Kashmir or a chance to live with safety and with food in our bellies in their own country."

No longer enraged, the girl says quietly, "They should've seen how the group I was with came to this country, how we ran through snow, were fired on, across border after border after border, abused, slapped."

Chanda's sister-in-law takes the bag the girl has been filling and begins to add heaps of red strawberries into it. "You hear about such things every day—people wading through filthy sewers and flooded rivers, leaving dead or dying people behind on mountainsides to be picked at by crows and vultures." She leans closer: "Now listen, you are a Pakistani and so am I. It's my duty to help you. If you need anything . . ."

But the girl is staring past her shoulder with disbelief in her eyes. Chanda's sister-in-law turns around and the bag of strawberries falls from her hand as she watches the building collapse several miles away in the distance. With a soundless shout the girl pushes her away and begins to run towards the door. She shouts again, failing once again to produce noise, as though her words are unable to cut the air. She runs along the road that will take her to her destroyed home, the locket leaping around her neck. There are several people outside the shop and since some customers have also entered the premises, Chanda's sister-in-law cannot go after her, which would obviously hint at some connection between her and the girl. She watches her disappear from her life. She lets out a moan at the opportunity she has just lost.

"Now what *have* I come out for?" says the woman who is standing at the counter, thinking aloud. "I am so forgetful. If I don't lose more things it must be because my belongings have some determination of their own to stick by me." Her daughter—dressed in a sparkly orange frock, the colour of Irn-Bru—pulls at her veil and tells her she wants two ice-lollies, one strawberry, one lime, but is told to behave herself or she'll be given away to a white person who'll make her eat pork and drink alcohol and not *wash* her bottom after going to the toilet—forcing her to use *only* toilet paper. The child is disturbed by the horrors disobedience can lead to and agrees to accept only one lolly, moving towards one of the glass coffins and looking in, chin resting on the edge of the freezer.

Chanda's sister-in-law comes and stands behind the counter, smiles emptily at the customer. Presented with all the choices below the Perspex sheet, the customer's little girl forgets the white horrors and lifts two lollies out after all. The mother sees this and shouts: "If you don't behave, I'll not only give *you* away to the whites, I'll give away your brother too. They'd make sure he doesn't learn to drive when he grows up and has to sit in the passenger seat while *you* drive. Do you *want* a eunuch like that for a brother? House*husbands*, if you please! The mind boggles at the craziness of this race." Visibly disturbed, the girl shakes her head and puts the lime back. The mother, meanwhile, has spotted another example of bad upbringing: "Oi, you," she shouts at the boy wearing the green shirt of Pakistan's Cricket World Cup team, "I am talking to you, whoever you are. Yes, you, green. It is not a cupboard, it's a fridge. Decide what you want first and *then* open it." She shakes her head at Chanda's sister-in-law: "The way he was just standing there taking his time, the cut-price Imran Khan. You are too kind, sister-ji, letting them get away with murder." She narrows her eyes: "Just tell me it was him who scattered those strawberries on the floor over there and see how I teach him to clean up after himself, I don't care whose son he is."

"I'll clear that myself," Chanda's sister-in-law says quietly, unable to stop thinking about the lost girl. The leaves of the strawberry plants are hairy like grape foliage, reminding her of the vines that used to grow in her childhood home in Pakistan. Her father had planted them but her mother always complained of the leaves they dropped on her clean floor. When he fell ill she saw her chance and cut them down. She was halfway through when suddenly the courtyard was filled with about a dozen sunbirds, screeching and circling the fallen arbour. They had fed on the grapes and had probably made nests somewhere under the large leaves.

The girl with the locket had been like that minutes ago; you grieve in that manner only when your home is destroyed. In his room her father screamed and waved his hands in the air like birds above his bed but her mother kept axing and sawing.

The sister-in-law looks at the column of dust rising towards the sky in the distance, like a battle between djinns in the desert. *We'll find another suitable young woman*—she tells herself.

Cinnabar

Shamas waits for Suraya at the *Safeena*, the interior filled with the previous six-hours'-worth of midsummer heat and with the odour of paper and ink. Today was one of those hot days that are a reminder that the world is powered by the sun. But the first thunderstorm of the summer has begun, the raindrops coming down fast. It looks as though the heat and the sunlight would be scrolled up and put away for the next few hours, the shower washing away the constellation-like hopscotch grids that the children had drawn on the pavements.

He stands at the window and watches the Cinnabar moth that's sheltering against the pane on the other side; its forewings are the darkish brown of milk chocolate with markings in an arresting red, one of those vibrating shades that you can get drunk on by just looking, but the hind wings are entirely red. He remembers Jugnu smiling and saying the Cinnabar have been paying attention to the way Pakistani and Indian women dress: the upper body is covered with the *kameez*-shirt which is made of a fabric printed with designs—flowers, geometric shapes—while the *shalwar*-trousers single out one of the main colours of the *kameez*.

The rain sounds like the stridulating of grasshoppers. Bubbles— nothingness lightly wrapped around nothingness—dot the lake's surface out there. He blinks and now Suraya is running along the edge of the lake, her veil blowing about her, and she smiles at him as she spots him in the window, strands of her hair and the red-silk scarf rising up into the air behind her, the scarf that she must love so much, wearing it as she does all the time. The water and the afternoon sky and the stones visible in the shallower parts of the lake are all grey, blue-black, white, and in those shallow areas the mosses too look dark, those long emerald-green and slimy strands which trailed between the toes of his children like thongs of delicate sandals when they paddled in the water with the hems rolled up.

She lets out a surprised cry when he moves forward into the rain and takes her into his arms, the rain falling on them both. With a laugh she pulls away from his kiss and brings them both into the shelter of the *Safeena*, the world out there gleaming as though just finished and taken off the easel.

"I looked but couldn't find the gold Koh-i-Noor pencils that I said I'd get you so you could begin writing poetry again," she says, shaking water drops out of her hair.

But with quick speed he takes off her clothes, the dusty and stained lampshade filling the interior with yellowish candle-warm light, her skin the colour of paled jasmine. On her elbows on the snake-and-ladders rug, her lips married to his, she suddenly lets her head loll back away from him, disengaging their mouths, and he goes down past her navel to the pubis. His abruptness and speed make her release a sound of surprise and protest occasionally but then her breathing stills like a river and the pairs of deer in their red flame-of-the-forest bowers on the walls turn their necks to look at her.

"Your husband telephoned last night."

She has been rearranging the clothing she's put back on, and turns to face him only after several seconds. It's as though the true meaning of what he's just said becomes clear to her very slowly like a bubble rising in honey. "I love my son, my dear dear son, and my husband, Shamas," she says weakly.

"When you decided to sleep with me the first time, was that a kind of down-payment? Giving me a glimpse of what was to come if I married you?"

She steps up to him, and her hand moves several times towards his shoulder, to touch him, but she withdraws it in the end. "Allah placed you in my path that morning on the bridge to help me when you retrieved my scarf. I knew you were a good man . . ."

"Someone easy to manipulate?"

"I had no choice. I would do anything for my son and husband. Love is the only thing that inspires boldness in a woman."

"I thought you were being bold because of what you felt for me, while all the time you were just boldly degrading yourself for the love of your husband and son."

"A man is allowed four wives simultaneously, Shamas. You could . . ."

"Had you worked out all the details? What was the plan?"

"I swear by my eyesight that there was no real plan. I eventually wanted to tell you everything."

"Let's leave love aside—I am no fool—but did you even like me or care for me a little?"

She looks away, but then says with sudden rancour in her voice:

"Did *you* have a plan: what did you think the outcome of our meetings would be? Were you going to leave your wife for me?" She seems to think that she shouldn't expect from him a song—a lament—about the suffocations of marriage and the heroic defiance involved in refusing its hypocrisies, because she continues: "I know without you having told me that your wife is the most important fact of your life. I made decisions in a dazed state just like you." She continues in a more amenable tone: "Shamas, you know that a man can have more than one wife . . ."

Yes, he knows that. A man came to Muhammad and said he was unhappy. The Prophet advised him to get married. He returned some time later, married, but still complaining of unhappiness. Muhammad said, "Get married again." The man was back after a while, twice married—and happy.

"I know you are angry, Shamas. Don't think I didn't care for you—I haven't slept with anyone besides my husband."

"I am just trying to understand what you were doing. How were you hoping to have me divorce you after the marriage?"

"I didn't think that far ahead. I didn't know what I was doing then just as I don't know what I am doing now. I close my eyes and wish all of it into non-existence, beginning with me going to the house of the enemy that day in Pakistan. I walk around missing my son, my husband, mourning my mother, begging forgiveness from Allah for committing sin with you, and, yes, I ask Him to forgive me for deceiving you."

"I don't think you are to blame. And don't forget you went to that house to save that young girl's life." He turns towards her where she's lowered herself onto the rug beside him: he touches the edge of her veil.

"I wonder sometimes about my motives. It was perhaps all vanity on my part. I wanted to be the centre of attention in that small restricted place, wishing people would think I was brave enough to save a girl's life, exposing the criminal acts of her uncle, and, perhaps, even bringing an end to a decades-old feud. Maybe all this is Allah punishing me for my pride and vanity. I was so tired of living in that little place, I wanted to be looked at, appreciated, wanted stimulation."

"These are very human failings. Don't feel bad."

She talks on in a low monotone: "I could speak English, I was quite pale-skinned, I had more knowledge of certain things than anyone else in that village. I pretended to be superior at times. That my mind had access to the higher secrets of life was, of course, a charade, a pretence." She gives a little laugh to ridicule herself. "Knowledge! I was corralled up in that wretched third-rate Islamic school for most of my learning years, committing to memory the names of all the Prophet's wives. I know how pedestrian my intellect and my understanding of life really are, how basic and limited my knowledge of life is. I was—*am*—terrified of having my ignorance exposed whenever I talked to someone who is *really* educated, someone like you."

"I don't know anything."

She ignores him again, "Of course I *could* have been something. But to become that would have required long demanding work, a life dedicated to the pursuit of it—"

"And even then nothing is guaranteed."

"I liked the look of awe and admiration on my husband's face when I quoted—not always accurately—something from one of the poems I knew because, yes, it flattered me a little, and then the very next moment I was filled with shame and disgust, because I know no one acquires real knowledge because of *vanity*."

"Don't torment yourself like that."

"Do you know what the matchmaker said to me back in spring, after I rejected every prospect she had presented me with? I said none of them were good enough for me, but she smiled and said, 'On the contrary, my haughty and proud beauty. I have a feeling that you want someone to whom you could feel superior. You feel that these *are* too good for you.' I wonder if there was an element of truth in what she said."

"Forget about all of that and try to think reasonably about the *future* now."

"The future? I fear that if I stay away from my son for too long one day I'll be told that he remembers me only when he is reminded of me by others, coaxed into thinking about me." And then she says suddenly, "My Allah, Shamas, why didn't you stop me just now when I was talking so disrespectfully of Islam? What is wrong with me sometimes? And you make it possible for me to think and talk like that: now I know what your wife means when she says your talk led Charag, Mah-Jabin, and Ujala astray." She buries her face in her hands. "What would Allah think of my disrespectful talk? My being apart from my son and husband is a punishment from Him. Oh you don't know how much I love them."

"Please don't cry. And I know how much you love your son and husband: you were willing to turn yourself into a"—he cannot bring himself to call her a prostitute—"into a . . . into . . . one of those women in order to be rejoined with them."

"A man is allowed four wives, Shamas. You will be in the prayers of all three of us for the rest of our lives. I'll ask your wife myself, explain my situation to her."

"No. Don't even contemplate approaching Kaukab. I am sorry but what you want will never happen." They sit apart but are alert to each other like animals quivering in a forest. "I won't marry you on principle: one of the things I find repulsive about Islam is the idea of a man being allowed four wives."

"Please don't say such a thing about Islam. Do you want to go to Hell?"

"Not for that, no. And, Suraya, how do you know your husband won't get blind drunk again and divorce you one more time? He was drunk last night on the phone."

"He couldn't have been. He says he's stopped drinking."

"He hasn't. You can't go back to him. Here's yet another reason why I won't do what you say: because I don't want you to go back to him. He could beat you. Pakistan is not just a wife-beating country, it's a wife-murdering one: he could *kill* you in one of his drunken rages."

"Sometimes I feel I'll welcome death. May Allah forgive my ungratefulness. Shamas, let me talk to Kaukab just once . . ."

"No!" The word comes out louder than he intended and she flinches.

"Oh no, did he ever hit you when he was drunk? Did he beat you?" He takes her into his arms as the sudden realization dawns on him that he must have. "Where did he hit you, where, where?" He kisses her face repeatedly while she struggles to get away. Her cheeks. Her lips (from between which he had drawn her wet tongue into his mouth, only half an hour before, and held it there while he climaxed inside her like an ewer of milk emptied in one long splash after another). "Here? Did he hit you here?" He kisses her breasts that with an amorous hum at his fingertips he had stroked that first time here at the *Safeena,* her horse-brown nipple, telling her that in a Sanskrit poem a woman's nipple is described as being so firm *that a teardrop falling on it may rebound as fine spray.* "Here? Here?" But a realization has come to her too now, suddenly:

"My Allah, if you knew the truth when I arrived here this afternoon then why did you kiss me, touch me—*fuck* me? You wanted to dupe me into thinking you didn't know anything yet, to satisfy your lusts one last time before confronting me. I am sure you would have had an idea by then of how much it had cost me in self-respect every time I lay down with you, and yet you still . . . You vile beast!" She hits his head with her fists again and again, trying to break free. "You monster! You deceived me, you heartless bastard! And you talk of principles!" He clings to her under her weak blows: "I am sorry, I am sorry. I love you." She buries her nails into his shoulder: "Stop lying, you don't love me. Otherwise you'll do what I ask." And when he says, "Do you think I tell everyone I meet about Jugnu and Chanda, about my poetry, about my father—about my life?" she stops her struggle, letting him tighten his embrace around her, and then lowers her face lifelessly onto the side of his neck where she lets out a howl. Leaning back, he lowers them both to the rug and they lie side by side as though felled by two arrows.

"He couldn't have been drunk last night, and he says he won't lift a finger to me in the future. He's learned his lesson, Shamas. When I moved out of the house after the divorce, living in a rented room, he came to see me every day, repentant, making a long and tiring journey to the city where I was. I had taken a job as a receptionist in a hotel but when the manager fired me, for shaking hands with a male guest, I expected recriminations from my husband, thinking he would doubt my virtue once again, would quote Mohammad—peace be upon him, peace be upon him—who said, 'He who touches the palm of a woman not legally belonging to him will have red-hot embers put in the palm of his hand on Judgement Day,' but he believed me when I said that I had forgotten myself for only an instant when I extended that hand to the male guest. He has changed. I trust him and I trust Allah."

The man on the telephone last night was drunk, but Shamas lets the matter drop for now. "Why didn't you tell me everything days ago?" The blood in his body had felt brighter over the past few weeks but now he feels each wincing vein losing light moment by moment.

"I didn't think you cared for me enough yet. I thought I had to . . . *be* with you a few more times." She's looking up at the ceiling. "In a way I am glad you found out everything on your own. It's stopped me from sinning further. I would have gone on sleeping with you for a while longer, not sure how you felt about me yet. And also, you were hope. If I didn't tell you anything, then I could keep thinking that when I eventually did tell you, your answer would be yes."

He turns his face to look at her, towards that body that smelt differently in different places, cloaked in a complex veil the way a single flower can produce as many as a hundred chemical compounds, with scents mixing and combining in patterns that change over time, with parts of a blossom smelling differently from other parts, the smells sending out a variety of signals to the visiting insects, one telling them that *This is food,* another that *Eggs may be laid here,* another that *This groove leads to nectar.*

He says: "Forgive me for accusing you of manipulating me, because I myself contemplated deception. While lying with you here earlier, making love, I thought for a moment that I wouldn't tell you this afternoon about your husband's call, that I'll wait until you yourself decided to reveal your plan to me at some future date. I knew I'd lose you this very afternoon if I told you I knew what you wanted from me, and that my answer is no. I didn't want to lose you, your company . . . and, yes, your body."

She waves her hand in the air: "That's all over and done with." And sitting up, she says, "I have to go. What's your answer?"

"I can't do what you want. But I *will* help you begin custody proceedings for your son."

"That's out of the question." A look of fear crosses her face. "The case could go on for years, and if I lose they'd never let me see my boy out of vindictiveness. I know of women who have never been allowed near their children. You've forgotten what Pakistan is like. I sometimes wonder why my mother sent me to that country." She's silent for the next few moments and asks: "Why did you marry *your* daughter Mah-Jabin to someone in Pakistan?"

"It's complicated . . . She wanted to go . . ."

He wants to touch her—wishing to siphon some of her pain into himself—but knows he's not allowed; he mustn't. (For many years now, similarly, every time he touches Kaukab he feels he is committing a sin.) He cannot bear the thought of not being able to see her anymore. In the future how would he know what has become of her (just as he doesn't exactly know what's befallen Chanda and Jugnu, where in India his aunt Aarti is)? He tells himself once again to stop being selfish, to stop thinking about the consequences of her departure on his own spirit and inner life. What matters is Suraya and her predicament.

"Please don't make me look for someone else," she says. "Please don't make me humiliate myself with another. Please."

As though a storm has carried her away, she'll leave in a while and he'll never see her again, will be alone with the Cinnabar moth dressed like a woman from the Subcontinent. She'll vanish from his life, a small figure dressed in blue hurrying through the rain, in the grey, blue-black and white downpour, leaving him behind surrounded by the wallpaper deer in their flame-of-the-forest bowers, out past Scandal Point and then under the high cable that brings electricity to the *Safeena* and is twined this month by the pure-white-flowering bindweed, the arrow-shaped leaves dripping with rain.

"No."

"Would you like some time to think about it? Ten days, a fortnight?"

"My answer would still be no."

"Say no *then,* not now. I have ordered the Koh-i-Noors for you: they'll arrive just in time and I'll bring them. Meet me here one last time, by our *Safeena,* our Scandal Point. Let's decide on a day."

She kisses him on the forehead before leaving. She is a believer, and sex outside marriage is one of the greatest sins in Islam. He has an image of her going home after their meetings and frantically scrubbing herself.

He stands at the window, and the sight of his face—reflected ghostlike on the glass pane—fills him with disgust: she must have loathed him secretly, at what she had to do to regain entry into her real life. How the feel of these hands must have repulsed her! In her eyes he was a beast letting loose his lusts on her flesh. Licking those orchid-sap stains from her breast and thighs. He hates himself for acting like an animal, a bull rejoicing in the cow. Clouding the glass with his breath, he makes himself disappear.

Before she left, she asked to be forgiven for her husband threatening him with violence over the telephone last night; and she said she forgave him for deceiving her earlier this afternoon. But he cannot silence the accusations inside *himself* the way it is said that deer are troubled by the musk that springs from their own bodies, that sometimes, driven insane, they begin to describe circles around themselves, start to run madly in the deserts and the forests in the hope that they may locate the origins of that encircling perfume, that they may discover the reasons why it clings and seems to chase them.

There is dandelion fluff caught in a spider's web, out there, looking as though the arachnid had taken off a fur stole and hung it in one corner of its dwelling (as little Ujala said once; or was it something he'd read in *The First Children on the Moon*—he is aware that a part of his consciousness is influenced by his father's magazine, looking at the world as though it is a bright toy). A lapwing sounds from somewhere around the lake—. . . *bewitched . . . bewitched . . .* The high bindweed has folded its flowers to prevent the rain from diluting their perfume and nectar. Now and then giving a lazy flutter to its brilliant cerise wings, the Cinnabar is still there: the wind has changed direction and the creature is now being lashed by water drops; he goes out and brings it in, placing it on a shelf beside a book with a bluebell-coloured jacket, reminding him also of the blooms of a Pakistani jacaranda tree. The colour of her veil.

There is *nothing* he can do to help her.

There on the opposite shore of the lake, in the dense trees, is where the ghosts of the two murdered lovers are said to wander, calling out to him, aglow, giving out a light without heat like fireflies. Pale eyes change colour soon after death—Caucasian pupils appear a greenish-brown—and he wonders what colour Chanda's eyes became after her murder, she whose eyes used to change with the seasons. Her ghost's belly is said to be brighter than the rest of her, an indication that it contains a luminous child, the child that died with her.

Time makes memories of everything. Would he forget Suraya, her memory coming to him only occasionally? But he doesn't think he has enough time to be able to forget her, because many decades are needed for such processes, and he is too old now. This one will go with him to the grave.

At Scandal Point

Beside the *Safeena* stands a leafless tree resembling an antler, as though a deer buried there is beginning to emerge free of the earth's grip, and it is there that Suraya awaits Shamas's arrival. She shakes order into the garlands printed on her clothing, the August sun blazing around her. How hot it burns. A summer breeze comes in from the lake's surface, from the sharp slopes of tight purple heather and patches of willow herbs with bright pink light clinging to them.

The agreed hour has come and gone. So his answer is no? But even now there is a vague hope that perhaps he'll come here eventually—having changed his answer to yes after all. She tries to hold back her tears when she realizes how absurd the thought is. And now, as the drops of sweat slide down her body, activating the nerve-endings, there is a surge of anger: how dare he reject someone as intelligent, beautiful and desirable as her, how dare he not come! And she recriminates herself for her temper—Satan the Stoned-One is aware of her pride and vanity and takes full advantage whenever he can. Yes, you need to be confident and self-possessed in life, but only a little. There are limits you shouldn't go beyond. There are some substances that are regarded as medicines up to ten drops, but are included in the list of poisons on the eleventh.

Her quick temper is a trait she seems to have passed on to her little son. "Why did you go to that house anyway," he said last night on the phone. "It's all your own fault." Shocked by the authority with which he accused her, she suspected that her mother-in-law had started filling the boy's head against her. He must hear things around the house and streets all the time too. Had he said something as objectionable and insolent as that to her while she was in Pakistan, she would have slapped him, hard, knocking all the brazenness out of him. When he grows up will he torment her with his accusations, ever wilder, ever more obscene? She shudders. She fumes at his grandmother, and her husband, he who had dared to hit her, beat her. Three days ago, she had found herself fantasizing for a few moments about how delicious it would be to taunt her husband, to torment him, torture him, by giving him all the details of her lovemaking with Shamas, telling him he was a better lover than him. But—she had mused—surely that would jeopardize my getting back together with my son. But then she had come to her senses: *My Allah, Suraya, you love your husband and are a worshipper of Allah—where have such thoughts come from!*

She hears a sound nearby and looks up, her heart full of hope, but it's only the wind brushing past the reeds.

She's dizzy from the sun. The thought suddenly panics her that Shamas has been waylaid by some friends of her husband's. *My Allah, he's lying in a ditch somewhere, dead to the world.*

Her hands tremble, the Koh-i-Noor pencils rattling slightly in their box.

No, no, Shamas is not lying somewhere, dead or dying—she reassures herself, with no cause for this optimism but the compassion of Allah.

But now, once again, there's anger: what if he hasn't come to any harm but has rather become afraid that he *might* be beaten up by her husband's friends, and has not come to see her out of cowardice?

The anger at him is such that it makes her want to go to his house immediately. But, suddenly restored to sanity now, she knows that she must resist the impulse—any confrontation would endanger her chances of being accepted by Kaukab. Over the past four days she has found herself circling his house at odd hours, but every time she has remained clearheaded enough to withdraw. Once she caught a glimpse of the woman who must be Kaukab.

She recognized the roses and the jasmine in Kaukab's front garden: they were added to the bath water in which was washed the corpse of the girl beaten to death by the exorcist.

Another sound and Suraya tells herself not to look up and have her hopes smashed again—*he's not coming, Suraya, but you are a strong and resourceful woman: with Allah's help you will cope with anything: You don't need Shamas*—but her resolve fails within seconds . . .

Leopold Bloom
and the Koh-i-Noor

Semen was found on the mosque floor late last evening.

It's almost a year since Chanda and Jugnu disappeared. This time last year they were in Pakistan. Shamas looks down at his own and the missing couple's house, from the slope at the back, at the base of which the narrow lane and the stream are. Here the ground rises to form an angled back-drop of sycamores and hawthorns that throw shadows through every back window at sunrise, the earth here deep with zigzagging twigs, green and scarlet berries, mouldy winged samara and rain-rusted leaves lying under the trees like *The Moral:* at the bottom of a fable. The scent of hawthorns in bloom in May is as thick inside the house as out, the air drowsily astir in summer with the weightless seeds of the poodle-tail dandelion clocks.

Yesterday morning—a few hours before his meeting with Suraya—he went into the mosque to consult the cleric about Muslim divorce laws, to see if there was any possible way out for Suraya other than having to marry someone and obtain a divorce from him. The cleric wasn't in the building, though children were chanting their lessons. Shamas thought he might be upstairs and was moving towards the stairs when he heard a child's cry from behind a closed door. "Uncle, I don't want to." He went into the room and saw one of the junior clerics, a bachelor in his fifties, with his erect penis in a child's mouth.

Shamas shouted out and grabbed the man. Soon every official of the mosque was in the room and Shamas was told respectfully to go home, that the matter would be handled by the mosque. He left, insisting the man should be handed to the authorities, but by early afternoon, as the time approached for him to travel to Scandal Point to meet Suraya, concerned that the police had not approached him for a statement, he returned to the mosque only to discover that nothing had been done.

He came home and called the police himself to report the assault: he had to wait for an officer to visit the house. He would make it to her just in time, he reassured himself—but when the police did arrive he couldn't get away from their questioning and procedures.

As the investigative process got under way, other details emerged of previous assaults on children involving the same man. A group of mothers had, two months before, confronted mosque officials, saying the man had assaulted their children, but they were told that the scandal would give Islam and Pakistan a bad name, that the man would be prevented from doing it again, that if the police got involved and shut down the mosque no one would teach their sons to stay away from the whore-like white girls, and that their own daughters would run away from home and wouldn't want to marry their cousins from back home, that the Hindus and the Jews and the Christians would rejoice at seeing Islam being dragged through the mud. Some of the men had just laughed at the women and told them to go away and get the dinner ready for their husbands; others were even more contemptuous and told them to stop cackling like hens in the place of worship, adding that a woman should be a creature of the home and the night, and had no place outside in the world of men.

The mosque denied any attempt to cover up the man's activities. "This is the house of God and if anyone had known about it, it would not have been tolerated," the cleric said to the police. "The females say they complained—but then they get excited over everything and are not very intelligent, they don't know what they are saying."

There was no way for Shamas to contact Suraya and arrange to meet elsewhere. It was early evening by the time he was free: and by then it was too late. He tried to telephone her several times but there was no answer: she was either not at home or chose not to answer.

Police were sure that the samples they took from the floor of the room in which Shamas came upon that terrible scene were the assaulter's semen.

He was devastated that she got his final answer in such a cruel manner, and he has been wondering whether he should try to contact her again today—just to explain his non-appearance. But, surely, a telephone call from him now would raise her hopes for the first few seconds as she hears his voice. And then he'll have to dash them again.

He doesn't know what to do. He stands still, unwilling to move any muscles, almost believing himself to be a column of separate parts that would scatter at the smallest movement or vibration.

She had said: "I had to degrade myself with you. In our religion there is no other way for me to be united with my beloved son." She of course regretted the first thing, not the second: a system conditions people into thinking that *it* is never to blame, is never to be questioned. *We have to beg,* say the beggars, *the accursed belly demands food:* it is the fault of the belly, not the unjust world that doesn't allow enough sustenance to reach the bellies of everyone through dignified means.

He climbs down into the back lane, carefully leaping over the stream, and goes into Jugnu's back garden. The deep blue of a peacock's neck, a denim jacket of Jugnu's was washed by Chanda and hung out to dry in May last year: a wren began building a nest in one of its pockets and the garment was allowed to remain on the line, Shamas taking it off only in October, removing from the pocket the small bowl constructed of one dead leaf each of maple and sycamore, one of elm, which he recognized due to its lopsided nature—one-half bigger than the other—and three leaves from the apple foliage; there were dandelion whiskers, and several consecutive layers of spiders' web trying to separate which was like pulling apart a sheet of two-ply tissue paper or entering a well-starched shirt. There was a piece of the purple thread that Kaukab had used to sew a *kameez* a few months earlier. The earth around him was covered with yellow leaves being dropped by the trees, the edges of everything giving out pulses of sunlight because last night the glint-slippered frosts were abroad. Berries, like chewy pearls, were everywhere. And no one knew where Chanda and Jugnu were.

Shamas crosses over into his own back garden, thinking about Suraya waiting for him at Scandal Point, beside the *Safeena*, holding the Koh-i-

Noor pencils in her hand. Years ago at the *Safeena,* while he was sitting in convivial geniality with the shop's owner, both locked in a habit of concentrated silence, a recently read paragraph or poem always in their heads like tealeaves releasing flavour in two cups of hot water, Jugnu had come in with a butterfly net to ask if there was an Urdu-language *Ulysses:* "A moth circles the light in the brothel sequence. I wonder which Urdu word for moth they would use—*parvana* or the more prosaic *patanga*?" Shamas said he remembered a path by Browning *where lichens mock the marks on a moth, and small ferns fit their teeth to the polished block,* but he didn't recall a moth in the Circe chapter of *Ulysses.* "Are you sure you are not thinking of the kisses that flutter about Bloom in Nighttown? *He stands before a lighted house, listening. The kisses, winging from their bowers, fly about him, twittering, warbling, cooing.*" Jugnu joined in with a laugh of pleasure: "*They rustle, flutter upon his garments, alight, bright giddy flecks, silvery sequins.* Yes, but there is an *actual* moth in that chapter also. Bloom wears the Koh-i-Noor diamond on the fingers of his right hand at one point in that chapter."

"I cannot think of anyone more appropriate than him to have that jewel," Shamas had said.

And now he goes into the kitchen through the back door, and moves towards the pink room in order to consult the Urdu *Ulysses.* "*Parvana* or the more prosaic *patanga*?" he mutters and looks up to discover that Suraya is sitting in there with Kaukab.

They are looking at a photograph of Ujala, and Kaukab has obviously just told Suraya something about the boy, because Suraya says, "I wish I could say something to make you feel better."

"Don't blame yourself," Kaukab says. "My wounds aren't the kind that heal easily."

They hear him come in and both stand up, Suraya looking him squarely in the eyes.

"And this must be your husband."

Kaukab smiles at Shamas. "This is Perveen. I saw her admiring my roses from the footpath and we ended up talking. We have been sitting here for about an hour and a half, finishing off the strawberries I bought yesterday." She indicates the two bowls on the coffee table, swirled pink and white with the cream and berry juice. "We even said our prayers together."

Perveen. Shamas had told Suraya that her name was the Persian word for the constellation of Pleiades, the Seven Sisters: "As is the other common girl's name—Perveen."

"She just moved into the area two days ago," Kaukab tells him.

"Now," Kaukab turns once again to Suraya, waving Shamas away, overexcited by the company she has found unexpectedly this afternoon, "I must tell you about Mah-Jabin. She's sitting over there in America as we speak, wearing immodest Western clothes, no doubt."

But Shamas remains where he is, trying to understand what she is doing here. His heart beats so loudly he fears his eardrums will split.

"You said earlier that you had sent Mah-Rukh, sorry, Mah-*Jabin,* to Pakistan to marry. Why?"

"Well, I feel I can tell you these things, Perveen, but you must promise not to tell anyone. What happened was that Mah-Jabin fell in love with a boy when she was young, and when he married someone else, well, she insisted on being sent to Pakistan."

Suraya lifts her eyes towards Shamas for the briefest of moments, and then looks back to Kaukab: "You are right: it *is* complicated."

"Such a nice boy she married, but she abandoned him." Kaukab's eyes fill up with tears. "He wrote to her earlier this year, but when she came home for a visit, way way back at the beginning of spring, she threw the letter away—unopened. Imagine, Perveen! I must show you a photograph of his. I used to keep it here in this room but then I put it away upstairs because it pained me too much to think how my daughter had pained him." And now suddenly she turns to Shamas: "My Allah, Shamas, we forgot to tell you that Nusrat Fateh Ali Khan has just died. Perveen just told me."

"Yes," Suraya says to Shamas. "A woman went by, weeping out in the street, and I asked what the matter was."

Is she lying? Is "Nusrat's death" a coded way for her to refer to their first night together and how nothing came of it eventually? Is she here to torment him?

"And Meena Shafiq rang me just now to let me know," says Kaukab.

The news is genuinely devastating: "Who will sing about the poor, now?" he whispers in shock.

"And about the women," says Suraya—his whispers are audible to her.

"And in praise of Allah and Muhammad, peace be upon him?" adds Kaukab.

Shamas looks at Suraya: "How did it happen?" He is troubled by how familiar she already is to him in the surroundings of his house. He shifts his gaze to Kaukab: "How did it happen?"

"In a hospital, hooked up to a dialysis machine."

"Probably unsterilized equipment," he thinks out loud. "The hospitals there . . ."

Kaukab is immediately indignant: "I knew you would find some way of badmouthing Pakistan in all this." She turns to Suraya: "See, Perveen, this was what I was talking about when I said he had turned my children against me." She stands up, almost in tears. "I'll go and get that photograph of Mah-Jabin's husband. You'll see for yourself how handsome he is, Perveen, and then you'll agree with me that it was totally unreasonable of Mah-Jabin to leave him. I'll let you decide."

Shamas enters the room the moment Kaukab goes into the staircase: "What are you doing here?"

"I had to see you."

"Are you sitting here making fun of her, a foolish old woman?"

"I don't think she's foolish in the least. Do *you*?"

She takes a step towards him but then they both hear Kaukab's voice from the stairs: "I have just remembered that the photograph is actually down there, hidden in one of the books."

In the time it takes for Kaukab to re-enter the pink room, Suraya quickly hands him an envelope—the faint rattle tells him that it contains a small box of Koh-i-Noor pencils. He pockets it and she whispers, "Come to the *Safeena* at dawn tomorrow, please." Her voice glows with emotion, a voice reeling with contrasts, at once caressing and corrosive.

Kaukab, smiling now (she's like a child after too much sugar), sends Shamas upstairs—"Leave us women alone"—and begins to hunt for the photograph. "Yes, indeed: while he pines away for her in Pakistan, she's in America, her long long hair cut short like a boy, wearing jeans and skirts. Why can't she wear our own clothes, like you, for example—the very personification of Eastern beauty—?"

He stands on the stairs and tries to hear what Suraya is up to; but at a sound from Kaukab—"Let me fill up the bowls with more strawberries and then I'll come and tell you all about my brother and a Sikh woman called Kiran . . ."—he withdraws upstairs. Kaukab is, on the whole, wary and quite guarded when it comes to revealing information about her family to other women, not knowing how this or that fact will be interpreted or retold, and she has been distressed by how some of the secrets have been turned into gossip in the neighbourhood; and now, Shamas understands, that she has seen this "newcomer Perveen" as someone to whom she can present her side of the family truths first, before she can learn the others' versions.

He can hear her through the floor: "My brother is now a widower, and when he came here for a visit last year, I kept a vigilant eye out, in case Kiran tried to entice him. Men are nothing more than children when it comes to these matters. You and I both know how wily a woman can be when she wants to."

No, he mustn't assume that Suraya is here to sabotage his marriage. Perhaps she has decided after all to begin a legal battle for her son and wants his help. He'll do all he can, write to MPs, find the best lawyers. Or perhaps she just wanted to see him for one last time, and hand him the pencils. The original Koh-i-Noors—from the factory in Bloomsbury, New Jersey—were given fourteen coats of golden-yellow lacquer, had their ends sprayed with gold paint and the lettering applied in 16-carat gold leaf, but these modern mass-produced ones are said to be no less exuberant when light plays on them. He tears open the envelope but it doesn't contain a box of pencils. *Home Pregnancy Test*—says the wording on the box. He opens it and, after a few minutes of consultation with the leaflet inside, realizes that the test in his hands is positive.

"She left as soon as you went up," Kaukab tells him when he rushes downstairs. "Nice woman, very beautiful. I wanted to show her the lovely embroidery patterns that Charag used to draw for me when he was a boy . . ."

He wants to run after her but restrains himself because Kaukab would be suspicious.

Tomorrow at dawn, at the *Safeena*?

No, he must pretend that he has to go to the mosque, to see how matters are there, and then telephone her from a street telephone-box.

"You just can't believe your luck that you have the chance to defame and ridicule Islam at last," Kaukab says to him bitterly as he tells her he is on his way to the mosque, having given Suraya enough time to drive back to her house. "I feel sorry for the poor pious cleric-ji, who has to interrupt his worship and do the rounds of the police station because of that junior cleric."

He is suddenly filled with rage. *I don't think she's foolish in the least. Do you?*

Kaukab meets his fierce look equally fiercely, and continues: "You want to go back in there and unearth more shameful things, no doubt. I always wanted my husband to frequent a mosque, but never thought it would be like this."

He closes the door, resisting the urge to bang it as loudly as he can, and steps outside. But Suraya's telephone continues to ring interminably without answer.

Tomorrow at dawn, at the *Safeena*.

You'll Forget Love,
Like Other Disasters

Shamas learns that a galaxy was stolen during the night.

Some figures came out of the warm night. They waited behind a screen of camomile and foxglove to let a freight train cross the tracks two or three feet away from them, the dust-covered petals shaken loose by the draught and flung onto their faces. And then they crossed over into the open countryside beyond to move towards the section of motorway cordoned off for repairs, sweating freely under their clothes in that damp herbal darkness. They bent on the tarmac and, working with cheap toy flashlights, prised out the cats' eyes embedded in the motorway lanes, reaching back and dropping each star-like bead into the rucksacks fitted onto their backs. The silent group of thieves worked undisturbed for many hours in the darkness full of the late-summer heat and in the morning the authorities discovered that more than three thousand sockets had been emptied.

The police remain perplexed, Shamas heard on the radio as he woke up, the motive for the theft of the galaxy incomprehensible, the case one of those cases that will probably remain unsolved.

Walking towards Scandal Point to meet Suraya, Shamas sees that the honeysuckle and the woody nightshade are displaying both flowers and berries, as though torn between the seasons. The year is about to enter its last phase.

He tried to telephone her last night but there was no answer.

To think of Suraya is still to bring about a chemical change in the blood, an instant physical lightness slow to ebb like the effect of an intoxicant, and there have been mornings when he has known upon waking that he has dreamt of her, even if he couldn't recall the details.

There is a faint citrus smell in the dawn air as though he is in a room in which an orange has recently been eaten. Soon, come autumn, the sun would be cooler and the sky would darken daily. Kaukab's roses and jasmine—the ones "Perveen" had been pretending to admire while she loitered outside the house yesterday—will die for another year in about five or six weeks, each round rosehip with its tall crown of long hairy sepals looking as though a berry has fused with a grass-hopper. Their colours would be as bright as sunlight on a bag of boiled sweets.

He cannot contemplate a termination, but what is the alternative? They will have to talk. A child isn't what even she wants. That was not why she was with him.

Surely she could not have lied about the pregnancy? Perhaps she wants to hurt him—plant pain in *someone*—for the injustice she has suf-fered in recent months. Powerless, demeaned, and discarded, her spirit poisoned—she must dream of revenge and mayhem. He goes under a birch tree whose foliage will begin to yellow soon and by November will lie on the ground under the white-skinned trees like bags of potato crisps spilled by children—oh, how everything must remind her of her son! The boy is said to have—beautifully—observed on the telephone during the summer that "Little whales live in our garden hose, spouting arcs out of its punctures when it is in use."

He feels ashamed for entertaining the thought that she might be lying. No, everything he knows about her tells him that she's not lying. The trees drip last night's raindrops on him as he goes. In a few weeks it would be like being surrounded by wounds—the red leaves of autumn. The light is already mellower, each ray only half full: the summer was a time of things *in* light, while autumn is light *on* things. Kaukab was preoccupied with thoughts of "Perveen" all yesterday evening: "She said she lived on Habib Jalib Street . . ." (She doesn't—the house she inherited from her mother is on Ustad Allah Bux Road.) "Shamas, she was as beautiful as your mother, may she rest in peace, but she seemed Allah-fearing with it, not that I mean to speak ill of the dead . . . She is a widow, her husband was a poet she said . . . I wonder, Shamas, if her parents or older relatives worked with us in the factories back in the '50s . . ."

Coming home from work two days ago, walking slowly through the town centre, Shamas noticed that the photographer to whom all the Asian immigrants used to go to have their portraits done, back in the late 1950s, and the 1960s and 1970s, is selling his shop. He must have thousands of negatives, chronicling the migrants' early years in this town, he had remarked to himself in passing; and now—as he walks towards Scandal Point to meet Suraya—it comes to him that the town government should buy the negatives from the photographer for its archives. Today is Saturday, and so first thing Monday morning he'll see what has to be done to set the process in motion, and later today he should visit the photographer in town to tell him not to dispose of the negatives until he hears from him next week. The negatives are far too important to end up at a landfill site.

Suraya. He remembers something Kaukab has often accused him of in the past: that he retreats from the problems around him by thinking about his work. And now he wonders if he's trying to drive Suraya from his thoughts—yet another disowning and banishing of her. No, the thought of the negatives came to him just now out of its own accord—that's all.

He edges away from a small Japanese knotweed tree of whose pale cream flowers—looking as though dusted with custard powder—he had tried to discover the smell of a few years ago, and found himself taking in a lungful of decay, suppuration, the shock throwing him back on his heels where he had reached up with his neck stretched like that of a hanged man's. Perfumes come from plants; it's animals who produce disagreeable odours, humans included. Musk, honey, milk—these are as much an exception in the animal world as those tropical plants said to produce blossoms smelling of festering flesh or this Japanese knotweed around whose shimmering flowers he had cupped both hands that day, the way a young man kisses his first girl. He'll never now kiss her mouth again while his penis is engorged and sticky at the tip like a bull's muzzle, or lie with her head on his chest while from somewhere nearby comes the summer noise of a bee that's got stuck inside a snapdragon flower, a panicked wing-thrash, as it tries to back out. According to her, what she did with him was a "sin," and she, according to her, will have to bear the "stigma" of that sin "till Judgement Day and after." She'll view the pregnancy as the beginning of her punishment.

There must be a way that the baby in her womb can be saved. He will not—cannot—marry her, but perhaps she could have the baby and live here in England while they begin a custody battle to get her boy away from that wife beater.

Will he have to tell Kaukab eventually?

He has been into the town centre to pick up the Saturday papers and is now walking towards Scandal Point and *Safeena*, hugging to himself the heavy news of all the world.

He arrives at Scandal Point, but there's no one there. He waits for a few minutes and then sets off in the direction where she usually parks her car. The lake is striped Kashmir-blue where it reflects the dawn sky, and here and there on a higher wave a patch of red is burning from the east because the sun is rising—red as the beast blood that was poured into the mosque at the beginning of the year. The glitter is uncomfortable on the eye, and heat seems to come off it whenever the head is aligned with it at its brightest.

More details of the unconscionable crime he witnessed at the mosque involving the little child—no older than Suraya's son, surely—have been emerging. It turns out that the junior cleric has been to prison for assaults on children at a mosque in the Brick Lane area of London. He had assaulted a seven-year-old girl and the mother had called the police. As the court date approached, a petition supporting him was circulated on mosque-headed paper. *We the undersigned support the respected Imam Amjad and want him to return to his job as soon as possible. We have every confidence in his ability as a cleric . . .*

The parents of his victims were under enormous pressure not to go through with the court case. When the date was arranged the father went to the police and said he did not want his girl to go to court—her chances of marriage would be ruined, she will be tainted by the scandal, the reputation of her sister too ruined. The people at the mosque had written to his parents back in Pakistan, asking them to tell him to drop the case against the holy man.

But in the end the family did have the courage to go through with it, and the man was convicted of one count of indecent assault and an act of gross indecency. While he was awaiting sentencing the mosque circulated another petition for signatures. *We the undersigned continue to support the respected Imam Amjad. While we regret the circumstances which led to his arrest, we nevertheless confirm that if he is allowed his liberty we will have no objection to him being employed by the mosque . . .*

Despite their pleas, he was sentenced to six months and placed on the sex-offenders' register.

Shamas stands under the pine tree where Suraya's car was always parked during her visits to the *Safeena*—he can see the tyre marks from last time ("The marks left by the passing of a python are exactly like the treads of a jeep's wheel," Jugnu said).

The man was released after three months and the police were alarmed when they learned that he was back at the mosque, but they were re-assured that he was not allowed anywhere near the children. Soon he moved on to a town in Lancashire and began attending the mosques there, leading the prayers at some. From there—after another incident, his followers threatening the parents of his little victim with a gun to keep quiet—he came to Dasht-e-Tanhaii.

And here he has been caught.

It remains to be seen whether someone would approach Shamas in order to dissuade him from testifying.

Perhaps Suraya has decided to park elsewhere, and so he sets off again towards Scandal Point, madly. His temples are burning and he is sweating, unable to think about where she is or what's going to happen in the future.

He returns to Scandal Point but she is still not there, and, after a wait, he sets off on one of the many paths that lead to the *Safeena*—impatient to see her, hoping to catch her as she arrives. The leaves of the rowan trees, there ahead of him, will begin to turn many kinds of yellow next month, from bright amber to the pale brown of a parchment lantern over a weak bulb, and almost as many kinds of red—sienna through to vermilion. The colours would be a reminder that what sunset is to the day, autumn is to the year.

Perhaps she has had a miscarriage during the night? Is she at the infirmary at this moment? Perhaps he should go home and try to ring the Accident and Emergency department?

No, no, she'll be here. He goes past a bank of late-summer wild grass and his dawn shadow is sliced up into thin uniform strips on the tall narrow leaves like a sheet of black paper coming out of a paper shredder. Once, pointing to the drawing of a porcupine-like clump of grass in a book of butterflies and moths, Jugnu said, "It could be argued that this species has taken part in *all* stages of civilization's progress: used for making spears, as support for vines, and, finally, wind instruments for music." Shamas is sure he has seen that species growing behind the church of St. Eustace, and now his mind turns yet again to the controversy that the vicar has generated over the last few days. The reverend told his 200-strong congregation not to associate with two people who have left their spouses to live with each other, that the two—although regular church-goers—are adulterers who would go to Hell if not persuaded to repent. His diktat, he says in *The Afternoon,* is guided by Christian love for the couple and a desire to bring them back to the church.

According to *The Afternoon,* he had responded to an immense amount of gossip by issuing instructions in the parish newsletter. *In relation to the distressing news about two people in our church rebelling against God, all members are reminded, sadly, of 1 Corinthians 5 vii, about not associating with them.* He followed this by naming the two lovers in church and telling worshippers that if they loved the couple and did not want them to burn in Hell, they would support his decision. Then he published a clarification on how church members should behave towards the couple, making the points that 1 Corinthians 5 vii is *not* optional; that it is not loving to offer hospitality and comfort to someone in rebellion against God, because that would tend to confirm them in their disobedience, which leads to eternal death; that invitations to share fellowship should be conditional on repentance first being fully shown.

Before leaving the house over the past few days, Shamas has been hoping he would not run into the vicar. He doesn't want to risk hearing the man speak of the matter lest some phrase or reasoning of the holy man may apply to Chanda and Jugnu, lest he, Shamas, be given a new insight into the motivation of the two killers, a disturbing piece of knowledge he would later wish to expel from his consciousness.

The bodies of the two lovers could be anywhere—here in England, in Europe, in Pakistan. Illegal immigrants come into the country in lorries and trucks and planes and boats without anyone knowing anything about it. If the living can be brought in, why can't the dead be taken out?

The summer's ending and soon it would be like being surrounded by wounds, the leaves of autumn. The van the two brothers owned is still there outside the shop, used by the father to bring in supplies from the cash-and-carry, though it is hard to know how the couple manages to keep the shop going on their own. Kaukab says she has heard that a new boy is at the premises these days; walking by she has caught a glimpse of him amid all the sacks and boxes—it is someone they have taken on as help, no doubt.

Behind him someone clears his throat, bringing him hurtling forward from the summer to the present moment—the summer's almost-end. "Brother-ji."

He turns and is face to face with a stranger. "Yes?"

The man is smiling under that moustache as fine as mink, the hair spreading out a little because the lips are stretched, and he places a hand on his shoulder in a good-natured Pakistani manner. "Allow me to introduce myself . . ."

Shamas doesn't catch the name or the beginning of the cascade of pleasantries that follows it because he is alarmed by the fact that the hand on his shoulder is holding a burning cigarette, an inch away from his cheek, his eyes. And in the second or two that it takes for it to become clear that what he has mistaken for a cigarette is in fact a pale-apricot Band-Aid wrapped around the man's index finger, the name has been spoken; the ripple of panic on his face has also caused the man to remove his hand and take a step backwards, embarrassed at his over-eagerness, or perhaps offended by being rebuffed.

Shamas gives his name and, transferring the bundle of newspapers to the other side of his body, frees his right hand for a handshake. The man's aftershave or cologne has a citrusy note, like raindrops flavoured by falling on lemon trees, like a room in which someone has recently eaten an orange. Didn't he smell it earlier—was this man walking behind him, without him being aware of it? "What can I do for you?"

"Nothing, brother-ji. I saw you just now and decided to come over to say *salaam-a-lekum,* a little hello. I am well aware, Shamas-ji, of the kind help you have provided for us Pakistanis through your office and am a great admirer of yours. I just wondered if I could be of any help to you in this difficult time."

For the briefest of moments but comprehended perfectly during it—as when a summer insect flies across a lit television screen in a room that is otherwise dark, the components of the insect's flight seen in a sequence of perfect silhouettes—Shamas wonders absurdly whether this man is an apparition seen only by him, sent to bestow benevolence. But the moment passes and the insect disappears into the darkness it had come out of. "Difficult time?"

"I meant the difficulty you are having with your daughter and your younger son. They have left home, yes?"

Shamas takes a step back, in shock and incomprehension. "Forgive me but I have to leave."

"We know these are delicate matters but we feel we have to offer you our services. We are aware that the girl and the boy have left home. The girl has cut off her hair and wears Western clothing now."

These things are known to everyone, of course; there is nothing sinister in that. Such knowledge comes into the neighbourhood's eyes innocently: it's no different than Kaukab's comment about a woman she doesn't know but who walks by the house daily that she's stooping more and more these days. No, everyone knows that Ujala and Mah-Jabin have left the parents' house; but what "services" is this man referring to? Shamas wonders if this man has mistaken him for someone else. And who is this "we"?

The man has noticed his puzzled look and clarifies: "What I mean to say is that we can bring your children back. We run a small discreet operation: no one official will ever know about us—we have been so quiet even you hadn't heard of us until now. We have ways of infiltrating women's refuges where the girls go to hide, and by using the National Insurance numbers we can find which city the runaway boys are living in. Manchester, Edinburgh, Bristol, London: no place is far enough. We charge a small fee, to cover expenses, but we won't ask *you* to pay anything, as a sign of our respect for you. We know you have helped people all your life; even back in the early days here in England you were helping the immigrant factory workers with jobs, housing, pay, unions, and learning English. It's all well known."

"It was nothing."

"You are too modest, *jannab-sahb*. But now the Almighty Allah, fate, and our good fortune has arranged it so that we can be of some use to *you*. It's our duty and your right. It doesn't matter where the children are, we'll find them discreetly: we could bring a chick out of its egg without breaking the shell. We made a few mistakes at the beginning, like the time we gave the address of the women's refuge that a man's wife had run off to, claiming he was violent towards her, forgetting that a woman should choose the poison being offered by her husband over the milk and honey of strangers—and then he broke in and put a bullet into her head. But now we are more careful."

"I don't need my children brought back from anywhere. They are not runaways," Shamas states firmly, understanding everything now. The news of this gang of bounty hunters had come to him at the office last week and he had initiated enquiries, asking the office to gather information which could be presented to the police. This man has obviously found out that questions are being asked and is here to try and dissuade Shamas. Would he try to bribe him, believing that a dog with a bone in its mouth cannot bark?

Shamas looks him square in the eye. "I don't need anyone to kidnap my children. Now if you'll excuse me I have to be somewhere urgently."

The man opens his heavy arms—the bones in them must be the size of monkey wrenches—with a glint of a gold chain at the wrist and, as though through a barrier of pain, says: "Kidnap? Shamas-ji, that is how white people would see it. They of course don't understand our culture. The children and runaway wives *have* to be brought back."

Standing here face to face, Shamas doesn't wish to counter him or explain anything to him: he'll dismiss everything Shamas says and soon it will be as though when the two of them opened their mouths they revealed not tongues but index fingers pointing and jabbing in the other's direction.

"They *must* be brought back. Girls can become prostitutes if they are on their own and the boys drug addicts. They can be taken in by unscrupulous individuals. There is a saying in Urdu: *Dhukhia insaan to sher ka bhi bharosa kar leta hai.* A lonely and distressed person will trust even a man-eating lion. In the past twelve months we have saved forty-seven of our youngsters from such a fate, and six wives who had left their husbands. One boy had decided to become a . . . a . . . a homosexual—please don't mind my bad language."

In the past twelve months alone? How long has this been going on? There is a sickness and a tightening at the base of Shamas's throat. He wonders what else this person is involved in. Contract killing? Did he have anything to do with Chanda and Jugnu's disappearance? Shamas is sure no one at the office knew anything about this before last week: when people come to the office asking for help because a daughter has left home or a son, they are told plainly that since the children are of age there is nothing legal that can be done; nor is it legal to disclose addresses and telephone numbers of women's refuge centres. Do they call this man and his associates after they leave Shamas's office in disappointment?

The man seems not to have read Shamas's silence as hostile. "We'll need photographs of Mah-Jabin and Ujala, of course, and National Insurance numbers. Credit card details too prove useful. Very little force would be used, I personally guarantee that."

Shamas's skin has become chilled: the man knows Mah-Jabin and Ujala's names. "I *know* where my children are," he hears himself telling the man. "Now excuse me. I really must leave."

"We'll be gentle. We do what the parents say. One mother and father wanted us to bring back the girl—who had run away a week before her arranged marriage to a decent-enough cousin from Pakistan—and they said we could use as much force as we liked but were not to hit her face because that would show in the wedding photographs and video. If we had to we should hit the body—which would be covered up with the wedding gown—or we could hit the head—where the veil and the hair would hide the bruises."

"As I said, my children are perfectly happy and so am I." He is trying to suppress his anger, his earlobes hot.

"You may be happy but is your wife?" A voice comes from behind Shamas.

He turns around and sees that two men are standing ten yards away from him, and behind them, a further ten or so sun-filled yards along, on a narrow cement path that cuts through the swathe of wild grasses and late-summer's imperfect blossoms, is a car, three of its four doors open. Maple leaves glisten above it, those at the lower edge of the canopy moving rhythmically to and fro on their long stalks like the pendulum of a clock. All this is glimpsed in the sweep of the gaze, but Shamas's eyes have returned to the two men because they have begun to walk towards him.

And the man who had been talking to him takes a step nearer to him too, aggressively. The two men arrive and in turn take his right hand into their own in an enforced shake, smiling.

He is not used to this: the people he has dealt with up until now have left their authority at the door when they entered his office. All three of these however are standing too close to him, and he is starting to tremble, experiencing a kind of vertigo and an unpleasant lightness in his feet—an awareness of being close to the edge of something.

He wonders whether Suraya's husband could have sent these people.

Maintaining his composure—he does not wish to appear undignified in front of these strangers—he steps out of the cordon they seem to have made around him and begins to walk away at a controlled pace. But they, obviously unconcerned about what he may think about them, break into a little run as they try to keep up with him and he is brought to a halt as all three overtake him and block his way. It could almost be playfulness—but he is beginning to think that it is not a game but a blood sport.

One of the two who had been waiting behind him earlier says: "Shamas-ji, you are happy with the situation but your wife came to us several months ago, a year and a half ago to be precise, to see if we could track down her son Ujala, and before that, four or five years ago, she had wanted us to see if your daughter Mah-Jabin hadn't fallen in with bad company. She told us in passing that she was devastated when Mah-Jabin left her husband, despite the fact that like every other decent mother she had told her daughter that the house you are going to—the house of your husband and in-laws—is Heaven but you are not to desert it even if it becomes Hell, that as far as the parents are concerned a daughter dies on the day of her wedding."

The second of the new arrivals says, "Your wife did not want you to know about the fact that she had visited us obviously because you don't have a mother's heart in your breast and wouldn't have understood. A mother misses her children when they run away so she wants them back."

"Some women in the neighbourhood had put your wife in touch with us—she is, of course, a very polite and pious lady. In the end, on both occasions, she didn't want to go through with it, but we were very distressed by her plight. She said her children were the other half of her heartbeat."

"Now," says the second new man, his face pitted around the mouth, scars from the beard of acne he must've had as an adolescent, "is it fair that you wish to deny *other* families the service your *own* family contemplated using not long ago? Why are you trying to blacken our name, asking awkward questions through your office? We are but humble slaves of our community."

The more the man talks the more terrible it is for Shamas. Once again, and for an instant, he thinks this isn't really happening, that his total disbelief will presently set reality straight and make these men vanish. He looks at the talking man's empty hands as they are balled into fists that are now being aimed at his face, his head, his ribs. The newspapers fall from his grip. The other men join in with blows of their own. When he cries out in pain, they hit him harder, on the kidneys and belly, and he does not know where to put his hands. A metal finger ring grazes his face and the pain is as though a line had been drawn on his face in sulphuric acid.

The blows came harder and faster but then, as though he is being hit by a single person, they begin to come after measured pauses, the men deciding, calculating carefully where to hit him before doing so—they are obviously people who understand the reality of violence and inflicting pain.

He can no longer breathe through his nose and as he lies there, the newspapers, torn or whole, scattered all around him, he feels a mouth draw close to his face and say,

"This is just a mild warning. Next time we'll deal with you in a Pakistani way. Watch out or I'll crush you like this"—he makes a fist and squeezes it tighter—"and lick you off the palm of my hand."

"And don't go to the police about this—unless you want people to find out about what you have spent the whole summer doing with that whore of a woman at the bookshop."

Another voice adds, "In that small room it must've been hot as a pistol that's just been fired but, no doubt, the sweat these two worked up kept them cool."

"He said earlier he had to be somewhere. Maybe the dirty shameless bitch is waiting for him over there as we speak, her fat tits at the ready, the knot of her *shalwar*'s drawstring loosened."

There is the sound of laughter. "Perhaps we should go and see."

"Look at him. He's trying to growl at us. I think we are hurting his feelings by talking about her in this manner. She's obviously so pure that angels can use her clothing as prayer mats. In fact that *is* why she'd take off her clothes and put them on the floor—to let the angels praise Allah on them—while he shoved his cock in her mouth or got her arsehole ready with fingers dipped in oil."

One of Shamas's eyes is looking into the ground and the men vacate the second eye's view, moving away. There is a red pricking in both his eyes, both have caught a fresh glimpse of the humiliations Suraya went through with him in order to be united with son and husband. How she must have loathed him during the hours she spent with him, he who was under the impression that she was with him out of her own choice, had yet to be told the truth about her circumstances by her!

He lies there with an ear pressed to the ground (down there where Chanda and Jugnu are turning into clay) as though trying to listen out for something, as though he's a traveller in a fairytale who's heard someone call out to him while he was crossing a forest, someone buried alive by a sorcerer who will be freed and jump out of the hole when the traveller digs deep enough.

He feels the sun creep up on him. Someone with a stick-crazy dog will come upon him soon, he reassures himself; those animals and their masters are constantly taking each other places, the dogs' fur covered in inch-long bits of grass like wrong-coloured stitches on a garment; the dogs wrapping their leads around their owners, revolving and describing circles like a lighthouse's beam. Or one of those figures he always sees from a distance, busy with a boat and its triangular sail at the edge of the water, their legs spread like a wishbone, ripples of breeze running across the material of the sail like the flank of a cow twitching away flies, in Pakistan.

Shamas lies on the grass after the voices of his assailants have receded into the distance, the newspapers rustling around in the descending silence, touching his skin, a ripped-up piece dyed crimson red with blood—his, for he can taste the salt in his mouth. He cannot keep his eyes open and feels very sleepy all of a sudden, very tired, eyes heavy and unable to focus. He makes an effort to move his legs but is unable to and closes his eyes . . .

And then with a great lunge of effort, like a hosepipe whipping into an arc of frenzy as water enters it at great pressure, he makes his body stand upright in tearing eagerness, jerking his head up away from the ground with a burst of energy: in a congestion of tender impulses, he tells himself that they are definitely on their way to harm Suraya—she who is so gentle and careful that she touches everything as though it were a part of her—and he must stop them.

Suddenly life matters again.

He can see the three of them walking towards the car and is surprised that he hasn't been lying here for longer. He limps after them in enthusiastic dizziness, everything a blur and everything perfectly clear. His progress wavers because he cannot walk in a straight line. He has to alter his direction every other second to bring them to the centre of his vision. They slide in and out of view periodically, in unexpected directions and diagonals. He drops and picks up again the torn bundle of newspapers that he had obviously felt compelled to collect and bring with him, not wishing to waste them, not having any memory of the time he made the decision to gather them up from around him before setting out. Perhaps he has vomited—his breath smells—but he has no memory of that either.

He steadies himself and moves towards them like a bubble flowing helplessly towards a drain. His heart clubbing away inside, he is not sure whether he is groaning but they do become aware of him eventually and stop and turn around.

AUTUMN

Ìris's Wings

Kaukab feels herself being watched from above.

The Prophet, peace be upon him, said that whenever a man's earthly wife makes difficulties for him, his seventy-two houri wives—waiting for him up there in Paradise—sigh regretfully. If ever her man wishes to copulate with the earth wife and she makes excuses or shuns him, the houri wives curse her all night.

The houris reserved for Shamas are cursing Kaukab from up there, because she has just stumbled out of the room where Shamas is lying, a month after his beating. Twenty-five of the past thirty days he has spent in hospital. He still gets delirious sometimes and has attempted to undress her just now, asking her to touch him between the legs, fondling her breasts, wanting her to show him the scattering of moles on her upper thighs that he loves. More than once over the previous weeks while she was visiting him at the hospital, he asked her—in delirium—how she feels about another baby. And several times he called out to someone or something called "Pleiades." And twice he tried to struggle out of the hospital bed saying, "I have something urgent to attend to at Scandal Point." The one in Shimla?

She has of course refused him intimacy before, but each time she has pretended—yes, pretended, she admits tearfully—that it was not a sexual advance, a request for access to her body, and has therefore remained relatively free of guilt, and free of the fear of Allah's retribution, but the recent touches and caresses have been explicit.

Shamas is bruised everywhere on the surface and there are innumerable internal injuries, the doctors saying he is lucky to be alive, and his faeces has been quite liquid like bird droppings since the attack that he has failed to explain to anyone, not remembering anything about it, some people in the neighbourhood saying that without doubt the perpetrators belonged to Chanda's family, that it is their revenge for the fact that, come December, their sons are facing a life sentence because of Shamas's brother.

A woman from the neighbourhood—who recently has been accompanying Kaukab to the gynaecologist because Kaukab has reached that age where her womb is slipping out of her vagina and must be either surgically removed or stitched back to the inner lining of her body—said, "When I heard the news my heart was as a porcelain plate dropped from a high terrace. May these bad times be short-lived and Allah take you both into His compassion once again soon."

She has just given him lunch and is now bringing the tray downstairs, the plate glowing in the enclosed staircase: it is part of an old set and she knows that bone china is partly bone, and goes yellow with age due to the phosphorus in the bones. That afternoon a month ago, when he came home clutching tattered newspapers to himself, he looked as though he'd been in a room full of glass cases when an earthquake had struck, and that those cases had contained venomous snakes. His face was swollen and when she saw him there was a split-second of confusion as to his identity before she recognized him—by his clothing. He was dribbling as though an egg had just cracked in his mouth.

Her womb—the first dress of her daughter, the first address of her sons—is a constant source of pain these days and she comes down the stairs carefully. She tells herself that she must bear up patiently, that a person is like a tealeaf: drop it into boiling water if you want to see its true colour. She reads verses from the Koran when the pain looks as though it is about to increase.

By the white forenoon
And the brooding night!
Thy Lord has neither forsaken thee
Nor hates thee.

Since midmorning there has been a distant buzz in the air from the grass-cutting machines at work on the meadow-like slopes behind the house. The wildflowers there are receiving their second cut of the year, and, all afternoon, a scent which is a compound of sap and shredded petals has been swirling down the hill, having a leavening effect on the atmosphere.

She'll make some rice pudding for Shamas this afternoon because he has asked for something sweet, and goes to check that there are pistachios in the cupboard. And maybe she should taste Shamas's food—despite the fact that it is Ramadan and she's fasting—to make sure that the things like spices and salts are in proportion. Allah—ever kind, ever compassionate—says that if you are a slave, a servant or a wife, and your master, employer, or husband is a strict man, you are allowed to taste the food you are cooking for him during your Ramadan fast to see that the salt and spices are according to his preference, to prevent a beating or unpleasantness. Shamas doesn't mind, but—since he is not well—perhaps her violating the fast would fall into the category of wifely devotion and love, and be excused.

There are no pistachios, and she wonders if she should go to the shops to get them, though Shamas's claw managed to scratch her painfully between the legs before she escaped; as it is, nowadays it's hard for her to even stand up sometimes.

Kaukab hasn't informed her children of their father's beating because she is afraid they would believe the rumour of Chanda's family's involvement and do something improper or illegal. Her children are mild-mannered with the exception of Ujala, but that sight upstairs will move anyone to do something drastic. She imagines various horrible scenarios like one of her boys ending up in prison like Chanda's brothers for having committed a violent crime.

"O just think how that girl Chanda managed to destroy her entire family," a woman said recently—the day Shamas got beaten up, in fact.

That the man who was equally responsible for the ruin of the shop-owning family was dear to Kaukab did not prevent the woman from saying this out loud in front of her, because everyone knows that Kaukab had disapproved of the two sinners. Kaukab and the women had been sitting in Kaukab's front garden—which is the sunny side of the street in the afternoons—and peeling and preparing vegetables, discussing various matters. Just then a bird had started to shriek somewhere nearby, so that

Kaukab and the others had had to cover their ears; and then realizing that the bird was in the lilac tree beside the garden gate, a woman threw an enraged slipper in that direction. They were stunned when a rose-ringed parakeet—"Here in this country?"—emerged and flashed away, the slipper getting stuck in the branches, a few heart-shaped lilac leaves falling out onto the ground. The bird paused for a few moments on a telephone wire to smooth its plumes, sprang up and then disappeared into the sky. "They were said to be flying about on the edges of Dasht-e-Tanhaii but now they are spreading into town, it seems."

And then suddenly everyone had their mental activity arrested for a few seconds because they had seen Shamas standing at the bottom of the garden, past the lilac tree, his face and hair bloody, clutching torn newspapers to himself. The women sat as if painted in a picture, wonder settling on them in layers. There were a dozen or so flies around his blood and wounds. And then Kaukab, her tongue feeling dry down to its very root, rushed to the gate and opened it to let him stumble in, the others running forward to assist or staying behind to clear a path for him through the bowls and platters of onions and chillies and potatoes and spinach, the sparrows flying away where they had been pecking away at the peels and the discarded coriander leaves.

Someone ran into the blue kitchen with its yellow tables and chairs to call 999 in rudimentary English, speaking to a white person for the fourth time in her life, wondering whether she should add the word "fuck" into her speech now and then to sound more like a person who belonged to this country, because she had seen her English-speaking children use that word with great confidence, whatever it meant. Kaukab hadn't been apprehensive at Shamas's absence from the house: she had gone to sleep after reading the Koran until one o'clock the previous night and she had slept through the alarm that should have awakened her for the pre-fast meal and the dawn prayers. She woke up at ten minutes to nine and saw that Shamas had bathed and gone out. She hadn't missed him at all, it being a habit of his to spend time in the town library on Saturdays, or take a bus out into the woody areas of the county, or go into his office to do some work—sometimes do all three.

Kaukab cannot find any pistachios in the cupboard. Of course, to make rice pudding without the avocado-green and hot-pink of the pistachios is like making the children wear clothes without colours and sequins on a festive occasion, a festive occasion like Eid which everyone in Pakistan must already have started preparing for, the way people here start getting ready for Christmas weeks beforehand, almost everything in the year planned with that festival in mind.

Pain shoots between her legs, and so she needs to hear Ujala's voice on his answering machine and moves towards the pink room where the telephone lies; but there is a knock on the door and she finds a neighbourhood woman holding a bunch of roses wrapped in a newspaper, the strong thorns sticking through the paper here and there.

"I have just pruned my roses, Kaukab, but I didn't want to waste these blooms. I thought they would brighten brother-ji's room, may Allah give him health. How is he? Be careful, they are sharp."

Kaukab exclaims with delight and takes the spiky package from her. "He's resting. But isn't it a bit early to cut back the rosebushes? I don't do mine until the middle of October."

"It is early, but the builders are coming to do some work at my house and I don't know if I'll get a chance later on. You know what they say about builders and djinns: once they've entered a house they are hard to get rid of." Instead of a gardener's leather gauntlet, she is wearing oven gloves for her pruning task, and the cloth they are made of looks Pakistani to Kaukab: a web of embroidery studded with little mirrors like dewdrops. She must have made the gloves herself because there is no home oven-cooking in Pakistan and so no oven gloves of any kind have been conceived.

Kaukab remembers from her childhood the cakes that Shamas's father used to bake with live coals heaped around the pan, may he rest in peace, remembers how the vanilla perfume would roam through the winter streets of Sohni Dharti and find all the children like someone expert at hide-and-seek.

"I would like to smell these roses," Kaukab says, "but I won't. Rose essence is used in several sweetmeats and I am afraid Allah might think me a conniver, think I am smelling the fragrance of these roses just to get closer to food during my fast."

The woman is sitting at the table and, having taken off the oven gloves, is helping Kaukab remove some of the leaves from the rose stems and arranging the flowers in the vase of water. "Allah is compassionate, Kaukab, and in any case He knows everything in our heart."

"He dictated it all to the angels who jotted it down in the Book of Fates."

"I was just thinking of that Book earlier in the morning, Kaukab. I thought if only I could get a look in its pages I'd know how long I'll have to wait for any news of my son, or I could flip back a few pages to go into the past to see what happened to him, where he is." She breaks off and twirls a rose in her hand, blinking fast to prevent tears.

Gently, Kaukab rubs the woman's shoulder. "You mustn't despair. Allah will come to your aid."

"I told him that if he wanted to go on holiday he should go to Pakistan and stay with his uncles. But he said he wanted to go to a different place, telling me that the point of travel was to 'discover new things'—whatever that means. In the end I was happy that he was going to Turkey, a Muslim country." The woman stares at the pink roses. "He disappeared almost on arrival in Istanbul a week ago. The police found a body in the Bosphorous yesterday and tests are being carried out to discover the identity. It is possible he was killed for his passport."

Kaukab nods. She has heard that a British passport can fetch £5000 in poorer countries.

"I know I must have faith in Him, Kaukab, but my heart sinks at the thought of what might have happened. Abdul Haq, from Gulmohar Street, was lucky but will my son be? Haq recovered last year from his fractured skull which he got after visiting Istanbul's historic mosques. They had drugged him and then bludgeoned him, taking his passport. Accepting the hospitality of a kind local who offered him tea was the last thing he remembered." The woman lowers her voice to an almost inaudible whisper. "Who knows what has happened? Only yesterday *The Afternoon* said that a rotting corpse has been discovered under the debris of a tower that was blown up back in the summer."

"We mustn't allow ourselves to despair of His mercy, sister-ji. Tower, what tower?"

"It was in the paper, but no one knows much about it yet. It was a dark-skinned boy, they say, a Pakistani or Indian or Bengali. It's possible that he was an illegal immigrant but who can tell?"

"May Allah treat the poor boy's soul gently," Kaukab whispers. "He must be known to a few other illegal immigrants in the town, but they can't come forward to say they knew him because they fear they'll be detained and sent back."

The woman sighs and places a hand on Kaukab's. "You are so good, Kaukab. You have had tragedy in your own family and yet here you are, thinking of others, consoling me. You haven't forgotten His goodness. And of course the same is true of Chanda's mother—she's been so forthcoming with reassuring words too." She places a rose into the vase. "Incidentally, Kaukab, last night I couldn't sleep and so, at about three, I decided to get up to read a few pages of the Koran and pray for the safety of my boy. I was in the bathroom, doing my ablutions, and through the window I saw Chanda's mother standing outside Jugnu's house."

"Next door?"

"Yes. The poor woman obviously wanted to see the last home her daughter had had, to stand in front of it and grieve. She couldn't do it in the daylight hours because people would have found it strange, thinking she was being disloyal to her sons. The things we poor mothers have to do, Kaukab!"

"I don't think it's wise for her to be out at three."

"She wasn't alone. She had with her that young man who they have employed as help at the shop. She was pointing out various things to him—no doubt telling him little things like which was the room filled with butterflies."

"I have heard that they have employed someone. I personally don't go there anymore as you know, but Sadiqa from number 121 said she had seen him a few times but wasn't sure who he was. She was beginning to think it might be a nephew brought over from Pakistan."

"Maybe that's who he is. I don't know."

The telephone rings and as Kaukab gets up to answer it the woman gets to her feet too, saying she'd better get back and finish cleaning up the garden.

Someone from Shamas's office is calling to say that the photographic negatives which Shamas had wanted the town council to purchase from a photographer in the town centre have been destroyed. He had asked Kaukab to telephone his office yesterday about the purchase, saying that the idea had come to him some time ago but that he had forgotten about it due to his injuries. It was a matter of utmost urgency that the photographer be contacted. He hoped it wasn't too late, that the man hadn't consigned the whole irreplaceable lot into a rubbish tip. But apparently it *is* too late. A new shop has sprung up where the photographer's studio was, and he himself is said to be holidaying in Australia after selling the light-fittings and chairs and gilt-frames to a junk shop and throwing away everything else—the backdrops, the pictures, the negatives, the soft toys that distracted little children, the feather boas.

Kaukab carries the vase of roses to the bottom of the stairs and looks up, hesitating, summoning the courage to take it up. Because of her pain, it had taken her a full five minutes to carry the lunch tray up to Shamas earlier, and a full five down. She enters the stairwell which is dark because the bulb died out last week with a small metallic sound and it is situated too high on the ceiling for her to replace—if only her children were living at home. She arrives on the topmost step and, under her breath, tells Allah she loves Him as He's always taken care of her.

Shamas's eyes are closed when she comes in. His forehead is bruised an unlikely green and there is a bump the size of a plum above the left ear. His skin is bleached in several places, the colour of Imperial Leather soap. She looks away from him, as she has frequently done over the past month, sparing herself the sight; it is too distressing to contemplate and yet she is crushed by guilt every time she does avoid it.

"That was Saleemuzzamaan from your office," she says quietly, to see if he is awake, looking around to find a place for the roses, "on the telephone just now."

He opens his eyes.

"He said to tell you that they have made enquiries and that the negatives have been thrown away."

She places the roses on the shelf and stands there, not wishing to move any closer to him, fearing he would become affectionate again, the condemnation and abuse of the seventy-two houris ringing in her ears. Some vulgar people ask that if a pious man will get seventy-two wives in Paradise, how many men will a pious *woman* receive? That of course is the height of ignorance and indecency: a pious woman cannot bear the thought of letting a man other than her husband touch her—so in Paradise, where there is nothing but ease and satisfaction, why would she be put through the torment of being groped and fondled by strange men? In Paradise everyone will have at least one companion, for there is no celibacy in Paradise, and so the pious woman would be happy just to be given an eternal place by her earth-husband's side after Judgement Day. Kaukab sighs. Allah is all-wise. The couple will become young again and eternally beautiful and purified. There will be no urine, no faeces, no semen, no menstruation; erections and orgasms will last for decades, and men will often hear their earthly wives say, "By the power of Allah, I could find nothing in Paradise as beautiful as you."

Shamas tries to move his lips to convey a smile to her.

She smiles back, hoping he has not noticed that she is wearing her outdoor clothes: England is a dirty country, an unsacred country full of people filthy with disgusting habits and practices, where, for all one knew, unclean dogs and cats, or unwashed people, or people who have not bathed after sexual congress, or drunks and people with invisible dried drops of alcohol on their shirts and trousers, or menstruating women, could very possibly have come into contact with the bus seat a good Muslim has just chosen to sit on, or touched an item in the shop that he or she has just picked up—and so most Muslim men and women of the neighbourhood have a few sets of clothing reserved solely for outdoors, taking them off the moment they get home to put on the ones they know to be clean. Kaukab has been wearing one of her outdoor *shalwar-kameez*s for five days now because she has to clean Shamas after he has emptied his bowels. One day he had diarrhoea—like an hourglass—and her hands were covered with the filth, but things are better now. She would like to use water to wash the sphincter as prescribed by the Prophet, peace be upon him, but that is impractical, the water hurting the bruised areas, and so she has been reduced to using toilet paper. So each time she touches him afterwards she can't go past the fact that he is unwashed and unclean.

Shamas calls her to himself and she sits on the bed for a while before leaving—it's time for the third of the day's five prayers.

"I wish you could remember who did this to you," she says from the door. "They say it was probably the work of Chanda's family. And I don't mean to cause you pain by saying this, but I blame Jugnu for doing this to us. If he had stayed on the decent pathways of life then none of this would have happened."

"It wasn't anything to do with Chanda's family."

"How do you know who it was? You say you were grabbed from behind and passed out after being hit on the head with something heavy. You are just defending Jugnu, reflexively, as always, that's all."

He can't tell her the truth. Helplessly, he watches her leave—not knowing what he can do to alleviate her suffering. He closes his eyes. Out of the fog of the painkillers her words about the photographic negatives now come to him but he is not certain what she was referring to.

He does however remember everything that happened that morning and hasn't told it to anyone lest his attackers reveal the truth of his affair with Suraya to Kaukab. It'll destroy her.

And he hasn't wanted the children to know about it because they might come to visit and ask intelligent questions about the events of that morning—why, when, how? Someone might catch him out.

But even if he wanted to tell someone about what happened, he is not sure he would be able to find a voice in which to do it. The very minor fracture in his trachea is beginning to heal but he's having trouble speaking. He is not entirely mute but there have been bouts when he couldn't put a sentence together without stuttering or stammering.

As soon as he is well enough to walk (the doctors say it could take several weeks), he'll go to Suraya's house. He has failed to show up twice for a meeting with her. What happened to her that morning? Did his assailants make it to the *Safeena* while she was still there? He feels nausea.

What has Suraya done about their baby? He hopes, for her sake, that she isn't pregnant after all, that the pregnancy test was inaccurate. His liaison with her has complicated her life needlessly.

Chinks between the blankets are letting cold air in. He can hear Kaukab moving about downstairs, it being a small house, so little that all the doors slide into walls: Kaukab, mixing up English expressions, had said once, "There is not enough room in here to swing a door." He can't remember what he had been thinking about before falling asleep but now he does: Suraya had said she would welcome death, and now he's afraid that she might try to kill herself—perhaps she already has. Suddenly he is convinced she has committed suicide; and he wonders whether he himself hadn't died by the lakeside that morning. The two ghosts that are said to be roaming the woods near the lake—surely they are he and Suraya, their baby glowing inside her womb, his hands burning, giving out light, from the newspapers he's carrying, the searing pain of the world? No, no, he must stay lucid: he must get up immediately and try to obtain all *The Afternoon*s for the days he's been bedridden—to see if a suicide has been reported. He must get up immediately. He tries to fight the drugs and stay awake but, like a doll that must shut its eyes whenever it is horizontal, he cannot help but sleep. Yes, yes, he tells himself as he drifts off: he'll find her the way Shiva had found Parvati when she had walked away from him after a quarrel: he'll follow her footprints on the ground, a row of paisleys—like the ones on her jacket.

Kaukab looks out to see if she can find someone on their way to the shop, to ask them to get a packet of pistachios for her. All ears, Adam's apple, and brittle vanity, a teenager goes by but he is going in the opposite direction; he is smoking and she resists the urge to tell him like a good aunt that he should be fasting.

Kaukab shakes her head to drive away the smell of food from her head, the smell of Shamas's lunch—it has mostly evaporated but the tip of its long tail is trapped under the lid of the enamel pan in which the leftovers lie. An Eid card has arrived from her father in Pakistan, full of pop-up doves in flight and minutely detailed palm fronds and jasmine garlands: it is impossible to open without risking a rip to the various tines and frills that stick to each other like eyelashes after sleep.

She goes to the window and looks out and sees a newspaper photographer taking a picture of the vicar outside the church; it is typical that the white people are treating their holy man as though he is ridiculous for having stood up against the moral vacuum of this obscene and degraded country. For once she would like to go from her house to, say, the post office without being confronted by the decay of Western culture.

Jesus Christ must be spinning in his grave.

Why is she stranded at a point in life where just about everything has stopped making sense? She begins to cry, wondering how what He does to humans can be called justice. Why has He chosen this life for her, written down such things under her name in the Book of Fates? May He forgive her for these thoughts. Yes, His justice cannot be defined by human terms. Let's imagine a child and an adult in Paradise who both died in the True Faith. The adult, however, has a higher place in Paradise than the child. The Child shall ask Allah: "Why did you give that man a higher place?" "He has done many good works," Allah shall reply. Then the child shall say, "Why did you let me die so soon that I was prevented from doing good?" Allah will answer: "I knew that you would grow up to be a sinner, therefore, it was better that you should die a child." Thereupon a cry shall rise from those condemned to the depths of Hell, "Why, O Master, did You not let us die before *we* became sinners?"

It does seem unjust to us humans but we cannot fathom His ways, she tells herself. Stella, her ex-daughter-in-law, once told her that her middle name—Iris—comes from a beautiful girl of Greek and Roman myths who had iridescent wings, but lack of sufficiently varied pigments had meant that she is rarely depicted in paintings from ancient times. This is a little like how things are with Allah. We humans just don't have enough shades and tints at our disposal to make a picture of Him. Here Kaukab is, away from her children, away from her customs and country, alone and lonely, and yet He tells her to have faith in His compassion. And that is what she should do uncomplainingly, reminding herself that she is not lost, that He is with her in this strange place. And yet she doesn't know what to do about the fact that she feels utterly empty almost all the time, as though she has outlived herself, as if she has stayed on the train one stop past her destination.

Dard di Raunaq

Ki pata-tikana puchde ho—
Mere sheher da na Tanhaii ey
Zila: Sukhan-navaz
Tehseel: Hijar
Jeda daak-khanna Rusvaii ey.
Oda rasta Gehrian Sochan han, te mashoor makam Judaii ey.
Othay aaj-kal Abid mil sakda ey—
Betha dard di raunaq laii ey.

The words of the Punjabi song come to Chanda's mother as she prepares to open the shop, the yellow leaves of early November scraping
on the road outside because they are being blown about by the breeze.
Fossilized dragonflies: there are faint marks on her cheeks and temples
from the creases on the pillow where she had lain awake most of the
night.

You ask for my address—
The name of my town is Loneliness
District: The Relating of Tales
Sub-district: Longing
And its post office is Condemnation and Disrepute.
The road leading to it is Devoted Thought, and its famous monument is
    Separation.
That's where Abid, the writer of these lines, can be found nowadays—
There he sits, attracting everyone to a lively spectacle of pain.

She stacks the shelves with items taken from brown cardboard boxes. It is forty minutes till opening time, when the shop will at once fill up with little children ready to buy sweets and chocolates by the handful, it being Eid today. In ten or so minutes she will be able to track her own little granddaughters above the shop as they thump the floor, running about to put on their frocks and veils stitched with sparkling *gota* and *kiran*. All dressed up, bespangled and a-clink with toy jewellery and glass bangles, they will come downstairs to get a blessing from their grandmother on the happy day.

A woman, smiling, knocks on the glass of the entrance door, and they exchange Eid greetings as she lets her in—the woman has run out of honey to marinate the chicken for tonight's dinner.

As Chanda's mother is pointing towards where the jars of honey are kept, another woman enters and gives them both her Eid greeting: "Though, of course," she continues, "what is the point of Eid in this country—no relatives, no friends, no going up to the roof to see the Eid moon the night before, no special Eid programmes on the TV, no balloon sellers in the streets and no monkey-wallahs with their monkeys leaping about dressed up like Indira Gandhi in a sari and a black-and-white wig? In short, no *tamasha*, no *raunaq*."

Except *dard di raunaq*—thinks Chanda's mother, remembering the Punjabi verses from earlier. A spectacle of pain.

The woman with the honey agrees with the newcomer. "We are stranded in a foreign country where no one likes us. I heard someone say only yesterday that our poor Shamas-brother-ji was beaten up by, who else but, white racist thugs."

"By the whites? *One* of the rumours I have heard is that the people from the mosque had him beaten up, to stop him from testifying against the man who he is said to have seen abusing a child."

The new customer has come to pick up the mince meat which she had ordered over the phone and which Chanda's father had prepared last night and placed in the freezer. "This *is* cold. I feel for poor brother-ji's frozen hands. Why don't you hire a full-time assistant?"

"Sister-ji, don't be inconsiderate," the woman with the honey says. "Why should they hire an assistant? Next month there will be a trial and then, Allah willing, both the boys will be back here and take over the reins of the business from their aged mother and father."

The other woman looks ashamed and says to Chanda's mother, "Forgive me, sister-ji, I didn't mean to imply that your sons would never return. They are going to be acquitted, of course they are. And from December onwards, brother-ji would never have to touch these hatefully chilly pieces of meat. Allah will deliver both your boys to you safely. Just you wait. But when I referred to a full-time assistant, I was thinking of that boy I saw here three days ago. I thought it was someone you had hired part-time, to relieve the load a little."

Chanda's mother takes an invisible blow to the stomach and holds her breath. "I don't know who you are talking about," she manages to say in a tiny voice.

The other customer joins in with a frown. "I saw a boy here last week too, sister-ji, at the back. No?"

Chanda's mother has become a reed that's sounding the plaintive note. "It must have been a customer who had wandered back there. We haven't hired anyone."

On their way out, the two women laugh. "That's who it must have been—a customer. Anyway, sister-ji, I heard poor Kaukab is having problems with her foetus-container, that it's slipping out of her. Is it true? They had to pin back mine last year but then I made the mistake of lifting a heavy plant pot in the garden and the whole thing came undone again. I'd better pay Kaukab a visit soon to warn her not to exert herself too much after the operation."

After the two customers have left, Chanda's mother bolts the door and has to steady herself against it, feeling as alone as the young Joseph at the bottom of the well.

So: people have seen that boy—the fake Jugnu—here? No one must know that they have had anything to do with him—or have a hand in his version of what happened to Chanda and Jugnu. He will say that he and his lover had been on the run in Pakistan, moving from city to city, town to town, because they had wanted to get married against the wishes of the girl's family who were hunting them in order to kill them—one of the many hundreds of "honour killings" that take place over there every year.

They haven't managed to find a counterfeit Chanda. And until they have found a girl, the boy must not be spotted here. They have rented him a room in a faraway street and he has come to the shop on three occasions so that the family can go over the finer details with him.

Under cover of darkness, Chanda's mother had taken him to Jugnu's house and pointed out which window belongs to which room, what piece of luggage was found where, which door was normally used by the couple to enter and leave the house.

But from now on, the boy must not come here. The family will pretend to be as shocked and surprised as anyone else by his tale when it is made public. He wants a down payment but they'll give that to him the day before he (or he and a female) presents himself to the station—while she and Chanda's father and their daughter-in-law are sitting by the telephone, waiting for a call from the police to tell them of what has transpired.

Falling asleep last night she had had a few moments of panic, thinking about the dead body found under the rubble of the building that was blown up earlier in the year: an illegal immigrant, in all likelihood—what if this fake Jugnu of theirs takes it into his head that the mangled boy is his lost brother and goes to the police to make inquiries, not caring that his true story would contradict the tale Chanda's family has concocted? She imagines him asking the police to check if the dead boy has a single gold hair amid the black ones on his head. So far he has given no indication that he knows of the newspaper reports—he can't read English very well and, even if he did, he would think buying *The Afternoon* an extravagant waste of 45p. He is insecure about—if not frightened of—talking to white people, so if he hears about the story it will be from an Urdu- or Punjabi-speaker. From now on they must make sure he doesn't talk to Pakistanis and Indians. They must frighten him into not contacting anyone about anything: *Some careless word of yours could easily reach the authorities and have you thrown out of the country—without you first having earned the money our plan will bring you.*

She leaves the door to continue the work she had interrupted to serve the early customers, the sound of her granddaughters reaching her through the ceiling as they get up to begin celebrating the festival—this *dard di raunaq,* this Eid of unhappiness. But five minutes later and it's her daughter-in-law that has come down the stairs, pointing at the shop's entrance as she rushes towards it, shouting: "She's outside. Open the door and stop her."

"Who?" she asks her, but the daughter-in-law—her breathless haste upsetting a stack of Metro Milan joss-stick packets, which tumble to the floor from the shelf in a fragrant primary-coloured heap—is struggling with the door.

"*Who* is outside?" she repeats and then the olive-green boxes of Kasuri *methi* fall from her own hands: Chanda? "My Chanda? Where?"

She runs to the door—murmuring, "My Allah, does Your kindness towards Your creatures know any limits?"—and follows the daughter-in-law outside. The road is empty, and the daughter-in-law is looking around, now rushing to stand in the middle of the leaf-strewn road, now coming back to its edge.

"You saw my *Chanda*? Where? Just now?" Some hours are potent beyond measure, making wishes—uttered by heart or tongue—come true, regardless of whether they are genuinely meant.

Instead of answering, the daughter-in-law whispers to herself: "But she was right here, a moment ago." And to her mother-in-law she finally explains, trying to keep exasperation out of her voice, "No, not *Chanda*, mother-ji. It was the girl who came here back in the summer. I told you about her. The illegal immigrant." She goes to stand in the middle of the road again. "Where has she gone? She couldn't have gone far in the time it took me to come out here. She wears one of those lockets containing a miniature Koran."

Chanda's mother lowers herself onto the front step, moving aside to let the daughter-in-law go back into the shop. The young woman mimics in passing what she had said earlier: " 'You saw my *Chanda*? You saw my *Chanda*?' " And hisses: "For God's sake! She's *dead*."

Chanda's mother stays on the front step for five minutes, looking dazedly ahead but then the daughter-in-law comes back down full of remorse and places a hand on her shoulder, telling her to come in out of the cold. "I am sorry, I forget sometimes that things have been just as bad for you. If not worse. I am losing a husband, but in your case it's two sons and a daughter. I am sorry." She tells the daughter-in-law not to worry about her, sends her up to dress the little girls and begins to rearrange the joss-stick packets on the shelf, mechanically picks up the olive-green Kasuri *methi*.

The light of the world has gone out. Above all she has to beg forgiveness from the souls of Chanda and Jugnu, for the elaborate lie she has helped construct in order to save her sons. If only there was a grave: she'd go and bury her face in the earth where they lie waiting to be questioned by the angels on Judgement Day.

She stands in the shop, holding a dozen bottles of rosewater, and brings Chanda's face before her eyes. How to explain the bond she had with her daughter? There she was, thinking that she had had her last ever period more than seven months ago, that that was it now as far as menstruation was concerned—her breath changed odour, her heart palpitated, her hands and feet became chilled—but then one night she dreamt of Chanda and woke up to find herself flowing again from down there, the place that, in her case, had proved to be the portals both of life and of death: Chanda came out of there, as did her killers.

WINTER

A Thousand
Broken Mirrors

December; and today was the last day of the trial. It lasted a total of five days and the jury returned the verdict two hours ago. The outcome was what most people expected. There were no last-minute witnesses bursting into the courtroom. There were no new pieces of evidence. Though of course there were some people who thought the verdict would go the other way. Someone even floated a rumour that Chanda's parents had paid a young man to say that he and his girlfriend had bought Chanda and Jugnu's passports from them in Pakistan and had entered Britain with them. It is said that Chanda's parents had paid a substantial amount of money—the amount varies from person to person—to the young man for telling that lie to the police. But he had taken the money and disappeared, never arriving at the police station—Chanda's parents had not received the telephone call from the police they were expecting, telling them that the trial was being postponed, cancelled, because they had received some new information.

Shamas stands outside the courts, waiting for the bus that will take him home. The sun has vanished completely and, here and there, there is a rain of cold thin droplets that gusts of wind push closer together so that briefly they look like pale-blue veils and banners floating away in the air, swaying. The trees toss as though rubbed with itching powder.

He stands holding the black flower of his umbrella, beside the shop called The Enchanted Forest that sells sawdust-filled hummingbirds in

glass jars like sweets by the dozen, flamingos so life-like they can be mistaken for artificial, trout with carnation gills, and hornbills posing on sea-
kneaded driftwood, and where the tawny lioness in the window becomes
a striped tigress when the sun is in the right place and the bars of the shut-
ters throw their shadows onto it.

Only this week has he been able to get out of bed following the assault.
And the first thing he did was to go to Suraya's house—the house she had
grown up in, her mother's house, the house where Shamas and she had
made love on two occasions back in the summer. But it turns out that she
has sold the house. He doesn't know where she is. He rang the infirmary
because he remembered wondering in his weeks'-long delirium whether
she had killed herself, whether she had had a miscarriage. He even went to
the cemetery to see if he could find her mother's grave—in the hope that
she would visit—but to no avail.

It's December and this morning there was a layer of ice on the puddles
as thin as the glass light-bulbs are made of. Kaukab has been unable to
attend the trial because her condition is worsening. She needs surgery for
her womb but the doctors have been unable to find a place for her at the
hospital; the operation will be in January. She is in severe pain, he knows,
and having to nurse him back to health has not been easy.

He raises a hand in greeting on seeing Kiran walking towards him, the
misty rain accumulating on her umbrella, too insubstantial to collect into
beads and slip down the outer slope like children sliding down a hill.

His heart kicking, he listened as the jury convicted Chanda's brothers
today. Feeling weightless and heavy at the same time, he heard the judge
say that the killers had found a cure to their problem through an immoral,
indefensible act; a cure, a remedy—and their religion and background
took care of the bitter aftertaste. Their religion and background assured
them that, yes, they were murderers but that they had murdered only *sinners*. The judge said that Chanda and Jugnu had done nothing illegal in
deciding to live together but, Shamas knows, that the two brothers feel
that the fact that an act is legal does not mean it's right.

Kiran was at the courts too today. Charag, his former wife Stella, Mah-
Jabin and Ujala have been attending the trial too; they are staying with
some friends while in Dasht-e-Tanhaii. He was surprised to see Kiran
there this afternoon but appreciated her gesture in coming.

"This cold weather," she says quietly upon arriving to stand beside him, shaking that head full of greying hair, the hair that she used to weave into a plait strong as a leather belt when younger, coiling the locks and fastening them with a series of diamond-like rhinestone pins.

"This morning I discovered a single icicle, thin as a thermometer, outside my window."

"Do you remember the year when winter unexpectedly arrived in September and everywhere the rain being held in the bowls of garden flowers froze into ice? About twenty years ago."

"Was it really that long ago?" From this existence of two moments, we have to steal a life.

"Shamas, I haven't heard whether the police have found out anything about who assaulted you."

"No. I didn't see who it was, so there are no leads. None of my children had been told about it, but they found out when we met at the courts this week. I am mostly healed but they were still shocked by my condition. They gave me a headache as they asked me a hundred concerned questions. Had the police done this, Had the police done that?" They had offered to drive him home, but he didn't want their company—afraid that a shrapnel of the truth might be extracted from him by them.

The bus is almost full and they have to sit upstairs. Their bodies become warm soon after the journey begins while, outside, the rain intensifies, big drops that each hit the windows diagonally and break into a row of six to eight smaller drops, sticking there to the dry glass that is vibrating like a harp string.

"Your sons reminded me of you—the way the elder stands, the younger's way of talking. I can see them in you."

"The children will come home tomorrow for a few hours, much to their mother's satisfaction. They are terribly missed by her." His distorted reflection in the steel tubing of the seat in front reminds him of the time he saw Jugnu leaning over a scarab beetle: his face was being reflected in the insect's polished silver back.

"I wanted to come to the courts yesterday too," Kiran says.

Someone rustles a broadsheet newspaper at the back and it sounds like a peacock dancing with its tail fanned out, the feathers aquiver.

In the seat in front of Kiran and Shamas a small boy of about eight or nine (the same age as Suraya's son, surely) is talking to an adult man, an uncle or father; he's eating an apple, journeying bit by bit along its equator, and his talk is obviously a complaint about school, "Everyone these days is doing the sideways thumb-flick thing when they want to point to someone standing next to them, copying the new boy in class . . ." He stops to take a bite.

A new boy in class? Shamas's heart begins to beat faster as it occurs to him that the new boy could be Suraya's son: could it be that she has managed to bring her son to England? Which school does this apple-eating boy attend?

". . . who's called James Hamby. Everyone thinks he's so cool . . ."

The new boy is obviously not Suraya's son. Just for a moment back then Shamas had had an image of himself standing outside this boy's school to meet Suraya as she comes to pick up her son. His heart is hammering inside his breast—from now on he'll see everywhere a possible map that'll lead him to her. He fears he's going to end up wandering around this town, muttering her name.

Kiran says, "I know how painful the past few days have been for you. When they set up home together, there were rumours that Chanda's family would soon poison them both. Of course, it didn't happen—our neighbourhood runs on gossip."

"Kaukab, I know, sometimes blames Jugnu and Chanda for what happened. They tried to turn their back on the world, on the world's trouble, and found themselves stabbed in the back."

"Meaning: No one on the planet has yet earned the right to be that innocent?"

Shamas nods, but his attention is drawn towards the people waiting to get on the bus, out there, now that they are approaching a stop: no, Suraya is not among them. He turns to Kiran. "Do you know this Punjabi couplet?

Kuj Sheher de loke vi zalim san
Kuj mainon maran da shauk vi si

It's by Munir Niazi."

Kiran translates the words into English, "*On the one hand, the city sur-*

rounding me was easily provoked. On the other, I was curious about ways of dying. Though, of course, it's their curiosity about ways of *living* that led to Chanda and Jugnu's death."

"The second verse should be, 'On the other, I was curious about ways of living.' *Kuj mainon* jeen *da shauk vi si.* They did not have a death wish. They had a *life* wish."

"Jugnu, with a blindfold of butterflies on his eyes," Kiran says after a while.

"Why weren't they careful? Even animals know to retreat from obvious danger. For all his love of the natural world, Jugnu should have remembered that all animals retreat from fire."

"All, except moths."

The sky is getting darker. Evening is on its way, planting flags of sadness as it comes.

Kiran says, "You mustn't feel too sad. In this life we are duty bound to dig up a little happiness. Remember Kaukab's brother visited England last year?"

Shamas looks at her.

"I met him," she says quietly.

Shamas nods: "I thought you would be curious." He smiles at her: "I hope Kaukab didn't see you two together."

Shamas glances at the newspaper in front of him. He cannot remember the last time he looked at the news. *A seventeen-year-old Palestinian girl was beaten to death in the Gaza Strip by her father for having lost her virginity . . . The Bahamian authorities found 56 Haitian migrants and the body of another on a desolate shore six days after their sailing boat foundered, the US coastguard said yesterday. The survivors said about 130 people were on board when the 30 ft boat left Haiti for Miami ten days ago . . . In Saudi Arabia, a fifteen-year-old boy has been publicly beheaded for changing his religion from Islam to Christianity . . .*

Shamas waits to see if she would resume telling him about the lost lover. There was a shameful expression on her face when she mentioned him, mentioned her search for happiness. Perhaps she thinks people would judge her? The world doesn't rub salt into our wounds exactly: it has coated us with salt so that whenever we happen to get injured it is doubly painful.

"How is your father, Kiran?" he says to indicate that she doesn't have to continue with the earlier subject, in case she has begun to regret having confided in him during the minutes away from him. "Is he still finishing every sentence with a laugh as though ridiculing his illness?"

Kiran however does wish to return to the earlier topic, and says, "I didn't meet him while he was visiting your house. Remember he left Dasht-e-Tanhaii to go to London, to spend his last two weeks in England looking up old friends in the capital. Well, one day I received a letter from him—from London—saying he was coming back to Dasht-e-Tanhaii just to see me. The look on my face had alarmed my father. 'What was in that letter?' he asked, having seen me reading it earlier. 'Has someone died?' I wanted to say, no, someone dead has come alive."

"He wrote to you and came back to Dasht-e-Tanhaii? I didn't know that. Did you know he had named his daughter after you?"

"No, I didn't, but he told me when we met. You knew?"

"Yes, but I didn't want to mention it in case it hurt you. I am sorry."

"There he was, at the doorstep one day soon after the letter. All my life I have looked at other men with the hope of catching a fleeting glimpse of one of his gestures, a skin-colouration like his, a smile resembling his. Now, there was the accumulated sadness of compromises in his features that comes to everyone in old age."

"I don't think he knew you had gone to Karachi."

"No. I told him last year." She is sitting stiffly, spine held away from the back of the seat. "He brought for me what he called 'the five arrows of Love, the mind-born god': there was a red lotus, a deep-red *asoka* flower, a coral-green froth that was mango blossom, yellow jasmine, and a blue lily."

"Yes. Spring is the time associated with romance and they were the five flowers of the Subcontinental spring."

"He stayed in a hotel and I visited him at various places in town." She looks at Shamas. "What must you think of me, Shamas? An old woman living in the past."

"Most people live in the past because it's easy to remember than to think. Most of us don't know *how* to think—we've been taught *what* to think instead. And, no, I don't think badly of you."

She doesn't say anything more and looks out of the window, craning her neck occasionally to keep this or that in view as the bus rushes along the road.

Two days ago, Shamas thought for a brief moment that he recognized Suraya's paisley jacket in the window of a charity clothes shop—but on second glance they turned out to be someone else's footprints, not hers.

The bus passes an electrical appliances shop that has a poster claiming that theirs is the *Best deal* ON/OFF*er*. The photographs of the immigrants are lost forever. A jeweller's shop will open soon in the place where the photographer's studio used to be: empty wristwatch boxes and little finger-ring cases are arranged in neat rows in the window, the lids open: a miniature cinema theatre of satin-and-plush seats. A chair can be glimpsed inside, for the customers to sit in, its tall ornately moulded back bringing to mind the frame of a mirror.

"When he left me in England all those years ago," Kiran says, "he said he'd be back in twenty-five days. When we re-met, he said if he were a religious man, he'd believe that God had turned those twenty-five days to twenty-five years as a punishment for not saying 'God willing' after telling me about his return. I told him that as far as I was concerned, he didn't go even after he'd gone."

"I never understood why you hadn't married anyone else."

"There were other possibilities. I'd get frightened of the loneliness of old age, and the members of the Sikh community would try to match me up with people. Some good, some not. But." She waves her hand in resignation. "There was even a white man I had gone to school with and had been terribly in love with as a girl. I was the only Asian in my school, and I used to wonder why no one had ever asked *me* out on a date. I approached that boy to see if he'd go out with me but he said no. And when I asked him to explain, he said, 'Well, you are a darkie!' The word 'Paki' wasn't invented until the 1970s, otherwise he would have used that. When he said that to me, I suddenly realized, 'Of *course* I am a darkie.' And because I loved him I didn't want him to be called a darkie-lover, and decided to stay away from him. He said, 'It's a pity you are a darkie, because if you were white you'd be really pretty.' And then some years after we left school we ran into each other . . . but nothing serious happened. The Sikh friends and acquaintances still try sometimes—they mean well, I suppose—but these days it's mostly widowers and illegal immigrants."

He wonders how long Kaukab's brother had stayed with her last year and asks her.

She is silent and then says, "He was still here around the time Chanda and Jugnu died—late summer."

"Do you still write to each other?"

She gives no answer.

He sees a tear slide down out of her eye and, appalled at his insensitivity at asking her so many intimate questions, he says, "I am terribly sorry." And this after she has shown him the great kindness of coming to the trial.

"I have been crying for a while: the tears've caught up with me only now."

She doesn't say anything further and Shamas looks away, out where the rain and the ice-clusters have stopped falling, and a day-moon is shining in the winter sky.

Kiran, composed now, sighs and paraphrases what she said earlier, "I met him on five occasions around Dasht-e-Tanhaii, and a sixth time in my house. That was the last time. I kept his presence in England from my father, and—during that sixth meeting, when he came to the house—I also tried to hide the fact that he was in there. He came very late at night and I took him upstairs . . ."

"You don't have to tell me any of this, Kiran. I know it must be painful."

"You are too kind. But please let me talk. I was upstairs with him. We poured all our longing into those moments. When we made love, it was as though we were trying to kill each other. And then I heard footsteps coming up the stairs but it was too late . . ."

"Your father managed to climb the stairs?"

Kiran places a hand on her breast. "I know I have let you think I came to hear the verdict today as an act of friendship towards you."

"Didn't you?"

"I was there because of Chanda's younger brother—Chotta. I thought you knew about me and him. We tried to keep our relationship a secret, but *some* people in the neighbourhood found out. I've always wondered if you were one of them."

"And he walked in on you while you and . . ."

"I had given Chotta a set of house keys. He saw us and went away shouting abuse, pulling off and shattering all those mirrors I have hanging in the staircase. A thousand broken mirrors: there was an eternity's worth of bad luck in his wake. It all awoke my father. I had to tell him everything. I resisted at first, saying, 'I cannot tell you what I have done.' But he retorted, 'A good person cannot do what others may not know.' I am sorry, Shamas."

"You don't have to apologise, Kiran. Who am I to deny you the comforts of a companion?"

She buries her head in his shoulder.

He places a hand on her head. "Did you love Chotta?"

"I've cried for him, which is the same thing, isn't it?"

"I don't know."

"And I do *have* to apologize to you, perhaps even ask for forgiveness. You see, that night was the night Chanda and Jugnu are thought to have been murdered. I ran after him when I had put on my clothes but couldn't find him anywhere. He must have been in a rage. I don't doubt for a moment that I contributed to the anger he unleashed on Chanda and Jugnu. I am terribly sorry." She looks at Shamas and then withdraws her gaze from him. "Please say something."

A bird sits on a bare tree outside, as though waiting for it to grow leaves and flowers.

Kiran is saying, "He refused to see me all during the coming weeks. I'd stop in the streets on seeing him but he would turn back or slip into a lane. I caught up once, tried to put him in good humour with a dozen cajoleries, but he said women were nectar-coated poison, puffs of coloured dust, dancing butterflies, and pushed me away."

"When did you begin seeing him?"

"I think it must've been around the time Chanda and Jugnu began seeing each other."

"And it also *ended* the night their story ended."

"The fact that they were happy while *he* had just been betrayed must've made him resent them, perhaps."

Daylight has faded altogether now; the road outside has become a river of car headlights heading home. The bus passes the Ali Baba carpet warehouse. Plastic fish are strung by their mouths on a sagging string above the fishing equipment shop, looking like the washing line of small mermaids.

Chanda and Jugnu are out there somewhere.

And Suraya.

Perhaps she returned to Pakistan? But: an unmarried woman with a child in her womb—she'll be arrested for the sin of fornication. No, no, she's still here in England.

Perhaps she aborted the child to be able to go back: her husband was about to marry another woman, and so she did all she could to be in Pakistan to disrupt and prevent the wedding—?

He has tried to get information from Kaukab about "Perveen," but apparently she has not been in touch since that first time. "Other women of the neighbourhood got to her, no doubt," she said with regret. "Telling her lies about me, turning her against me. And, between my own illness and your injuries, I haven't had time to go to her street."

Kiran asks, "Do you want to know how it began?"—and goes on without waiting for his answer: "I heard a knock—very gentle—on my door one night. It was about ten o'clock. I opened the door and he asked me if he could come in. I recognized him from the shop, and although I was taken aback by him asking to be let in, I brought him into the kitchen. He said he wanted to talk, but he kept his eyes on me quite blatantly as I moved about making tea, and it was only after a while that I realized he was drunk. And it must've been soon after that that he stood up, eyes still trained on me. We both knew what he wanted to do but neither made a move for many minutes. Things refused to come to a boil. My father asked from his bed who was at the door, and I said no one. That was his prompt. The fear that I would shout if he came near me was what had kept him from making a move but now he knew I wouldn't. So he lunged." Without looking at Shamas she says, "I didn't resist."

"I think I understand why you didn't go to the police to offer information or come to talk to me."

"It was because people would have called me names."

"I wouldn't have."

"After Chanda and Jugnu disappeared there were rumours about Chanda's family's involvement. Chotta had refused to talk to me or see me after that terrible night but it was several weeks later that he came around one day and confessed to the murders. I never saw him again. I am so sorry."

"Are you saying you could have helped put the whole matter to rest sooner?"

"No, no. He told me everything *after* the policemen from England had got their testimonies from the people in Sohni Dharti. I am sorry."

"I don't know what to say. You did what you had to do to save your name, Kiran. Even *he* tried to preserve your good name: what happened with you that night isn't mentioned in any of the testimonies—that that was part of the rage unleashed on Chanda and Jugnu. He didn't tell it to anyone."

The bus is pulling up at their stop. They both go down the stairs and the winter's chill hits them in the face when they get out. Each day after the trial, Shamas has gone home and told Kaukab the details of what happened at the court. Based on what he learns at the court, they put together the sequence of events that led to Chanda and Jugnu's murders, adding new details each time he returns from the hearing, moving the narrative of the couple's last few hours forward each day. But he'll have to keep secret what Kiran has just told him.

He and Kiran stand together for a few moments before going their separate ways.

"Do you know what he was doing, drunk, knocking on my door at ten o'clock that night?"

Shamas looks up at the sky where the moon is the colour of garlic peel, with a morning-sky blue girdle around it.

"He had mistaken my house for the prostitute's next door, and when I answered he had decided to try his luck with me."

"This December is harsher than last year's."

"Well, *we* are older and weaker by another year, remember." She smiles. Shamas smiles in return and tells her to tread carefully on the rain-slippery roads as she walks away.

After a sentence has just been written down, a sense of unfinished business compels the tip of the pen to return to that place back there where an "i" is still to be dotted, a "t" left uncrossed; and during a distraction, the mind is vaguely aware that somewhere in the room there is an apple not yet eaten down to the core, a cup of tea with two sips still remaining in it; and so now, now that the conversation with Kiran is over, he is aware of a similar dissatisfaction within him. He locates it: he had wanted to ask her whether Chanda's brother had ever discussed with her the matter of Chanda and Jugnu setting up home together. He and Kiran were lovers: the matter would have come up. How did he view his own illicit and, yes, *sinful* encounters with Kiran while condemning Chanda and Jugnu for the same thing?

As he watches her recede in the distance, he wonders whether she had told him the truth: he wonders whether she knew about the details of the murders many weeks or even months before the British police got their lead in Sohni Dharti. She just didn't come forward because she was afraid of what people would think of her.

And just now on the bus, she was no doubt unable to face him with her guilt and had lied about it.

Nothing is an accident: it's always *someone's* fault; perhaps—but no one teaches us how to live with our mistakes. Everyone is isolated, alone with his or her anguish and guilt, and too penetrating a question can mean people are not able to face one another the next day.

And he is not sure whether he will ever be able to confront or compel her to admit the truth.

They are trapped here with each other—locked up together in solitary confinement—and there is no release.

How Many Hands Do I Need to Declare My Love to You?

I begin this action with the name of Allah, Kaukab whispers in Arabic. It's midmorning and she's begun preparing the evening meal: this house—so full of disappearances for so long—will have people in it tonight. She wonders if she had been smiling a little in her sleep last night—the daylight hours still numb from yesterday's verdict.

Magpies, chuckling and cackling woodenly, dart in and out of the hedge outside, their markings panda-like, their tails turned up like a spoon in a glass.

From a carrier bag she takes out the *karela*s: the six-inch-long bittergourds, pointed at either end, the skin covered in tough green sine-waves like backs of crocodiles cresting the surface of a swamp. She counts the gourds and they are ten. A sufficient number: one each for the six adults, and one for the little grandson in case he wishes to experiment. And that still leaves three to prevent embarrassment and regret in case someone wants a second helping. She begins to prepare each gourd in turn. Feeling drops of moisture exploding in her face like fistfuls of rain hurled by the wind, she scrapes off the tough ridges onto the flattened carrier bag, and then carefully introduces a long cut into the skin of the gourd by running the tip of the knife from top to bottom. Inside, the seeds are large, square, and scarlet, embedded in white flannelette pulp. Her thumb gouging the vegetable delicately, she removes the seeds so that the gourd is empty. Each lime-coloured purse is to be filled later with half-cooked mince meat, wound about tightly with a yard of thread to prevent any spillage, and then cooked until the skins have softened and the mince inside fully ready. She drops the skins into a bowl and sprinkles salt over them to draw out the bitterness.

A little dance of rhythmically raised and lowered arms always accompanies this dish: one end of the thread has to be located and pulled out, the vegetable spinning on the plate like a kite-flyer's spindle. Kaukab has never *stitched* the openings shut with a needle as some women do: she knows some metals can be poisonous and doesn't want the risk.

The perfect hostess, she makes a mental note to put out a saucer on the dining table just before the meal begins, to receive the oily threads.

In a large pan the size of an elephant's footprint (as Jugnu used to refer to it), Kaukab soaks some basmati rice. *Bas*—scent; *mati*—earth. She inhales the scent of Pakistan's earth deep into her lungs. She washes the starch out of the grains by gently rubbing them until the water is no longer milky and the rice looks like little stones at the bottom of a clear rain-fed stream.

Nusrat Fateh Ali Khan's voice, singing Allah's praises, fills the air from the cassette player on the refrigerator. Nusrat is gone, leaving his songs behind, the way when a snail dies its shell remains.

The three cassettes, Pakistani imports, had cost £5 from Chanda's parents' shop two years ago; these twenty or so songs would have cost about £45 from white people's music shops in the town centre, Nusrat being famous among them these days too. Kaukab had shuddered at the price when she was told about it: tonight's lavish meal—stuffed bitter-gourds, grilled chicken, mutton-and-potato curry, *pilau* rice (in case someone doesn't feel like eating chappatis), chappatis (in case someone doesn't feel like eating *pilau* rice), *shami* kebabs, cauliflower-and-pea curry, fruit salad, sweet vermicelli decorated with edible gold leaf, all spiced and flavoured with the finest and freshest spices—will cost just over £39. It would feed six people and a child tonight and the leftovers would be consumed by Kaukab and Shamas over the next day or two.

Islam is said to forbid music, Kaukab remembers as she marinades the chicken breasts with natural yoghurt mixed with Australian wildflower honey and the juice of two lemons, puréed onion, grated ginger and garlic, but she has always reminded herself that when the holy Prophet Muhammad, peace be upon him, had migrated to Medina, the girls there had welcomed him by playing the *duff* drums and singing *Tala'al-Badru 'alayna,* which is Arabic for *The white moon has risen above us.*

From the cupboard under the sink, with its dark light of a forest floor (Jugnu again), she takes out the packet of desiccated Arabian dates that she had hidden there: hidden there from herself, dates being a weakness of hers. She steadies herself against the counter as she straightens—the bending has resulted in a spike of pain in her lower abdomen.

She opens each date to check that it doesn't have insect eggs inside, takes out the stone, and then washes the flesh before dropping it in a bowl of hot water. As she discards any insect-riddled fruit, she remembers being a young girl and joking with her friends that they shouldn't throw away fruit from the sacred land of Arabia just because of a minor impurity, that they should remember the story of the Pakistani man who went to Saudi Arabia to perform the pilgrimage and, in feverish delight at being in the holy land, began to kiss the words written on the walls along the road: Arabic to him was what the Koran was written in—he didn't know that it was an everyday language too—and what he took to be verses from the Koran was actually an advertisement for hair-depilatory cream. Kaukab sighs as she remembers her girlhood, and only then is she disturbed by the realization that she has just thought of something irreverent if not offensive to Allah.

She shakes her head.

Muslims must be alert against such thoughts: Satan, the Father of Woes, is always around, ready to urinate in your mind through your ears the moment he feels you have let your guard down!

To drive away the Accursed One, she revolves sacred facts about the Koran in her head: the text is composed of 114 chapters, 70 of which were dictated at Mecca and 44 at Medina. It is divided into 621 divisions, called decades, and into 6,236 verses. It contains 79,439 words, and 323,670 letters, to each of which attach 10 special virtues. The names of 25 prophets are mentioned: Adam, Noah, Ismaeel, Isaac, Jacob, Joseph, Elisha, Jonah, Lot, Salih, Hud, Shuaib, David, Soloman, Dhul-Kafl, Idris, Elias, Yahya, Zacharias, Job, Moses, Aaron, Jesus, and Muhammad. Upon all these be prayer and peace, especially on Muhammad. There are no butterflies in the Koran but nine other birds or winged creatures are mentioned: the gnat, the bee, the fly, the hoopoe, the crow, the grasshopper, the bird of Jesus, namely the bat, the ant, and the bulbul . . .

The dates, cleaned and stoned, will be cooked in creamed milk into which vermicelli—shining like a fairytale princess's golden hair—will be added. With the potato peeler she shaves a heap of thin waxy crescents from a dried coconut, to be added to the syrupy vermicelli along with rose essence, pink-husked pistachio nuts (and the dates brought back to plump fullness by the boiling water). A square of gold leaf is safe from damage between two rectangles of rough paper: it is to be stuck onto the surface of the prepared dessert. The gold leaf flutters, aware of the slightest air current, when Kaukab lifts the top paper rectangle at one corner for a little peek. It is almost as though there is something not-quite dead between the pages of a book, a brilliant trapped moth.

The food she is making is more than enough for six people, but, who knows, perhaps Allah has written in the Book of Fates that Jugnu and Chanda—safe and sound—are to walk in on the family just as it is sitting down to eat; in that case there won't be any leftovers for tomorrow or the day after.

She opens the front door to throw the date stones into the rose beds. They might germinate there next year. Tall sky-touching palms, the sons and daughters of trees growing over there in sacred Arabian soil. But she has to close the door immediately because the Sikh woman Kiran is coming down the slope with the maples, between the church and the mosque.

She crosses the kitchen and throws the date stones into the flowerbeds in the back garden. The sycamores and the hawthorns on the slope behind the house are bare. She recalls how, back in spring, the hawthorns' clotted five-petalled profusion had weighed heavy on the branches like snow. The dangling arm-long sprays had overlapped like feathers on a bird's body. And thinking about the white hawthorn blossoms, she remarks that their scent is not too dissimilar to a Pakistani beauty soap that, according to the advertisements, was *the choice of nine out of ten film starlets.* The air now smells of freshly cut wood and the sun is a white hole in the sky.

There is a knock on the front door just then—and she is paralysed, absolutely sure that it is Kiran. What does she want? The knock sounds again and she opens the door to find

Ujala.

"Oh my life!"

A chunk had been bitten out of her life when he walked away from her, away from this house, and with the Ganges flowing from one eye and the Indus from the other, she wraps her arms around him, opening her hands wide to touch as much of his back as possible. When she releases him he doesn't say anything, just gives a little flick to get his long hair out of his beautiful antelope eyes in that arrogant-seeming gesture of his. She brings him in and wants to take his face in her hands, to kiss him again and again. Get drunk, my heart. Go mad, my eye. But then she remembers what a woman had once told her at the shop concerning the latest Western theories about the bond between a mother and her son: "They say all mothers secretly want to go to bed with their sons. A bunch of people in suits and ties was talking about it on television last night." Kaukab had felt repulsed, her mind spinning with revulsion at the idea: these kind of things were said by vulgar hawkers and fishwives in the bazaars of Pakistan, but here in England *educated* people said them on *television*. To speak in this manner about a mother's love! This immoral and decadent civilisation was intent on soiling everything that was pure and transcendental about human existence! Mothers did check that their baby boys' penises were stiff first thing in the morning but that was nothing more than a parent's concern for the child, to see that everything about him was in order, developing satisfactorily; and women also quietly began to look for signs of nocturnal emissions in the bed linen and the pyjamas when the sons turned thirteen or thereabouts, and, once again, that too was no different from the eye a mother kept on her *female* children's development.

She backs away from Ujala, who has yet to say anything.

Eight years!

"You look—" she begins but stops to wipe her tears with her veil.

"How do I look?"

Like a dream walking is what she wants to say. "I knew you were coming, but I didn't know when. I said to myself he should hurry up and get here." She wants to use the English expression "the sooner, the better" but wonders whether it isn't actually "the better, the sooner"; she decides not to risk looking foolish in his eyes. With such tiny things is a semblance of dignity maintained, is a liveable life assembled. She moves forward and takes the boy in her arms again but he makes an attempt at release after only a couple of seconds, his head averted a little in discomfort. She lets go, the noise in her head louder than a tin roof in monsoon—thoughts, fears and words appearing and popping like bubbles.

The heavy stone of silence is back on the boy's lips as he takes a chair.

"Would you have breakfast? No? Tea? I am making vermicelli for you. When you were little you used to call it 'princess's hair.' " She is afraid he will snap at her, tell her to stop digging up the grave of the time that has passed, the days that have died. But he smiles at her politely, his eyes haunted, his look colourless. One night while she was pregnant with him she had dreamt there was a rainbow in her womb. What has stolen his colours?

"How did you get here?" she asks.

He is silent as though his tongue has become fused to the roof of his mouth.

"A woman in the street told me yesterday she thought she saw you in the town centre," she says. "Was that you?"

He takes a deep breath and shrugs.

"I told her she must've mistaken someone else for you, some non-descript boy who reminded her of *me*. I said to her, 'Was he a handsome boy? Don't go by *my* looks, sister-ji. My sons are very very beautiful.' " She hopes he will let her look at him to her heart's content. How long has she waited for him to return, those long years, her eyes painted with the kohl of longing, a glittering sequin of hope stitched onto her drab veil. His face, once round and healthy, looks thin and drawn: the full moon has become the crescent.

"Where are you going?" she says in panic when Ujala makes to get up. "You've only just arrived. You can't leave. By Allah, I won't let you . . ."

"I am not leaving. I would like to go upstairs and sleep for a while. I have been up since before dawn."

A shiver runs through her on hearing his voice, the ghost of a reflex from the times she called his answering machine, fearful that he might pick up the phone.

"I'll come with you and get you an extra blanket. We don't have central heating so the rooms are cold, especially upstairs. The kitchen stays warm."

She climbs the stairs ahead of him—red pain shooting up between the legs because of the speed of the ascent. Upstairs, she gets one of her new blankets out of its nylon zipped-up bag from the cupboard. "Warm as July." She smiles as she hands him the blanket.

"You didn't go to the trial," he says abruptly. "They burned parts of the bodies. Now we know for sure."

"I didn't go," Kaukab says. "No." The scent of naphthalene balls escapes from the cupboard—a protection against Jugnu's moths. Pointing to the jar full of one-pence coins in the corner, Kaukab says to the boy, as though distracting a child: "That's yours. Do you remember?"

"I remember. Do you recognize the jar?" he approaches it and strokes it with his hands. And without waiting for her to answer, goes on to explain: "It's one of a pair. Jugnu knitted copper wire around the other one and then broke the glass with a hammer to make a cage to hold the Great Peacock moth female. She had hatched ahead of the males, and hung in that cage, sending out chemical signals." Kaukab watches him as he speaks almost as though he is in a trance. "The males hatched and followed the scent to her, flying up through the attic and then down into his bedroom where the cage was hanging."

"It was his first night next door."

"He woke in the morning to find them clustered around her, the cage completely covered with vibrating velvet. The Night of the Great Peacock Moths," he whispers, and then in his normal voice says, "You once told me that back in Sohni Dharti a man had committed suicide by boiling a few handful of coins in water for a long time and then drinking that water."

She nods. "The boiling metal turned the water poisonous, yes."

He unbuckles his belt and undoes the top two buttons of his jeans to enter the bed.

Kaukab turns to leave the room. "What an awful story to remember." She wants to examine his face, to understand why he had made that comment about the suicide, but she hears him taking his pants off, the slide of fabric against skin, and therefore cannot look in his direction. "Are you sure you will be comfortable in this room? The kitchen is directly below and I am going to be cooking all day: the smell of spices will rise right through the floorboards and the carpet."

"Close the door as you leave."

Downstairs, she lets out an inward sound—echo, and then echo of echo—a cry in the forest of old age, loneliness. He is out of reach, no doubt holding her responsible for Chanda and Jugnu's disappearance. She senses loathing in him, a wall-like hate in whose foundations lie the bloody cut-up bodies of the two lovers. She thought he would be happier than he is. She'd thought he'd ask her, *Did you miss me?* And that she would answer: *No more than I'd miss my eyes.* They haven't seen each other for eight years and have, therefore, a total of sixteen-years' worth of life to catch up on, but he has barely said a word. Mah-Jabin and Charag have sent her photographs of him during his absence, but they stopped when he found out and threatened to cut himself off from them too.

It had taken her decades to rebuild the happiness she had lost when she moved to England: she had built it around her children, and, yes, around Jugnu, but she had never realized how loosely woven a thing it was, how easily torn.

She breathes in against a wave of tears and sits there for a few minutes before getting up carefully. There is a lot to do. She had peeled the potatoes last night and covered them in water to stop the rusting, and the base for the *pilau* rice was readied last night too: just a matter of reheating it half-an-hour before it's time to sit down at the dinner table and dropping the rice in it. An illiterate woman came by yesterday to ask her if she would read a letter from her brother in Pakistan, and she and Kaukab had spent the afternoon chopping up all the onions that would be needed today.

And the dozens of cloves of garlic got peeled as though all by themselves when the matchmaker stopped by in the evening and the two of them talked as they worked, the topics under discussion varying from recipes to djinns, from the new fabrics to become available in the clothes shops to all the successful marriages the matchmaker had arranged this year, the most recent one of a woman named Suraya about whose beauty she never tired of speaking.

After the dawn prayers today, Kaukab sat down with a basket and extracted the peas from each peapod with the skill of a pickpocket.

The mince for the *shami* kebabs was boiled with split chickpeas, cinnamon sticks and other spices, two days ago, beaten in a large black-stone mortar with a heavy wooden pestle until it had the texture of wet sand

and came out from between the fingers in sculpted waves when squeezed in a fist. It was patted into small discs: they are in the fridge now, and all that remains is to dip them in egg and shallow-fry them in sunflower oil minutes before eating—the egg coating would seal the mince in the thinnest omelette imaginable. For the fruit salad, she would enlist one of the other guests when they arrive: the fruit—apples, pomegranates (the very last batch of the year), pears, grapes, and peaches that look as though they are apples made out of the finest pink suede—must remain fresh and crunchy. There is coriander and mint chutney to pound in the small marble mortar the size of a green-pigeon's nest—oh, Jugnu! Oh, my Jugnu!—that she had been given as a present by a woman returning from Pakistan five years ago.

She takes the coat Ujala has left on the kitchen table and carries it into the pink sitting room. The smell of cooking mustn't get into the clothes. The whites call the Asians "smelly" but they do have a point: the coats are hung in the kitchens and the pungent smells of the spices get into them. The Asians who have moved out to the suburbs also call the Asians in this poor neighbourhood "smelly" and "stinky." Some of the women in this neighbourhood are from villages where it is common practice to put butter in the hair: the smell is often rancid. Kaukab makes sure Shamas's coat and hers are never in the kitchen.

The extractor fan has been on for over an hour now and will continue to work into the evening.

She wonders if she should ring Shamas at the office and let him know that Ujala has arrived. But she is still a little apprehensive about the telephone because two days ago, when she had dialled a wrong number, she was told to, "Get off the phone and go back to your country, you Paki bitch." She is glad Shamas doesn't drive: accidents happen, and you never know what kind of person you would have grazed the vehicle of or offended with your way of driving, what kind of name he or she would choose to call you in public.

From the floor she takes up the glove that had fallen out of Ujala's coat pocket and places it on top of the coat next door. The wool is bright green, vivid red, a deep yellow reminiscent of linseed oil. Children's primary colours. In winter the tiny mittens and gloves are all across the town centre, lone and lost, along with dropped mufflers and misplaced pompom hats. It is almost as though there is a conspiracy among the toddlers to replace the colours now that the hanging baskets containing the annual flowers have been taken down for the year, the wrought-iron brackets affixed to lamp-posts remaining empty until next summer.

She had turned off the cassette player when Ujala arrived, but now she switches it back on: so as not to disturb him, the volume is turned low, like the faint whiff from a long-empty scent bottle. She cuts the cauliflower into florets, and as she washes them in a basin her hand becomes a starfish, the florets among which it moves appearing like a coral reef. Getting the mutton-and-potato and the pea-and-cauliflower curries started and kneading the dough for the chappatis takes her to one o'clock. Turmeric has dyed the tips of her fingers golden as though with the yellow dust of lotus blossoms. She wipes the table until it is as wet and clean as an eye. It is time for the noon prayer, but before that she tiptoes upstairs and, asking herself to be courageous, goes into the room where Ujala is asleep and carries away the jar of coins. She hides it under the sink, his comment about the suicide flying inside her head the way the silver ball zigzags inside a pinball machine. She had heard somewhere that one Japanese emperor had taken his life by inhaling gold leaf, and she wonders whether the edible gold leaf could be used by someone for similar purposes. Having performed her ablutions, she says her prayers on the velvet prayer-mat, bending and straightening with immense pain, and afterwards she opens the front door to see if there is anyone outside the church—in order to ask them to go in and see if a Song of Solomon cake can be bought: it has all the spices mentioned in that Christian poem and it has been a favourite of Ujala ever since he tried it at a school fair. She doesn't have time to look in the direction of the church because she finds Mah-Jabin sitting on the doorstep, a bunch of Madonna lilies—coned-up in red paper—held against her breast like an infant.

"I rang the bell," Mah-Jabin says as she gets up.

"I was saying my prayers. I didn't hear anything at all."

"I hope I didn't disturb you. I knocked too," the girl says apologetically, placing the lilies on the table.

"My mind wandered during the prayer twice. There is nothing that torments Satan more than the sight of a faithful in prayer. He succeeded in distracting me today. I began wondering about what kind of gold leaf the Japanese have?"

Mah-Jabin smiles. "Are we having vermicelli for dessert?"

"I was just asking Ujala if he remembered calling them 'princess's hair.' "

Mah-Jabin, unwrapping the lilies, looks at Kaukab. "He left before the rest of us were up. When did he come?"

"He came around ten. Mah-Jabin, he looks so thin."

Ujala is as healthy as a footballer, as a ballet dancer, but Mah-Jabin doesn't wish to contradict Kaukab so early. She goes into the sitting room to get the vase. The pink tulips had turned violet as they had dried up in dying, a petal here and there leaning away from the cup of the others like a resting insect that hasn't quite succeeded in shaking its wings into perfect order upon alighting.

After the lilies, Mah-Jabin goes upstairs to the bathroom (where all those years ago she had sat with a knitting needle, not knowing how to proceed). She takes off the silk scarf and hangs it from the hook. The fabric was bought from an Asian material shop, just two feet of it, where once she would have bought it by the yard to make *shalwar-kameez*s. She laughs whenever her fashion-student friends make a fuss because they have to undo a few inches of a seam that has been placed wrongly. Growing up she had seen her mother—and the other women in the neighbourhood— rip up seams, put them down again, and cut and recut sleeves, necklines, hems by the dozen. Kaukab, who has never bought any Western shirts and trousers and has never paid a seamstress to make her a *shalwar-kameez*, had once claimed that in her life she had stitched five-hundred kilometres of seams.

She stands motionlessly. The stress of the previous days, and the lag brought about by the fact that her usual routines have been broken here in Dasht-e-Tanhaii, have combined to produce a kind of delirium: she fades and comes into focus with the rhythm of this mild fever, now suddenly conscious of her weight on the floor, now unconvinced of the reality of things. And now, remembering something, she opens the narrow angular cupboard in the corner that houses the immersion heater swaddled in insulating pillows of shiny silver nylon. "Hello, spaceman." It was in here that she had tossed her husband's letter—unread and crumpled-up—during the visit back in spring. The spaceman was to take it up in his rocket: toxic waste to be dumped into some distant black hole. But it is still back there, and just when she reaches in, out of curiosity, and has pulled it forward a little she hears Ujala's voice. She quickly lets go of the balled-up paper and closes the hatch. Ujala enters the bathroom just as she turns around. He is smiling, and, his arms extended towards her, he comes closer and begins to feel for the clasp of the Venezuelan necklace she is wearing. A row of seeds threaded onto cord, he had bought it for her two days ago.

"I have to return it to the shop. The seeds are poisonous, it seems. There is a note in the shop window, asking the customers to bring it back for a refund, and they have also advertised in the papers."

"Seriously?" Mah-Jabin cannot help laughing as she takes off the necklace hurriedly. It tangles in her hair and Ujala's attempts to free it make it only worse. He looks anxious for a few moments as though they won't ever be able to get rid of the lethal seeds from around her neck, from around his fingers. She calms him and they collapse against each other, smiling and tumbling like kittens, the moments a ball of yarn between them.

Shortly before she left England to get married and settle in Pakistan, Ujala had come home in the middle of the night, having slipped out soon after Shamas and Kaukab went to bed. He was twelve and had clearly been experimenting with alcohol out there on the hills or beside the lake. Mah-Jabin had taken him to his bed, quietly, not wishing to awaken the parents. The smell of beer from his mouth revolted her. He wept against her, begging her not to go to Pakistan and leave him alone here; he said that Charag was a shitty swot but she was his friend, his only *friend*, his *only* friend: "What will I do without you here? No, I am holding on to your leg until you promise to stay. I mean it: I'll hold it as long as I have to. Just watch me." She hissed at him to lower his voice, but he kept talking, the placement of words in each sentence in slight disarray—the way the drunks talk, the way their mother speaks English (once, when she had a headache, she had told the children, "Make noise silently!").

A few days later, he had had his face slapped by her in fury. She had returned from the town centre with a new suitcase and found Kaukab in tears in the kitchen. Without needing a word of explanation, Mah-Jabin had rushed up to his bedroom. "I want you to stop accusing Mother and Father. They are not forcing me into an arranged marriage. I am going because I want to." He said she was stupid not to see that they weren't giving her the advice she needed, didn't tell her openly what she was getting herself into.

Free of the Venezuelan seeds, Mah-Jabin goes downstairs, telling Ujala to come to the kitchen as soon as possible so that they can help their mother with the meal.

Several separate foods will come together to form a meal in three stages, and Kaukab's plan is to, over the next few hours, bring them each to within twenty minutes of completion. The bitter-gourds are almost ready, secured in the violet thread that Kaukab had used to sew herself a frilled tablecloth not long ago, and she tells Mah-Jabin how difficult it had been to settle on that colour as the thread with which the sewing would be done. "Because the pattern on the fabric was yellow splashed with violet, a yellow seam would stand out when it passed across a violet patch, and the reverse would be true if the thread of the other colour was chosen."

"What you needed was a transparent thread: something which the spiders should get together with the fishing-line manufacturers to develop: thin enough but sufficiently strong."

Ignoring her frivolous comment, Kaukab looks around and says, "I've always wanted this kitchen to be bigger." She is draining the water off the potatoes and putting the yellow wedges into the pan where the curry base is sizzling. "It is going to fill up this evening, and everyone will have to sit cramped around the table."

"We can eat in the sitting room," Mah-Jabin suggests. "We'll move the table in there." She slides open the door and looks in to confirm that there is enough room in there. When Ujala comes down—he is putting on a sweater and his face emerges out of the neck-hole like a diver coming up and breaking the water's surface—the brother and sister move the dining table and chairs into the centre of the next room, pushing the coffee table with the vase of lilies to one side. The Koranic verses hang in their black frames against the pink walls that are lined up to waist-length with bookshelves. "I used to cut the bookmark ribbons off Father's books to tie up the hair of my dolls," Mah-Jabin says. Ujala takes the latest issue of the Muslim women's magazine Kaukab subscribes to—the monthly *Veil*, published in Pakistan—and puts it in the pile where the previous issues are kept.

"It doesn't do any harm," Mah-Jabin whispers: she had seen the distaste on his face when he picked up the magazine full of orthodox rants and strictures, apocalyptic visions and prophecies.

"I think it does."

She looks away. "It makes her happy."

"I don't think it does. I have never seen more misery and guilt on her face than when she has just finished reading something printed in there. It's turned her into a selfish monster. *She* is the reason why Father won't openly condemn the idiocies of Islam. He thought it would hurt her. She and her like don't do any harm? She has harmed every one of us. She won't allow reason to enter this house." Mah-Jabin leaves the room and he stands looking at the verses on the wall. For millions of people, religion was often another torture in addition to the fact that their lives were not what they should be. Their world is pitiless from womb to tomb, everything in it out of their control, almost as though the life-lines on the palms of their hands were live knife-cuts, a source of pain since birth. This world gives them terrible wounds and then the holy men and women make them put those wounds into bags of salt.

He follows Mah-Jabin out into the kitchen. A ladle in each hand, Kaukab is stirring two pots simultaneously. "I should have made some chickpea stew as well, Charag's favourite, but it is not the easiest thing to digest and I didn't want him getting a stomach ache."

"But chickpea stew looks, smells and tastes so nice, though," Mah-Jabin says, as she takes one of the ladles from Kaukab.

"Yes," Kaukab agrees. "Jugnu said: 'You'll regret it if you don't eat it, and you'll regret it if you do eat it . . .' "

The air in the room changes. Mah-Jabin winces inwardly and takes in a breath at the mention of the dead man's name. Kaukab slowly looks over her shoulder at Ujala, who is sweeping the area of linoleum that has been exposed now that the table is gone. He had stopped but now resumes the strokes of the long-handled brush, the nylon bristles red as a fish's gills.

"Don't worry about the stew," Mah-Jabin says, as she picks up the cauliflower pieces and adds them to the pot. "You've cooked enough food for today. It's a feast."

"A feast?" Kaukab says. "It cost £39."

"No, Mother," Mah-Jabin shakes her head. "The *ingredients* cost that much. You should add the cost of the planning, the organization, and the cooking that has gone into it all. A meal like tonight's, if we were to pay a firm of caterers for it, would cost hundreds. Hundreds. And the food probably wouldn't taste half as good as yours."

Kaukab smiles. "I am just an ordinary woman. Your cooking is much better."

"But I learnt it from you."

"Would one of you stop licking the other's pussy for a second and tell me where the dustpan is."

Mah-Jabin turns around, stunned. "Ujala!"

He stands there with his jaw clenched, the eyes bright red.

"How dare you talk to your mother and sister like that," Kaukab says to him. "I wish I had never come to this country."

The tears spill over onto his cheeks but he is still breathing like a bull, the jaw pulsating. "What the fuck *is* all this for? What are we celebrating with this . . . this *feast*? May I remind you that yesterday it was confirmed that Uncle Jugnu and Chanda were murdered, chopped up and burnt."

Kaukab turns back to the pans set on the hobs. "We are not *celebrating* anything. My children were coming home after a long time, so I thought I'd cook something . . . Then I started thinking about the favourite dish of each one of you . . ."

"Did you, even for a *moment*, stop to think that it might be a little inappropriate—your seven spiced-and-saffron'd dishes, and tandoori chicken, with a choice of chappatis and rice?"

"Ujala, please stop it." Mah-Jabin takes a step towards him. "Mother has been working on this for two whole days now."

Kaukab is frowning. "As I said it's *not* a feast. Only a few dishes I cooked. It's *not* a party. And yes, when someone mentions saffron you are bound to think the meal is luxurious and special, but I've always put a little saffron in my rice, a festive occasion or ordinary day."

"Let's hope you stop at saffron and don't start putting any other ingredients in the food," Ujala says.

"What does that mean?" Mah-Jabin looks over her shoulder. She turns to Kaukab: "What is he talking about?"

Kaukab too is puzzled: "What other ingredients? It's Charag who doesn't like cumin seeds in his food, *you* eat everything . . ."

"I was thinking of that powder a Muslim cleric gave you, after you had gone to him to tell him how unruly your son Ujala was, how he had done nothing but quarrel with you ever since he entered his teens. Remember?" He smiles contemptuously at Kaukab. "The holy man read special verses of the Koran over some powder and asked you to secretly mix it into your son's food. 'With Allah's help the child will be obedient within thirty days,' he said, or something along those lines."

Kaukab looks ashamed. "I didn't know what else to do. I . . . I . . . How did you find out?"

"You put things in my food!" he shouts. "If you lot had tails they would wag every time you approached a man with a beard."

"I asked Allah to help me through that holy man. And it worked, thanks to His blessing. After I started putting the sacred salt onto your plate, you did become very kind and affectionate, mindful of the respect you owed your elders. But then, for some reason, you disappeared and I haven't seen you since then. And I have felt you moving and walking about in the world the whole time. They take the baby out of the mother but not all the way out: a bit of it is forever inside the mother, part of the mother, and she can hear and feel the child as he moves out there in the world."

"Do you want to know why I left? Do you?"

"I do know now. You must've seen me putting that blessed and consecrated salt in your food."

Mah-Jabin approaches Ujala and places a hand on his shoulder. "What difference does it make, Ujala? It's all harmless and it makes her happy."

Kaukab looks fiercely at the girl: "Don't patronize me, Mah-Jabin."

Ujala removes Mah-Jabin's hand from his shoulder. "Yes, I saw you putting that thing into my portion of the food but I didn't leave because of that." He turns to Mah-Jabin: "I *did* think it was all harmless at first, but then I found the place where I had been hiding that stuff and had it checked out. It was a bromide, the thing they put in prisoners' meals to lower their libido, to make them compliant. That was when I left."

Mah-Jabin gasps and looks at Kaukab.

"It was just some *salt* over which the cleric-ji had read sacred verses," Kaukab says. "And it worked. His behaviour was exemplary then. Any decent mother would have been proud of his conduct during those days . . ." She talks but cannot ignore the horror in Mah-Jabin's eyes, and asks: "What's a libido? What's a bromide, Mah-Jabin?"

Ujala crosses the kitchen and goes out of the house, leaving Mah-Jabin and Kaukab where they are.

"Mah-Jabin, go after him. Take his coat and go after him. Bring him back . . . Yes, yes, put on your own coat too . . ."

"Mother, did you know what that powder was?"

"I told you it was just *ordinary* salt over which some verses of the Koran had been read. What is a bromide?"

"I'll tell you later. I'd better go after him."

Alone, Kaukab suddenly sees for the first time the amount of food in the kitchen. There are bowls, plates, saucers, basins, *katoris*, pots, *kamandals* and glasses on every surface, full of ingredients large and small, black cardamoms, green cardamoms, clove, cinnamon, mace, cumin, coriander seeds, saffron, yoghurt *raita*, green chilli, red chilli, onion, red onion, garlic, honey, gram flour, wheat flour, chicken pieces, mutton cubes, potato wedges, cauliflower florets, peas, beetroot, kebabs, basmati rice, bitter-gourds, vermicelli, cream, sultanas, dry coconut, lemons, fruits, dates, pink-husked pistachios, rose essence (the sweat of Prophet Muhammad, peace be upon him), lettuce leaves detached whole and curling like seashells, salted butter, unsalted butter, clarified butter. She feels shame for having forgotten that all this might appear inappropriate so soon after the confirmation of Jugnu and Chanda's death. How insensitive would she—and therefore all Pakistanis and Muslims as a result—appear to the white girl Stella? A rush of blood to the head had resulted when she realized that her family would be together under the same roof for the first time in many months—many *years*. But now it is a possibility that Ujala would disappear again. What *had* she added to his food? What is a bromide? Is it some kind of poison?

She lets out a whimper.

She switches off the gas from under the pots and begins to clear some of the surfaces, thinking fast about how she can scale down tonight's meal, her mind occupied by the complex culinary algebra. Just the mutton-and-potato curry and the *pilau* rice? But the white girl Stella doesn't eat meat. So: the cauliflower-and-pea curry and *pilau* rice? But Shamas doesn't like cauliflower, so she would have to fry the *shami* kebabs for him. She could freeze the almost-ready mutton-and-potato curry and use it at a later date . . . What had she fed her son? Is he ill as a result of it? She leans her head against the wall. There would be no fruit salad and the vermicelli would have to go without the sparkling gold leaf that the grandson would have enjoyed looking at . . . She reminds herself that her plan was to put the immersion heater on around about now so that the water could warm up for when the guests needed to wash their hands. Slowly she climbs the stairs and goes into the bathroom to switch it on. In the hatch she finds the piece of crumpled up paper and pulls it out, puzzled. Flattened, it looks like a soft square popadum. The handwriting looks like little black ants stuck to the popadum. . . . *It is a story of love* . . . She doesn't know who this paper belongs to.

The Television keeps informing us in the news bulletin that we are defeated yet again. The newspaper headlines scream. They say we are defeated, irrelevant, finished. And the reins are now in the hands of those who neither say their prayers nor keep the fast. On Allah's vast earth, we small and humble Muslims are everywhere in ruins. Our lives and our lands lie like a pile of rubble. Our women have become disobedient like Western women. Our children seduced by the West into being strangers.

The heads that had never bowed before anyone but Allah are being cut off.

Kaukab frowns at the page. It reads like the text of a Friday sermon at a mosque. But what is it doing here?

It is a story of love. The caravans of the lovers of Allah are being ambushed again and again and looted. Those talking—they who "claim" to be the possessors of wisdom—say, "We should realize that we are weak and should bow down before the strong."

From Adam to today, from Noah to Ibrahim, from Ibrahim to Lot, from Christ to Muhammad, peace be upon him: the believers carried the truth to streets and lanes. They were stoned. They were taunted. They were ridiculed by those who refused to believe. The Liars activated the laws against them. The non-believers said we won't believe. The believers said we will believe even if they kill us, even if they burn our buttocks with live coal. (Remember the tip of my cigarette on your skin, Mah-Jabin? Keep that fire in mind. The fires of Hell are a thousand times hotter.)

Kaukab lets out a cry, and quickly turns the page around to see who this letter is from. There is no name. But, of course, she knows it is from Mah-Jabin's husband: who else would write to her in Urdu? If so then what does the reference to the cigarette-burn imply: had his cigarette accidentally come into contact with Mah-Jabin once?

So: Is this temporary setback—the fact that the Muslims are humiliated everywhere on the planet—a defeat of the faithful? The earth and the sky say no it isn't. The universe says no it isn't. He who created the universe says no it isn't. Those who side with the Liars, those who laugh at the true believers, those who wrinkle their brows every time Allah's name is mentioned, those who claim to be God themselves—they are made an example of in the afterlife, and they are forced into burning flames day and night. This is the punishment for those who resisted the truth. They'll have spikes in their flesh. (Remember the sewing needles in your thighs, Mah-Jabin?)

Kaukab reels and lowers herself onto the edge of the bath. Mah-Jabin has always let it be understood that her husband was a loving and caring young man . . .

Yes, we—the good—do stray from the path occasionally. Satan made me enter the room where Chanda was asleep during her and Jugnu's stay with us. I had been unable to bear the burden of need ever since my own female deserted me. Satan made me approach her bed and beg her for comfort. Satan told me she was from the West and therefore would have easy morals. She said she would make a noise and awaken my father and Jugnu in the other room. I came to my senses and left. And in the morning—as if to remove temptation from before me—Allah made Chanda tell Jugnu that she was homesick for the West, and they left that very day. I remained on my prayer mat all day and well into the night, thanking Allah for having removed temptation from before my eyes, but His kindness towards my soul was unending: I was still on my prayer mat, in the middle of the night, when the telephone rang and Aunt Kaukab wanted us all to know that Jugnu and Chanda were lovers, sinners. Allah, the merciful, the Beneficent, saved me from polluting myself in that polluted stream! I haven't told you any of this before but now I want you to know in order that you may be wise to His ways.

Kaukab, not believing what she has read, rereads the lines. She realizes now that she is not to blame for the fact that Chanda and Jugnu had left Pakistan earlier than they had planned. But there is little comfort in the alternative, real, sequence of events. "Poor Chanda." She sits with her hand in her head. "My poor Mah-Jabin." Suddenly she gets up and, a last attempt at resistance, looks behind the drum of the immersion heater. Could this letter be a trick of Mah-Jabin's? A forgery to torment her? A plot hatched by Mah-Jabin and Ujala and Charag and the white girl Stella and Shamas to humiliate her, to ridicule her faith? But there behind the drum is the crumpled-up envelope the letter had come in. She recognizes it, remembers that it had arrived back in spring. The stamp portrays a tree ablaze with pink-white blossoms in the distance and in the foreground a sprig containing a ruffled orchid-like flower and a leaf resembling the imprint of a camel's foot: it is *Bauhinia variegata,* the wording informs along a vertical margin, and horizontally that the stamp is one of the MEDICINAL PLANTS OF PAKISTAN. She drops the envelope and continues with the letter.

We stray but we beg for forgiveness and are pardoned because we are good. The world is lit only with the light of our love for Him, we, the men who were submissive to Allah, and the women who were submissive to their men.

The book of History is recording everything, and He is making a list of the believers and a list of the unbelievers. Try thinking about which list your name is going into, Mah-Jabin, and be afraid. What kind of End awaits you after this short life of fifty or sixty years?

Having read to the end, Kaukab picks up the tattered envelope from the floor and places the folded sheet of paper into it. She sits there, staring at the stamp depicting the pretty flower of the tree that is valued for, among other things, its effectiveness against malarial fevers, the ability to regularize menstrual dysfunction, and as an antidote to snake venom.

The sun rounds the corner and begins to sail at the front of the house. She sits there, wondering if that's who she is, if that's what her image looks like in the mirror: a mother who feeds poisons to her son, and a mother who jumps to conclusions and holds her daughter responsible for the fact that her marriage ended disastrously? The realizations are still new and she is not sure what effect they will have on her soul after she has lived with them for an hour, a day, a month. The bitterness of the poison is as yet only testing her tongue and mouth: what will happen when it soaks into the veins?

She hears a car pull up outside and, from the bathroom window, she looks down to see that Charag and Stella have arrived. Charag opens the back door of the car to let the eight-year-old son out. The temperature has plummeted over the past two days and Kaukab is pleased to see that the grandson is wrapped up against the December cold. The end of the woollen cap doubles in a band across his little forehead, over the ears and back along the nape of the neck, for extra warmth. When they were still married Kaukab had once seen Stella and Charag arrive for a visit—and Charag had kissed her on the lips out in the street. Kaukab had backed away. Must they display such lewdness in public? (Chanda and Jugnu at least spared her such obscene behaviour outdoors.) And right there in front of the little boy too, who would no doubt begin to chase girls as soon as he is in his teens and be sexually active by the time he is fifteen, thinking display-of-wantonness and sex-before-marriage was the norm and not grave sins! The little boy would no doubt marry a white girl and his own children would too: *all* trace of modesty and propriety would be bred out of them. Is this how Charag's grandchildren would think of Charag?—"My mother and father are white, and my mother's people are all white. I look a little dark because of one of my grandparents. He was a Paki."

The grandson flings his cap onto the linoleum the moment she lets the three of them in. She apologizes for the kitchen smelling of food and asks them all to take their coats into the next room. Before closing the outside door she runs her gaze in a sweep across the street to see if Mah-Jabin and

Ujala are returning. She hugs the little boy and kisses his head, face and both hands.

"What's that?" Charag points to the crumpled letter that Kaukab only now realizes she still has in her hand.

She quickly puts it into her cardigan pocket. "A letter from your grandfather in Pakistan. He says he is disappointed that your son—his great-grandson—didn't begin Koranic lessons at the age of four years, four months and four days, as is prescribed for every Muslim child."

Stella is looking into the room next door. "Have Mah-Jabin and Ujala not arrived yet?" The dining table in there is paved with plates. The table-cloth is obviously from an Asian fabric shop, the beautiful material—patterned with movements of flower-heavy creepers—that the Asian women make their clothing out of, the colours often bright, the shapes exquisite, and which, Charag once said, had made his adolescent self look at Matisse more carefully.

"They have gone for a walk," Kaukab says as she strikes a match to relight the hobs. She tilts the matchstick downward so that the wood beyond the head tempts the fire into remaining alive. "Please, go into the next room and stay there. I don't want the smell getting into your clothes." She was hoping to take Mah-Jabin aside as soon she came back to the house—to let her know that she has found the letter, to ask her to explain the truth about her marriage in Pakistan—but it's unlikely that she would have a chance to do that over the next few hours. And she has yet to explain to Ujala that it wasn't her intention to harm him with the sacred salt. Those damned scientists, how they love to analyse everything! As she takes the lids off the pans one by one, she is reminded once again—having forgotten it when she read that letter upstairs—that she has to scale down the evening meal. Suddenly confused, she wishes Mah-Jabin were here to be consulted, and she calls out to Charag in the next room so that he can go out and look for his brother and sister. But he doesn't hear her.

Switching on the television in the next room, Charag is startled by the loud burst of noise that comes out: the volume is turned too high. He decides not to ask Kaukab whether his father's hearing is deteriorating: he had asked once but Kaukab had denied it and seemed to consider the inquiry impertinent. A son may not notice his father's inadequacies. Tonight he will contrive to show Shamas how to access the subtitles on the remote control: white, green, yellow, red—each person speaking a differently coloured sentence.

A black-and-white Tarzan movie is found for the little boy and Stella sits with him in front of it with the assurance that he'll like it. "What does he turn into?" he asks after a while and he loses interest immediately when he is told that the character doesn't *turn* into anything, isn't transformed into a monster or otherworldly creature, that he remains a human being. But then he looks up, points to Tarzan and says, "He speaks like Grandma Kaukab!"

The three of them go back into the kitchen just as Kaukab is opening the door to Mah-Jabin.

"Ujala is still at the lake," she announces, and, holding Kaukab's eye, makes the smallest possible movement of the head to convey reassurance, "He'll be back in a moment, Mother. We walked all the way to the *Safeena.*"

With her arms around her little nephew, Mah-Jabin buries her lips into the soft skin of his neck. How old would her child have been now had she not lost it?

Stella tells her she has the beginning of a cold: "There was a spectacular storm scene in the play I went to not long ago. Wind machine, real water for rain."

Mah-Jabin smiles and lowers the boy onto the floor and turns brightly to Kaukab. "Let's get the food ready. Fasten your tastebuds, Charag and Stella. No doubt, you two haven't been asked to help with the preparations because Mother is too polite . . ." Stella is assigned the task to locate the cellophane bag of crushed summer mint from the ice-compartment and add them to a bowl of yoghurt. The beaten pulp is frozen solid in the cellophane like a creaking chunk of tundra with prehistoric algae in it, and there is no adult way of breaking it apart: it has to be done clumsily the way a child would do it.

Leaning into Mah-Jabin at the first opportunity, Kaukab tries to tell her that she knows the truth about her marriage but all she can say is, "Would you believe me if I told you I didn't know what was going on?"

Mah-Jabin knits her brows and puckers her lips into a silent *Shhh,* and whispers back, "It's OK. We'll talk later. I think he knows you thought it was just ordinary salt."

"I am not talking about Ujala," Kaukab says, and wonders if she would know how to broach the subject of her marriage with Mah-Jabin later. "But, for the record I didn't know anything about that too." Her eyes are red.

From her coat pocket, Mah-Jabin takes out a pack of tamarind pulp: "I thought we could add it to the chutney, Mother. I stopped by at a shop on my way back."

Kaukab is immediately concerned. "You went into a shop?" She knows the women of the neighbourhood know the girl is divorced, and is sure they would have made comments about her to each other—comments about her character, about her Western dress and cut-off hair.

"Yes. Chanda's parents' shop is closed. I went to the one in the next street." She unwraps the tamarind. "A woman came in while I was there, a wealthy-looking, well-dressed woman. She must've heard that somewhere around here two brothers had killed their sister, and, not knowing that I was the niece of the dead man, she began berating the two murderers. She said, 'People like that are ruining the name of Pakistan abroad.' She was visiting from Pakistan, staying with her relatives in the suburbs who had brought her to our neighbourhood for amusement—if their suppressed smiles were anything to go by whenever a woman entered the shop with bright village-like embroidery on her *kameez*—to show her how the poor Pakistanis lived here in England, the factory workers, the bus drivers, the waiters. She couldn't hide her contempt for us. Apparently she had been called a 'darkie bitch' by a white man in the town centre during her first week here and was resentful. She said, 'The man who called me that name was filthy and stinking. And he would not have called me that name if it had not been for the people in this area, who have so demeaned Pakistan's image in foreign countries. Imagine! *He* thought he could insult *me*, I who live in a house in Islamabad the likes of which he'd never see in his life, I who speak better English than him, educated as I was at Cambridge, my sons studying at Harvard right now. And it's all the fault of you lot, you sister-murdering, nose-blowing, mosque-going, cousin-marrying, veil-wearing inbred imbeciles.'"

Kaukab shakes her head in disappointment. "We are driven out of our countries because of people like her, the rich and the powerful. We leave because we never have any food or dignity because of their selfish behaviour. And now they resent our being *here* too. Where are we supposed to go? The poor and the unprivileged, in their desire to keep living, are being disrespectful towards the rich and the privileged: is that it?"

"She was very elegant, not at all like people who have made their fortunes quite recently and are intent on showing it off."

Kaukab bangs the wooden ladle on the rim of the pan—to free it of the sauce clinging to it, but with a little more force than necessary so that it emphasizes her disapproval: "What's all this talk about old money and new money? If it's new money it's tainted with the blood and sweat of the poor people who are being used and abused in the present, and if it's old money it's tainted with the blood and sweat of the poor people who were used and abused in the past. The legs of the rich people's thrones have always rested on the heads of poor people." She turns back to her work: "I haven't lived with your father for four decades and not learned a few truths."

She wishes she could've said all this in English so that Stella would know she was intelligent, a thinking person. Yes, she had grown to like Stella eventually. She remembers when Charag had come home from university years ago to tell her that he was in love with a white girl who was expecting their child. After the initial shock of the revelation had worn off, Kaukab had walked to the train station to get on the train that would take her to Charag and his white girlfriend and their unborn child. How her selfishness had blinded her to the immense love her son must feel for the girl! Kaukab had grown up being told that what the two of them had done before marriage was wrong, wanton and depraved, but she had made sure her own children grew up with the same message: and if what had occurred was hard for *her* to accept, how hard it must have been for her son, how great the love that made him act against her teachings. Even in Pakistan everyone loved someone before marriage, but from a distance: a surreptitious glance answered by an eloquent smile. The West just gave a person the permission and opportunity to *act* on those feelings—it wasn't her son's fault. On the way to the train station, she longed to nestle her future daughter-in-law in her arms, call her by her name, Stella, but at the ticket-office window she lost heart on being told that she would have to change trains, fearing she would be lost without her lack of English as she searched for the correct platform, too humiliated by her pronounced accent and broken words to ask someone to guide her to the connecting trains. And where and how do you get a taxi in a strange city? She was a beggar who did not want to stretch out her hand because that hand was dirty. And so with eyes veined with carmine, she waited for Shamas to come home: as soon as he returned she asked him to take her to her son.

"This curry is done. Now I must see if there's enough dough for the chappatis. Who wants chappatis instead of rice?"

Charag has been peeling and cutting fruit into a salad bowl that is now filled up with the sweet chunks—the colourful heap of peels beside it looks as though the flags of a dozen nations have been shredded—and he now asks from where he is standing at the dresser, "Where are the lemons? And why is there such a feast being laid out for tonight?"

"It is not a feast," Mah-Jabin says quickly. "As Mother explained to me earlier, and as I explained to Ujala not long ago when he asked me the same question beside the lake, Mother just decided to cook the next few days' food in one go. She happened to be in the mood."

Kaukab looks at Mah-Jabin with gratitude. "I'll freeze them in silver-foil containers."

Stella nods. "It's a good idea." She points to the eight-year-old: "He asked me recently, 'Why is Grandma Kaukab always cooking?' "

Kaukab is moved that the boy had noticed her, had paid enough attention to her to have identified a trait of sorts. She wants to kiss and nuzzle him but stops herself in case the whites have come up with a theory about *grand*mothers and *grand*sons too.

"It would be a feast if I were making something special: these foods are everyday." She has found another reason to bolster the lie Mah-Jabin has told to save her. She wants to make a humorous comment at this point: "But, yes, being a housewife *is* difficult. I sometimes say to myself that if I had studied medicine I would have had to take the exam just once and be respectfully called a doctor for the rest of my life, but in domestic life you have to take and pass exams *every* day, and even then appreciation isn't guaranteed." She is in the process of mentally translating all this into English to be able to tell it to Stella, when Ujala returns.

Head drooping like an elongated sunflower, he seems as gaunt and withdrawn to Kaukab as before when she dares to take a quick peek at him, but he joins in with the tasks and even carries and lifts up the eight-year-old to the cooker to let him look into the pot in which the bitter gourds are sizzling. "What are they?" he asks the child.

"Starfishes!" the boy exclaims on seeing the plump pointed gourds that have browned on cooking and now do look like dismembered starfishes.

"That's right. We are having starfish curry," Ujala says.

Over the next hour—while December's darkness falls outside—the kitchen is animated as voices rise and hang in the air for short periods—a mouthful of food taken directly from the pot resulting in a bout of praise for Kaukab; the grandson spitting out a mouthful of half-chewed M&Ms like coloured gravel; Charag smiling and telling Mah-Jabin to finish the apple she has left to brown on the table ("Apples don't grow on weeds, you know—as Mother always told us"); the threat of a tantrum from the child, followed by a counter threat of punishment from one of his parents, a fawning taking of the sides by the grandmother, the young uncle, the aunt—but these are short lived and the air becomes tense and subdued quickly: yesterday—with its verdict—is like a colossal block of ice that's still too near, breathing chilly air on everyone's skin. The house, as it floated through time, has arrived at an iceberg, and no one is sure whether it will ever move away from it, leaving it behind. Now and then, to relieve the silences, Kaukab says, "Allah is great!"

When she goes upstairs to the bathroom immediately after Charag has been there to wash his face, she notices that the linoleum is warm where he had been standing just now, and she has to steady her heart with joyful fingers—her cold cold house is full of her children again. There's warmth in unexpected places.

Shamas comes home just as Kaukab is telling Stella about a woman in the neighbourhood both of whose identical-twin daughters became pregnant at the same time: one of them has had the baby in the seventh month, and now the news has to be kept from the other in case she too fails to carry the pregnancy to full term; luckily the still-pregnant girl lives in America so it's easier to hide the truth. Every time Kaukab has spoken to Stella, she has surreptitiously breathed into the hollow of a hand and sniffed it to see that her breath isn't stale, and she has missed the sarsaparilla root that is thrown into the brass or earthenware containers which hold a household's drinking water in Sohni Dharti, to sweeten the water so that its scent will freshen the mouth when the water is drunk.

Shamas realizes that the grandson is about the same age as Suraya's son. He tries to drive the thought away.

He knows he's going to end up wandering around this town, muttering her name.

He looks at Kaukab when she is otherwise occupied, to see what kind of a day she has had. The last few days—if not the last few months—have been devastating for her, he knows. Each day after the trial he came home and told her the details of what happened at the court, and she had been inconsolable. Last night he wondered whether he should add to that story of Chanda and Jugnu's last few hours on earth what Kiran had told him on the bus, weave that dark thread into the already-dark tale. But he feared how Kaukab would react—she would see Kiran's secret affair with Chanda's brother as proof that she was a woman of loose morals, that her family had been right in the 1950s when they refused to let her marry her brother; perhaps she would accuse Kiran of lying about her brother's secret visit to Dasht-e-Tanhaii—? But, he must admit, he had also envis- aged the opposite reaction: that she would insist Shamas not reveal to anyone the details of Kiran's love affair with Chanda's brother or the night she spent with her own brother: "People would gossip and point fingers at the poor woman. You have no idea how easy it is to ruin a woman's life." Now, as he steals glances at her, he wonders which of the two Kaukabs is the real one.

She seems contented, her children around her.

The pots sing on the fire. Dipped in beaten egg, the *shami* kebabs drip like a cow's mouth from a drinking pail and they are noisy when lowered into the oil which crackles like cellophane. Everyone except Kaukab and Mah-Jabin sits down and eats from the yellow plates arranged on the table in the next room. In the kitchen, Mah-Jabin asks Kaukab to join the oth- ers too—seeing as she has been on her feet all day and also has the pain in her abdomen to consider—but Kaukab bats down the suggestion, and then Mah-Jabin tells her that she *will* come to Dasht-e-Tanhaii to be with her when she has to go to the hospital for the operation in January, that she has arranged leave at her work. Kaukab tells her to lower her voice—"There are men within earshot, and this is women's business."

The mother and daughter, with a Lakshmi-like abundance of arms and hands, have filled all the plates and, while the kebabs are taken steaming to the table in batches by Mah-Jabin, every other minute a new chappati is ready from Kaukab's hands. Growing as it does from two whorls at the crown of her head instead of the usual one, Stella's hair is often unruly, and with a touch of his finger Charag removes the irritation of an escaped strand from across her cheek, an action he—at one time—would perform with his tongue, kissing her face afterwards.

Kaukab asks Mah-Jabin to go join the others when the initial servings are over and the meal enters a more relaxed phase, the food unfolding warmth in the eaters' bodies.

Shamas unspools the thread from around the grandson's "starfish leg."

The spicy cauliflower goes into Stella's mouth and comes out through her eyes as water.

Tiny beetroot stars—that Kaukab had punched out of the beetroot slices with a cutter—are lined up in a growing necklace where they are being discarded towards the edge of Ujala's salad.

There are white specks associated with calcium-deficiency on Stella's fingernails, and Kaukab is privately taken aback when she notices them for the first time as she takes a chappati to the table: she is ashamed whenever these marks appear on her own nails, yet another proof for the white people that the Pakistanis are unhealthy people, disease-riddled, filthy bearers of epidemics like the smallpox they brought with them to England in the 1960s. Ever since Charag and Stella arrived she has been worried that she has forgotten to brush her teeth in time for their arrival, to get rid of any bad odour before the white girl came.

Stella tells them all about the fair she had taken the child to not long ago. Eating from cellophane bags stuffed like pillows with candyfloss, they went into the tent where a Sleeping Beauty lay on a satin-draped bier. The body was a wax statue and, as proof that the princess was dead to the world, the impresario pierced it through the gown with a long pearl-headed hat pin. To approach the sleeping body was to become a child that had awakened from a nightmare and gone into the parents' room for comfort, or, Stella thought, a thief that had broken into a house with its occupant asleep unawares.

Kaukab says the princess should have had a few scented geraniums scattered about the palace corridors so that the intruders brushing against them would wake her up.

Surrounded by hair as long as a wild horse's mane, the face on the bier belonged to the woman who was hiding underneath the wax body—and they saw her drunk when the fair closed, staggering about the cobbled square, weeping with her wig in her hand and shouting abuse at passersby.

Halfway through the meal, Charag reminds Stella that there is a gift for Kaukab and Shamas in their car, and when Stella gets up to go to the car, Kaukab asks her to remain seated: "It's too cold outside—cold as outer space. Charag should go." Stella is wearing a skirt, her legs visible below the knees, and Kaukab doesn't want anyone in the neighbourhood to see the exposed skin and comment on it: when they were still married, she had asked Charag to tell Stella to not dress in that immodest garment—at least during her visits to this neighbourhood—but nothing happened. She hadn't expected Stella to begin wearing the *shalwar-kameez* and the head veil (though nothing would have pleased her more; many white women do abandon their old way of dressing upon marrying Muslim men) but she didn't wish to see female flesh on display.

Charag gets up and goes out to the car, returning with a small brown-paper-wrapped square fastened with a cord. "It's a surprise, Mother. Open it."

Kaukab unknots the thread, remembering the first time she had made a knot in something in Stella's presence: she had suddenly gone numb, wondering if there was a *Western* way of tying a knot—more sophisticated, *better*. Perhaps the way she tied knots was an *ignorant* way of tying a knot?

"I bought all the photographs and negatives from a photographer in town the last time I was here. They are from the '50s, '60s and the early '70s, of Pakistani and Indian immigrants," Charag says. "I met this woman at the lake who planted the idea in my head that perhaps I should try to incorporate into my art the lives of the people I grew up amongst—examine and explore them."

"And going through a box, he found this," Stella smiles. "Extraordinary."

It is a photograph of the family—Charag and Mah-Jabin, as children, sitting cross-legged on the ornate rug on the studio floor; Shamas standing and looking impossibly young; Kaukab, seated on a reproduction chair, pregnant with Ujala, the stomach swelled out like a bulb, like the middle of a vase. Kaukab smiles as she holds up the framed picture for everyone to see.

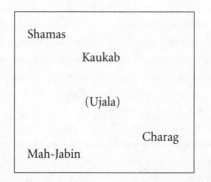

Shamas

    Kaukab

   (Ujala)

         Charag

Mah-Jabin

"I remember making this shirt for you, Charag." Kaukab smiles. "You complained the collar was too stiff. The fabric was crisp as a new bank-note."

"It was completely by chance that I went in, to rummage around but then the photographer said he would be going out of business later in the year. Look at Mah-Jabin's two plaits! How pregnant were you then, Mother?"

"Don't be vulgar," Kaukab frowns. "Later Mah-Jabin would demand I make only one plait, saying, 'On the way to school the two brothers walk either side of me and each flicks one of them whenever he feels like it.' With one plait she managed to cut the difficulty in half."

Shamas can scarcely believe what has occurred. When the photograph is passed to him he, instead of looking at it, asks Charag, "Where are the others? Are they in a safe place?"

Kaukab's bright glance appeals to Stella against the impossibility of men. "Who cares about the others? Look at the one in your *hand*."

"No, no, they are an important document," Charag says. "They are safe, Father. I might want to do a series of paintings based on them."

"I wanted the town to buy them, but as long as the people in them are celebrated somehow and not allowed to be forgotten it doesn't matter who has them." He places his hand on Charag's shoulder. So the pictures have been saved!

Charag wonders whether his father has so far been indifferent to his paintings because he thinks that his work does not contribute anything to society. Shamas had never encouraged him to become a painter, despite seeing examples of his talent around the house since childhood, despite the fact that his India-ink drawing regularly accompanied Jugnu's *Nature Notes* in *The Afternoon;* and Shamas had disapproved when he *did* become a painter. Had Shamas—who had known politically committed artists in Pakistan—thought that the artists in England were engaged in a comparatively trivial activity?

Shamas looks at Charag, a bird in his chest pipping proudly: *My son . . . My son . . .* He hasn't known how to read Charag's paintings in the past— they seem too personal to the boy to hold any interest for Shamas—but now, now that he has mentioned that he might do something with the photographs of immigrants, Shamas knows he is maturing as an artist, becoming aware of his responsibilities as an artist.

Which to hold dearer: my love for you, or the sorrows of others in the world?
They say the intoxication is greater when two kinds of wine are mixed.

Good artists know that society is worth representing too.

"Did you see Charag's picture in last Sunday's papers?" Stella asks Shamas and, against a mild protest from Charag, gets up to bring the magazine section of the paper from her shoulder bag, and there he is on the front cover, photographed with two other young painters. The child looks at the photograph and shouts, "That's Uncle Philip and that's Uncle Toby."

Although complimentary on the whole, the article does contain criticism of Charag's work: he himself can deal with that criticism but he had wanted that article kept from his father because he didn't want to appear a failure in *his* eyes.

Ujala scans the article, reading aloud. "It reads: *In certain art circles you are regarded as contrary if you are still putting paint on canvas. But for me painting is still an intelligent option, says the 32-year-old Charag Aks. The painter is sitting in his flat with a chocolate biscuit in one hand, amid paint-spattered monographs and volumes of critical theory . . .* The paragraph goes on to describe one of his paintings and ends like this: *There is nothing showy here; it is a rhapsody in restrained form and colour. He is following a very tough discipline. It was the combination of these qualities that so inspired the art collector Marshall Gaffney that he commissioned a year's worth of work from him. The resulting paintings, eight in all (including a 4-foot nude entitled* The Uncut Self-Portrait*), are part of the Gaffney Gallery's second Young British Artists exhibition, which opens in London in January.*"

Kaukab, smiling proudly, takes the magazine and looks at Charag's photograph. *The Uncut Self-Portrait* is pictured inside too and she closes the magazine when she sees it. Charag has painted himself without any clothes standing in a pale grove of small immaculate butterflies, fruit- and flower-heavy boughs, birds, hoopoes and parakeets and other insects and animals, the mist rising from a lake in the background—and he has an uncircumcised penis.

He sees the distress on her face and says, "What I am trying to say is that it was the first act of violence done to me in the name of a religious or social system. And I wonder if anyone has the right to do it. We should all question such acts."

"That such wickedness can be!" Kaukab says quietly. "Why must you mock my sentiments and our religion like this?" Outside the window a large moon has appeared, its mountains and valleys a greyish black-and-white, very faint, as though it were a bad photocopy. She wishes she could fly away out of the window.

"It's a *metaphor*, Mother, and, Mother, I didn't mean to offend you. Forgive me, but why does everything always has to do with you? Jugnu taught me that we should try to break away from all the bonds and ties that manipulative groups have thought up for their own advantage. Surely, Mother, you see the merit of that."

"Jugnu died because of the way he lived," Kaukab says.

"He didn't die, Mother," Mah-Jabin says quietly. "He was killed."

"It is healthy to have a boy circumcised," Shamas says, merely to come to Kaukab's aid. "The Western doctors say it."

"So if the doctors find out tomorrow that circumcision is unhealthy, would the Muslims stop it?" Ujala asks without looking up, face remaining tilted over his food.

"Of course not," Kaukab says.

"I didn't think so. And, incidentally, would these Western doctors be the *same* Western doctors whose advice that first cousins shouldn't marry each other, you lot *ignore*?"

"I fail to see what I could have possibly done to be humiliated in this manner again and again," Kaukab says.

"I know circumcision is probably healthier," Charag says quietly, "and we have had our own son circumcised, but we didn't do it because of a religion. I am sorry if you are offended but I can't paint with handcuffs on."

"I think your conduct is most regrettable. What point are you trying to make with that picture? That a religion that has given dignity to millions around the world is barbaric?"

Ujala sits back in his chair and considers Kaukab. "Dignity? Mother, are you aware that Muslim women cannot marry a non-Muslim? Their testimony in a court of law is worth half that of a man. Non-Muslims living in Muslim countries have inferior status under Islamic law: they may not testify against a Muslim. Non-believers are to be killed: of the seventeen great sins in Islam, unbelief is the greatest, worse than murder, theft, adultery. In Saudi Arabia, following a saying of Muhammad that 'Two religions cannot exist in Arabia,' non-Muslims are forbidden to practise their religion, build churches, possess Bibles." His voice has risen a little and the eight-year-old looks furiously at him, and, chest out, says, "Stop shouting, you!" Ujala reaches across the table and ruffles his hair, "Sorry," his fingertips briefly tickled by the penny-size area at the top of his head which always resists flattening, sticking up like the crest of a thistle.

"How do you know all this all of a sudden?" Kaukab, who was on her way out, turns around and asks Ujala.

"I've read the Koran, in English, unlike you who just chant it in Arabic without knowing what the words mean, hour after hour, day in day out, like chewing gum for the brain."

Kaukab says, "What I don't understand is why when you all spend your time talking about women's rights, don't you ever think about *me*. What about *my* rights, *my* feelings? Am *I* not a woman, am I a eunuch?"

Ujala continues, "A religion that has given dignity to millions around the world? Amputations, stoning to death, flogging—not barbaric?"

"These punishments are of divine origin and cannot be judged by human criteria."

He looks at her. "If I changed my religion in a country like Pakistan what would happen to me, Mother?"

"Please let's continue with our meal," Shamas says, not wishing to be reminded too much of his father's death.

To give the impression of normality restored—because all this must be making the white girl uncomfortable—Kaukab moves forward to gently touch one of Stella's earrings: "Very pretty."

Stella turns her head at an angle to bring the jewelled glyph into light. "My mother passed it on to me because it is too heavy for her now that her earlobes aren't as firm. It stretches her skin and there are three wrinkles above the hook like the eyelashes painted on a doll's face."

"Very pretty. Look, Mah-Jabin."

Mah-Jabin obligingly pretends to admire the jewel—making sounds to drown out the beating drums of battle, the roar and smoke of the clash.

But despite all this, Kaukab is unable to convince herself to abandon her argument with Ujala; she is too wounded to be diverted, even if it's she herself who has been trying to create the diversion. She turns to Ujala: "Why would you want to change your religion? Islam is the fastest growing religion in the world."

Shamas has heard this several times from various sources but has never been able to find definite proof—but he won't say anything now to add to Kaukab's distress. She's continuing:

"No one has ever heard of a Muslim converting to another religion."

That Shamas knows to be false—but he concentrates on his food.

"I might want to change it because Islam further deranges an ignorant and uneducated woman so that she feeds poison to her sons," says Ujala.

Everyone looks at him—everyone except Kaukab.

"What are you talking about?" Charag says.

"I love my children." Kaukab looks at Ujala and holds his gaze.

"I am sure you think you do," he replies.

"Be quiet, Ujala, please," Mah-Jabin says. "If Mother is uneducated there are reasons. She has little English and she feels nervous stepping out of the house because she is not sure whether she can count on a friendly response—"

"Let's drop the pretence," Ujala interrupts. "She would have been exactly like this if she weren't here in England. What were her achievements back in Pakistan, a country where she *can* speak the language and count on a friendly response . . ."

Mah-Jabin's shakes her head: "If she is the way she is, it's because she has been through what she has been through. You wouldn't say this if you knew fully about the place of women in Pakistan. You—"

Now it's Kaukab's turn to interrupt: "There is nothing wrong with the status of women in Pakistan."

Ujala smiles triumphantly: "See, Mah-Jabin? Tell us, Mother, were Chanda and Jugnu sinners?"

"If you think I condone their murder, you are wrong."

"But were they dirty unclean sinners?"

Kaukab looks around like a trapped animal. "Yes."

"So: you are sorry they were murdered but they *were* sinners. It's like a judge saying, 'Let's give the criminal a fair trial, and then hang him.' Have they gone to hell, now that they are dead? Yes or no." He has been holding a spoon and looking at it whilst speaking. His face reflected in the curved steel of the spoon like a distorted portrait reminds him of the time he saw Jugnu with his reflection on the polished silver back of a scarab beetle.

"What do you want from me, from us?" Kaukab says, wishing to end this conversation, this battle without visible bloodshed. "Do you want your parents to say that everything they have ever done is wrong? You'd like to know what mistakes they think they've made in their life? Well, the biggest mistake of my life was coming to this country, a country where children are allowed to talk to their parents this way, a country where sin is commonplace. But I had to come to this country because your father was a daydreamer and got himself into trouble with the government. Once, when I said we have a child now so please think of the future—

think about saving money for the child's education, about building a house—he replied that by the time this child grows up the whole world would have become Communist, and things like education, healthcare and housing would be free."

Shamas is avoiding everyone's eyes, simply because he wants this episode to be over quickly and not because he is ashamed of what he had once believed—still believes—namely: that a fairer, more just way of organizing the world has to be found.

Ujala says: "There couldn't have been a more dangerous union than you two: *you* were too busy longing for the world and the time your grandparents came from, they and their sayings and principles; and *he* was too busy daydreaming about the world and the time his grandchildren were to inherit. What about your responsibilities to the people who were around you here in the present? Those around her were less important to her than those that lay buried below her feet, and for him the important ones were the ones that hovered above his head—those yet to be born."

Mah-Jabin shakes her head at him: "I think it's inaccurate to say that Father was daydreaming. It is a noble idea: to make sure that no one has too much until everyone has enough."

"Of course it is," Ujala says, "but what did he do to achieve that end? He didn't contribute much, if anything."

Shamas has accused himself of this always—he didn't do enough, if anything.

"Father did contribute. When he came here he got workers at his factory to join the unions; he also battled with the unions because they weren't accepting foreigners into their ranks," Charag says. "He's been involved in such works all his life."

Kaukab is distraught: "How they all come to the rescue of their father, refusing to hear a bad word against him, and yet they abuse *me* openly."

Ujala sighs and gets up to stand at the window. There are still many things to say. He feels like a wind-up toy stuck against a tuft of carpet: standing still but full of energy. Everything is suddenly quiet. All evening a winter wind has been blowing around in the streets outside, carrying and making sounds, shaking the Hawaiian grass-skirt of the willow tree in the garden four-doors-down, hurling the frost-stiffened sycamore leaves onto the back lane where they smash like crockery, and rustling the long grasses on the hill beyond, but now all the airborne songs have died down and the twenty maples lining the side-streets are stiffly shaking the last of the wind out of themselves.

Shamas and Stella begin to clear the table and Kaukab sits down sideways on a chair (to keep her legs free in case she is needed and has to get up): she begins her meal, the food served onto the grandson's leftovers. Mah-Jabin sits with the nephew at the coffee table: the boy is fascinated by the rotary dial of the 25-year-old telephone, which these days is found mostly on children's toys. This phone rings instead of chirruping, its receiver heavy the way only the receivers in public phone-boxes are these days, most modern phones being light as a grasshopper husk. Mah-Jabin realizes now that she never telephones home if she knows there would be idle or free time after the call to dwell on the conversation: she always makes sure there is an activity lined up for immediately afterwards. With the dining table clear, Charag goes into the kitchen with Mah-Jabin to bring out the gold-leaved vermicelli. There he asks Mah-Jabin what Ujala had meant by his remark about Kaukab poisoning her sons. She resists but finally tells him the truth.

Kaukab had watched Charag follow Mah-Jabin into the kitchen and known he had wanted to be alone with his sister to ask him what Ujala had meant by poison. When they don't return immediately—how long does it take to pick up a dish and a stack of bowls and spoons, after all?— she strains her ears to see if they are whispering in there.

When Charag enters the room, carrying the dish of vermicelli, the look on his face tells Kaukab that Mah-Jabin has told him everything. And as if to confirm, Mah-Jabin—following Charag with the spoons and bowls— avoids her eyes guiltily. The girl has applied the gold leaf to the surface of the vermicelli very clumsily, tearing the delicate sheet here and there so that it looks like a blistered mirror.

"I know you all think me the worst woman in the world," Kaukab hears herself speak, "but I . . ." And speaking evenly she tells everyone, turning now to Charag, now to Shamas, breaking into English occasionally to include Stella, that she hadn't known the salt given to her by the cleric-ji was a bromide—whatever a bromide is—and, she sees herself reaching into her cardigan pocket many seconds before her hand actually makes that movement: she takes out the letter and says: "And, Mah-Jabin, I know you think I've kept at you unreasonably to return to your husband, but that's because I didn't know any of these details. I know I can't seem to move without bruising anyone, but I don't mean to cause pain."

Mah-Jabin has recognized the letter and moves forward to take it from Kaukab's hands.

Kaukab leaves the room and hurries upstairs, wishing to be alone. She closes the door to her bedroom and locks it, getting into bed with the intention of staying there for only a while but opening the door more than an hour and a half later. She must get downstairs quickly, she tells herself as she steps onto the landing, because otherwise Mah-Jabin would start doing the washing up: there are too many dishes and pots today for her to ask the girl to wash them.

She comes downstairs to find Shamas bringing the chairs back into the kitchen. The dining table is already in its usual place. "Have Stella and Charag gone?" she asks. He gives a nod, and when she asks him where Mah-Jabin and Ujala are he tells her that they have gone too: "They all drove away together. Mah-Jabin knocked on your door before leaving but you didn't answer."

"Where have they gone? When are they coming back?" Kaukab finds herself asking in panic. "I have things to say to Mah-Jabin—tell her that the *next* husband I find for her would be decent—and I have things to say to Ujala. I hadn't expected a happy farewell but at least a tender and affectionate one." She rushes to the front door and opens it, looking around desperately. A sandalwood-coloured cat that has been standing in the garden flashes out of sight at the appearance of the human, very fast, as though it had been at the end of a length of elastic stretched to the limit. "How long ago did they leave?" It was all over so quickly: this morning she had thought she would have many hours with her children, whole days with Ujala: she feels the crushing disappointment she felt as a child whenever she accidentally swallowed whole the sweet she had hoped to enjoy sucking the flavour out of slowly.

The bitterly cold air spills into the house like a sea. Shamas asks her to calm herself and makes her sit on the chair for a few minutes. Stony-faced, she does what he says but then gets up to begin the washing up, waving away his offers to do it all for her. She rubs the pans mechanically until she can see her face in them and then stops as though that was what she'd been looking for. There are fifty-five items to be washed altogether and the leftovers are to be put into dishes of manageable sizes and fitted into the fridge. She says her night prayers at ten, and although she is silent, her faith is not mute: he can hear her screaming as she sits on the prayer mat. Without a word exchanged they both work until eleven at night when the kitchen and the sitting room are back to their normal shapes, the drawers shut, the cupboards stacked with pots and pans, the floors clean, and the Madonna lilies glowing on the central coffee table.

As Shamas drifts towards sleep he hears Kaukab's movements in the next bedroom.

And in the middle of the night he opens his eyes because he has suddenly become aware of sounds from downstairs. The winter nights are deceptive, he reminds himself: although it is dark it must be nearly dawn—Kaukab has no doubt gone downstairs to say the first prayer of the coming day. But then he notices that it's 3 a.m. Too early for the dawn prayer. Even though it is not uncommon for one of them to get up in the middle of the night to go downstairs and rattle the aspirin bottle, he decides to go downstairs to take a look nevertheless. At the bottom of the black staircase there is an envelope-thin slit of light from the door to the kitchen, and on the very last step there is a miscalculation by him—he thinks there are no more steps left—and his foot falls through the ten or so inches of air to land with a thump on the floor, a feeling not too dissimilar to mistaking an empty stapler for a full one and punching it with force. It seems she hasn't heard the noise and doesn't react when he enters. She remains motionless but says quietly of the pan on the cooker: "I am waiting for it to cool. It's still too hot to drink."

"Milk?" And when he moves towards it she comes at him from behind and pushes him sideways, his right hipbone hits the wood of the dresser and he jack-knifes with pain. His hand had been about to close on the handle of the pan and the pan tilts off the hob: a transparent sheet of stretched water emerges, and within this long waterfall a thousand one-pence coins clattering to the linoleum.

A circle of steam expands towards the four walls from the spilled water.

She scrambles for the pennies on all fours. "Get away from me." She tries to shake his hand off her shoulder now that he has staggered forward. "I am going to drink this water." She turns around and a lioness's paw scratches his face because he tries to drag her away. "You brought me here. To this accursed country. You made me lose my children."

He is terrified. Someone in Sohni Dharti *had* committed suicide by drinking the water in which a handful of coins had been boiled, the relatives mistaking his broken footsteps for alcohol and putting him to bed so he could sleep it off.

She looks wildly at him: "I hold you responsible for the fact that my children hate me." She catapults forward but his arms are ready to grip her from behind, keeping her a yard or so away from the coins overlapping like fish scales. There is no longer any danger because all the water has been spilled, but a revulsion in him must prevent her from touching the coins, a fear of death-contamination—and she seems to want a contact with them for corresponding reasons.

"Yes, I hold you responsible. Have you read what that beast nephew of yours did to my daughter, my better-than-flowers daughter?" She loosens his grip from around her waist and gets up, the tail of her *kameez* and the top of the *shalwar* soaked in the poisonous water. "I want you to know that Mah-Jabin's chances in life were ruined by you, her father. You didn't want to move to a better neighbourhood, and no decent family was *ever* going to come to ask for the hand of a girl living in this third-class neighbourhood of people who are mill labourers or work at The Jewel in the Crown and The Star of Punjab. You have to think of these things when you have daughters. I asked you to put aside your principles when there was talk of an O.B.E., just for the girl's sake, just so there would be at least *something* attractive about her to other people, your photograph in the Urdu newspaper for all to see, but you said no, said you neither seek honour among men nor kingship over them. I swear on the Koran I didn't want any of these things for myself but for the children. I wanted Charag to become a doctor so people would say Mah-Jabin is a doctor's sister, but that dream of mine failed too. And how am I going to find another man for her *now,* now that her brother's picture *is* in the newspapers but for disgusting immoral wicked reasons. I can only hope no one sees that magazine. How will I face the decent God-fearing people of this neighbourhood if the news of that debased picture ever gets out? How I hate you for allowing Satan to plant his seeds in my stomach."

Shamas knows that she's referring to the belief that Satan shares the sexual intercourse of a husband if he has omitted to read appropriate Koranic verses before penetration. And the penalty is great if the husband has not read specific verses at the precise moment of ejaculation: Satan's seed enters the woman's womb along with the man's and the resulting child is predisposed to Satanic deeds.

He listens as she talks in a monotone. There is a half-penny coin in amongst the pennies, a coin out of circulation now, not seen in a while. Coins in the rotted pockets of some buried bodies have helped the police to narrow the time period within which that person might have gone missing. What was in Chanda and Jugnu's pockets when the bodies were dismembered?

"Charag didn't get into medical school because he was unable to concentrate on his studies in this house: the woman next door had begun making jeans for a garment company and had that industrial sewing machine installed in her kitchen, so that for twelve hours a day there was a buzzing noise in every room of this house. It would not have happened in a better neighbourhood. And Ujala grew up among the dole-collecting sons of factory workers and ended up thinking like them, leaving school at fifteen. In a better neighbourhood he would have had better examples all around him. You nearly called me a snob last month when I said I didn't want one of Ujala's old school friends in my house, but that wasn't because he is on the dole and his father works in a mill, it was because that boy is said to be an expert thief who could, if he wished, even steal the kohl from your eyes. I would have missed the women I know in this neighbourhood had we moved elsewhere, but I would have been prepared to make that sacrifice for my children. Tonight, you were more interested in the fate of *other* photographs than the one of your own family."

"They are an important document."

"So is the one of your own family."

The top layer of coins has lost its heat to the air but those buried underneath are still warm, a coil of vapour rises from them as when a biscuit not long out of the oven is broken in two: he has taken the glass jar (the twin of which, he remembers, was used to fashion the cage for the Great Peacock moth) from which the money came and is filling it up again, scooping up the slithery discs. The steam is a tangible soft pressure on the face:

at one point it is no less repugnant than as if it were rising from the opened gut of a slaughtered animal, but the moment passes. And now there is that swan wing that was flexed up at him, brushing his face one summer night this year: he had been returning from a late meeting at the town hall and the milky bird sitting in the middle of the street collecting the day's warmth from the tarmac.

He follows her up the stairs. She climbs sideways, like someone very old, holding onto the handrail: the steroid injection in the kneecap last year has relieved the arthritis somewhat but that leg is still not what it once was: in time one learns the individual failures behind the standard attitude actors and children-at-play assume when imitating old age. He watches as she changes into dry clothes and gets into bed. Would she like some hot milk? The fire on?

Downstairs, he dries the kitchen floor and sits looking at the jar of coins (while the little girl next door coughs in her sleep). The sight of the coins revolts him, a threat, and after quietly climbing the stairs to check on Kaukab, he gets dressed and, picking up the jar, steps out of the house. He can't bear to have them under the same roof as him. It wouldn't take him long to drop the coins into the lake. But less than a minute into his journey the cold forces him back into the house. December sucks warmth out of his body in white plumes as he goes. He climbs the stairs once again and, having checked on Kaukab, goes to the wardrobe where he keeps the whisky. Out on the landing he drinks two gulps and he places the bottle in his coat pocket before setting out for the lake once again. He had once overheard Charag say to Stella that he was glad Islam forbade alcohol "because otherwise I am sure both my mother and my father would be alcoholics." The maples along the sloping side-street between the mosque and the church had begun to bleed drop by drop at the beginning of autumn and now they are almost empty, skeletons of their former selves. The moon floats on the water's surface in a roadside pool, and the stars are closer to him on this bitingly cold night than the sparkling veil on her head is to a bride (as Kaukab once said) as he walks on towards the lake.

. . .

Kaukab, unable to gain more than an hour's sleep, sits up, the house empty of her children. There are searing convulsions in her belly like the "three-day pain" a woman suffers after giving birth, the womb going mad looking for the baby it had contained until recently.

She wishes she had the Book of Fates for a few minutes so she could flick through the golden text, looking for happiness, while moths hit the windowpanes of the house loudly, to get at the light emanating from Allah's ink. If only the angels would accidentally let fall the Book and it would land in her garden encircled by a brief nimbus of pure gold brightness. As it dropped through the dark air it would attract the attention of moths from the warmer corners of the universe, and they would follow its journey as though they were being sucked into a vortex. They would be hovering above the Book as it lay in her garden, those otherworldly moths, in an excited dance like sparks above a fire, the wings thinly haired like the back of a man's hands. She would go down and pick it up, waving the insects aside with her free hand, maddening them with the smell of spices that still clings to her from earlier today. The Book would be very cold from its journey through outer space, and she would quickly step back into the house with it, clutching the secrets of her destiny to her body. And when she opened the pages the luminous words inside would light up her face—she'd feel the pressure of the light resting on her skin, as she looks for happiness.

She'll find the page where the family had gone to have that photograph taken (as Allah willed and the angels wrote down with quills plucked from their wings).

Turn a few pages, and here she is six years ago, looking out at the young man who had been Ujala's school friend—her boy-doll of a son Ujala—going by the house. Ujala had once swapped a coat with him for a pair of shoes the way young people do sometimes. And she had noticed with a pang that the coat was too small for the boy who wore it now, and she was reminded of how much Ujala too must've grown in the years she hasn't seen a new photograph of him. At that age boys get bigger and taller at such a rate that they outgrow their clothes during the time it takes to buy them at the shops and to unpack them at home.

Moving forward, she'll look for the day last year that Chanda and Jugnu are supposed to have died—just to prove to herself that the courts had made a mistake, that Allah is compassionate and merciful. But what if it's all true? What did Allah have in mind by having the two lovers killed? She remembers a couplet of the Mughul poet Ghalib: *My destiny's script—due to the carelessness of its writer—is covered all over with smudges of spilled ink: these dark spots are the black nights I spend away from my beloved.*

No, no, she mustn't complain even for a half moment about the amount of unhappiness He has written in the Book for her: she must remember that Hazrat Rabia—may Allah hold that esteemed daughter of the dawn of Islam in His light till Eternity—had once confided to a friend that the amount of happiness in her life was beginning to trouble her: "I wonder if Allah is angry with me for some reason. Why hasn't He sent any tribulations my way for a while so that I may please him by triumphing over them or bearing their burden without losing faith in Him."

And suddenly now she is afraid: how could she have entertained those thoughts about the Book of Fates? No human is ever to set eyes on it. Such flagrant disobedience! No, no, if the Book ever fell to earth, she would bring it in and then wait for the angels to come looking for it. She'd know they have arrived because the noise of the moths outside the window would lessen—their light would attract some of the moths away from her house. Would they look a little like the ones she has always imagined? During the 1965 war between India and Pakistan, some of the bombs that the Indian jets had dropped on Pakistan had not exploded upon landing, and several clerics had said that they had personally seen angels appear and intercept the bombs in midair and carry them in their arms to gently place them on the Allah-beloved soil of Pakistan. Would they match the angels' descriptions Kaukab had read in the newspapers at the time? An iridescent cloud, up there in the sky, would retain a precise cut-out where one of the angels had flown through it. They'll settle on the mosque roof, no doubt, as they wait for her to bring them the Book, the air bright around them, the hems of colourful silk-and-brocade robes resting on the black tiles, for the Muslim angels aren't dressed in white like the Christian ones, nor are their wings plain white: the feathers are green, blue, red, orange, yellow. Birds of Paradise! They have diamond sprays in their chiffon turbans and their cheeks are as though dyed vermilion. Some would be reclining on the roof, others looking in the direction of this house— she is sure they could see through the walls, possessing eyes powerful enough to spot a candle flame on the moon—and a few would have taken off their wings and would be rubbing their shoulders as though for relief, as though the wings are too heavy, the flight to earth too long. She is not sure she would be able to see them because some clerics maintain that angels or the spirits of holy figures cannot be seen by women, who are inferior to men, but then she remembers that the Koran plainly states that Moses's mother had received a divine message from Allah, a revelation, just as all the prophets had, who were all male.

Kaukab gets out of bed, performs her ablutions, and opens her Koran.

No, she doesn't need a peek into the pages of the Book of Fates.

She has *this* book.

Yes, it's not our place to say "Why?" or "How?" to Him; we can only say "Help!"

A Leaf from the Book of Fates

On the last day of his life, Jugnu was awakened an hour and a half before dawn by the sounds the peacocks made as they entered his back garden.

A man was hurrying towards the mosque because the cleric had collapsed with his left hand on his heart, and the peacocks—who were roaming the dark streets—were made to scatter in every direction by him. The peacocks were a nuisance—liable to scratch the paintwork of cars, and last week they had entered the mosque and several had snatched up rosaries, the beads dangling from their beaks as they were chased out and down the street.

A few of the birds now entered Jugnu's back garden for safety amid the branches of the apple trees. The birds had appeared in the neighbourhood a fortnight ago—no one could tell where they had escaped from. They spent most of the daylight hours in the lakeside woods and in the secluded hilly meadows around the neighbourhood, away from humans, but they came out to the streets at dawn. Their presence in the neighbourhood was disturbing to some. The faithful have always been ambivalent towards peacocks because it was this kind-hearted creature that had inadvertently let Satan into the garden of Eden. Disguised as an aged man, Satan had asked to be admitted but the door-keepers had recognized him and refused, but then the peacock—who had watched the entire incident from its perch on the boundary wall—had gone down and lifted the bedraggled old man with its feet and flown back in with him.

Leaving Chanda asleep, Jugnu got out of bed. He approached the window and its dimly lit view of the peacocks. A pale summer moon was decomposing in the dark blue sky, which, at dawn, in an hour and a half, would be painted with a light as red as a Kandahar pomegranate. Jugnu was wearing an improvised *dhoti*: it was his habit, upon getting up in summer, to tie around his waist the light sheet of linen he had slept under.

Jugnu and Chanda had arrived home from the airport after ten last night, and, exhausted from the long eight-hour flight, they were asleep in each other's arms just over an hour later; Jugnu had often remarked that an aeroplane journey was surely worse for the body than a ride on a primitive bullock cart along rutted backwoods-village roads. As her dark-green eyes closed last night, Chanda had no inkling that she would never see Jugnu again.

They hadn't unpacked. And upon getting up and going downstairs on this the day of his death, Jugnu began to open the suitcases and he soon became engrossed in the notebooks in which he had recorded the information about Pakistani lepidoptera during his visit. He had witnessed a Paradise Flycatcher tear up and feed a Common Mormon to its fledglings in the Kaghan valley. After the monsoon shower in the Salt Range of the Punjab, he tracked the south-easterly drift of Blue Tigers, and he managed to observe the annual migration of the Pale Lemon White through the Khyber Pass.

In the kitchen patterned with rows of cedars—more gift-wrapping than wallpaper—he opened one of the many small cardboard boxes that contained the butterflies he had brought from Pakistan.

One box—which held several Common Guava Blues that had been caught in the guava orchards of Malir and Landhai, just outside Karachi—would be found on the kitchen shelf when the police forced their way into the house thirteen days later—because the couple had returned earlier than they had planned, no one would miss them till then.

As there was no food in the house, Jugnu boiled some water and drank a cup of black coffee while he waited for the first sign of life in the house next door so he could go and borrow bread, milk and eggs from Kaukab. He went outside and hesitantly approached the denim jacket that had been hanging on the line since spring because a wren had built a nest in one of its pockets. He noted that the bird family seemed to have thrived in his absence.

Going past the lily tangle of the garden next door, he dug up an onion from Kaukab's small herb patch for an omelette, his hands glowing in the gloom-rich corner. He didn't know that he was being watched.

All but two of the peacocks had dispersed by now, and they were sitting near Jugnu, also watching him. But they too had vanished by the time he came out of the house for the second time (the suitcases lay in the kitchen like gutted carcasses) to knock quietly on Kaukab's door because a light was now on in there.

There was no answer.

On the small patch of grass in front of the back door there was dew, and Jugnu, using his hands as a brush, wiped the words *The Vision* onto it. The words were a clear green amongst the silver-grey-green beads. It was a message for Chanda: Jugnu had decided to walk to the farm of that name where fresh bread was sold at this hour. He'd buy other provisions for breakfast from there too.

The farm was a mile away, beyond the lake and its xylophone jetty. The family that owned it also bred orchids in a glasshouse presided over by a lightning-shattered elm. Since long before Jugnu knew them, they had been trying to breed a flower resembling the one to be found at the centre of a gold-and-ruby Fabergé egg. The dazzling heirloom had travelled through the decades and each new generation of those tenacious yellow-haired giants seemed obsessed with creating a living copy of the jewelled sculpture. "But that flower is the work of the imagination," Jugnu had once said to them with a smile. "It's like trying to live a life described in a beautiful poem or a perfect novel." They came to the neighbourhood of Asian immigrants every year to invite children to take part in the annual "worm-charming" competition held on the farm. There could be up to fifty-million earthworms beneath an acre of land; and each team of children was allocated one of the tablecloth-sized squares in a field. The ground was beaten with sticks, pounded with fists, stamped on, until the vibration brought the worms to the surface. There were prizes for the most earthworms collected (the record had been standing at 763 per-square for several years), for the longest earthworm, and the heaviest. But the mothers in the immigrant neighbourhood were always apprehensive about letting their children take part because the field where the competition was held was next to the cemetery and they did not want their children to handle anything that could have fed on corpses.

Jugnu took his keys and came out of his back garden. The barber's son—having driven his taxi all night—was just pulling up outside his parents' home when Jugnu emerged into the street. The old man sat in the car next to the son, who, as testified by the black-and-white photograph that hung in the barbershop, looked exactly like his father when he was young.

Jugnu stopped because his way was blocked by the car door opened on the pavement side. And with a greeting and a smile, he reached in and relieved the old barber of the box he had been holding on his lap. There was a scraping of claws inside when the box tilted in his hand. A strong smell of bird-droppings and feathers came from the box which told Jugnu that on his way home from his night's work the son had collected the father from an all-night quail fight. Some members of the older generation indulged in this passion which was illegal in England but wasn't prohibited back in the Pakistani, Indian and Bangladeshi towns and villages they came from. Most young men, born here in England, were uninterested in the activity, but there *were* younger men at these fights here in England: they were the sons-in-law (mostly nephews) the older generation had imported from the villages back home for their British-born daughters. And increasingly the other young men present were the asylum seekers and illegal immigrants.

The birds were starved for a fortnight and fed on seed soaked in alcohol just before the fight, the men handling the Islamically unclean bottle of alcohol with rags, and then spurs were attached to the back of the birds' legs.

"The box contained dying blood-soaked birds," the barber's son would say later, in the months to come, "and I was afraid Jugnu would grow suspicious and land us in trouble. He was an educated man. Not like us: the sons had failed their O-levels just as, in another time, another country, the fathers had failed their Matriculations."

The barber's son let Jugnu help his father—in spite of the fact that the old man was overcome by disgust when he saw Jugnu, whom he considered a loathsome and immoral sinner.

After helping the old man out of the car, Jugnu carried the box of quails to the front door. The son was about to drive off but then the car stopped: the window was rolled down and the son told the father what he had just heard over his communication radio—that the cleric at the mosque had collapsed of a suspected heart attack. The barber, fishing in his pocket for the key to the front door, was shaken by the news. During Jugnu and Chanda's stay in Pakistan the cleric had had a most-holy dream, a dream that had had an electrifying effect on the Muslims of the neighbourhood; and it had also been mentioned in letters and telephone calls to Pakistan, India, Bangladesh and Sri Lanka, where too it had proved sensational. A saintly figure, holding a thousand-bead jade rosary, had appeared and told the cleric to write a letter to the American president, inviting him to convert to Islam. The holy man was standing in a mosque carved out of a single pearl that was—it was the cleric's understanding in the dream— washed twice daily in rose water. The saint told the cleric that he had pleased the saint by his unwavering piety, and that—as a sign of his plea- sure towards him—it would be at the cleric's prompting that the Ameri- can president would convert to Islam.

The barber bid a perfunctory, distracted farewell to Jugnu, after saying, in a voice full of awe, "Only the pious die on a Friday." And he'd claim later that when his fingers touched Jugnu's—as he took from him the box con- taining the wounded birds—Jugnu's hand had felt cold and stony, like a dead man's.

After seeing the old barber to the front door, Jugnu continued on his way towards the maple-lined side-street that rose between the church and the mosque.

He stopped before he began the ascent because at the corner he noticed the ladder rising towards the sky. The previous month—while he was in Pakistan—the workmen who came to replace the telephone pole had dis- covered that a letterbox was fastened to it, as red as a fire engine and hot under the summer sun despite the shade of the nearby maple trees. They did not have the official keys needed to release the clips and decided to ease the box over the top of the pole and slip it down the replacement like a wristwatch. The new column turned out to be thicker nearer the base and the box rested twelve feet above the ground. It would remain in that position for several months and a ladder was put up for the posting and collecting of letters. Some people in the neighbourhood would see it as a blatant and obvious attempt by the whites to stop the Asian people from keeping in touch with their families back home. Bindweed raced up the ladder and pole, the tendrils candystriping the rungs, the beautiful white flowers lolling in the air on delicate branches that were full of sculpted heart-shaped leaves.

Just under two weeks from that day, Kaukab would drag this ladder trailing a straggle of dusty green hearts into the front garden of Jugnu's house and set it against the top window, sending a boy up to have a look through the window—wishing Ujala was home so she could send *him* up instead of having to ask someone else's son.

Standing there, he was smiling to himself when Naheed the seamstress hurried out of her house and asked him to please go up there and quickly post this letter, brother-ji. In the months to come she would debate with herself whether or not to let anyone know that she had been one of the people who had seen Jugnu during that predawn hour. The letter was to her sister, who lived in Bangladesh, and she wanted it kept a secret from her husband: during a visit to Pabna over a decade ago, the man had been accused of assault by Naheed's younger sister, and, shouting down the girl's claims, he had forbidden Naheed to communicate with her family. Naheed wrote to her parents and sister whenever she had the opportunity and posted the letters while he was asleep, on occasions going out into the street in the middle of the night.

If I tell the police about having met Jugnu, she would write in a letter to her sister several weeks after that dawn, *he would want to know what I was doing out at that hour, talking to other men. And the police visits to the house and questionings would abrade his vindictive nature.*

As for the barber and his taxi-driver son—who were the other two people to have seen Jugnu by that time that day—they would not wish to get involved because they feared the quail fighting would land them in trouble with the law.

After posting the letter for Naheed the seamstress—a letter that had been sealed with dabs of chappati dough because the tube of glue was somewhere upstairs and Naheed hadn't wanted to go looking for it lest she wake her husband—Jugnu continued up the maple-lined street, towards the corner where the mosque was situated.

The street lights were still on and they cast an apricot glow on the pavement.

As Jugnu walked past the mosque door, Shaukat Ahmed, who had a knitwear stall in the covered market, came out and, on seeing Jugnu, asked him grimly to step in and look at the cleric. ("I always thought he was a doctor!" he would say of Jugnu later.) The cleric was talking slowly with his last breaths, and wanted to be laid out on his prayer mat. He used a cured deerskin as prayer mat and Jugnu brought it to him from where it lay folded and spread it.

As the news of the cleric's death spread in a short while, there would be a large gathering of people in the mosque, but when Jugnu went in there was only a handful of people, listening to the cleric, the American president's letter crumpled in his right hand.

Everyone except Jugnu was terrified by what the old man was saying: The "bearded figure" in his dream, referred hitherto as just a saint, had been none other than the Prophet Muhammad, peace be upon him. The cleric had kept this fact from the Muslims due to humility: "I did not want to appear to be a braggart. I am not one of those over-zealous men to whom Gabriel would appear to be a poor catch: they would want to track God."

Jugnu left the mosque after the misunderstanding about him being a doctor had been cleared up.

To contemplate that the Prophet Muhammad can be wrong—on anything—was to risk a deep spiritual trauma; and so, after the cleric died, soon after Jugnu departed, the men who had been present at the deathbed decided that what the dying man had revealed to them should never be made public. These men would not come forward to testify officially that they had seen Jugnu that dawn. They would have, of course, talked to some of their most-intimate friends or to their wives about meeting Jugnu in the mosque if they had decided to keep quiet for some other reason—say, that they did not want to get involved in a murder inquiry. But this was a matter of religion.

All except one of them would remain utterly silent. And the one who would speak would say to his wife, "When I saw Jugnu I knew he was as good as dead. I knew Chanda's brothers were waiting for them to come back from Pakistan to kill them. Had my sister set up home with someone that shamelessly, I would have dissolved them both in acid much sooner."

It was only when he had got up to say his predawn prayers that the cleric remembered that he hadn't opened yesterday's post: he found the letter from the American president, politely declining to convert to Islam.

The world's most-powerful country was not to be headed by a Muslim anytime soon! Everyone in the neighbourhood knew the details of the dream, and some of the faithful had made plans in anticipation of the President's assenting reply. When the prophet Suleiman (or King Solomon, as the Christians called him) had sent a letter to Bilquis (the Queen of Sheba), inviting her and her people to submit to worshipping only Allah, she had decided to pay him a personal visit; and while she was journeying towards him, Suleiman had had his djinns transport her throne to him so that she would know that he had Allah on his side. The people in the neighbourhood had wondered whether the President would turn up in Dasht-e-Tanhaii upon receiving the letter, and they had wondered if Allah would command a few of His djinns to transport some famous American landmark or other to this town. How would the Statue of Liberty look up there on the highest hill, next to the Iron Age fort? Was the earth in the town centre strong enough to take the weight of the Empire State Building? Was the Golden Gate Bridge long enough to span the lake, a girdle around the embedded giant's waist?

Having left the mosque on his way to The Vision, Jugnu had to walk past Chanda's family's shop. Chanda and Jugnu had returned to England earlier than planned, but their killers knew that they were back because the taxi driver who had driven them home from the train station last night had casually mentioned the fact over his vehicle's communications radio. Chanda's brothers happened to be at the taxi firm in the town centre and were told the news. The police would never find out who it was that had driven the couple home from the station. The taxi place was staffed mainly by illegal immigrants who were either too afraid to come forward with leads—because the police would surely detain and deport them—or they had moved on to another job or another town by the time the police came to make enquiries.

Chanda's elder brother, Barra, he who was born holding in his hand a piece of clotted blood, was already awake because when the cleric had collapsed at the mosque earlier, someone had run to the shop and rapped on the door to get a packet each of star anise and cinnamon to make a fortifying brew for the patient. Through the glass of the window, Barra saw Jugnu go by in the half dark.

During the police questioning soon after the couple's disappearance, the two brothers would declare that they knew absolutely nothing of Chanda and Jugnu's arrival back in England. But during their talks—part boasts, part confessions—to family members and close friends back in Pakistan, they would admit that Barra had seen Jugnu go past the shop during that early hour.

Jugnu, being watched by Barra from the window, stopped when he noticed the time on the clock-tower that stood in one corner of the Mount Pleasant primary-school playground. It was a quarter to five—fifty-five minutes to sunrise. His wristwatch showed Pakistani time and he took a few seconds to wind the hands back. Barra went into the room of his younger brother—Chotta—in order to wake him. "You preferred being murderers to being the brothers of a sister who was living in sin?" one of the people they would tell the truth to, over there in Pakistan, would ask them. "Yes," they would say, "because it was we who made the choice to be murderers. We are men but she reduced us to eunuch bystanders by not paying attention to our wishes."

When both her marriages in Pakistan failed and she came back to England, Chanda had been asked by her brothers and father to consider wearing the all-enveloping *burqa*. The men said they felt awkward and ashamed when they were with their friends on a street corner and she went by. "We see the looks in their eyes—some pity us, some blame us for not having found you a better life," they said. If she wore a *burqa* no one would know it was her as she went by. The shop was named after her— Chanda Food & Convenience Store—but the sign above the entrance was painted over after she came back trailing the stink of failed marriages. The old name, it was felt, would needlessly remind people of the girl, their next thought probably being, "Chanda—the twice-divorced girl." *I feel I am being erased,* Chanda wrote in her diary angrily.

Chotta was not in his room when the elder brother Barra entered it. Barra knew where he could be—in Kiran's stealthy arms, in the room next to where her bed-ridden father lies—and he left the house to go fetch him. He went in the opposite direction from Jugnu, and he didn't yet know that he had seen Jugnu alive for the last time. On his way to Kiran's house, he had to go past the mosque and he met and exchanged greetings with several men who were gathered outside in the half dark, mentioning examples of the just-deceased cleric's holiness to each other.

Some of the men who were gathered outside the mosque had remonstrated with Chanda's brothers in the previous months for allowing their sister to cohabit with a man she wasn't married to. Many people who saw Barra in the gathering beside the mosque would vouch for his whereabouts to the police later, not knowing if their sighting was of any value. Shahid Ali, who worked the night shift—6 p.m. to 6 a.m.—in a factory (and drew unemployment benefit too), would say that on seeing Chanda's brother that August Friday, he had remarked to himself that no wonder what the cleric had been promised in his dream hadn't come true, that the vision of the saintly figure had proved to be false: how could it not when the world was full of such shameless people? " 'We are a people so undeserving of miracles,' I had said to myself with regret."

Haidar Kashmiri, who had gone to the shop earlier for the spices, saw Barra and thought that he had found a packet of star anise on a shelf somewhere and had brought it over, not having been able to locate it earlier.

People had already begun to doubt that a holy man had appeared in the cleric's dream.

"But he insisted the figure in the dream was a most-honourable being," Zubair Rizvi says, "seated in a mosque that was so beautiful that the gaze became glued wherever it landed, with flowerbeds brimming with *gul* and *rehan*, with *lala* and *nargis*, *nasreen* and *nastreen* and *yasmeen*."

"He listed it all, down to the smallest detail," agrees Ijaz Rahmani. "He said the air was full of birdsong, the laughter of *andleeb*, the uproar of the *kumri*, the wail of the *koyal*, the beckoning of *kubk* and *daraj*."

Barra nodded and said, "He could have been mistaken. He was a mere mortal—"

But he was cut off by Naveed Jamil who thought it disrespectful to allow such speculation: "I am not shameless like certain other people present here that I should not object to this kind of talk, and right outside the mosque too. There was nothing mere about that mortal. He told us several times that whilst he was praying alone in there, fairies came bearing presents, left them beside him and then hid. He never accepted any of the presents, saying, 'Take them away, girls, daughters. A rosary in my hand, a prayer mat under my feet, a mosque-floor under the prayer mat—I don't need anything else.' "

If Barra felt insulted at being so interrupted, he didn't give any indication; some of the younger men present outside the mosque had gone to school with him and remembered his short temper of those days. " 'Do that again and they'll be tracing you in chalk!' was what he would say when provoked as a schoolboy," Rashid Uddin the left-handed would recall later. "But that was no more extreme than anything the rest of us said. Youth provokes you into picking fights with everything in life."

That hour, no one was sure whether Chanda's brother was aware of the fact that, at the barber's shop last week, Naveed Jamil—the man who had cut him off just now, and more or less referred to him as "shameless" to his face—had said that Barra's wife was not a virgin on the wedding night, that she was split well before the "night of breakage." Every gathering in this neighbourhood is full of such broken glass—a person has to pick his way carefully across resentments, allegations, slights to honour and virtue. Naveed Jamil had many years ago wanted to marry Chanda but her parents had turned him down: his lowly origins were said by many to be the chief obstacle—his father had been a hookah mender in Cheechokimalyan.

Barra left the mosque's vicinity and was seen walking along the road with the cherry trees. Kiran's house was situated in that direction. He had known for some time that the Sikh woman was Chotta's secret lover, but he hadn't broached the subject with him. And since he had never had the occasion to talk to Kiran, he began to feel awkward as he neared the house because the nights she shared with his brother were a secret, and she'd be embarrassed to know that he was aware of them; she could also turn aggressive out of fear of exposure and accuse him of trying to tarnish a decent woman's name. She was a Sikh, after all, and their women were known for a certain earthy spiritedness. Some people in the Muslim community were aware of the clandestine love-affair, and hoped that Chotta would do the right thing and ask Kiran to convert to Islam and marry her. They—and Chotta himself—saw nothing in common between his secret nights with a woman he was not married to and Chanda setting up home with Jugnu. "I am a sinner," Chotta had said in the past, regarding his fondness for alcohol, "but I am not an apostate. I *know* I am sinning. That's the difference."

As things turned out, Barra didn't have to knock on Kiran's door. A dark-blue wave of peacocks ran towards him from behind with their dot-of-oil-on-water's-surface tail feathers in disarray. He stopped and turned around. The birds were being scattered by Chotta, who was running towards him, out of breath. He arrived, pale as death, and grabbed him by the upper arm.

"Come with me, over by the lake," he said. "I think he's dead."

When Jugnu knocked on Kaukab's back door—soon after being awoken by the peacocks, a few hours before he died—she was not in the house, though the light was on.

She had got up, unable to sleep, and gone out—to see the man Chanda was married to. She had run into him the previous week and asked him to do the decent thing and divorce Chanda "so she can marry my brother-in-law." The man was aloof and said he would see what he could do when Chanda returned to England. She asked him where he lived so she could send Shamas to talk to him.

He worked in a factory and left for work at an early hour and Kaukab, lying awake all night, thought in the dark about Charag and the news about his vasectomy.

The previous week, coming home from the town centre with a few things from Marks and Spencer, Kaukab had seen a woman from the neighbourhood walking towards her, and recognizing her as the woman who had once bristled upon seeing her with a Marks and Spencer carrier bag, telling her that as a Muslim she shouldn't buy anything from that shop owned by Jews, Kaukab had stopped on the bridge above the river to conceal the bag with the St. Michael logo in her coat. When the woman neared, Kaukab realized it wasn't the same woman, but she saw that the man standing on the bridge not far away from her was Chanda's third husband. Naturally, she changed colour when she saw him. She approached him and introduced herself. "*You* have forced her into that sinful situation," she told him. She reminded him of how much Allah hated the unjust, and she demanded to know his address. He seemed taken aback by the force of her will and told her where he lived when she asked him.

He had been living in England illegally already for three years when he married Chanda. He had arrived in Britain on a three-month visa as part of a television crew from Lahore, ostensibly to film a drama serial for a television production company, but had then "disappeared." In reality there was no serial: the actors, the crew, the photographers were all young men and women who had paid thousands of rupees to the people who ran this and other similar immigration scams. He washed dishes in a restaurant but Chanda's parents had agreed to the match because they were desperate to see their twice-divorced daughter married again and settled. "Life weighs as much as a mountain," Chanda's mother had said, "so how will she be able to bear the burden of it on her own?" The father had agreed: "Even a tree dries up if it's on its own." They knew they had to trust Allah and not despair because to be the parent of a girl had been a trial since time immemorial. Chanda's mother would quote the Pakistani poet Hasan Abdi:

The walls carry the scent of humans—
Had others been imprisoned in this dungeon before me?

They both kissed the marriage certificate. They envisioned a happy future at last for their girl but it was like trying to project a film onto a spider's web, because it was obvious from the start that the man had married her simply to gain British citizenship. Chanda's brothers and parents were courteous—even respectful—towards him, and he too acknowledged and returned their kindness during the year or so it took for his nationality to be finalized. But after that he changed, saying they should buy him a car, that the shop should be signed over to him, or he would divorce Chanda. Chotta hit him one day over an insult and he disappeared soon afterwards, having emptied the cash register of everything it contained.

Chanda's brothers had accepted the contempt he had repeatedly shown them during the previous weeks. They had been brought up to believe that a man must respect his brother-in-law because he has taken the burden of your sister off your hands, that he is to be feared lest he take offence at anything you've said and abuse or divorce your sister. Language reflected this matter: anyone who made himself too comfortable at another's expense was told to mind his ways because the world wasn't "the house of his family-in-law." And there was deeper humiliation too: the word *sala*—"brother-in-law"—was a term of abuse all over the Subcontinent: to call someone *sala* was to say, "I fuck your sister and you can't do anything about it!," "You can't stop me from trying my manhood on one of your women!" What could be more humiliating to men who had been brought up to defend their women's honour above all else? A man's brother-in-law was a swear-word made flesh, and, frustratingly, he had to accept it.

Just before dawn on the day of Jugnu and Chanda's death, Kaukab arrived at the man's house. "You have played your part in this sin for long enough," she told him when he came to the door in a vest, holding a shaving brush. He had to be at work by five.

"I want you to present yourself to your wife's parents as soon as possible and formally divorce their daughter." She gave him the shop's telephone number, but he said he already had it written down somewhere, although he did accept the phone number of Chanda and Jugnu's house when Kaukab said he could call her directly if he wished. He went to get a pen and she stood there. On the opposite side of the street there was a giant advertising billboard depicting a blonde woman in a lace brassiere, and she remarked to herself that living in England was like living in one big brothel. The billboard of the woman with the lace brassiere had been daubed by some lover of Allah with the words "Fear Your Creator" in another location closer to the mosque. When he came back, she told him: "A word of two syllables, spoken three times—*Talaaq, Talaaq, Talaaq*— and you would have made God happy. He is compassionate and forgiving." She left only when he promised that he would stop by at the shop after work.

He didn't.

Kaukab thought she was doing the right thing by approaching him to demand he release Chanda. The Prophet, peace be upon him, said, "He who is a go-between in a fair action has equal merit with the performer and shall meet with reward in Paradise." She was out there when Jugnu knocked.

Chanda's brothers, when they confessed to the murders during the visit to Pakistan, had said: "It was a matter of honour." Everyone present had agreed. Such killings were not uncommon in Pakistan, but the killers usually killed openly and were proud of their deed. Some even presented themselves to the police afterwards and said they had done what needed to be done and were now ready for whatever punishment the law of the land thought they deserved. The law of Pakistan was almost always lenient with them and they were out of jail much sooner than those who had committed other kinds of murder. And in their streets and neighbourhoods, their act gave them a certain nobility in the eyes of those around them. Chanda's brothers, on the other hand, had insisted they hadn't killed her and her lover. They knew the law of this country would not view their crime indulgently. They boasted of having killed her and Jugnu—but only in Pakistan, where the laws and the religion and the customs reinforced their sense of having acted properly, legitimately, correctly. The people who learned of their crime patted their backs and said they had fulfilled their obligation, that such sons were born only to men among men and women among women. They said that he who committed the great dirty sin of sex outside marriage was nothing less than evil; it would not have surprised anyone if bats flew out of the gashes when such a person was stabbed and slain. The friends in Pakistan told them that they had acted wisely by not telling the truth to the English police:

"They would never understand your reasons. The West is full of hypocrites, who kill our people with impunity and say it's all a matter of principle and justice, but when we do the same thing they say our definition of 'principle' and 'justice' is flawed."

Here in England, the judge, batting down all talk of "code of honour and shame" would call them "cowards" and "wicked" on the day of the trial. *The Afternoon* would say, *They were the kind of people who don't realize that not everything in life is to do with them. In short, they were not grown-ups. They thought the world revolved around them.* A distinguished Pakistani commentator on the Asian radio too would be forthright: "Some immigrants think that just because they belong to a minority they are nice people, that they should be forgiven everything just because they are oppressed." As for the murderers themselves, after the verdict had been announced they would begin to shout in the court the litanies, including words like "racism" and "prejudice." The judge's remarks would be deemed to have "insulted our culture and our religion." They'd said England was a country of "prostitutes and homosexuals." Being led away, the younger, Chotta, would shout: "It's a kangaroo court!"

"Come with me, over by the lake," said the younger brother, pale as death, scattering peacocks as he came running, on the last day of Jugnu and Chanda's life. "I think he's dead."

The two brothers hadn't seen each other since late the previous day in the town centre when Chotta had by chance run into Barra who was returning from a visit to his wife at the abortion clinic. She had had the pregnancy terminated as soon as the tests revealed that the embryo was female. The couple already had five daughters and they did not want a sixth one. The woman often worried how they would ever find suitable matches for the five girls when they grew up because no one would want to marry someone whose aunt had set up home with someone out of wedlock.

When they met in the town centre, Chotta had been alarmed by the tired and distressed look Barra wore. When he commented on it, Barra replied: "I decided to walk home instead of getting on the bus, to clear my head a little." But the truth soon came out as the brothers walked along the street: "I am ruined. The doctors now say they made a mistake: it was a *boy* she was carrying, not a girl."

The news devastated Chotta too. And Barra went on speaking quietly to himself with tears brimming in his eyes: "They killed my son, they killed my son." There had been a mix-up at the laboratory, and now it was too late. "The security guards were summoned when I began to shout. It was only they who stopped me from punching the doctor."

Chotta offered to drive the elder brother home from the town centre but was turned down because the family van that week was full of the stink of meat. "I'd feel nauseous," Barra said. "In that case," said Chotta, "get into a taxi." He accompanied him to the taxi office and that was where they were told that their sister and her lover were back in England. Although they were given the information casually and in passing, they had both wondered whether there was a malicious intent: this was a taxi firm run by Bangladeshis, and they were a treacherous and wicked people, having broken away from Pakistan to found their own country, the treachery and betrayal of their race going back even further to the time in the eighteenth century when, just before the battle of Plassey, Mir Jafar, the commander-in-chief of Saraj-ud-daullah, had signed a secret pact with the Englishman Robert Clive, and ensured him a victory over the good Siraj, a victory that marked the beginning of the British Raj in India and the beginning of the end of the Muslim rule. Yes, every time there was news of a cyclone devastating Bangladesh, killing hundreds—sometimes thousands—of people in one fell swoop, the brothers at the shop would hear several of their Pakistani customers mutter under their breath that it was Allah visiting his vengeance on the damned Bangladeshis for first helping to put an end to Muslim rule in India, and then, in 1971, breaking away from the Islamic Republic of Pakistan.

At the taxi office, on being given the news about Chanda, the brothers had protested that a male stranger should not have uttered their sister's name with such familiarity: "No one can talk to a man about his women-folk." It was a fleeting glimpse of the nightmare: the brothers knew the kind of crude talk that went on among the gathering of young men in such places—they too had been participants in many—and they had suspected for a while that their sister's character and virtue—because of what she had done—was probably discussed in demeaning and suggestive terms behind their backs.

"We have to do something about her," the elder said to the younger as he got into the taxi to go home.

Chotta had come into the town centre after closing up the shop at nine because the seat covers of the family van needed changing. It was the only transport the family had, and in addition to personal travel it was used for the twice-weekly visit to the abattoir. The meat for the consumption of Muslims had to be slaughtered in a specific way: the animal had to be alive when its throat was cut and blood had to flow out of its body while it was still alive—the animal could not be stunned unconscious before being killed, as was the practice among non-Muslims; and all butchering from start to finish must be done by only a Muslim. The previous week, after the brothers had killed the lambs and sheep in the abattoir and brought them home in the van, blood and fatty liquid had somehow leaked out of the plastic sheets and stained the seat covers. No amount of washing could remove the unbearable stench from the fabrics and it was decided finally to purchase new ones. Chotta had driven to a friend's warehouse but they hadn't been able to find the correct size. He was on his way to the pub when he met Barra.

The pub he had been walking towards was a few streets away from the taxi office: it was known for its peaceful atmosphere, and the word was that the whites in there never displayed any unpleasantness towards the dark-skinned people; as a result, it was frequented by many Asians. However, after the taxi carried his brother away, Chotta decided to walk into a pub that was known for having bigoted people among its clientele, but it was nearer and he needed alcohol quickly. And although nothing untoward happened during the following hour or so, he remained tense and a little on guard. He was there until just before eleven, drinking alone, mourning his brother's loss, thinking about Chanda.

He drove home but did not go upstairs, where everyone seemed to be asleep. He went to the shelves and helped himself to a bottle of vodka and continued drinking in the dark, sprawled on the battered chintz sofa at the back of the shop, the smell of blood coming to him constantly from the old seat covers of the van which lay in a heap nearby. At around two, he came out of his stupor and went to Kiran's house, the half-empty bottle swinging from one hand.

Having let himself in with the key, he went upstairs and found Kiran naked on the bed with another man. He staggered down the stairs, shouting, and was out of the house before she could dress herself to follow him. Her father heard the noise from his bed of affliction in the room downstairs and added alarmed calls and enquiries of his own to it.

Chotta made it back to his house but this time he didn't go in: he went into the back garden and began to dig out the pistol he knew was lying buried there in a box, the pistol that he and Barra had acquired around the time they went into that heroin-smuggling deal. He put the loaded pistol in his waistband—it was too big for the pockets and he hadn't known how to carry it but then he had slipped it there because he remembered that was the way it was done in the movies. He was on his way back to Kiran's house, saying "bitch" and "whore" to himself repeatedly, when he changed direction and found himself going towards where Chanda and Jugnu lived; what he had been saying had changed to "bitches" and "whores" some time ago.

He went around the back, cleared the stream in one leap, and climbed the slope with the hawthorns and sycamore trees. He didn't know what his next step was going to be, and he fell asleep sitting in the darkness, the empty vodka bottle rolling quietly down the grassy slope and shattering on a stone jutting out of the stream. He didn't wake up at the noise. The flock of peacocks rushing up the hill—after they had been shooed out of the way by the man on his way to the mosque because the cleric had just collapsed—roused him an hour and a half before dawn, just as it did Jugnu. He saw Jugnu appear in the window of his bedroom soon afterwards.

He sat and watched as Jugnu came out of the house wearing nothing but bed linen around his waist, a reminder that he had been lying naked beside his sister all night.

He watched him dig up the onion.

He watched as Jugnu unsuccessfully knocked on the back door of his brother's house. And after Jugnu had gone out of the lane (he stopped briefly to push away with his foot those shards of the broken vodka bottle that were lying in the middle of the lane), Chotta approached the back door, tried it but found it locked, and it was when he turned around that he saw the message Jugnu had left for Chanda in the dew on the grass: The Vision—they shone a clear green in the sea of dark diamonds.

He went up the slope, knowing a way over the hill that would get him to the path that led to The Vision quicker than the roads and streets Jugnu would be taking. He had to hide beside the path for ten minutes before he saw Jugnu walking towards him in the distance.

He brought him to the ground with two blows of his fist, but when he pulled the gun out he discovered that he couldn't decide where to shoot: the gun was pointed one moment at Jugnu's face, the next at his heart, the next at his groin. Jugnu had recovered somewhat and, rolling over, was soon on all fours, trying to get up. He was hit several times in quick succession at the base of the skull with the gun's handle, and the blows stopped only when Chanda's brother realized that his hands were wet with blood. The blood was phosphorescent, glowing the way Jugnu's hands did.

Chotta was so taken aback by this fact that it was a while before he realized that Jugnu was no longer moving. He didn't know what to do about the corpse, and dragged it into the bushes. Leaving it and the gun there, under the foliage, he rubbed the bright liquid off his hands with some soil. He needed to talk to his brother and ran towards the neighbourhood.

As he neared the shop, Shafkat Ali, who was coming from the direction of the mosque, saw him and shouted to him that cleric-ji had just died. "Only the very fortunate people die on a Friday: it's not for the likes of us sinners," Shafkat Ali said; and in addition to that he casually told him that his brother Barra was in the gathering outside the mosque.

When the two brothers arrived at the narrow birch-lined path and went into the bushes, Jugnu's body was not where it had been left. The elder brother could smell alcohol on Chotta's breath.

"The thought came to me that there was no corpse, that it was just a drunkard's hallucination," he would say later, during his confession in Pakistan. "But then we found the gun. It was covered with blood—though it wasn't luminous: I thought that that *was* the alcohol talking. But then I saw that the grass was dotted with bright spots of light here and there." That too wasn't shining blood: the bright flickerings were in fact the fireflies about whose presence in Dasht-e-Tanhaii there had always been much speculation, many sightings.

It was obvious that Jugnu hadn't died: he had recovered and had wandered off somewhere. The two brothers thrashed through the August leaves, flowers, and branches as they followed the drips of real blood. Barra went over the places Chotta had already searched, knowing he was drunk, saying, "In your condition you couldn't find a mosque in Pakistan, or prayer in the Koran."

They saw movement in the distance, in a thick patch of wildflowers— one of those little places of extreme beauty that Dasht-e-Tanhaii hugs to itself—and when they approached it, their nerves taut, they found two teenagers making love. The lovers ran away into the foliage, gathering clothes, shoes, underwear, stopping now and then to pick up a dropped belonging, protectively shielding each other's naked flesh, turning around each other like two leaves brought together by autumn wind.

It was twenty minutes past five o'clock—twenty minutes till dawn— when they realized that the trail of blood led back to the lovers' house.

Jugnu had taken the shortcut over the hill—the very shortcut that Chotta had taken earlier—and gone back home, to Chanda.

As the brothers went up towards the crest of the hill, they passed several peacocks that were displaying their tails, the huge fans shimmering in the pale darkness.

The two men climbed down the other side where the sycamores and the hawthorns were and when they arrived in Jugnu and Chanda's back garden the message in dew was still there, the drops each carrying a piercingly bright highlight. The door was open. They went in tentatively and heard footsteps coming down the staircase.

"Where is he?" Chotta asked Chanda when she came down.

"He's upstairs," she replied quietly after the initial shock.

She had awakened shortly after Jugnu left for The Vision and, coming downstairs, she had opened the back door to fill her lungs with the early air of a summer-dawn. She saw the words in the dewdrops and knew Jugnu had gone to buy breakfast. She left the door ajar and began to attend to the suitcases, carrying them upstairs and taking things out of them. Because they had left Pakistan unexpectedly, she had had to pull some of her wet clothing from the washing line in Sohni Dharti and put it in the suitcases still wet. She took out the damp garments—the *shalwar-kameez*s, the see-through head-veils, the chadors and wraps of thick cotton—and brought them down to spread them on the line strung across the room next to the kitchen: the washing line in the back garden had been out of use since spring because of the wren nest in the denim jacket that hung from it. She filled the room with the colourful garments and the long swathes of brilliantly dyed fabric. When the brothers came in, she had been oiling her hair upstairs, pouring the fragrant liquid onto the scalp as though she were adding oil to a curry—generously. She had used the same brand all her life, the same one as her mother's. It smelled more beautiful than the fabled roses of Quetta, which she had had the chance to smell during her visit to Pakistan: she had gone to that mountain city with Jugnu in search of butterflies—they had seen the famous silhouette of the dead girl that appeared in the vast Koh-e-Murdar range of mountains outside Quetta at sunset, her dishevelled tresses, her face in profile, her torso with conical breasts.

Her brothers dragged her back up the stairs but Jugnu wasn't there.

"Where is he, girl?" Barra shook her. The younger spat on the bed she had shared with Jugnu, the sheets awry, and said: "Where is he hiding?"

She had lied to her brothers, of course: Jugnu still hadn't returned from The Vision, but she thought they would be less abusive towards her if they knew her man was upstairs. "Get out," she said in an even voice when she saw Chotta spit on the bed, "or we'll call the police!"

"Are you threatening us, you shameless whore?" said Barra as he slapped her.

"You think the world is heart shaped?" Chotta said. "Some people aren't as lucky as you, and have problems. Tell us where that Hindu bastard is!"

The brothers checked the rooms but couldn't find Jugnu. "Oh fuck!" Chotta exclaimed suddenly. "I don't think he's here. He's still outside, bleeding. For all we know he hid behind the fans of the peacocks when he saw us and we walked right past him."

"Bleeding?" That her brothers had had a violent encounter with Jugnu somewhere out there was now obvious to Chanda and she was about to shout in panic when they all heard a sound from the gate at the entrance to the back garden. The horror of what might have happened to Jugnu earlier was clear to Chanda when Chotta pulled out the gun and held it to her head. "Shut up!" he whispered. A milk van went rattling by at the front of the house.

After the noise receded, Chanda said: "Tell me where Jugnu is."

They told her they didn't know where he was, that they hadn't seen him since he left for Pakistan three weeks ago.

She began to weep, aware that they were lying, and she made a lunge for the stairs, managing to get to the ground floor in a few seconds but they were soon beside her again, blocking her path to the outside door. She shouted that she would ring the police. To stop her shouts Barra blocked her mouth with his hand as they dragged her towards the cellar door. "We had to keep her there and go out to look for Jugnu. One minute she was struggling with us on the steps," Chotta would say later in Pakistan, "the next she suddenly went limp. I didn't connect this to the crack I'd heard only a moment ago. I couldn't understand what had happened and thought she had fainted. But then I saw that her neck had a small protrusion. Barra had broken her neck."

"What's done is done," said Chotta after the next few moments had passed in silence. "Let's stay calm."

Barra nodded, letting go of Chanda's wrist. The limp hand fell to the floor beside her where she was lying. The girl's eyes were open, their colour changing from second to second, very fast.

"He's out there somewhere," said Chotta. "He could have called the police, and they could be on their way here."

There was a sound from Chanda's mouth at this moment, the weakest of groans. Barra leaned to her face and said, "If you can hear me, beg Allah's forgiveness for your sin before dying. And beg pardon from us and your parents for all that you put us through. And don't forget your husbands, ask forgiveness for the times you may have overlooked their concerns and comfort. The soul will leave the body easily if you repent before dying."

"She's gone," said Chotta who'd been looking for signs of life in her body. "What do we do now? I don't want to go to jail." He shook and opened the canister set on a shelf in the cellar, and giving it a sniff he discovered that it was motor oil, used to power *The Darwin*. There was another one of petrol because the Sheridan Multi-cruiser ran on an equal mixture of oil and petrol. He would say later in Pakistan that, just at that moment, he was overcome by the enormity of what had happened, the great difficulties that still lay ahead: "I felt like a spider caught in its own web." But, as it turned out, things went their way. Barra would say, "What appeared to be an impossibly huge mountain from the distance, turned out to have paths all across it once we got closer."

It was just as the sun was rising above the hills that Barra left the house, to search for Jugnu, the sky turning the blood-red of anemones in the east. Chotta stayed behind in case the wounded man turned up, Chanda lying on the cellar floor, the two cans set beside her, still full. "I thought the police had arrived when I heard the door open twenty minutes later," he would say in Pakistan. Barra would interrupt him and say, "But it was only me, coming back. I didn't find him but while going by our shop I saw that the newspapers had been delivered, and I picked up two batches of them where they had been lying on the doorstep, and carried them to Jugnu's house, to wrap up her body."

The message in the dew was already beginning to evaporate.

They decided to leave her in the cellar until that night: they'd bring the van and carry her out to the woods by the lake.

Chanda's mother telephoned the newspaper delivery people when she opened the shop at just after six-thirty, to complain that they had got their order wrong, that some of the papers had not been delivered that morning. Both Chotta and Barra were back in the shop by then. Barra stayed at the counter to help his mother because his wife—who was the one who usually stood at the counter with the woman at that hour—was in hospital, recovering from the abortion.

Chotta went to bed. They were both agitated all day, and Chotta was eager to go to Shamas's house to deliver the bag of chappati flour Kaukab had ordered over the telephone. His mother told him it could wait till the next day when he would be making the door-to-door rounds in the van to deliver the sacks of rice, potatoes and onions, but he went anyway, despite the fact that the shop was busy with the people who had come to say the funeral prayer of the cleric-ji.

Chotta would say in Pakistan that he had hoped Kaukab would tell him if anything was suspected, if Jugnu had turned up during the day.

"But the woman didn't say anything unusual, just took the delivery of the flour. She was kind and very courteous towards me because she sided with us when it came to the whole affair." So Jugnu was still lost out there somewhere. As planned, at around one o'clock that night, they took two of their butcher knives and a cleaver, a saw, two hammers, a large box of black bin bags, a shovel and a Chinese-made Diamond Brand axe—one of the thousands imported each year and selling in hardware stores for £4.50—and went back into Jugnu's house.

They were in the woods until five, using the implements, digging, burning with the help of Sheridan's fuels, dismembering and burying her changeable eyes, her hair, the flesh orchid of her womb.

They didn't know where Jugnu was. Two days after they disposed of Chanda's remains, they went into the house to see if they had cleaned up everything properly, because someone at the shop said that her little son had gone into the back garden to look at the wren in the denim jacket and noticed a funny smell coming from the house.

Kaukab too noticed that faint smell, but she thought it was probably one of Jugnu's creatures that had died in his absence, or that the fridge full of butterfly and moth cocoons had broken down. One year he had bought a chameleon—against her protests, because it was a chameleon that had bitten through the water-skin of Hazrat Abbaas in the desert, causing him to go without water in the burning sands of Karbala—and it crawled somewhere under the floorboards and died. The whole house stank for days.

The house smelled of death when Chotta and Barra entered it at around two that night—a smell they knew from their butcher's trade, and from the hours they had recently spent by the drowned-giant's lake. It was a dead peacock. The brothers were crossing the room downstairs, the room hung about with the monsoon washing, when the telephone rang from somewhere behind one of the yard-long veils and chadors. They were paralysed with shock. It rang two or three times before Chotta could move to pull it off the hook. That was when he saw Jugnu's body, on the floor behind a blue-and-green dotted veil that was suspended from the washing line, the edge touching the floor. Next to him lay the bright corpse of the peacock.

Jugnu had been in the house all along. He was there when the brothers came in through the open door that first morning. He had made it back ahead of them and gone through the coloured cloths to connect the phone. He died there, before he could call the police. Chanda didn't know he was in the house any more than they did.

After the British police had collected the testimonies of the people in Sohni Dharti, they would check to see if any telephone calls had been made to Jugnu's house at that particular hour on that particular date. They would learn that the call was from Chanda's husband. Drunk in the middle of the night, he had decided to use the number Kaukab had given him: "I wanted to tell her that I wanted her back. But no one answered, and I woke up with the receiver in my hand, the mouthpiece full of bubbles from my saliva, as though someone was trying to shout through water on the other end."

"It was doubly fortunate that we went in because we saw something else," Chotta would say in Pakistan. "When wiping a shelf with a rag, to get rid of any fingerprints on the wood shortly before we carried Chanda's body out, I had let fall all the dust of the shelf onto the small table standing below it. The gun was on that table. And I picked it up just before we left the house with her body. On this return visit to the house, I saw that there was a perfect silhouette of the gun on the table. The fine waft of dust from the shelf had fallen onto the weapon and the surface surrounding it. It was like a stencil."

"And as for peacocks that burst out when the police forced their way in the following week," Barra would say, "we have no idea how and when *they* got into the house."

The birds urinated on the dinner plate, picked pinned butterflies off the frames and ate them, spitting out the pins everywhere the way humans spit out fish-bones, and the female laid an egg in an open suitcase. The males had got into a fight, over food, over the female, ripping each other with their snake-killing claws and beaks, and the liquids seeping from their wounds and gashes would mean that the blood samples found on the floor would never prove to be conclusively human, conclusively Jugnu's.

The house itself—the house of Sin, the house of Death, the house of Love—went through a destiny of its own, shut up, abandoned to dust and insects. The police dug up the back garden.

A spider's web—sagging under the weight of a hundred dewdrops, no two the same size—had hung between two apple trees in the garden, and the late morning sunlight was a deep translucent yellow—as though the sky was being seen through a bar of Pears soap the day Chanda came to the house for the very first time. It was March. The sparrows were about to begin shedding the extra five-hundred feathers they had grown at the start of winter to keep warm, to return to their summer plumage of three-thousand feathers each. The apples had not yet put out their shell-white flowers (the blossom would be out in May, and Chanda would be dead by the time those very flowers became fruit in the autumn, the apples that would continue to lie in a circle of bright red dots under each tree until the Siberian snows of this year's January).

Her veil caught on a branch (as though she were being clairvoyantly prevented by the tree from advancing any further, as though the crop of fruit last year was not apples but crystal balls full of blood, predicting red rage and red death), but she freed herself and moved towards the door.

On her upper lip there was a mole the size of a kiwi seed; and her eyes always changed colour in keeping with the seasons: in spring they were the bright green of budding leaves, but in summer they were darker, the colour of mature foliage, and while they were a pale yellow-brown at the beginning of autumn when the leaves were beginning to turn, with hints of pinks and reds here and there, they became and stayed wholly brown for the rest of autumn and winter, the cycle beginning again the following spring.

She knocked several times on the door but there was no sign of life inside the house; she hesitated and then went in.

Inside, the walls were decorated with pinned butterflies in glass frames that appeared to be strays from Paradise. The girl—carrying the little wooden stars—didn't yet know that some of the butterflies she was look-ing at had stood at the centre of man's interest since their discovery, the glinting creatures named after the heroes and heroines of Greek mythol-ogy and the queens of the great maritime powers, that at one time some of the rare specimens had been paid for with gold and others used as royal gifts. She moved around the room, slowly, and then came to a standstill. There were ten dead butterflies on the sky-blue table before her. They were large and belonged to the same species, the bodies as long as match-sticks, the wings breathtakingly lovely to her, and she—the girl dressed in straw-yellow—lowered her head to examine them. The charcoal-black forewings were rounded ovals while the outline of each hind wing was tear-shaped and had three thin spurs protruding from the base; the forewings were marked with white bars, and each hind wing—although the same colour and pattern as the forewings on the whole—had a circle the size of a ten-pence piece on it, divided into three vivid bands, one berry red, the middle one blue, and the lowest yellow, a thin streak from this yellow band emerging and flowing deep into each of the three spurs.

She contemplated them with a serious and absorbed expression as though about to whisper a magical formula to reverse death. And, inex-plicably, as she looked at the ten luxuriant insects, she began to think of how her mother, after she had washed her hair, liked to prepare a brazier of smouldering incense, cover it with a small upturned basket and then lie down for half an hour with her head resting on its base, her eyes closed in lassitude, her long hair collected about the sloping sides of the basket, the warm fragrant smoke escaping through the weave to simultaneously perfume and dry the locks, a few stray wisps of the smoke climbing onto her forehead and dancing there as though, below, her brain and thoughts were on fire.

Wondering what had triggered the memories concerning her mother's hair, the girl realized that the wings of the dead butterflies issued a fine odour, the scent of garments stored in jasmine and sandal, of dark hair dried in incense and gentle musk.

The girl's face hung above the ten butterflies and the sky-blue rectangle of the table's surface, and she wondered where Jugnu was. She was eight when Jugnu arrived from America—twenty-three years younger than him—and had grown up thinking of him as an uncle like almost every other child in the neighbourhood. She had sometimes heard people say that his was an unconventional family. Once a woman said it wouldn't surprise her if she was told that some member of this family, after he had died and been made ready for burial, had suddenly sat upright to tear the shroud away from him, not wishing to be bound by any tradition or custom even then. He loved butterflies and the butterflies loved him equally in return, gathering around him as though around a rose, and, said a number of children, although they were his passion, whenever their fluttering hampered his daily routines he collected them all in the palm of his hand and swallowed them, but he soon began to miss them and, growing sad, brought them out of his mouth one by one to fly about him once again.

Just before Chanda entered the back garden, Jugnu had been studying the charcoal-black butterflies that lay on the table. *Bhutanitis lidderdalii*. Bhutan Glory. A relative of the Festoon butterflies, the species was extremely precious and listed in the *Red Data Book: Threatened Swallowtail Butterflies of the World*. It lived in the eastern part of the Himalayas, in Bhutan and adjoining Assam, and also in one locality in Burma, its natural habitat being mountains and mountain valleys where tall trees grew. They liked to flutter about in the high crowns and laid their eggs on poisonous lianas. The Bhutan Glories had a fragrance which even lingered for some time after they died, and Jugnu had dipped these ten live specimens in dry ice to induce deep sleep in order to study the scent-related mechanisms. Having finished, he had put away his microscope and the notebooks, leaving the butterflies to revive in their own time, and had gone upstairs.

While he was up there, the heat from Chanda's face had roused the Bhutan Glories.

Failing to find her full voice, she let out a small startled cry when a "dead" Bhutan Glory gave a rustling spasm, flapped its white-striped wings and—all compressed power—lifted itself from the surface of the blue table to—extraordinarily, without losing any of its elegance, in spite of the recent somnolent state—begin dipping and swilling about through the interior, and it was followed immediately by another and then one by one the rest as though they were all threaded at regular intervals onto an invisible string, were the bowed tail of an unseen kite that swayed and undulated.

The bag of star anise fell from her hand and the spice—an ingredient for the food of some of Jugnu's butterflies, and for which he had telephoned the shop earlier, saying they were to send it to his house if someone was coming this way—scattered on the floor.

"I didn't know they were alive, that I hadn't just dragged them out of their graves," she explained to Jugnu as he helped her gather the wooden stars a few minutes later, all ten of the Glories scraping their wings against walls, probing the objects in the room and the ceiling above them, slowly whisking a million molecules of perfume into the air.

Beginning in about a month, they—Chanda and Jugnu—would lie in the various rooms of this house on secret trysts, the windows curtained and the clocks daringly put away the way they are in casinos—but they wouldn't know in enough time that they were gambling with their lives.

They contrived to meet for sensual dalliance in other places too, in the age-old manner of lovers, Jugnu telling her about Keshav Das, the court poet of Rajah Madhkar Shah of Orchcha, who wrote in the sixteenth century of how every day in summer the cowherds gathered on the banks of the Jamna, the girls on one side, Krishna and the crowd of boys on the opposite side: the two groups dived into the water and after a while emerged once again on their own side of the river, each lover having met and entwined with the beloved under the surface, their longing satisfied for now, the disapproving world unaware that any contact had taken place.

GHOSTS

Carrying the jar of coins, Shamas nears the lake. The sand lines on the shore emit a pale brightness like the dry smears of grainy starch left on the knife that has been used to cut potatoes. Is it here that the ghosts of Chanda and Jugnu are said to roam? The lake reeks of minerals, the deep centre of the mass rising in response to the tug of the moon, making a sudden and momentary hill of water that causes the leaves floating on the surface to roll down towards the margins, the leaves that would stick coldly to the bodies of children whenever they braved the chill and went swimming in early autumn, marking them like fawns, and which they would pluck off each other when they emerged onto the land.

Standing here at the edge of the lake in night darkness with the long jar of coins that shine in the moon, he could be a figure out of a fairytale published in *The First Children on the Moon*—perhaps a fisherman who is releasing back into the water a fish that is in reality a marine princess whose grateful father would then give him a boon, bestow on him the ability to bypass reality. He walks along the water's rim until he comes to a point where the water is deep and lowers the jar into the lake. It sinks, sending up a noise of bubbles. The water is full of large stones here—each the size a horse's egg would be if horses could lay eggs (as the child Ujala had once described something). He turns back, crossing leapingly the little wet patches of the sand as though jumping from one square of a hopscotch grid chalked on a pavement to the next. While the moon dances on the waves, he goes past the *Safeena* and takes a mouthful of whisky at the xylophone jetty where lovers have carved English, Hindi, Bengali, and Urdu initials into the wood. When Kaukab was screaming at him earlier tonight he had thought, for one terrible moment, that, in addition to everything else, she had somehow found out about Suraya: rumours do begin and widen their rings with time. He sets off again, under the tall pines that the children are fond of climbing, Charag once saying that when he was up there he felt like a bird clinging to a giraffe's neck. The night-air is frozen solid by now but, as he walks, the heat of his blood melts a burrow for him to slip through, the lake continuing to dream audibly in the darkness. He stops where the path forks and, instead of beginning the journey that would take him back home, he takes the path that leads to the cemetery, the narrow passage that is lined in summer with thimble-shaped foxgloves attracting gauzy Peacock butterflies. Could Suraya be visiting her mother's resting-place in the darkness—avoiding him? Climbing a hawthorn-planted slope that is increasingly steep under his feet, he ends up suddenly lost in the fringe of bracken whose tips curve like violin necks, not knowing when he had left the path that in late summer is covered with the red paste of dropped hawthorn berries. He is very high up and can look down on a stretch of the lake shore that would take five minutes to walk along. He is lost, alone here with his mind. Every now and then he steps into a stream, one of the many that go towards the lake and the paths of which the children know the way they know the lines on the palms of their hands.

He is lost. His hands are trembling with the cold and as he puts them into his pockets he discovers a matchbox in one of them. Charag had put the coat on to go outside into the cold for a smoke. He takes the matchbox from his pocket but there isn't any strength in the fingers for a forceful-enough strike: he just sheds a little three-dimensional constellation of orange sparks at each attempt. He achieves a flame successfully with a deafening hiss the sixth or seventh time, and raises the light in the air to see where he is. The oval flame colours the smoke that feathers out of its circle of light. Further match-heads unfurl a path of light along the soaked frost-singed grass for him. He is shivering. He decides not to screw the lid back onto the bottle after he's taken a mouthful. It's hard to believe even in the existence of the sun at an hour like this.

He stops: there, ahead of him, is movement in the darkness.

He stands still—there is a throb of expectancy in the air, a slight quiver. He walks towards where the movement had been and the boy turns when he hears him approach. It's the Hindu boy whose lover was beaten to death whilst she was being cleansed of the djinns. The whites of his eyes are shining in the moonlight: he looks away in the direction he had been earlier, enraptured by something.

Shamas stops where he is, not wishing to frighten him by moving towards him.

"Can you see her, uncle-ji? She's there, look."

"What are you doing out here at this hour?"

He points into the trees. "Can you see her ghost? I am with her too. Both of us there."

There is of course nothing there. The boy has become unhinged. "Ghosts? People said it was my brother Jugnu and his girlfriend Chanda. Jugnu's hands glowing as always. Chanda's stomach glowing brightly because of the baby she's carrying. Three ghosts. Two adults and an unborn baby."

The boy shakes his head. "I heard about that. But it's not them. It's me and her: her stomach glows because that's where on her dead body my letter was placed, the letter I wrote to her on the day of the funeral. And my hands glow because of the orchids I am carrying for her."

The boy is hallucinating perhaps, or sleepwalking. "You should go back home, *put*. It's cold."

"I know you don't believe me, uncle-ji. But it is the two of us, over there." He is far away, staring blankly.

Shamas moves closer and manoeuvres his face in front of the boy's face until their eyes finally engage: "You are not dead, you are alive—standing beside me. Come with me, I'll walk you home. Remind me where you live?"

The boy looks around to find his bearings, and then sets off, Shamas accompanying him in silence, knowing he mustn't leave him.

They emerge onto a lakeside road, the boy having led him out of the forest he had got lost in. The boy motions with a hand towards a house on the other side of the road: "She was married to the man in that house. He is obsessed with the idea of having a son but so far none of his wives have given him a boy."

It's beginning to snow.

"He married again not long ago."

Shamas looks up at the house. And there standing in the upstairs window is Suraya.

She withdraws as soon as their eyes meet but he is sure it's her, her eyes emitting a light stronger than the moonlight, than the falling snow. Tears? She was wearing her yellow jacket. Paisleys. The paisleys that Parvati's footsteps formed when she hurried away from Shiva after a quarrel.

Wasn't there a curve to her belly—or is he mistaken?

He turns but the boy has disappeared from his side.

Shamas looks at the number of the house and, walking away, reads the name of the road from the sign at the corner. "Neela Pathar" Road. The snowflakes are settling on him, a thick crust of them growing on his shoulders. Does Suraya know that the man she has married has no intention of divorcing her soon, that he wants to see if she can give him a son first? Perhaps she didn't tell him why she wanted to marry him beforehand, thinking he would refuse to marry her under those conditions. She herself has no intention of bearing a child for him—she just wants him to divorce her so that she can marry her original husband again, to be with her son again. But the man has married her solely because he wants her to have a child. He must be forcing himself on her every night, taking her violently. What is she going through?

He hears footsteps behind him and, without stopping or glancing back, he knows that Suraya is following him through the falling snow. He should continue, continue, away from this road where someone who knows her might see them talking. He takes the turning and finds himself walking towards the lake, where the giant lies buried below the water, trapped but still alive. He looks back but she is not there—she has not been keeping pace with him. But he continues because she'll know where to find him. At the *Safeena*. Their *Safeena*. Their Scandal Point. He'll wait for her there. There is so much he has to tell her. The third time they met they had talked about the fact that the people from the Subcontinent love wordplay, take great delight in language. And a few hours ago he had had cause to remember that: when his grandson—who is the same age as her son—wanted a drink and asked what choice was available, he had been told there was Vimto, but he had pulled a face and said, "Vomit!" Has she been following the details of the murder trial? Did she hear the rumour that Chanda's parents had paid a young man to go to the police and say that he and his girlfriend had bought Chanda and Jugnu's passports from them in Pakistan and had entered Britain with them? But that he had taken the money and disappeared, never arriving at the police station? And now there is another rumour that yesterday Chanda's parents received a package in the post containing the money they had paid him: there was a note saying he was sorry not to have found the courage to do what they had asked but he didn't want to keep their money.

He arrives at the bookshop and turns around. She is still not here but he knows she's coming—even if she's got lost, even if she is unclear about where he is, she'll know eventually to make her way to the *Safeena*, the way he himself had known back at the beginning of summer that she would be here waiting for him when he left Nusrat Fateh Ali Khan's performance. He stands in silence, not knowing what he would say, how he would begin, when she comes. There's no sound except the waves caused by the heart-beat of the trapped giant, and as he waits the snow intensifies. He stretches out an arm to receive the small light snowflakes on his hand. A habit as old as his arrival in this country, he has always greeted the season's first snow in this manner, the flakes losing their whiteness on the palm of his hand to become clear wafers of ice before melting to water— crystals of snow transformed into a monsoon raindrop.

And now he hopes she *has* become pregnant by him during the summer, that her new husband—thinking he himself is the father—is leaving her in peace because of it.

Shamas's child is already saving her, already lessening the amount of pain in this Dasht-e-Tanhaii called the planet Earth.

The First Lovers
on the Moon

As lightly as ermine moths, the snowflakes float around the boy who was to have been the counterfeit Jugnu. He moves through the all-knowing silence of the winter morning.

There is a wind stiff as wood. He hides from its blows in a shop doorway, sitting in a crouching position, the way dead bees and wasps curl in on themselves. Rich as ink, he feels a drop of blood trickle down from the back of his nose into his throat. He dreams of a sun, sending out rays like the spokes of a bicycle wheel.

A bright-green rose-ringed parakeet makes a shrill noise as it darts through the snowflakes to the left of him.

He gets up and walks along the streets where the shops are being opened but he stops to look in through the glass pane of the newsagent. In the local paper there is the picture of a Pakistani man who was found dead in the snow by the lake—someone quite prominent and respected, it seems.

According to the Book of Fates, *He'll look at Shamas's photograph only for a few moments before moving on, but this delay will mean that he'll run into the Pakistani girl with the locket containing the strands of his brother's hair, the girl Chanda's sister-in-law had met at the shop back in the summer. Coming along through the snowflakes, her head lowered and neck withdrawn into the shoulders against the cold, she will enter the street from the far end, the end the boy is walking towards.*

They'll collide at the corner in less than a minute and it wouldn't have happened had the photograph of the dead man not held his attention for those few moments—she wouldn't yet have arrived at the corner . . .

She's walking close to the wall, sheltering against the wind, approaching the corner. She remarks to herself that the snow is as bright as a full moon.

He looks at the face in the newspaper. It is the first day in over a fortnight that he has dared to venture into the town centre, afraid of other people, of being recognized. Someone could follow him and inform Chanda's family of his whereabouts—they must be deeply angry at him for not having gone through with what they had planned. He hasn't been able to sleep much and keeps thinking some calamity is imminent, dreaming again and again of rocks and stones being hurled at butterflies. But at dawn today he had told himself to go out into the world again. If a calamity is coming then where else would he rather be than with his fellow humans? What else is there but them?

He moves away from the newsagent's window and resumes his journey along the snow-covered street.

London—Dasht-e-Tanhaii
October 1991–April 2003